Emily's Letters

Vicki Reddin-Gauthier

Sandfire Publishing

Sandfire Publishing
2677 Buntain Rd.
Hunter River RR#3
Prince Edward Island, Canada
C0A1N0
Contact: vickirg@gmail.com
Sandfire Publishing is a registered trademark
Copyright: Vicki Reddin-Gauthier
www.vickireddingauthier.com

Copyrighted material used with permission:
"You Still Move Me". Written by Dan Seals. Published by Pink Pig Music. Non-exclusive license to reprint the lyric of Dan Seals' work.
"The Way" Written by Anthony M Scalzo. © Bible Black (ASCAP) Administered by Penny Farthing Music (ASCAP) c/o The Bicycle Music Company. All Rights Reserved. Used by Permission
"It's Five O'Clock Somewhere". Words and music Donald Rollins and Jim Brown. Copyright © 2003 Warner-Tamerlane Publishing Corp., Songs of BDAS, and Sea Gayle Music. All Rights Reserved. Used by Permission by Alfred Music and Clear Box Rights, LLC

Cover Photo: Brad Fremlin. Author photo: Sue Woodworth
Cover Design: Katie Perry, www.littlebikedesigns.com

Library and Archives Canada Cataloguing in Publication
Reddin-Gauthier, Vicki, 1955-, author
    Emily's letters / Vicki Reddin-Gauthier.
Issued in print and electronic formats.
ISBN 978-0-9947288-0-7 (paperback).--ISBN 978-0-9947288-7-6 (pdf).--
ISBN 978-0-9947288-5-2 (ibook).--ISBN 978-0-9947288-4-5 (epub).--
ISBN 978-0-9947288-3-8 (kindle).--ISBN 978-0-9947288-1-4 (mobi)
    I. Title.
PS8635.E334E45 2016   C813'.6   C2016-905474-8
                                                    C2016-905475-6

Published in Canada. Printed in Canada.

Dedicated to the family of George and Fanny Gallant whose creativity has given me the courage to jump out of the fishbowl and take a look around in the bigger ocean.

Resting at the People's

Emily bent over the tombstone and adjusted the circle of pearls left for Kate by some unknown mourner. Kate's headstone featured a big chubby cherub standing on top of the cold grey granite. Someone, maybe the mourner, had wrapped the necklace around the cherub's clasped hands. The wind must have taken it for a spin, because now one end looped over an angelic little ear, too. Not quite to Emily's liking, the cherub or the pearls, but she didn't have much say in any of it, as these tributes were chosen by Kate's two children, Lori and Sam, and the anonymous pearl donor.

Emily picked up another unpaid job when Kate died: tend the headstone; sweep away the grass cuttings in the summer and the leaves in the fall; make sure the ornaments, teddy bears, St. Christopher medallions, and rosaries did not drift over from the other graves and clutter up Kate's space. With all the aging Islanders, the People's Cemetery would soon become overcrowded. Maybe the grave diggers should start constructing condominium graves, build up instead of down. 'Rack 'em and stack 'em,' Emily thought, 'Oh well, never mind. So long as Kate's is comfortable, a nice place to visit, and not too muddy. This red Island mud sticks to everything.'

Emily heard lots of stories about the big controversy while hanging out at the oncology unit with Kate last winter, some of them tales of woe and some downright funny. The people of the People's Cemetery, the living ones, wanted to be free to express their heartache, to love and care for and nurture their dearly departed's eternal home, or its symbolic representation here on earth, at least. Holy Mother Church wanted a clean, uncluttered space. As a graveyard decorator, the Catholic Church leaned towards minimalism.

In its own time, the Church reached a compromise with its parishioners, many of whom had lost children too young and too soon and needed to at least pretend to comfort their babies. The Church recognised that there is no harder loss than to lose a child, so it agreed to permit adornments as long as said adornments decomposed at a faster rate than the contents of the grave.

1

'All well and good,' Emily grumbled to herself, 'but I would appreciate it if Kate's neighbours' loved ones would take better care of their graves.' She dug up a stray candle and a plastic Jesus who had landed on its head in Kate's freshly turned clay. 'Clean lines, soft colours, and natural fibres for Kate. No plastic.' Kate and Emily would have placed their vote with Mother Church on the plastic issue, if they'd ever had a choice. 'A complete ban *must* be in order. Plastic never decomposes.'

After rejecting the cut glass vase she intended to leave by Kate's tombstone, Emily hauled out the tidy bouquet of lupines, loosened the ribbon, and scattered the flowers all over the grave. She realized their seeds would never survive all the summer's mowing or cold winter frosts, but she liked the idea of a lupine garden atop Kate's grave, come next spring. She must remember to stop at Vesey's Seeds and pick up one of those little packets of seed with the picture of Anne of Green Gables on the front. Next time, she could scatter them on Kate's grave. That should do the trick.

Kate had always been the best Lupine Hunter. Every June, she traveled the back roads of Prince Edward Island in search of one more abandoned farm field, recently colonized by lupines. Kate kept a photo journal of her discoveries and a list of all the colours she'd found while searching for the illustrious, but not elusive, wild lupine. Where many Lupine Hunters discerned only purples and pinks, Kate's eyes distinguished: white, purple, mauve, lilac, lavender, fuchsia, pink, coral, peach, salmon, apricot, pale yellow, gold, sky blue, deep blue, navy, indigo, periwinkle, turquoise, baby blue, and teal. Not counting all the shades of green for the leaves and greys for the seedpods. With a little faith and some trust in Vesey's hearty little seeds and their high survival rate, by next June a bright and beautiful and brilliant lupine bed would show up to entertain Kate.

'Did you know, Kate, some of the townies like to come to the People's to get drunk on home-made wine? Here's a little history on your new home: at one time, vandals, determined to wreck the atmosphere of People's Cemetery, became a big nuisance. So the Church put the runs to them. Now, tombstone tipping is *passé*. I guess delinquents have moved on to bigger and better acts of vandalism. Today's kids are too tied to technology to bother with the outdoors at all, even in the pursuit of destruction. So you don't need to worry about them tramping all over you, Kate. Neither do I.'

Emily stretched, rotated her neck and head, yawned, and wandered off into the cemetery. What a lovely spot for wandering, meditating, crying, writing, praying, and, on a clear day, singing. Big old shady trees, gentle slopes, abundant grass, secluded shadows, undisturbed chair backs to lean on. 'You could think of a tombstone as a chair back,' Emily considered, 'if you want to, and are desperate to sit down, like I am.'

Emily wandered over to Chris' grave to say hi. Like John Brown's body in the old marching song, Chris' bones had been a molderin' in the ground for a long time now, twenty-seven years at last count. A few years after Chris' death, his family moved back to Ontario, leaving only this trace of their son behind.

Whenever she drove by Chris' tombstone, she remembered his funeral. As she had watched his friends lower his coffin into the black hole, she wanted nothing more than to throw herself on his casket. Three of her friends wrapped their arms around Emily, led her away, and made her go sit in her car. What did she know of funeral protocol? She was only twenty-one at the time.

Tessa's grave wasn't too far from Chris'—about ten years' worth of rows. Even though she wouldn't have accepted such proximity for Chris and Tessa in life, she liked the way they lay close together in death. All of her short life, beauty emanated from Tessa's living soul and drew people, especially men, to her. Emily couldn't compete. Thank heaven, she'd never been asked to. Tessa's grave was well tended with lush, green grass, much thicker than on Kate's. And the fresh scent of spring radiating from the deep red French lilac her sister Trudy had planted by her grave reassured Emily that Tessa would never be less than lovely.

A bit of the doldrums and spiritual weariness caught up to Emily, even among so many enlightened people and their hopeful epitaphs. The thought of a little laylay in the luxurious grass tempted her. Tessa's grave seemed like the right place to dream of fairies and rainbows and butterflies and babies. Her bed was too shaded and cold, however, and Emily couldn't get to sleep. The blanket of moss on Chris' overgrown grave bed looked soft and warm, as the late day sun highlighted the light green fibres of plant life there. She took a little lie down on Chris' moss, instead, and dreamed of motor bikes, aliens, and long blond hair flying in the wind. A good sleep, even if the dreams were a little odd. Like the pearl necklace.

3

Kate, Tessa, Chris. Three people she loved. Three people she missed.

Life Begins at Forty-eight

Emily let the letter from the lawyer fold over. Time to fulfill her dreams. The unexpected promise of tuition funds from Kate's estate would make all the difference. The last couple of years had been tough, and her move back home to Prince Edward Island hadn't gone quite as expected. Still, she determined to make a go of it. The money would not flow as easily here as in Vancouver, not that it had been easy in Vancouver.

She prepared herself to live with less; she didn't need much now. No more kids to raise, not even her ex-husband Roberto, who she'd kicked to the curb when she left British Columbia. Alleluia!

She'd be damned if she would work in a fish plant or clean toilets all summer to earn barely enough unemployment insurance to see herself through the winter. Subsistence earnings for her Island years would not do.

The night Emily took the call from Kate, telling her the cancer had returned with a full frontal attack, she hadn't ever imagined the last year of Kate's life would be so rough, or that her friend would suffer so much. She wanted to spend time with Kate so she hopped the next plane east, to support Kate in whatever way she could on her 'cancer journey'. God, she hated that expression! Turned out to be more like a roller coaster ride with a grand smash-up at the end than a journey.

A year later, she woke up at Kate's funeral and wondered, 'What the fuck do I do now?' The Cancer Year had been one big daze, and by the time Kate died, she felt washed up, burnt out, and at a loss to remember why she had ever come back to the Island, especially for such a lousy outcome. Now, four months after the funeral, Emily could focus on the plan. The hefty cheque would provide her the means to complete her long-neglected degree in Education; then find the dream job teaching early years kids. Her favourite mental picture showed her standing at the front of a class full of six-year-olds, all of them rapt and starry-eyed. Surely it wouldn't be difficult to find work.

Or not. She was getting ahead of herself. First, she needed to return to the classroom and learn. Learn first, teach next; quite a creed to live by.

She missed Kate's sound advice and gentle sense of humour. She wished Kate could be here now, watching the sun go down over Tracadie Bay. She longed to hear Kate's voice, if only once more.

One More Gift from Kate

Early the next morning as she lay dozing, Kate called out to her. 'What?' she thought, 'What do you want now? Can't you see I'm trying to get back to sleep here? But it can't be you, anyway. You're too dead.'

Kate: It's me alright. Remember when I was still in the land of the living, but too sick to go out much?

Emily: When? Before I moved home?

Kate: Yeah. We would get on the phone several times a week and talk until I was too tired to chat anymore. Well, I miss those times.

Emily: So do I.

Kate: I don't think I ever thanked you enough for coming back to the Island for me.

Emily: The money for my tuition was more than enough thanks.

Kate: It's only money. Without your kids or me, you will be lonely too often. I have a good idea.

Emily: You and I could have lived all day in the land of ideas.

Kate: This one is a doozer. Em, what you need is a good male friend. Since I'm not around for you to talk to when you're stuck home studying every night, he will let you talk to him instead—not that I am in the least bit replaceable. I'll pick someone younger for you. He'll have to be someone who doesn't know you like I do, so he won't know all your jokes. And he'll be able to tell when you're being funny, like I can. He will have to be an incredibly patient man.

Emily: But Kate, why a male? Girlfriends are awesome, but boys? Boys stink.

Kate carried on as if she hadn't heard her: He'll keep you company. You may have to write to him, hone your skills for your essays. You've been complaining about how scared you are to write, how out of practise you are. You can practise on him and give up that long-winded style you use when you gab on about your feelings. Some boys who grew up with computers are wired with super hi-speed microprocessors for emotions, and we both know all men have short attention spans when it comes to their feelings. So, I expect you to work extra hard to make your point in a few words, instead of going on and on, like you usually do. I'll find you one with a sense of humour. He'll need it.

Emily: Why can't I just write to myself?

Kate: Writers need someone to write to if they are ever going to learn how, Dummy. Writing to your own self won't work, plain old self-indulgent. You know that.

But I'll warn you: sometimes he'll pretend he can't read.

Em: Will he flatter me?

Kate: No-oo.

Em: What's the point? Kate? Are you there? Kate?

Kate: Yeah, I'm still here.

Emily: If he's younger, how will he ever understand me—this mature, complex, creatively-challenged individual?

Kate: Oh, it won't be that hard. He'll make up rules and you'll break them.

Then she said: And I will be highly entertained.

Quite the comic, that Kate.

First Day of School

Busy weeks followed, and as she hadn't heard from her friend again, Emily forgot about the details of her conversation with Kate. Emily knew that's what comes of not writing things down, especially dreams. She didn't forget Kate's generosity as she registered for class, though. She better start practicing taking copious notes, if she wanted to keep the professors off her case in the coming year.

The big day came on September 5th: First Day of School. How strange to be sitting in a hard chair facing the teacher after all these years! How weird to be in a class with all these fresh-faced young women, too. Emily wouldn't let it get to her. She always enjoyed the time she spent with her daughters' friends. Sitting around the kitchen with a bunch of yappy teenagers couldn't be much different, and she considered herself the master den mother of yappy teens. No problem.

This school thing looked like tons of fun! First Day would be perfect if she could share it with Kate. She couldn't conjure her up, though, as hard as she tried. The conversation must have been only a dream.

The crunchy leaves on campus brought back memories of the times she and Kate spent together at this University of Prince Edward Island, thirty years earlier. Emily recognized Main, Marion Hall, Dalton Hall, and Robertson Library. Now, with the Vet School and all, the campus held so many new buildings and so much less green space. Also, UPEI had built a new sports complex to replace the old hockey arena, where they used to freeze their asses off. Man, that old rink was cold! The coldest rink on the Island, or so they claimed.

To think the University had the audacity to tear down the old student union building, The Barn, where she and Kate would go to dance, drink, and smoke pot with the security guards. A lot of that going around back then: welcome to the seventies. All those good times happened before Kate ran off and married a sailor. Or moved to Halifax at least, settled down, and started a family. Lucky sailor, stuck in the Caribbean soaking up the sun every winter, while Kate watched the snow and ice pile up in the Halifax Harbour and fulfilled her baby care duties at her grungy Canadian Forces Permanent Married Quarters. The first time Kate told her what PMQ stood for, Emily did a double take. Was it the quarters that were permanent or the marriages? Only the Navy knew for sure. For Kate and her sailor man, neither the quarters nor the marriage proved to be permanent.

She was a great mom, was Kate. Emily didn't suck at motherhood, either. She hoped she would be able to use some of her maternal experience to get through her teaching degree. Forty-eight years of taxing her memory banks might make it tough to compete with all the young brain-iacs.

Sometimes she wished she'd had the foresight to take the Education program after she completed her BA. Wrapping it up in one year, instead of the two extra years now required, made much more sense. Or better yet, she should have done a five-year BEd degree rather than her four-year Bachelor of Arts. Oh well, hindsight was better than foresight by a damn sight and a whole lot cheaper. UPEI was notorious for changing the rules for teaching degrees, so what the hey!

There was this one guy. In her Early Childhood Development class. He raised his hand (good manners) to ask a slightly stupid question. He asked how old you had to be for the fart humour stage to end, because he hoped it wasn't any time soon. Got him a laugh, but Emily thought it was pretty corny. Obviously this guy didn't have kids, or he would have outgrown potty humour ages ago. After class, he strode into her space and started talking away, a mile a minute. And she thought he seemed like a quiet type. Apparently not!

Emily couldn't quite decide what to make of him. He looked to be about twenty years younger than she, young enough to be her son. He wore his hair long, or longish, for his generation. Shoulder length and blonde. Reminiscent of university lovers long past, or passed on. Too much dying going on in her generation, come to think of it.

His eyes were green, but not hazel, an unusual colour of blue green which changed with the light from celadon to cerulean to teal and back around again. Around six feet tall, he was the perfect height for her to walk comfortably by his side, as he kicked up the gold and red leaves with every step. Could have become annoying, except he reminded her of a child she once loved, with all the chatter and enthusiastic kicking and playing, and she liked the sound leaves make when they are crispy. His name was Luke.

Quite mystified and a little perturbed, she left him hanging around in the parking lot.

A few nights later Kate came to Emily again. She popped back into Emily's mind, (or wherever these conversations happen):

Kate: Hey, Em.

Emily: You again?

Kate: I've been thinking. How is the friendship going?

Emily: What friendship? Hasn't happened yet.

Kate: Remember that male I told you about? Keep your eyes open and you'll see him.

Emily: And what exactly are you planning now? You're not cooking up another one of those schemes of yours that always got me into trouble, are you?

Kate: He's about to create a little box where you can put your thoughts, out in cyberspace, but you'll only be able to send them if you write them down first. Also, you can ask him complicated questions like, 'What does lol mean? And btw?' He will possess the answers to important stuff you will need to know if you are ever going to enter the twenty-first century.

Emily: Does everything I put in the box need to be original?

Kate: No, Silly, you can send whatever you want as long as you respect the rules and remember to stick in some things you think he will enjoy, too: cars, music, funny quotes, even hockey stats.

Em: Will he always read my thoughts?

Kate: Sooner or later. I'll remind you, though, he is at a very busy time in his life, so you must be patient. It may more often be 'later' than 'sooner'. Remember how hard we'd cram for exams, and then, around midnight, we'd go shake it off at the pub...

Then they spent time reminiscing about university, exams, pub-crawls, and making music, before kids, jobs, and husbands taught them what 'busy' actually looks like.

Emily: Kate, I'm fretting again.

Kate: Didn't your mother ever tell you fretting is like picking at a zit? If you keep picking, you never give the ugly bugger a chance to heal.

Emily: I can't help it.

Kate: What's the story, Morning Glory?

Emily: That guy? What if he goes to the box one day, and I write something stupid? Or my thoughts are empty?

Kate: He won't think it's stupid. Or he'll check back another day. Don't worry; you don't need to put all your thoughts in this box. Some you can share with your other friends and, believe it or not, some you can keep to yourself.

Emily: How long am I supposed to use this stupid box?

Kate: For as long as you need to, of course! Don't be so whiney.

Emily: No point getting huffy, Kate. What does he get out of all this?

Kate: Oh, I don't know. Maybe some days he'll want to put something in the box, too. He'll figure it out.

Emily: What will his response to the stuff in the box be like?

And Kate said: Brief. If you don't stop asking questions, I'll hang up on you.

Emily did not want that to happen; Kate lived so far away now. She doubted she would ever hear from her again. So she shut up and listened. To the North East wind shushing through the autumn leaves, the sighing of the branches against her window, and the murmur of the tide as it caressed the shoreline.

Mustard and Beer

Luke sat at the picnic table and kept an eye on Emily as she walked across the sports field through the early morning mist. As he peeled the label off his bottle of Moosehead, he remembered a trick his brother, Tommy, had shown him. Dead simple rules to Tommy's game: whoever gets the label off all in one go with no raggedy edges wins. Bad habit that, beer bottle peeling. Beer drinking and label peeling—two grand clichés of Atlantic Canada, the beer capital of this great nation.

Man, the fog was thick and damp. Cut right through you. It was too late in the year for an outdoor Oktoberfest, but the frosh orientation committee insisted. Against his protests they delegated him sausage chef, since he was one of the older and supposedly more responsible freshmen, He felt oddly old as he fed the hungry freshmen and freshettes. Would he ever be that fresh again—or that drunk and stupid?

Fortunately for him, Emily kept him company much of the night, and the heat from her body and the barbeque kept the chill off.

He couldn't stop telling her stuff. At one point, when he was running off at the mouth again, he stopped to apologize for babbling on about himself and all the boring details of his life. Emily pointed out when a man and woman are getting to know each other, they often share a lot of personal stuff. That and Cracker Jacks.

Luke picked up his guitar and wiped some of the dew off on the last napkin which had a little mustard on it. Too cold and damp to keep the guitar out, but this one wasn't his Gibson, more like one of those Cracker Jack box ones. Emily told him when she was growing up, she would always find a tiny toy of some sort underneath all the gooey popcorn and peanuts. Half the fun of the box, by Emily. Sometimes she'd snag a little plastic guitar buried under the popcorn and peanut bundles. Luke had never heard of prizes in Cracker Jacks. Ah, the things you learn when you hang around with older women.

Whatever turned the tap on his runaway mouth—scorched sausage meat, cold night air, or hanging around older women—Luke couldn't remember sharing so much with a woman since he started dating his wife six years ago. Wasn't much to tell Siobhan because he'd known her most of his life, or at least known her brothers from hockey and seen her around lots. Siobhan knew him all too well, all his secrets, and he knew hers. But not Emily; Emily was new to him. New like a brand new debit card. Shit, he forgot to order one to replace the beat-up creaked one in his wallet.

Or new like a bright shiny penny, with her copper hair and all. A bit of a mystery. Emily disappeared into the fog. Gawd, he guessed he'd exhausted all his stories in one night. Not much mystery left to him.

A minute later, the motor to Emily's car turned over and her headlights shone faintly through the mist. She must have found her car without too much hassle. Luke hated hassle of any kind at 5 am. He tracked her car by its noisy muffler. Too late to tackle her on the football field now.

So he strummed a few out-of-tune chords, hummed a couple of lines of an old melody, and added some words:

She moves through the mist
Slipping away home
Fading with the sunrise
Leaving me alone
Lady of the mist
Where do you run to
In your dress so white
Bare feet flashing
In the early morning light
All I see is you leaving
All I hear is the leaving
And I wonder if
You'll be okay
When I find you
Again another day
She moves through the years
Head held high
In spite of all the tears
Till I lose track

14

Forget all about
What I learned that night
To hold her just once
Would have only been right
All I see is her leaving
All I see is her leaving
And I wonder if
I'll be okay
Knowing she'll be gone away
And I won't find her
No matter how long the days

His first attempt at song writing. Kinda sucked. Luke didn't think he'd put much effort into working out the tune or the beat or all the chord progressions. He wouldn't likely share it with Emily. Or his wife.

Maybe he should take the last burnt sausage and eat it out of his hands. That seemed messy and nasty, though, with no bun and no napkin. Could he navigate guitar, sausage, and beer bottle, *sans* bun? Definitely needed a bun. Now, Emily had nice buns. Luke bet they'd feel toasty warm on a cold night. He could have navigated guitar, mustard, sausage, beer bottle, and Emily's buns, if she hadn't left him by the barbeque, all by himself.

As he doused the coals with the dregs of his beer, he remembered how her eyes sparkled in the campfire light, like the eyes of a young chick. The effect seemed pretty cool for a forty-eight-year-old woman, till she explained about the artificial lenses they used to replace her old, cataract-covered ones. The twinkle was simply a trick of the light on shiny new plastic. Her jugs didn't disillusion him, though. A bit of a breast man, he bet hers felt and tasted like sweet, honey dew melons. 'Where'd that come from? Fuck I'm drunk.'

Emily also told him she started dying her hair after three pregnancies had darkened it from a warm copper to a deep dark mahogany. She didn't like mahogany. Not as a hair colour, anyway. Luke didn't give a care about the dyed hair. At least she didn't dye it pink and purple like Siobhan.

The air seemed extra shivery without Emily to keep him company. So he shut down the barbeque and fell up the steps of the apartment building.

Nothing like the wee small hours of a cold October night to fill you with longing; for what he couldn't say. Cracker Jacks? Sausages? Home?

He probably should mention his wife next time he and Emily talked. That might be a good idea.

Emily buried herself in her schoolwork, forever surrounded by books: school books to study and novels to fall asleep. When she wasn't reading, she was typing away on the computer, researching, or writing papers. Not much time—or energy—for writing anything fun, not even to her daughters out west. Her circle of study buddies reassured her she wasn't too old for this university life, mostly because they were almost as old as she, or even older.

UPEI offered a mature student program which allowed the fifty-plus crowd to audit a course for a much lower fee and get all the pleasure of learning, without the pressure of assignments, tests, deadlines, and marks. Doug and Betty attended a couple of her classes, including Early Childhood Development. They often joked, to the point where Emily thought she might puke, that they wanted to learn more about kids so they could do a better job with their grandchildren than they'd done with their own. Their favourite T-shirt read 'If I'd known grandkids were this much fun I would have had them first'. Each of them wore one: Doug's in blue, Betty's in pink, sometimes to Early Childhood class together on the same day. Yuck.

Betty and Doug did everything together. One of *those* couples. Doug's bushy eyebrows inch-wormed their way across his forehead, and on a bad day his moustache looked like mutton chops. Doug's sixties style sideburns reminded Emily of kinky pubic hair, except by 2004 his facial hair had faded from its original black to a dull grey to match the well-oiled hair on his head.

Betty's British Bulldog nose didn't add much to their image as a classic couple, either. After thirty-five years of wedded bliss, they looked much like each other, except Betty wasn't as hairy. Emily noticed it happens with dogs and owners, too, if they spend too much time together. Who wants to look like a dog?

Whatever dog they resembled must not be hypoallergenic as Emily sneezed whenever she came within sniffing distance of the two of them. Unless she was reacting to Doug's heavily doused self: classic eau de Old Spice. Betty and Doug's guts even matched. In a moment of wickedness, Emily imagined how their guts fit together when they performed their monthly 'romp'. Interesting visual. Or not.

Betty warned Emily sex wouldn't seem so damn important, once she got through menopause, and she felt blessed to have a husband to satisfy her needs every now and then. Betty figured if that part of your marriage still worked at her age, you absolutely shouldn't mess with it. Emily, no longer having a husband or any kind of sexual partner, wished Betty would keep her private life to herself. A bit of Island politeness surfaced, in spite of all her years in the wild, Wild West, so she listened and refrained from telling Betty she absolutely wasn't ready to think about middle age sex, or any sex at all between two people she barely knew. Besides, she never knew when she encountered people if they might make an interesting character for a story for her Creative Writing class. So, best to be polite. One glance at her own middle reminded her she had a few rolls of her own, which seemed to have taken up permanent residence. Who was she to criticize?

'So that's why it's called middle age! 'Cause you get so much more middle', she thought. Adorable as her middle might now be, she couldn't take the chance a man would laugh at hers. She would only be able to do it in a pitch black night, another excellent reason to avoid close encounters of the sexual kind with any of these frisky young men, especially the cute musician guy, Luke. As if she needed any more.

Although if he'd wear the cologne he wore the day they walked through the leaves...or the night they worked together on an assignment for Early Childhood class, when he leaned into her under the street light in the student parking lot, caught her as she climbed into her car, startled her with a kiss. Surprised by desire at her age. Imagine that.

No time for creative writing, either. Sex. Writing. Two things she had been waiting a long time to try again and enjoy again. Taking care of Kate hadn't even left any room in her head for fantasies, either. Cancer had a way of tampering with her libido, it seemed.

Had she had any decent sex since Chris died twenty-seven years ago? She couldn't remember. Roberto, her ex, wasn't good for much except procreation. There was one time in Mexico...

She put down her novel and decided to write about one time in Mexico, as if she was talking to that hot Luke guy. To see how far she would get, assuming he would never read it, she wrote:

Dear Luke

Last night, I finished a cop/adventure book by a woman named Sandra Burroughs. I noticed for a woman, she uses a lot of crude four letter words when describing the sex scenes. For the female's anatomy, words like 'quiff,' 'c--t'. Fuck, I hate that word. If you ever want to get back at me over some misdeed of mine, throw the c-word at me two minutes before my 8:30 class on a Monday morning. The only four-letter word Burroughs uses for the males is 'cock'. In fact, she describes the woman's parts way more than the man's. Her lack of imaginative descriptors makes me wonder if she figures men's appendages don't matter so much, as long as they know what to do with them to satisfy (or destroy) the central female character in her story. My, wouldn't men be disappointed if they ever figured out our little secret: their wonderful, worship worthy, Wet Willie isn't really a subject of adoration for most women? It might take the fun out of reading Burroughs' adrenaline driven, violent tales of murder and mayhem. For the men, anyway.

As I read along, I realized she only uses the crude words if she's describing an attack on a woman. When the two main characters eventually fall in love and do the dirty, the language is not so dirty anymore. Then it's all about caresses and tender glances and all that crap. So maybe there is a formula to her writing. Bet it goes something like this: crude words are for exclusive use of the aggressive, misogynistic villains; soft, tender words are for the big, brave hero. Either that or she's a man. (Since men favour crude words more than women do, unless women are pissed. Then they can out-curse any sailor. Research shows. So do I.) Could be she's writing under a pseudonym, and she is secretly a man named Sandy.

I've been contemplating how I would write sex scenes. I don't think I'd use four-letter words. Prick maybe, but that's more of a five-letter word—that and balls, also five letters. Ball doesn't quite work the same. Doesn't scan as well, and is usually inaccurate. Although men can function equally as well with only one. Or so I've heard.

This morning, when I was having sex with myself, I got to thinking about The First Time, trying to remember the feeling. It wasn't great for me. It isn't for many women. So I decided if I am to write about the first time, I'll make my central character someone who had her hymen ruptured by a bike accident, so I can get the blood and gore over with. My mind wandered off again. (Does that sometimes during sex. At least it wasn't counting the flies on the ceiling. 'Cause there aren't any this time of year. I used to do a lot of counting with my ex. It's not a good sign. So goes the quality of my sex life.)

So. Where was I? Oh yeah, thinking of our last Mexico holiday. Must be because of all the spoiled people, like Betty and Doug, who are getting another tropical vacation this year. As for me, like Jimmy Buffet, I keep looking for five o'clock. Could you please tell me where somewhere is?

Six years ago my family took a trip to Huatulco. Seems like a distant memory now. You didn't know me then. I hope to God I don't start marking time by when I met you. It could happen.

Huatulco is one of those intentional towns Mexico built in recent years to supply the needs of foreign tourists. So, no colonial or indigenous characteristics. The Bahais de Huatulco gave us nine bays to explore; the ocean, the scenery, and the friendliness of the residents compensated for the lack of heritage architecture and history. Plus, it's a university town and alive with young people and good food.

Of all the resort towns I've visited, Huatulco is my favourite. The main resort hotels perch on an ocean-side cliff and are built close to the ground with beautiful, Mediterranean lines. We were treated to a classical concert in the garden of one of them. White tablecloths, white chair skirts, white candles, white wine, black-tie musicians. A white three-quarter moon shining over one of the nine bays. Classical music by candlelight: as close as we could afford to get to the many refined experiences this resort offered.

This particular resort hotel is democratic enough to invite the riffraff from the town every Thursday for a night of music. Many of the high-end hotels are owned by Canadian companies. I'd like to think the Canadian influence is why Huatulco's resort area is more sympatico *with the surrounding landscape* than the American built resorts on the Yucatan. But then, I've always been a Canadian snob when it comes to architecture, democracy, and good taste.

One Saturday we took a tour up into the mountains. The vibrant little jungle bungalows there don't blend into the landscape so much as cling tenaciously to the mountain wall. The back of the house leans like a worn out child, while the front raises its inhabitants up on stilts, a more effective construction to keep the night creatures out. Stilts could also prove advantageous if the mountain decided to slide away. This mountain wouldn't, though: it's still heavily forested.

They say the black jaguar still roams these hills. The mountain and the jaguar keep each other's secrets, so it's unlikely you would ever see one. We didn't. But we saw butterflies. Lots and lots of butterflies.

Here the native people practise natural healing and drink copious amounts of moonshine they make for themselves out of cactus and several other mysterious exotic plants and animals. They also eat lots of mysterious exotic plants and animals, including cactus and crickets and wild boar. So did we, for lunch that day. You haven't lived till you've crunched on a cricket.

This little excursion included a walk through the woods to a waterfall, where we swam in the pool at the base where the water collected. A few brave souls in the group added to the experience by climbing a tree and clinging—and I do mean clinging—to a rope they found tied to the strongest branch, swinging out over the falls Tarzan style, and letting go over the middle of the pool to take a blissfully inelegant dive, seconds before they would crash into the stone cliff on the other side. The cliff kind of reduced the options, but my daughter Christina and my brother Dave both said it was terrifying to let go of the rope, even as the sheer face of solid rock came closer and closer, coming right at you. They are both bold people, not afraid to let go. Not like me.

So, I started thinking about the waterfall as I stared at the flies on the ceiling. I decided to write my first sex story, since I had enough unsatisfactory sex for one day and needed something else to do. Think I'll call it 'First Time'. Pretty obvious, eh?

First draft of *First Time*. Or more like:
Outline for First Time

The girl would have to be from Prince Edward Island. Let's call her Jane. She doesn't think she's pretty, as she inherited the standard Celtic combo of red hair, freckles, and blue eyes from her mom. She often thinks of herself as Jane of Green Gables, even though Anne's eyes were green. Weren't they? And that's about as innocent as this story is going to get. When I finish it, I don't think I'll save it for my Creative Writing course, although the Prof might appreciate the literary nod to L.M. Montgomery, if I even leave that part in.

So, she thinks she's a plain Jane. Jane's friends know different though, and they can't wait for her to start to see what they see so they plan a surprise for her eighteenth birthday. One of her friends—let's call her Anne—is quite an adventurous and capricious soul who had already traveled to Mexico several times with her family. On Jane's birthday her friends present her with a one-way ticket to Huatulco and promise to travel with her and help her find her way. So off they go. But they don't fly Air Canada because it's too unreliable, thanks to its poor labour relations. Besides, AC is so annoying and always loses your luggage. Doesn't matter how the girls get there, they just do, the six of them. Six eighteen-year-old Island girls on the loose in a little Mexican town called Huatulco. Without their parents. Uh oh.

There's a bar in Huatulco my three daughters fell in love with, where they hang scarves from the ceiling and let them blow around in the breeze from the fans and the night wind. The bar is decorated with leather chairs, paintings and souvenirs they sell, and T-shirts hanging on the walls—metalhead stuff, like Black Sabbath and Metallica. And they play old Bob Dylan tunes and Leonard Cohen. (His music travels the world. I've been trying to tell you.) My youngest, Bethany, got to tend bar one night with the young bartender, and crush on him, so she added it to her list of Huatulco favourites. If you ever get there, stand at the ice cream shop by the town square where the little kids play with their daddies every night, and look kitty corner and up. You'll see the balcony, which is most of the bar.

So...where was I? After a day of drenching their supple bodies in the sun, Jane and her friends gussie themselves up Canadian-style and head to this bar, whose name I need to Google. Or ask my youngest. She'll remember. In the hazy, sleepy atmosphere with the night breeze and the fans stirring the silk scarves, Jane eyes a young man. A dark and dreamy and handsome (Fetching? Attractive? Gorgeous? Princely? Help me out here, Luke.) young man, who orders her a beer. Or more likely, "Dos cervezas, por favor."

Now I forgot to tell you something. Mexican men love Canadian women. And they love red heads, and when they find out we come from this mysterious Island by the Atlantic Ocean, they love us even more. So this guy is sunk right from the get-go. After canoodling in the dark to Cohen's "I'm Your Man", Jane tells him she has to go. He reaches for her hand as she hurries down the stairs (She shouldn't have hurried. As I recall, those stairs are awful treacherous.) He calls out to her, "Wait! Meet me in the *zocola* (town square) tomorrow at ten, and I will show you something wonderful."

She wonders for a minute if it might be his cock (my first sex word); she had heard Mexican men are quite proud of their appendages. Still, he seemed like a humble, if gorgeous, sort, so she doesn't think it would be.

The next morning here she is, sitting on the bronze park bench, watching the magpies peck at the leftovers from last night's community party. Waiting. Jane is a little worried, because someone told her Mexicans are notorious for tardiness, and famous for living on Mexican Time. (It's kind of like Luke Time. Or Emily Time. A self-fulfilling prophecy.) But Miquel (I just named him. What do you think? Miquel is a good strong Mexican name. Think I'll go with Miquel, since you're no good at naming things, anyway.)

So, Miquel comes running across the *zocola* in his shorts and T-shirt, and Jane notices certain things she hadn't the night before. Beautiful calves. Dreamy eyes, black like agates. And black hair on his chest and his hands and his arms and his calves. In fact, he would be quite a hairy beast if he wasn't so fuckin' handsome. He can speak pretty good English. Many of the locals speak 'pretty good ingles' in Huatulco, evidenced by the signs at the market that say things like:

GOLD silver shop 40% OFF

GABRIEL THE OWL,

WE WON'T CHEAT YOU TOO BAD.

Anyway, Miquel doesn't have any trouble making himself understood. Men never do when they are interested in a woman, or so I recall. It has been so long...five long...Oh yeah, story. Focus.

Miquel notices something he didn't the night before, either. He notices the way the morning sun shines through the trees, catches strands of Jane's hair and sets them on fire, or so he thinks at first. The sun catches her hair, or her hair catches the sun. I'm not sure which; neither is Miquel. He mentions this to her, and she shrugs and says, "My hair has always had a mind of its own," as if it is a living thing. But her hair reminds Miquel more of a fire star than a living thing. An extraterrestrial fire star, one that came down from the heavens with the dawn.

Miquel wants to take Jane up into the mountains, where his great granny comes from. His old beat-up truck is lacking a muffler, so Jane isn't so sure. Until she remembers what her well-travelled friend, Anne, had to say about Mexican drivers. Besides them being ridiculously insane, they make sure three things work on their rigs. Brakes—check. Wipers—check. Horn—check. So she decides to make a change for Miquel and take a chance. She trusts him. She won't be disappointed.

It's beautiful on the mountain. The road swoops around the curvaceous mountain like a gentle and respectful lover. This is not an aggressive switchback mountain. More like a wise old medicine woman of a mountain. The native societies of this area are matriarchal, and their love of women shows: warm mother earth and warm mother people. Glimpses over the cliff let Jane see the river winding down from the crest of the mountain and into the hills and valleys of this Grand Old Dame.

Every now and then, Miquel stops at a way station and lifts Jane down from the dusty old truck. They stand together at the edge of a ravine and gaze out over the greens and blues and pinks and reds. Yes, the soil on this mountain is red, not quite as red as PEI's, mind you, but a lovely warm soft red; a colour much more suited to the tropics than to our northern climate. Either way, the earth reminds Jane of home and helps her relax.

Miquel finds the little path he has been watching for during their ascent into the clouds. He pulls the truck into a clearing in the forest. Miquel takes Jane's little freckled hand and stops for a moment to admire the contrast of his dark hand against her pale one. Like a true Mexican gentleman, he lifts her hand to his lips. (I know you won't like that part, Luke, much too mushy, but...)

Now it's time to guide her through the woods. The mountain grows not so much a jungle or a tropical rainforest as a southern pine forest with hardwoods and occasional cyprus trees, growing in among the vines and leaf cover. The walk is not difficult or hot, and the tall pines remind her of home. She can sense Canada in the green undergrowth, mixed in with the musty funky smell of growing and dying foliage, and the clean scent of the crystal clear stream they are following. The water is so clear she can see the gravel and stones on the bottom. Her mom told her the streams of PEI looked like that at one time. So translucent you could step in the cool, transparent water and tickle a trout swimming by; catch one by hand if you needed it for supper, simply by tickling. Jane will be tickled and caught today in this cool, clear water, in a way she has never experienced and is soon to discover. Because Miquel needs her like we all need each other when we are young and about to fall in love—in case you didn't know, Luke, or don't remember. Or weren't paying attention. Now I have to get Jane and Miquel down to the waterfall, so quit distracting me, would you?

Miquel parts some branches and points off to his right, and Jane catches sight of a magical little pool of clean, fresh water. Champagne bubbles swirl in the deepest blue she has ever laid eyes on. Green plants line the banks with little blue flowers in their midst, blue cornflowers like the ones we grow here on the Island.

At first, she thinks they are alone. Then a lilting teenage voice sings out, "Miquel! *Aqui! Aqui!*"

Jane's heart sinks and her red hair despairs as she spies a dark beauty on the far bank, beautiful in the way Miquel is beautiful: raven hair, agate eyes, and smooth, permanently tanned skin. Imagine her relief when Miquel yells out, "*Ola muchacha! Esta es mi amour, Jane. Jane, esta es mi hija, Marta.*"

Jane doesn't quite get this. Her Spanish is not only elementary, it's pretty well non-existent. She does understand this chica is Miquel's sister, though. She starts to breathe again.

Marta and Jane and Miquel take turns swinging out over the pool, like Christina and Dave did. Finally, none too soon as far as Jane is concerned, Marta takes her leave. I forgot to describe the waterfall. Well, it looks pretty much like a waterfall. It's not particularly high as waterfalls go, but it is high enough that you wouldn't want to fall over.

Miquel knows something she doesn't, and he can't wait to show her. He guides her once again. (She is a little blind and stupid out of her own environment, this Island girl. Like you would be if I ever took you to Mexico. You would be sooo much work. You can bet that will never happen.) Miquel doesn't mind being a good tour guide, though. Hospitality comes naturally to these mountain people, kind of like us on the Island, except they're not inundated with mass tourism, yet. Lucky not-yet-cynical folks.

Let's try that again. (You and tourists are the biggest distractions.) Miquel guides her once again. Behind the waterfall curtain into a secret cave hollowed out over time by the cascading falls. It takes her breath away. Literally and figuratively. She can't breathe. At first. It's a little claustrophobic, till you get used to it. Miquel stands by her and gets her to focus on his lips as he breathes in and out, in and out, like a feather in the breeze. (Only there wouldn't be any feathers in behind a waterfall. No birds either. I don't think.)

Miquel places her hand on his chest, and once she stops getting lost in those eyes, she can find the rhythm of his breathing. She gets the hang of it.

The water behind the water curtain comes to her waist and to the top of his thighs. I haven't mentioned he is about a hip's worth taller than her, have I? However high that is. The water tickles him in his private parts, but for her, her belly button is not particularly erotic, so she is as yet unaffected by the cool touch of the surface at the top of the little pool. Not so lucky, Miquel tries to hide his reaction. He just met her yesterday. Jane is so intrigued by the experience of breathing in mist and watching the colours the light rays make as they sift through the crystal curtain she doesn't notice Miquel's discomfort or embarrassment. And that's a good thing.

After a few minutes, Miquel starts to fear he has lost her to this mystical environment he takes for granted and she finds absolutely captivating. Jane remembers her manners, the many times she guided tourists at The Lake of Shining Waters, and the frustration of getting them to pay attention, so she comes back to Miquel. Can you blame her? He's hot. Hot, Hot, HOT. Hot Tamale hot!

Jane is wearing a bikini she bought especially for this trip. Her ivory skin is now golden from her days in the Huatulco sun. Miquel bends down and kisses her golden shoulders; the memory of the morning star fire returns to him. He nuzzles her neck, the hollow underneath her collarbone and the one above, as well. She touches his shiny wet hair for the first time, as he leans over her. His breath feels warm on her cool skin. All that time spent in a mountain spring under green overhanging boughs leaves them both cool and squeaky clean. This is all about to change. He brings his lips up to hers and...well, you know what happens next. And no, he doesn't kiss as good as you, Luke. No one does. I knew you'd ask. You're the best kisser ever. OK?! Get over it.

But he kisses damn good. His mouth has a way of finding her soft spots and exploring them to a point where she thinks they might melt, dissolve into him. Now he is sliding his hand into her bikini top and his fingers into her bottoms. He releases the ties at the back of her bikini and cups her cool firm breasts in his hand. Her nipples are cool, too. Cool and hard.

27

But not for long. Against her will, her better judgement, her embarrassment, and her natural shyness, her nipples respond. They go soft and warm and full in his hands, and next in his mouth. Now he comes back up for air and more mist-blessed kisses. Jane wraps her arms around his strong broad shoulders, pulls herself up to his chest, senses his soft black hairs tickling her already stimulated nipples. She sighs and holds him for a minute, her heart against his heart.

Hey, I just realized something! Men and women both have their heart on the left so when they are chest to chest they can feel each other's hearts beeping away, beep, beep, beep, in simultaneous synchronicity. How convenient is that?! Another example of God's infinitely pleasurable design! And when we face one another, we humans, we are a mirror image for each other. Like I will be to you one day, Luke, whether you see me or not.

This is not about you and me, Luke, and Jane and Miquel are a lot smarter—and freer—than you and me, so they go with it, wherever it takes them. The next place it takes them is his fingers into her bikini bottoms. Sliding along her hipbone till he finds the ties and springs her loose. Her sex has come out of jail and feels to her, as the water and his fingers lap around her core, as if she is home free at last. Away from her plain Jane name, Canadian winters, and all the stultifying Islanders. Away from all the cyber bullies of her high school years, with their gossipy chat groups—the modern day equivalent of the slate Anne of Green Gables broke over Gilbert's head.

Jane can't remember a time when she felt this glorious, or this sure, or this strong. See, that's what love does, Luke, when it's returned. It leaves her feeling every one of those things and more: sensual, shimmering, silvery, and slippery, like the water of the curtain.

Now she's Amazonian enough to wrap her legs around his hips. He finds his way to her wet (What? C--t? No fucking way. Quiff? Nope. Quimmy? Hmmm, Vajayjay—too childish and unsexy. Envelope? Purse? Puss?) Silk purse. You know? The one I've been trying to make out of a sow's ear since the night I first felt on fire for you; the night in the parking lot I will never write to you about.

28

He slides into the silk purse and experiences the deepest peace he has ever experienced, which lasts about five seconds before the adrenaline kicks in and takes over. Jane slides up and down on his (What? Prick? Cock? Member? Noodle? Dick? Hmmm...Dick and Jane...Oh no, different story. Sword? Peter?) Peter. Named after yours and every other man's. Is that your middle name, too? Miquel's is Jesus, pronounced Hey Suuz. Jane calls out his name and, as the tension builds, yells, "Jesus! Jesus! Jesus!" Or "Hey Suuz! Hey Suuz! Hey Suuz!"

Then, "God! Great God Almighty!" She's going back to her Catholic roots. Or not. She's just singing the praises of the force that gives us poor, snivelling humans a way to pleasure each other, sort of a trade off for all the death and destruction coming our way. Jane and Miquel are not thinking about death and destruction, not at all. Miquel is so close. Still, he's a gentleman. He wants to show her the best time of her young life, as if all the aforementioned isn't enough. He lifts her carefully off him, sets her back into the little pool in the little cave under the little waterfall. Her face falls, so he catches her up again and says, "No, No, don't cry! You are perfect. I want to show you how perfect you are."

He slides her up and over onto the rock shelf on the walls of this cave, places her where he wants her, and asks her to lean back, as he supports her with his thighs and his beautiful calves. He bows his head as if he means to make his confession to her, open his soul to her. He touches her with his tongue, where she has never been touched that way before, where he has never tasted before. When he dreamed about this moment last night, he wondered what a girl from Prince Edward Island, Canada, would taste like. What is the taste of blue skies and white clouds and green fields and red cliffs and butter cream sand dunes and evergreens and blue spruce and lilacs and lupines and peonies and pansies and blue cornflowers and devil's paintbrushes and red maple leaves and pure white snow and silver thaws? All the things Jane described to him that filled his dreams. Now, I am not going to tell you what that tastes like. That's private. Besides, you live here so you should know. If you don't, it's because you haven't been paying enough attention. Again. Pay attention, Luke.

Let's just say Miquel was very happy with what he found on the rock shelf behind the waterfall curtain. And so was Jane. And, yes, her sex was on fire. But it didn't melt. She didn't melt and neither did he. But they both felt...well...phenomenal. I'll leave it at that.

There are so many ways two people can pleasure each other when they are young and healthy and in love, or old(er) and healthy and in love.
Maybe I could rewrite this, take you and the sex out; share it with my Creative Writing Class next term. But then, she asks innocently enough, what would be the point?

Emily

Emily felt better, even though she would never ever be able to share this story with Luke. So she slept.

Sticky Buns

Emily handed in her last exam, exited stage right, and took the first deep breath she'd taken in weeks. As she shrugged herself into her coat, she felt two big hands clenching her neck. Luke, trying to loosen her up and get her attention. "You scared the shit out of me!" she hollered.

He had this way of coming out of nowhere, which she found more than a little disconcerting, and a habit of whispering in her ear, even when they weren't in class and supposed to be listening. It showed a rather infantile side to his character. Then she remembered he was only twenty-four, not much more than an *enfant terrible* himself.

He whispered, "I'm playing at the Student Union Building tonight. Why don't you come and listen to me? I'm doing the acoustic set before the big Christmas dance."

She said she couldn't see how that would ever happen and left him standing in the hall with his ball cap in hand. On the way to her car, Betty and Doug hailed her from across the parking lot. They talked Emily into going, reassured her the first set was for the mature students and those from the Seniors' College. There wouldn't likely be many of the young ones at that time, as it would be too early to get their drinking done at their apartments. University on a budget meant getting drunk before you hit the bars. At five bucks a shot, she couldn't blame them.

That evening, after a long luxurious bath, Emily contemplated her wardrobe. And then contemplated suicide. She wouldn't be bringing sexy back with any of these clothes. She wavered between an old sweatshirt and the standard little black number that might still fit her.

This had to be a very bad idea: she was too old to go chasing after some young buck. So she settled on jeans and a T shirt, hailed a cab in case she might want a few celebratory drinks, and picked up a fruit tray at the Superstore. Old people and musicians need to eat.

She waved to Doug and Betty as she walked into the SUB. She could spot Betty in her orange muumuu and Doug in his Hawaiian shirt a mile away.

Good lord, she hadn't seen a muumuu since the seventies! Betty's secret fashion ambition must be to channel Mama Cass.

What was it about this couple that brought out the inner bitch in her? Who knows. Maybe she just didn't want to think she'd ever get that damn old. 'How did that song go?' she thought. 'Something about being much too young to feel this damn old. About sums it up.'

They sent Doug to find them the best seats in the house. Not that any seat made of orange plastic could ever be called 'best', but at least theirs weren't cracked. Last week, when she and Luke were taking a study/coffee break, Emily (who thought that morning it would be fun to dress up for a change) hitched up her dress and sat on one of the plastic chairs, not realizing it was cracked till it pinched the cheek of her ass. Not one of her finer moments. Then, when she stood up to try to free her butt from the seat, the chair came with her. It wasn't *that* funny. It pinched like a son of a gun. She still had a skinny blue bruise on her left butt cheek. She had been half tempted to ask Luke to kiss her bruise and make it better. Shut him up, for a change.

Doug made sure their seats gave them the best view of the action. Not a big challenge: there were plenty of choices. Only a few old farts like them around and that young fart Luke on the little riser, still setting up. What time do these things get going? It said 8 pm on the poster so 8 it should be, in her humble opinion. Could she be getting 'this damn old', after all?

Luke gave her a great big grin and apologized for his missing band, as they all still lived over in Cape Breton. He treated her to a dozen Celtic songs she recognized and liked: songs like "The Fields of Athenry", songs her generation and her mother's generation and her grandmother's before her loved and kept close to their hearts. Emily expected as much from Luke, given he was a Caper. She forgot he belonged to a whole new cohort, who learned music from their iPods, not at their mama's knee.

She had a reasonably good time and wished she could stay longer for the main event, since the semi-famous band from Halifax headlined, and she'd like to sing along with their hits. But Betty and Doug kept going on about their monthly romp, and Luke was surrounded by a gaggle of young girls. She recognized some of them from class, but not well enough to talk to. All their gushing made it look like he wouldn't have time for her, even though Betty claimed he'd been watching her out of the corner of his eye all night. She wasn't buying it. Any of it. Watching Luke lap up all the attention was getting on her nerves. So rather than lose her temper, she bowed out gracefully and hitched a ride with a neighbour back to the lovely little house on the shore. And lay there unable to sleep. And unable and unable again, till her friend Kate came by:

Kate: What are you still doing up at three in the morning? You know how cranky you get when you don't get enough sleep.
Emily: The cat jumped up on the porch roof and started banging on the window. He made me get up and let him in.
Kate: That old trick, eh?
Em: Now I'm awake and have nothing better to do than think.
Kate: Oh oh.
Emily: My belly hurts.
Kate: Too many fudge squares?
Em: It might have been the cinnamon rolls from Winter River Bakery. So many people brought sweets to the Christmas party at the Uni. I contributed fruit. Good thing, eh?
Kate: You can't get those cinnamon rolls here, only in Winter River. Remember the day we bought those sticky buns from the bakery, parked by the side of the road, and walked up to Officer's Pond?
Em: Before you got sick the second time. Two redheads in the sun, trying to find what remained of the pond we remembered: weeds, wildflowers, and lots of mosquitoes.
Kate: Whatever happened to the sweet young family who ran the bakery, anyway?
Emily: Now that's another story. Their marriage flew off the rails not long after that—poor souls.
Kate: Remember how they kept plugging away, day and night? A bakery is hard work.
Em: Kate, I need to talk to you. You know that friend you sent me? What if I imagine him to be more sensitive, kinder, and more generous than he is? After all, he did take the last fudge square.
Kate: Well, the word up here is his mom is noticeably kind.

Emily: So I've heard. His brother, Tommy, is nice. He's staying with him in Charlottetown for the year. But Tommy's not him. Luke can be a little cynical.

Kate: You've always liked some edgy cynicism in a person.

Emily: What if he turns out to be, as the Brits would say, a perfectly unsuitable boy?

Kate: He's not a child now, even though he might like to be.

Em: Wouldn't we all? What do I do if he proves to be unsuitable?

Kate: Hmmm...I'm not usually wrong about people anymore...used to be when I was still in the world, but that was then. Let me think for a minute.

Ten days later—those people in heaven, they have absolutely no concept of time!

Kate: You could accept him the way he is and learn to appreciate the strengths he does offer. He's more focused and grounded than you imagined. His sense of humour is a good thing to bring to a friendship. He's not like you, except in the ways you've figured out. Consider it a blessing. He helps you stay sane at exam time. He makes you laugh. There's that.

Emily: Or I could trade him in. In fact, if this keeps up I may start actively disapproving of this boy. I know you don't approve of disapproval where you live.

Kate: Actually, there isn't any approval or disapproval up here. We leave it up to you earthbound types, since you all enjoy it so much. Try to be patient.

Early the next morning, just as the sun was rising, Emily called Kate to her once again.

Emily: Kate, I dreamed you walked into your little house at the beach, and you stood in the living room admiring the new paintings by Island artists and the new paint job—by me. Then I remembered you can't come to this house anymore, this house where you lived out your days. But I could hear you and see you as if you popped up, right there in the living room. I've tried writing to him like you said, but my words are too private and personal to share. Besides, he's too young. He's just a pup. I should write to you instead.

Kate: Of course, you can write me any old day. But you can't dump your new friend just to take up with this old one again. Remember in Brownies how we used to dance around the big toadstool and sing

> Make new friends,
> But keep the old.

One is silver
And the other gold.
Make new friends
But keep the old.

Emily joined in the old Brownie earworm as she and Kate made a round of it.

Em: I guess we did learn the most important stuff when we were little kids. And his hair is gold.

Kate: Emily, you always put way too much significance into hair colour.

I talked to Willie today and he says many people considered Anne perfectly unsuitable. In fact, they are still saying so four hundred years later. You know, all that talk about her being the 'corrupting older woman', etc., etc.

Em: Anne who? Cuthbert?

Kate: No, Hathaway, of course. Anne Hathaway's Cottage in England? Shakespeare was only seventeen when he got tangled up with her, but it didn't hurt his career one bit.

Em: I'm hardly Shakespeare. I wouldn't even want to try to be. All I want is to write stuff that makes him smile, or at least think a little.

Kate: Willie says that's all he ever wanted to do. He just used a lot of excellent words well and a little rhythm and rhyme, too.

Emily: Will you ask him if he ever experienced the sound of one hand clapping? Or dead air? Or the drunk at the bar phenomena—when the only one left besides the bartender is the drunk who keeps falling asleep and waking up long enough to yell at you, but you still have to finish your stand-up routine anyway? That's what it feels like when my new friend doesn't respond.

Kate: Look at it this way—he made you sit down and write this out today so he can't be entirely unsuitable.

Emily: Good point. What are we going to do about the sound of one hand clapping, Kate?

Kate: Hmmm, I'll have to go ask...

Emily: No, no, don't go. It's a rhetorical question. The sad thing is my friend seems to think all my questions are rhetorical so he doesn't answer any of them.

Kate: What do you want him to do?

35

Emily: To tell you the truth, I don't know. In my imagination he's listening, and that's a useful thing to do. But then, I could be deluding myself. I'm capable of it. In fact, sometimes living in Dreamland is more fun.

Kate: Remember how we both would give ourselves reality checks when I lived in the world? I'm so glad I don't do that anymore. Reality shmeality. Who cares about reality, anyhow?

Em: I still care. Or at least I think I do. What if I am deluded about this? Kate? Kate? It wasn't a rhetorical question. Kate?

Kate disappeared—again! When she came back:

Emily: Kate, last night I dreamed I was walking down on the sandbars with a bunch of clam diggers. We were sifting through the sand and sea, trying to find my new friend's baby finger a clam had bitten off. The clammers worried it might hurt his guitar playing; fingerless fingering might not work. Then I got to thinking about how vulnerable our appendages are. They could be attached one minute and the next thing they could fly off into the air and land somewhere in the ocean. Kind of like our children. Or the bakers' marriage.

Kate: Or like new friendships. I heard a rumour about your friend today.

Emily: Who did you hear it from?

Kate: Not sure who started it—someone who knew him in your dimension, or he might have known your friend before he was born. I heard it from a friend of a friend of a friend. Playing 'gossip' happens up here, too. Anyway, the story going around is he's meant to do more with music in his life, like sing more. Or write songs.

Em: Yeah, and I will write caustic lyrics to go with them. Ha ha.
Should I tell him?

Kate: Maybe not. It is only a rumour, and it may prove to be unsubstantiated. When you write to this guy, does he try to critique your writing or editorialize? Or encourage you to join writers' workshops or suggest books to read on the art of writing?

Em: No, thank God! He just lets me write.

Kate: That must be refreshing.

Emily: Mmmm, encouragement can be so constricting sometimes, can't it?

Kate: Then you best not tell him yet what they say about him and music. Better not encourage him.

Emily: Better not. He's got a big enough ego about his music as it is. Can't see how he'll ever make a teacher if he doesn't learn to share the spotlight. Maybe I'll ask him to sing in the choir; that might teach him to share.

So she did. More about that later—after Christmas.

Tessa

Speaking of Christmas, there's not much to say. Emily spent a miserable one. None of her daughters, Erin, Christina, or Bethany, could afford to come back East and, on her budget, she sure couldn't go out West. Kate's money would only stretch so far, and she had to be careful if she expected to make it through till summer. Her school friends and acquaintances had gone home or were spending time with their families. Emily didn't want to intrude, and she didn't want to head to Halifax to impose on her siblings, either. One quick trip over to visit her mom, and the rest of the holiday she spent reading, writing, and eating way too much chocolate. She would be glad to see the New Year and the new semester in.

One special thing happened for Emily over Christmas. One night, as she danced naked in the moonlight, she heard a voice on the wind. Sure enough, it was Kate:

Kate: Hey, Emily, I talked to your friend Tessa today.

Emily: Yeah? How's she doing?

Kate: Heavenly.

Emily: Oh Kate, how corny!

Kate: That's all I got. Sorry. She is a sweetie, though.

Emily: Funny, you two never clicked. Did it taking dying for you to finally connect?

Kate: Maybe. She died too young, before I got a chance to grow up a bit and stop resenting the time you spent with her. We were both young and foolish and capable of tremendous jealousy at the time.

Emily: I was thinking how Tessa loved to dance in the moonlight, too. Sometimes she even went *au naturelle*.

Kate: Like you?

Emily: She taught me everything I know. About moonlight and dancing, anyway. Don't tell God—or at least not if it's that Catholic God on duty tonight.

Kate: Remember the healing God they burned for a witch? She's on this shift. So I think we're safe.

Em: Did Tessa ever tell you the story her Baha'i friend Heather told about how, when Tessa lived at the palliative care home, Heather asked if she could be her best friend?

Kate: No, she didn't tell me. What did she say?

Emily: She said, and I quote, 'I can't be your best friend because I already have one, and she's almost more than I can handle.'

Kate: And that 'she' would be you.

Emily: Yup. Did she also tell you about "The Cherry Tree Carol"?

Kate: Nope.

Emily: When we were about thirteen or fourteen, we both sang in a choir. We were performing the Christmas concert. The Bel Cantos, we called ourselves— all dressed up in powder blue and royal blue sack-cloth dresses. The fabric scratched like potato bags and had about as much shape. We were so hot! Nana Mouskouri glasses and all.

Kate: I hear those are back in style again.

Em: Sorry to say.

Kate: No one has to wear glasses here.

Emily: Thank God for that!

Kate: Yes, you can.

Em: So anyway, the choir director, who also happened to be her father, picked Tessa to sing "The Cherry Tree Carol", while I was standing in the back row, praying, 'Pick me, pick me.' You talk about jealous! You and Tessa had nothing on me that night! Of course, she sang it beautifully, her voice so true, pitch perfect, and it didn't even matter to her. She sang solo because she felt obligated to for her dad. She might have even been a little embarrassed. Her crush was in the audience.

Kate: Joseph was an old man

Em: An old man was he

Kate: He married Virgin Mary
> The Queen of Galilee.
> He married Virgin Mary
> The Queen of Gal-li-lee.

Emily: Still my favourite carol.

Kate: Tessa did tell me another story, though. She told me how one day when you came in to visit her at the palliative care unit, she was all yucky and sick and fed up and all she wanted was to curse. You said, 'Go ahead. I'll curse along with you.' And you both cussed away, like mad hatters.

Emily: I remember now! She'd had enough of hospital food, hospital clothes, and hospital odours. She was sick to death of her body and how it kept misbehaving—sick to death of being sick. The F's were flying everywhere! Turned the air blue.

Kate: She said that afternoon was one of the few times she thought it would be OK to stop being brave for everyone.

Em: She was a truly brave soul.

Kate: Still is.

Emily: Her family was so good to her those last months. As was yours. All I did for either of you was help you curse.

Kate: That's alright. When it comes to the big C, no one ever feels they can do enough. She wouldn't want to leave you with any regrets.

Emily: After I left the hospital, I went down to Fran's—remember when Fran owned the clothing store—and bought Tessa a purple fleece jogging suit, on sale. When I brought it in to her at the palliative care unit, she was thrilled to own something comfortable and colourful to wear, deep purple against white bed sheets. Most of her beautiful, thick, ash blond hair had fallen out by then, but she still looked like the Queen of the May to me.

Kate: So that's where you got the idea to buy me a tracksuit!

Emily: Not very original, eh? Plus chemo often left you chilled. I bought you a coral one, coral and white. See, I told you coral and white would suit you better than purple and black. Kinder to your fair freckled skin.

Kate: Now that I'm up here, I can see your point. Not much black around this place.

Emily: Black's not my favourite absence of colour either, but Tessa looked stunning in black. It brought out the hazel in her eyes and the rich olive of her skin.

Tessa was always so quick to give, but so hesitant when it came to accepting gifts. That day was one of the few times I remember Tessa receiving a gift and simply saying, 'Thank You' instead of, 'Oh, you shouldn't have,' or, 'I don't deserve this, blah, blah, blah.'

Kate: Spiritual growth via a tracksuit.

Emily: Yeah, spiritual growth via a tracksuit.

Emily and Kate: Too funny.

A few hours later, Kate told Emily she had someone on the line who wanted to talk to her.

Tessa: How you doing, Em?

Emily: Hey, you! I've missed you so much!

Tessa: I know. Me, too! Guess what I thought of today? Remember how I tricked you into signing the Baha'i membership card?

Emily: You got me to read *God Loves Laughter*. Good trick. Any religion with humour as a founding principle can't be all bad.

Tessa: Shame you didn't stick with it.

Emily: I couldn't get past the anti-gay stuff.

Tessa: Em, honey, the Baha'i belief was never meant as a rejection of gays, just a prohibition against practicing.

Emily: I know, I know, every major religious doctrine seems to dictate that taboo. They must think they wouldn't qualify as a world-class religion if they didn't. Lately, they all seem to be rushing to stress a little point of clarification as to why gays can be gay and God still loves them, but they just can't practise love. Maybe I'll burn in hell, but I can't commit to a belief system that shuts people out for who they are.

Tessa: Are you finished yet?

Emily: Yeah.

Tessa: You won't burn in hell.

Emily: Well, that's comforting. If that's the case, I'll continue to be a religious voyeur for the rest of my life.

Tessa: Remember how God loves laughter?

Em: Yeah.

Tessa: He's just playing a little joke on humans with all that controversy over sex.

41

Em: Weird sense of humour.

Tessa: You get used to it.

The stars were shiny and bright at the beach house the next time the girls came to call.

Tessa: How's Bethany? I had so much fun teaching her "Brilliant Star" in Baha'i School when she must have been—what, three?

Emily: She's all growed up now and she can still sing all the words:

> Oh God
>
> Guide me
>
> Protect me
>
> Illumine the lamp of my heart
>
> And make me a brilliant star
>
> For thou art the mighty and powerful.

Tessa, you were always terrific with kids, so gentle and kind. Children need people like you in their lives.

Kate: Tessa spends a lot of time in the nursery. The little ones love her. Of course, everyone loves her. That's the way it is here. The kids think she's extra special.

Em: So do I.

Kate: Me, too. Thanks for connecting us, Emily.

Tessa: Hey you guys! You're making me blush! Spirit people blush, too, you know.

While Emily watched the moonlight dance over the water, she remembered the summer Tessa lived in the farmhouse down Eldon way. One lovely clear day, she dropped by to check out this house her friend kept raving on about. Tessa stepped down from the sun porch to greet her, wearing nothing but a big straw sunhat and a little teeny bikini. She was so gorgeous and tanned. Emily took a step back to admire her friend in her perfect state of health. Tessa attributed it to all the time she spent in the gardens surrounding the old house. She said they had been a bit of a tangled mess at first, but she had tamed them enough to let the plants grow big and tall. Sunflowers and hollyhocks reached for the sky, while columbines, sweet Williams, and bachelor's buttons filled the walkway with their colour and scent. Tessa said the best part was, now that the gardens were at least a little bit civilized, she could garden in her birthday suit, if she wanted.

Emily wondered if the neighbours down the road ever got a glimpse of Tessa's naked bum through the bushes, and if they cared. No doubt they would have an opinion, but she doubted they'd care—Tessa possessed an especially cute butt. Sometimes Emily wished she could see her adorable butt (only bikini clad), and her big sun hat, and those eyes sparkling with health.

When Tessa lay dying, Emily had often wished for vibrant pictures of Tessa to replace the ones of her poor body wasting away like an Auschwitz victim. But if wishes were fishes, she'd fill up the sea. Tessa would have told her not to wish her life away, anyway.

Christina's Crash

A few days later, Kate and Tessa showed up again to keep Emily company on a cold and lonely winter's night:

Emily: Hey, you two! Do you know anything about Christina crashing her brand new motorbike?

Tessa: Yeah, we thought we'd play a little joke on her. Tee hee. OK, so dead people giggle, too. We can't help it.

Em: That is not funny, you guys! She sent me pictures of the skid marks.

Kate: It was only a little scratch.

Em: It was only a little scratch on the bike and a big road rash on her leg.

Tessa: No big deal. And a motorcycle looks too new if it doesn't have the odd little mark or ding on it.

Em: Easy for you two to say. Neither one of you is much of a judge of how much pain a person should endure. The mechanics at the dealership could not believe she didn't drop the Harley. They asked her three times. She's lucky it wasn't raining, and it always rains in British Columbia, even in the middle of winter.

Tessa: I'll take the credit, thank you, since I arranged the dry pavement.

Emily: By the sound of it, she could have been killed. That old fella pulled out, panicked, and then stopped dead, right in front of her. Thank goodness she wore her black leathers, and her helmet protected her head. Her nana calls motorbikes 'murder cycles'. Poor Mom worries about Christina mashing up her perfectly proportioned face all the time, as it is. She was rushing to work, as usual. At least, she wasn't applying her mascara, like she does when she's driving her car, and it *was* the other guy's fault. You made him do that didn't you, Tessa?

Tessa: Yup, just going for a little dramatic effect.

Kate: How does she feel now?

Em: Real grateful. Glad to be alive.

Kate: And how did she feel when her idiot boyfriend broke up with her last week?

Em: Like she wanted to die. That heartache has all disappeared, thanks to the old guy who panicked. Still, you guys, it was a dirty trick.

Tessa: We made sure she didn't get hurt, didn't we? What more could you ask for?

Em: Good thing someone intervened. Thanks a lot, guys. I think.

Kate: No problem. Our pleasure. Anytime.

Emily: Thanks, but no thanks. Between you two leaving me behind here to sulk and Chris' close call, I think we've provided enough entertainment for you to last another lifetime.

Tessa: Eternity is a long, long time up here. Things are so glorious and divinely peaceful up here, we get bored sometimes.

Em: So deal with it.

Tessa: Aw come on, admit it, you got a thrill, too.

Kate: You did say life on the Island is too dull this winter and you're running out of stories to tell. We just gave you another one.

Emily: OK, I get the point. I'm way over it now. Chris, too. She did sound more serene last night. After that shock to the system, she got over the big break-up extra quick. He'll come back to her, at any rate. They always do.

Kate: Aw, but she may not take him back.

Tessa: Maybe not.

Choir

Emily woke up, rolled over, turned on the laptop, and wrote to Luke. She forgot about the gaggle of girls at the dance and wrote out her loneliness. She asked him to try her choir when he got back to school. He had better get at it if he still planned to pursue a music degree after he finished his BEd, like he talked about. He had a long way to go to get through all those degrees; but he was young, and must be independently wealthy. She hoped so. Besides, the choir could always use another tenor. So many of their members were getting old and/or dying. His reply to her: 'What's a tenor? Is that like a fiver? Or a tenner?'

'No, Luke.' Emily groaned to herself. 'It has nothing to do with money, Silly.'

'Gotcha! Of course I know what a tenor is. Just didn't realize I sing in a tenor's range.'

When she asked if he even knew how to read music, he typed: 'A little. Mostly I sing what I hear and play my guitar. Do guitar chords count?'

She wrote back: 'It's not that hard to learn how. Didn't you study some theory in music classes in elementary school?'

'Probably. I wasn't paying a lot of attention. Too busy playing I Wanna New Band with my buddies in the garage. Now I need to figure it out.'

'I don't mind teaching you. Choir would help too.'

'Great! You rock, Em.'

'OK, we'll sign you up in the new year.' She knew the conductor was desperate. If Luke was serious about becoming a music teacher, not just dicking around, he needed to up his game, if he could. A very big IF, one which required him to take his music and himself seriously. She couldn't see that happening any time soon. In fact, his first—and last—choir rehearsal proved her point.

Sent: January 15, 2005 9:45 pm
To: Emily
Subject: choir

You warned me we would be singing in Latin and this is the piece your choir is rehearsing for Good Friday, but this is something I need to know. How would you pronounce *Pia mater cum vi-de-bat. Na-ti poe-nas in-cli-ti?* Or *fac, fac, fac, ut te-cum lu-ge-am?* And what's the English translation?

> **Sent:** January 15, 2005 9:48 pm
> **To:** Luke
> **Subject:** choir
> Ha-ha. Very funny. I warned you Schubert had a dirty mind. Did I also mention some of the elderly Brits in the choir are the smuttiest of all? You should see them at the Christmas parties.

Sent: January 15, 2005 9:52 pm
To: Emily
Subject: choir
What I wonder is: how's your *cliti* tonight? Is it *in cliti* or *cum via de bat?*

> **Sent:** January 15, 2005 10:05 pm
> **To:** Luke
> **Subject:** choir
> Not too bad. How's your *poenas?* And your *bat?*

Sent: January 15, 2005 10:45 pm
To: Emily
Subject: choir
And what exactly is a *cum lugeam?* Is it a little like cunningulis?

> **Sent:** January 15, 2005 11:02 pm
> **To:** Luke
> **Subject:** choir
> Go to bed, Luke.

Sent: January 15, 2005 11:09 pm
To: Emily

Subject: choir

OK. But I can't sleep. Too much excitement.

Sent: January 15, 2005 11:12 pm

To: Luke

Subject: choir

Sheesh. Why don't we try a basketball game next time?

Cold Arses

They both liked basketball. Luke because he used to play, and Emily because she used to play and it was always warm in the gym. Sometimes, as a concession to Luke, she toughed it out at a varsity hockey game. She knew the rules and jargon—what Canadian girl doesn't? But, much as hockey was constantly promoted by the beer companies and corporate sponsors as Canada's game, it wasn't her game anymore. The NHL should never have established all those new franchises. Too many players and none of them with much personality to add to the story. Took the spark out of the game.

Besides, the hockey bosses set up teams in bizarre places like Florida. Operating an ice rink down south had to be like trying to freeze the flames of hell. What's the point of that? She would hate to pay the Tampa Bay Lightning's bill for electricity. It couldn't be good for the environment either, wasting all those hydro carbons on running the Zamboni, freezing the ice surface, and heating the dressing rooms to compensate for the cold, while the temperature is about one-hundred degrees Fahrenheit right outside the arena doors.

Luke didn't worry about any of that. Then again, he hadn't grown up with the greats like Bobby Hull, Bobby Orr, Jean Beliveau, and the Rocket, so he had no idea what he was missing.

Emily took a good look around the cottage one day and realized she hadn't stored enough wood indoors for the winter. She would have to wait for some fine sunny days, so she could chip the ice off the woodpile before she lugged some more into the cellar. The fine sunny days were few and far between; much as she hated to ask him for anything, she called Luke.

"Luke, they're calling for good weather this weekend, and I need a favour."

"What's up, my little Chickadee?"

"I need at least two more cords of wood inside, if I'm not going to freeze my arse off before spring."

49

Luke understood wood stoves, so he agreed to come and help Emily on Saturday. Kate's cottage was built in the Craftsman's Bungalow style, a story and a half that was quite popular with home builders on the Island in the nineteen thirties and forties. Emily loved so many of its details: wainscoting halfway up the walls; interior wooden doors with glass panes and handles; double pocket doors between the kitchen and dining room; an Enterprise wood stove; and, for the trim on the ceilings and stairs, Douglas fir imported all the way from British Columbia—quite an undertaking in 1930.

Emily's least favourite features included the outdoor wooden hatch and the set of red Island-stone steps that allowed her to step down into the hole in the wall of the stone foundation and enter the basement, so she could carry the wood in from the yard to dry. It didn't help that ice had formed on the steps since the last time she opened the hatch, sometime back in November. Treacherous. Kate's kids, Sam and Lori, needed to come up with something more convenient and up-to-date, if she planned to put in another winter here. But the rent was cheap, practically nothing, so she didn't want to bother them.

Luke tackled the woodpile with the ice pick. After an hour of chipping away, he was able to dislodge some sticks for her to carry down to the dark, cobweb-encrusted cellar. Hours passed in this patient labour. Emily paused to watch him when he turned his back to her. The man knew his way around a woodpile. Luke had stripped off his jacket and stood with his knees apart, swinging the axe to split some larger pieces, as the sun glinted off the blade. There was strength in those calves, and the sound of steel against wood sent Emily's mind back to another time. Same man, but a different place and time. Emily shivered as she felt goose bumps of recognition. 'Where did that come from?' she wondered.

By late afternoon, Luke had scattered the pile of wood all over the back yard. She grew tired of trotting up and down the slippery steps, and Luke couldn't find anything more to do out in the clean, fresh—and bright—air, no matter how hard he tried.

"Why don't you take a turn hauling some wood in?" she asked. "It will soon be dusk and I need a lot more stored inside."

"Oh sure, I'll go into the kitchen and make you a big stack in the wood-box," Luke offered.

"Come on now, you're not scared of a few spiders, are you? They're all hibernating down there, anyhow."

Emily forgot to mention the skunk, who had taken up residence in the far corner of the cellar, on the clay floor behind the old dysfunctional furnace. Too bad, because first trip down Luke tripped over it. His panic sent him scooting up the inside staircase leading to the kitchen. He would have been fine, except Emily hadn't lifted the hatch at the top of those stairs yet. In his panic, he cracked his head on the hatch, stumbled back down the steps, and landed about six inches from the little white-striped rascal.

"For fuck's sake, Luke, don't wake the skunk up, whatever you do! Hold still till I can get over there and pick you up."

"Why would you ever let a skunk in your cellar in the first place? What were you thinking?" Luke demanded, once Emily eased him out of harm's way.

"Not much choice, seeing as you weren't around to help me evacuate the little darling. Don't you know, when a skunk chooses your house to live in, it's a good omen. Skunks are able to repel all predators, so they make a good, strong protection totem."

"Well, this one is sure repelling me. Get me out of here, quick!"

"Here, lean on me till I get you up the stairs. Do you think your ankle is broken?"

"Nah, just twisted a little. Hey, this must mean I get to sleep over!"

"Not a chance in hell. You've got quite a goose egg on your noggin, too. I'll run you into Outpatients at the QEH. You might be concussed."

"Aren't you going to at least feed me first?"

"After I go soak in my tub. My muscles are crying out to me. Go lie down on the couch but don't fall asleep in case you actually do have a concussion and you're not just being a big baby."

Emily fell asleep in the bathtub instead, and didn't surface till an hour later. Then she had to pick something other than her dirty flannel shirt and down vest to wear and do her hair and fuss with her make-up. When she came downstairs, she flipped through the living room, shook Luke awake, turned on the stereo, and headed to the kitchen to start supper.

As she fried up the fish cakes, an old April Wine tune came on the radio. She sang along, forgetting for a minute Luke might hear her, *"When you*

51

won't dance with me. And you won't hold hands with me. And that's not the way to be. Girl, you're treating me bad. I used to walk you home, now I walk alone. And it seems that you don't care. And when we're at school, you say I'm a fool. Why must you treat me so unfair?"

Luke hobbled up behind her, pretended to lose his balance, and made Emily catch him in her arms. And danced with her. All over the kitchen and around the wood-box, picking hidden twigs and moss out of her thick hair as they twirled. He stopped pretending. Emily glanced at the clock as she leaned her head against his shoulder and made a wish at 11:11, the moment he held her hips and pulled her in closer. But as quickly as he started, he stopped, walked away.

Maybe she should change the subject. Find something safe to talk about, like the resident skunk. Luke asked her again why she hadn't gotten rid of the skunk in the fall. She said, "I didn't realize he had come in till he went into hibernation. I think he snuck in when I was hauling wood in one evening. Once he settled in, I figured it was best to let sleeping skunks lie. Sorry, I should have warned you. I forget he's there most of the time. All he does is sleep. I guess I'll notice him when spring comes."

"I'll borrow a live animal trap when it's time for him to come out of hibernation," Luke said, "and we'll go way back on a dirt road through the woods. They claim a skunk will travel a long way back to find its den, so I'll make sure we're far enough from the cottage before we release him."

"What should we name him?"

"Naming skunks is not such a good idea," he said. "Animals we name can stick around forever."

"Like you, Luke?"

"You know what Trooper said."

"Yeah I do. 'Here for a good time, Not a long time'. Someone else said that to me once. Can't remember who."

Not long after, Emily remembered who and when.

Just Goofing Around

Luke's brother Tommy was a wickedly entertaining social animal so he would often invite people over. Emily didn't mind going to his house. Tommy could put just about anyone at ease. Luke was long and lean and light; Tommy was stocky and short and dark. A little too weathered and worn to be considered adorable, Tommy possessed a working man's physique, Popeye-the-Sailor-Man forearms, and a pug nose, all of which he had acquired breaking up fights and bouncing drunks out of The Jolly Night in Sydney. Or the Jolly Fight, as the locals called it. He gave up bartending in Cape Breton to come to Charlottetown and work in a call centre. Not much of a profession, but there wasn't much work to be had in Cape Breton either, as far as that goes.

Nowadays, Tommy got yelled at on the phone all day, instead of busting balls and noses all night. He was easygoing so he took the change to a desk job in stride, and consoled himself that he could at least enjoy drinking at night, too, along with all the other 'lunes', and introduce the girls to some famous Cape Breton drinking games.

Emily knew a few drinking games of her own, and won the 'caps' tournament more than once over the fall and winter. Luke might show up in the kitchen for an hour or two, but sometimes he'd be in his room practicing his guitar, and sometimes he'd just be in his room.

When he would do stuff like that, disappear for a while and not speak, Emily wondered what got into her. Hitting 'send' was one thing, but talking to him in person was quite another. She didn't consider herself easy to intimidate, but she hated the sick feeling in her stomach. She couldn't identify it till she mentioned it to Betty, who called it butterflies, like you get when you're thirteen and the hottest singer from the latest boy band shows up in your home town. Betty thought Luke could pass as a reasonable facsimile thereof. Emily preferred to think Luke, with his astonishing eyes, dimpled chin, shoulder length golden hair, and beautiful bod, looked more like the late great Kurt Cobain. Only taller. He sometimes forgot to shave and was kind of scruffy like Cobain, too, and Emily liked that in a man. Occasionally.

Sometimes Emily would drop Luke off at Tommy's after class, and he'd invite her in. If it was only the two of them there, he might play her a tune. Occasionally, they'd even remember to study. She might get out the sheet music from choir and try to explain all the symbols and notations to him again. Lots of times he wouldn't ask her in at all, he'd just lean into her car window and say good night with that big stupid lazy grin of his. But he didn't repeat that kiss.

Still, too often, Emily found herself spending too much time with Luke. It took a few months for him to get around to mentioning his wife and young son waiting for him, back home in Cape Breton. He put it in one of his cryptic text messages, 'seeing the wife and kid Study Week. Can't wait.' Tommy had already dropped a few clues about a woman named Siobhan and his favourite and only nephew, Liam, during a round of 'caps' (which Emily won) so she didn't go all forensic on it.

She knew the whole age gap thing made it all together too ridiculous, anyway, but she might have liked to hear it from Luke first. Why didn't he just tell her his marital status when they met? Then again, why didn't she think to ask? He didn't wear a ring, but that wasn't uncommon in a region where most men made their living with their hands. Wedding bands and lobster trap haulers don't mix. That was her excuse for him, anyway.

Even so, Emily thought she was helping him. Sometimes he would act particularly difficult and self-protective, as men do to be annoying. He could sure use help with his ego, or so she thought. Plus, she needed some advice on the contemporary world of dating. One day when they were both sitting in the lecture hall, bored to tears, she thought she should suss out his self-protective nature so she slipped him a note:

Professor Edelmeyer
UPEI Research Lab
Somewhere on PEI

Dear Professor Edelmeyer

Question: How comfortable is a condom if you wear it all day?

It must get kind of, I don't know, dry or wet or sticky or wrinkled or something. This is serious research I am conducting here, Professor, and I need your help. We never used them back in the day. As I recall, we were more interested in freedom than protection. So I know so little about them. Next to nothing. I guess that makes me a condom virgin.

I'm willing to learn. You have more expertise in this matter than I, Sir, so I will rely on your input before conducting further investigative research on my own. (Plus, I count on you to keep me out of trouble and away from the SUB, if I think I should conduct research, but I'm already too drunk.)

Anxiously awaiting your reply, I remain your keen and curious student,

Emily

Luke caught up to her after class, gave a little 'ha ha', and announced his big exciting news. In spite of, or because of, his failed attempt at choir, he decided to pull together a new Island based band. This time he hoped it would be a badass rock band. He needed help with his song writing, given that he was not very articulate when it came to white-hot words, or so he said. So Emily wrote him some lyrics.

Sent: February 14, 2005 9:20 pm
To: Luke
Subject: i got a new band
Song for Luke's Band
    I got a new band
    I got a new band
    Yeah, me on the vocals
    Banging on acoustic guitar
    Hairy, oops, I mean Perry on the drums
    Matt MacDonald's electric guitar
    Bob on the keyboard when he can
    (Emily when he can't

Cranking out that "Freddie the Frog")

I got a new band
I got a new band
I get all the best parts:
Playing past the doorman's bedtime
Counting up the pay like I need it
Fixing the sound board, on demand
Unless maybe Perry can
I hope maybe Perry can
Oh no what if Perry can't

I got a new band
I got a new band
I get all the best parts:
Kissing the mike
Hugging the girls (but not Em)
One night stands
With the fans
(But not Emily)

I got a new band
I got a new band
Hope the amps don't
Give us too much feedback
Or the fans either
Not if it's negative
Some nights they might
(But not Emily)

Think I want a new band
Think I want a new band
I'll have to put us
On Facebook

Get myself a new profile pic
Don't know if I can do that
How can I give up the old one?
(I'm so hot in it
Don't think I can let it go)
If that's what it takes I

Don't want a new band
Don't want a new band
I'd have to play
Some original material
Write meaningful lyrics
But I so suck at written words

Think I want a new band
Think I want a new band
Maybe not
But I love the chords
I hear in my head
Besides I could pawn the words part
Off on other people
(Like Emily)
That way I get all the best parts
I want all the best parts
Em will get me the best parts

I want a new band
I want a new band
Think I'll call it Strychnine Passage
Leftover Crack or Pungent Stench
Or maybe Pond Scum
Old Woman's Porridge or Dredge

I want a new band

I want a new band
Practise in the garage
Teach my baby to sing
Earmuffs to protect his ears
Baby bowing to the Eagles
Wifey screeching Metallica

Got a new band
Got a new band
We three singing Buddy Holly
Give baby the Roots of Rock and Roll,
The Foundations of Life
So he grows up with the finest
Rock and Roll Pedigree
Oh yeah.
'Cause I'm a good Dad
'Cause I'm a good Dad

Do you think it's too long? It needs work. Actually, it's pretty bad. God awful. But I think it has enough comedy and tragedy to please your humungous, ever-expanding fan base (the tragedy is in the brackets of the lyrics—those parts are so sad.) It'll be fun improving it. It's a start, like your band.

By the way I am NOT going to be your super-groupie! But no doubt I'll dance. So I'm happy for you that you're doing this. You probably already knew I would be.

Emily

I've Got a New Band

Shortly before semester's end, Luke received his invitation to play the SUB. Emily connected with a couple of old friends, Trudy and Kara, and told them a little about this young man in her life and his big gig. It didn't take much to persuade them to go with her to his opening night. So Emily got to hear Luke's band live and in person for the first time, and not just practicing in Tommy's garage. Late that night, Emily tucked herself up in bed with her laptop:

Sent: April 25, 2005, 3:17 am
To: Luke
Subject: oh and i forgot—take my shoes off. too

Fuck I stink. Must be Bob Marley sweat...girl I wanna make you sweat. And you did, ya bugger.
Were you nervous? Couldn't tell. Wasn't paying attention. Must have been the shooters.

Hairy Perry looks like Animal from the Muppets. But then, don't all drummers?

You shouldn't be grabbing Judy's arse even if she can sing. Nice of you to let her though. Sing that is. Maybe. You might get the boyfriend pissed off. Don't want a donnybrook on your hands your first gig out, now do you?!

Kazoo Kazoo we are the singing Kazoos
Me and Trudy and Kara and You.
We'd never make any money
But we'd never be blue
Except youooouoo!
Drive us to the ferry
Couldn't you?
If you want to be part of
The singing Kazoos.

Band.

Might be the best offer you get, Buster.

Don't knock it! Best song of the night. And I wrote it.

That Kara is a party in a drawer. Or a box. Or a tire. Or something. Guess who Trudy reminds me of? Just Trudy. When I'm partying with her, I feel like we are five years old again. You know she can really fuckin' draw. Fuck I'm drunk. Musta been the shooters.

Loved the whole other woman theme in the song by The Trews you guys covered tonight:

Tryin' to build a bridge across my heart's divide
Caught between two opposite signs
I want it all and I can't decide
If I should leave you here or stay with you awhile

I love you, I love her, I need you, I need her
I'm always gonna love you, I'm always gonna love her
I guess I should just let this thing die
'Cause I am a man of two minds

Hey! That might be a good song for the Kazoo Band! We'd change all the 'hers' to 'hims'. I looked it up on YouTube—this guy used it at his wedding for the Mother/Son dance. We could become wedding singers, make up our own version:

I love you Mom, I love her, I need you Mom, I need her. I'm always gonna love you Mom, I'm always gonna love her.

Weird, huh? Incest or marriage? Dude! Make up your mind!

Why is the light upside down? Oh! It's not the lamp it's me. Ooops!

Anyway, they are just songs full of words. Some nights, words just piss me off.

60

Maybe they are pissing me off because my throat is sore. I might be tired. Wonder if I'm getting the fucking flu. It's not only words I'm mad at—I'm not too happy with my body, either. It keeps betraying me, doing stupid shit. It had better behave itself when I go south, whenever that happens.

Speaking of drinking, I'm glad I stuck to Jell-O shooters. That way I'm not very drunk.

Kazoo me Lukey Lou!

I'm back from worshipping at the porcelain throne. That's better. Man, Jell-O shooters sure catch up on ya. So do those Spanish Coffees. Oh yeah, I forgot about them. Five times the caffeine makes...I can't do the math, but it's a whole lot of wide awake. Maybe I am just a little bit drunk. Wired and drunk.

Thanks a lot for telling me I look tired. Haven't you learned not to make that comment? Don't you know what "You look tired," actually means in woman-speak? Try "You haggard, dowdy, dumpidey dump old thing." I might bop you on the nose if you keep it up!

You should write a song. You could start out with something shorter than mine. Four verses and one chorus. Not like the ten verses and three (or was it four?) choruses I wrote. No one has tried that many since "The Twelve Days of Christmas"—and the jury's still out on Twelve Days.

Iambic pentameter. Remember high school English class? My song is sadly lacking in it—or any rhythm at all.

Next time I'll pay more attention to the notes than the lyrics. Better go practise the Kazoo. Hope it's more forgiving than the Jell-O shooters.

Ciao

Emily

PS Fuck. It's Sunday morning already. And I'm almost sober and my head hurts.

> **Sent:** April 25, 2005, 4:48 am
> **To:** Emily
> **Subject:** Re: oh and i forgot—take my shoes off. too
> Judy? You mean the blonde who thought she could sing? Yeah she had a
> cute ass. But I don't remember grabbing it.

> The two girls pole dancing in front of us were entertaining.

Sent: April 25, 2005, 5:15 am
To: Luke
Subject: heads and tales
Pole dancing, eh? So *that's* where musicians' heads go when they're supposed to
be paying attention to the rest of us!

I'm sure they are glad you enjoyed the performance—got your eyes to wander
away from the guitars and the boys in the band. Hey, that's all you'll need to
make eye contact with us—we'll all pole dance for you—even me!

The girl in the grey coat who can't sing—at least not when she's drunk—and
doesn't know how to use the mike. That one. I was watching her struggle to get
to the end of the song when you ran your hand down her back. Ergo, coming
from a horny young gaffer like you, it should qualify as a grope.

It is my duty as your reviewer to keep your head on your shoulders, your feet on
the ground, and your hands off the asses.

Amanda is some flexible. No, wait!—that might be Natasha. Those girls look a
lot alike and I didn't get a peek at her face—I was too busy avoiding eye contact
with the band. Amanda leaves for work in the Mid-East real soon. I think it's
Saudi she's going to. Now don't go getting yourself all distracted by thoughts of,

'Nurse Amanda has to give up all her sexual freedom for two years, so she goes down...on the dance floor' fantasies. No, I'm not jealous—I could move like that when I was her age...well, maybe not. But I could move. Still can.

Who knows where Hairy Perry's head is, but it's a happy place.

I borrowed this lovely hand cream from a friend and now I can smell lavender as I type. Mmmm...yummy.

Your favourite—and only—music reviewer. And Publicist!

E

> **Sent:** April 25, 2005, 5:22 am
> **To:** Emily
> **Subject:** Re: heads and tales
> Don't remember running my hand down her back. What are you getting at? Spit it out.

Sent: April 25, 2005, 5:30 am
To: Luke
Subject:
The hand on the back? You made a gentle and natural gesture to help her get off the stage. Leave it to me to make a big story of it, eh?

I think it's sweet when you give people their fifteen seconds of fame.

I'm off to the dump today—woohoo! Gotta write my last exam, too! Quite the mix my life is, innit it?

E

The Ferry...

Like all good things, first year uni comes to an end. It would seem friendship with a younger man is in the same category. Luke, being a Caper at heart, has to go away, back home to Cape Breton and his wife and kid. His year at UPEI didn't produce the greatest results; he won't likely be back in the fall. Emily knows his yen to make music is stronger than ever, and for Luke time spent sitting in class steals time away from living the dream. Emily doubts the practicality of his dream when he needs to support his family, but it is not her way to interfere.

Instead, she drives him to the Wood Islands Ferry on May Day, the first truly reliable day of spring on the Island. As they drive through the awakening countryside, she sorts out her best intentions. She plans to keep calm and carry on, wave him off gracefully when they hit the dock. But what if she spills the beans?

In spite of the way his scent engulfs the air in her car and holds her heart hostage, she is determined to act nonchalant and stick to the 'casual good-bye' plan. Before that can happen, she has to get him and his cologne out of her car. Already those stupid pheromones are interfering with her resolve! When they arrive at the toll booth, Emily learns the ferry is conspiring against her too, as it is running fifteen minutes late.

Emily talks Luke into taking a walk to the lighthouse. She hopes the blue cloudless sky, the red sandbar running parallel to the barnacle covered pier, the red and white lighthouse that sits perched on the edge of the terra cotta cliffs, and the deep blue Northumberland Strait, might distract them both from her jitters. And she needs to breathe fresh, non-Luke-scented air.

As they stand on the cliffs gazing at the cloudy grey line on the horizon that might be the hills of Cape Breton, Emily doesn't want Luke to leave without finding out. This could be her last chance. Forgetting her best intentions, she maps out some hell-paving ones instead. She plans to link her arm in his, as they walk across the field to the parking lot...pull him in close for one innocent good-bye hug...whisper in his ear and ask him to demonstrate to her, in the name of science, how that first and only kiss could have been so amazing. Why not? So she goes for it. But she doesn't get to find out. Not at the ferry terminal, anyway.

Luke is very sweet about her sudden flight of broad-daylight, sexual assertiveness. He doesn't scold her; he laughs it off, as the bright red burn spreads from her shoulders up to her cheeks. He has his own casual goodbye plan in mind. So he reminds her he is happily married; walks her to the driver's side door; gently places his hand on her shoulder as he eases her back into the car and behind the steering wheel; and stretches the seat belt across her chest, snapping it in place for her.

Emily folds her arms against the steering wheel, tucking her head up into the cradle her arms make, and won't look up at Luke. But she watches him from her rear view mirror, as she pops the trunk open.

As she explains to Kate, as she dozes in her head cradle, all the nice stuff was before he grabbed his knapsack and guitar case out of the trunk and scuttled off up the ramp, onto the passenger deck. She can't see how his scuttling off like a friggin' tarantula will do anything for her peace of mind. Kate agrees with Emily that with Luke, it is all about the body language, and Luke's is full of contradictions.

Before Emily pulls away from the passenger drop-off lane, she winds down all the windows and replaces every ounce of air mass with salt-blessed breezes. She thinks about how the current in the air still moves for her when Luke walks into a room. It does for anyone: matter displaces air and humans all take up a certain amount of mass. She just never thought of anyone entering a room that way before. Or noticed it with anyone else. Or felt it or sensed it or something. But then, as the salt-kissed air replaces Luke's scent and mass, the air and Emily adjust to the space he stole from them and move on. Air is a tolerant element and Emily...well, Emily likes it better this way; it leaves more room around her for a life. She promises herself and the air in her car she is going to get one of those. Soon. Very soon.

...is About to Disembark

Luke leans over the rail of the ferry deck as Pictou Island draws near. Siobhan will be waiting at the Caribou terminal to meet him, but he needs a moment to think. The ferry ride is always good for sorting your thoughts. How will he explain what went wrong with his year? The waste of money will be hard for his parents to accept, given they had lent him a fair amount of it, and he is now no closer to having a means to repay them.

Learning to sight-read music hadn't worked out either, in spite of Emily's help. So pfftt! There goes that dream. The music he hears travels around comfortably in his head and is lost to him when he sees all those bars, clefs, key signatures, quarter tones, codas and dynamics on a sheet of paper. It's a long road from rock and roll chord progressions to classical notation and music theory, and he just isn't up for the journey. The short circular ride it takes notes to get from his brain to his voicebox and back to his ears seems much more efficient somehow, so who needs eyes? The effort needed to change the route music takes puzzles him, and he wishes he had paid more attention in grade school. The professors and Emily might call it sight-reading, but to him, music is all about the sensing, not the seeing. Luke can't fault himself for that. Not too much, anyway.

Another passenger throws chunks of his half-eaten hamburger into the sky for the seagulls to fight over. One gull looks overly anxious, and, sure enough, gets himself dive-bombed by a big aggressive bird. He careens onto the poop deck, shakes the blow off, and hops around for a minute, testing his leg to see if he is destined to spend the rest of his life as a one legged, lop-sided seagull. Luke finds the tippy bird-hop quite hilarious, till he realizes who the sad sack gull reminds him of. Himself. He remembers the high school hockey game when the big hulking goon from the Halifax team creamed him into the boards. Luke was so busy catching his wind he couldn't feel a thing till he pushed himself up to get back in the game. As soon as he stood on his right leg, he tipped over like the seagull, stared down at his leg, and saw the piece of anklebone projecting above his skate lace. Bastard!

'Have I ever told Emily that story?' he wonders. He wishes she was still here to talk to. 'I wish I may, I wish I might, have this wish I wish tonight'. She always makes him feel like he can do it, even when he knows he is too lazy or bored or disinterested to try. She never seems to suffer from any of that. Instead, she radiates energy, curiosity, and enthusiasm. Teacher's pet that she is.

Luke realizes he has run out of time when he hears the recorded voice come over the loudspeakers: "The MV Prince Edward is about to disembark. All passengers please proceed to the lower decks. The MV Prince Edward is about to disembark. All passengers please proceed to the lower decks."

For a moment, Luke regrets not giving Emily a proper hug in return. No point prolonging goodbyes, though. He told her before he wasn't made that way. He hopes she'll stay in touch and he won't be too lazy or bored or disinterested to reply. Christ knows where boredom and laziness got him at school. Nowhere. She is so much better with words, except for song writing. He has her beat there. Even so, Luke is a little jealous of Emily and her words and her good grades and the air she breathes, as he walks down the ramp to greet his little family.

Liam practically jumps out of Siobhan's arms and reaches his chubby little soft hands up to him. Luke snuggles Liam in close, breathes in his baby scent for the first time since Reading Week, six weeks ago. His heart gives a familiar hiccup of happiness.

Funny how Emily wrote his baby boy into her song, even though she's never met Liam. Funny the names she made up for his band, too. Luke smiles as he remembers his personal favourite: Pond Scum. Maybe he could send her a text.

Better Boyfriends

Emily needed a good cover after her failed attempt at seduction, so Luke wouldn't get too big feeling, or think she might actually fantasize about him. Later, after chatting with Kate, she decided to write a fantasy about her real boyfriends:

Sent: May 1, 2005 9:10 pm
To: Luke
Subject: my beaus
Hey Luke.

Do you watch "My Name is Earl"? I'd love to be able to write for that show. I'll have to add it to my bucket list. Remember the day our prof referred to working stiffs as people who live 'lives of quiet desperation'? (I can't remember who wrote that quote. Kind of glad *I* didn't. It sticks in the head too much. Oh yeah— Thoreau. Walden Pond and all that.) The setting for "My Name is Earl" is sorta the polar opposite of *On Walden Pond*. Trailer hood stuff. Their writers have a lot more fun poking fun at the proletariat than patronizing it, like our prof did. Earl's ex-wife Joy, who is now married to Crabman Darnell, had the best line the other night when she said to the hot illegal immigrant Carmen, "You just don't realize how much lies and deception it takes to keep a marriage afloat these days." Amen to that, Joy.

My boyfriend appeared on the next episode. My buddy Beau. Bridges that is. He plays Earl's father. Remind me to tell you the whole story some night. It's too old to take the trouble to type it all out. Let me assure you, he is a lovely man. Maybe you look like him—except you're blonde and he's grey. You both have a high forehead and similar chin and mouth—only yours is a bit younger looking. But your smile and expressions are quite different—his are bigger, and he raises his eyebrows more than you. Your brows aren't as bushy. He has this habit of

68

bouncing on the balls of his feet. He's got a little belly and you don't. Not that I noticed. Either of you.

Earl and Beau helped me get rid of my headache. Such lovely, funny men.

And then I listened to "I'm Your Man", a favourite from my other boyfriend, Leonard Cohen. The title should be "I'm Your Perfect Man", though. Oh, we women can only dream...Nothing makes my beating heart accelerate like my favourite short septuagenarian in his classic fedora, especially when he sings—or growls—his most seductive lyrics. Even if he is a self-proclaimed 'lazy bastard living in a suit'.

The other day, I heard a man on the radio who claims a man should have three different women in his life: a younger one to share the busy child raising years, an older woman to teach him the ways of women, and I can't remember the third (probably a porn queen to grow old with, or something stupid like that). I wonder what the three different men a woman needs would be. Maybe Earl, Beau, and Leonard: Humour, Chivalry, and Poetry. Hmmm...what if a woman could ever find all three in one real man...?

Not frickin' likely!

Just in case you ever get the mistaken idea my expectations of fantasy boyfriends are set too low.

Emily

Two weeks passed by. Two weeks without hearing anything from Luke, not even if he was dead or alive. Emily sent a couple of angry emails, to which Luke did not reply. Then she wrote some where she expressed her frustration with his slack approach to correspondence, and did not send them. Finally, she settled on this one:

Sent: May 15, 2005 8:52 am
To: Luke
Subject: guitar-playing fingers
Here's a quote from the Iris Murdoch book I read last night/this morning, as I tried to go back to sleep. The woman is at a punk bar in England in the late 70's:

> She pushed Jane up to the front, where Gavin spotted her and foregoing his angry pose for a moment, gave her a nod and a grin. She looked at him, transfixed. What was it about boys playing guitars? She answered herself: emotion. Would he be like that in bed?

Hey I didn't say it, Murdoch did!!

E

Sent: May 19, 2005 6:05 pm
To: Emily
Subject: re: guitar-playing fingers
I like to think I can transfix women with my fingers.

Miss you.

Luke

Sent: May 19, 2005 6:45 pm

70

To: Luke

Subject: how do I end up so uncivilized all the time?

What a freakin' day! I'm trying to get the cottage ready for Erin. I'm painting the spruce sub-floor since Kate's kids don't want to invest in the place and I can't afford flooring. Guess what colour? Spruce. And I sat on the wet floor and got paint all over the ass of my pants, not just my pants as it turns out but right through, so now I have a spruce green toilet seat and a spruce green ass and I can't get it off because it's OIL-based. Of course. And I got it on my favourite old flannelette nightie. And on my good tub 'cause I tried to wash it off even though I had no hot water for a bath 'cause my water heater is fucked. Again. And the hand (and ass) cleaner I have won't do anything with oil-based paints. Nuts!

And now I have to chuck out my best pair of old jeans 'cause I ripped them too. And I have practically no work clothes and way too many dress-up clothes even though I only get to play dress up once a week and I have to wear work clothes ALL the time when I'm working. Them and old nighties. Which I just ruined my favourite of.

I am the worst cutter-inner in the whole wide world, but I always end up doing it anyway because I don't mind the ladder, even though I get paint all over the ceiling. And Erin will *have* to comment because she always notices all the little paint flaws even though she hates painting and wouldn't even offer to help me once she gets here. And I can't get *that* paint off either even though it's latex. And it's making my hair white. Fuck.

And the compost bin blew over into the ditch and spilt lobster bodies EVERYwhere and I can't haul it up because the ditch is too steep and my leg won't work that way. Leave it there to feed the skunks, I guess.

And I just get to the point where I think, 'Go away, Luke, and stay away if you're gonna keep running and it won't bother me one way or the other', and you do something totally out of character like REPLY and here I go again. Or I start to think, 'this is boring', and you start paying attention. Or say something funny. Or sweet. Or decent. And we have these time-delayed fights where we never get to make up in person in the best way a man and a woman can make up. (I meant hug. What did you think I meant?) Yesterday I was praising the Lord and shouting, 'Alleluia you've finally moved away', and now I'm frustrated because we never get to talk. Hunh? When people care about each other, they want to talk. In person. Did ya not ever notice?

You make me crazy. And if you are thinking 'If I make you so crazy, why do you put up with me?' you already know the answer to that so I AM NOT TELLING YOU AGAIN.

And I jammed my finger in the door.

Lord knows why *you* put up with *me*.

There. Now I'm done. How was your Monday?

Sent: May 20, 2005 8:02 am
To: Luke
Subject:
In case you get involved in a high speed chase tomorrow, I'm sorry. I over-reacted.

You make me see the world as a funny place sometimes. I would miss that if you got mashed up in a great big crash.

Emily

Luke didn't respond.

Island Fantasy Ice Cream

Flora sends her grandson, Charlie, running over to Emily's with an invitation to supper. Emily baffles Flora sometimes, keeping in touch with that Caper, her former study partner. Flora assumed once the school year had ended, so would the friendship with the study buddy, as Charlie called him. It makes a body wonder if there is more than studying going on in the little cottage on the other side of the tree line.

As she sets the table, Flora pulls the brown cable knit sweater Kate gave her a little closer to beat the chill. She likes to use her mother's Limoges set when she invites company over. Not much point using fine china with only old Fred and young Charlie to feed. Too rough, the two of them. They would just find some way to chip an edge.

However, Emily has a dignity to her that reminds Flora of the women of her childhood: the aunts and grannies who survived the war years carried on, no matter what the hardship. What could Emily possibly be thinking? Flora can't fathom it. Emily would be better off reading a good book than waiting for that Luke to call. If she was in Emily's shoes, she would read instead. Flora loves the shape and texture and length and strength and precision of words. Living with so few neighbours gives her lots of time to read. Words can take you so many places and heal a lot of heartache.

It is almost dark by the time they clear away the dishes, so Flora thinks it best for young Charlie to lead Emily home. The skunks have been quite active the last couple of months; Charlie's keen eyes will give them enough advance warning to steer clear. Also, Flora heard the coyotes yipping the night before, and she doesn't want Emily to run into one of them in the dark. There was a time when you didn't have to fear anything more than a stinky spraying from the wildlife of PEI, but the coyotes changed all that.

Before supper, Fred had been telling Emily how the bear and the deer had gone by the wayside years ago, hunted to extinction—not that there was much to fear from the deer. The same couldn't be said of the coyote. The Eastern Coyote turned out to be a bigger, tougher character than his western cousin, much like Easterners themselves. The wildlife conservationists claim the coyotes had crossed with wolves somewhere on their trek across the country, from west to east, which made them at least as big as a German Shepherd and more aggressive than any other life form on the Island. Except for the humans, of course.

According to Fred's story, one pair of coyotes had been brave enough and bold enough to cross over the Northumberland Strait on the ice about twenty years ago. The coyote couple must have texted their relatives to tell them PEI was a good time, because now there are plenty of them, roaming the fields and catching the foxes' food and people's cats for their supper.

Thanks to the influx, the sheep farmers hire donkeys to keep the coyotes away from their flocks. The farmer down the road came across a pack of coyotes when he went out to the backfield to check on a pregnant cow. The farmer was too late. He found the poor cow lying on the ground in hard labour, as the coyotes pulled the calf right out of her uterus. Two of them were chewing away on the newborn calf's front legs. The cow was that tore up she'd had to be put down. The farmer said he still had a hard time putting those pictures out of his mind.

Probably that's where the coyotes crossed from in the first place—from Cape Breton across the Strait to the east end of the Island. Cape Breton humans have been known to text their relatives, too, to let them know PEI is a good place for a wild time. Too much sexting going on. There better not be any Island crossbreeding happening next door. Or wild times, either. If only Emily wouldn't drink. Ever. Not around Luke, anyhow. Something about the combination makes Emily come unhinged. In her humble opinion.

It makes one wonder what species the human pioneers who travelled to the Island had crossed with to make them fierce enough to withstand a land that must have seemed unbelievably harsh and bitterly cold. Tough bunch. Same went for Cape Breton Islanders, too. Two Islands with two tough breeds.

It's a good thing the aboriginals came over to the Island in the summer to teach the early pioneers how to survive. No doubt the M'ikmaq thought they were entertaining some not-very-bright tourists when the Europeans first arrived, because if the pioneers were tough, the M'ikmaq people were a whole lot tougher. Smarter too, as for the most part, they only used Prince Edward

Island as a summer camp; too harsh for a year round home, with all the northeast winds blowing off the water. She bet the Mi'kmaq's summer camp, on the Island they called Abegweit, felt disrupted wicked bad by her ancestors. Flora read all about it in a book by the Acadian historian, Georges Arsenault. Quite a story. She loves that Abegweit means 'cradled in the waves'. A beautiful image for this place she loves so well.

A couple of weeks earlier, Emily borrowed a book from Flora called *On Mexican Time*, which she remembers to return at suppertime. Over dessert, after Flora delivers her lecture on the dangers of coyotes and Islanders crossbreeding, Emily, Flora, and Fred move on to trading stories about travel. They have quite a lot in common when it comes to travel and food. Flora has grown fond of Emily. Emily earned her respect when she cared for Kate so faithfully. Flora had been quite fond of Kate, too.

Fred and Flora peer out the kitchen window as Charlie guides Emily through the little woods.

"Do you think she'll be alright living there all by herself, now Kate's gone?" asks Flora.

"Oh, I think she'll be fine. We'll keep an eye on her, you and me and Charlie. She should be okay. She lives well within shouting distance. I told Charlie he should sleep over on her couch tonight. Keep her company."

"Good idea. Coming to bed, Fred?"

"I'll be right up after I finish my ice cream."

"What kind are you eating?"

"Island Fantasy."

"Bring me up a bowl, would you?"

"Sure."

Fred trudges up the steep stairs, carrying her bowl of ice cream, and says, "Here you go."

Flora sets her book down on the quilt and watches as Fred tries to straighten up. How much longer can he manage those stairs with that back of his? Will he be able to continue to fish for a living? He's been at it since he started at fourteen, and fifty-six years seems a long time for any occupation. Funny how those Upper Canadians assume you don't work as much when you work in the seasonal industries. As far as Flora can see, a body works just as much, at least as much, every bit as much; you just spread it out over more years. Sometimes—too often—over an entire lifetime.

They could move their bedroom downstairs; convert the den or the pantry someday. Neither room is big, though, with only enough room for one single bed. That day might mean the end of the two of them sharing a bed. Aw well, when—and if—he retires, they could take another one of those tropical vacations, learn more about the native folk. Flora would like that.

"Fred, remember the time we went south and drank líquidos by the Mayan Ruins? Chichen Itza, wasn't it?"

"Yup. Where they claim the Maya sacrificed virgins and fed them to the gods of the *cenotes*."

"Snuggle in closer, Fred."

"Put your dish down."

"While I was waiting for you to come up the stairs, I got to thinking."

"Yes, dear?"

"What if I had been one of those sacred virgins? Don't laugh. What, you don't think it could happen?"

"I'm not laughing. But your butt cheeks are tickling my Elmo and giving me ideas."

"Well, how's this for an idea. You know how we found the little Mayan ruin the guide said would have been a common person's house? Remember the stone platform they used for a bed?" Flora pulls the faded old floral sheet down, to be a little more comfortable.

"Those Mayans could do just about anything with stone. Smart people."

"That wasn't exactly where I was going with this, Fred."

"No? And exactly where is your imagination taking you this time, Flora?"

"The Mayans must have laid a lot of straw down on those beds. What if you and I had escaped from the tour group that time and snuck away to the house with the platform bed? I can almost hear the ghosts of the Maya drumming a jungle rhythm as you laid me down on all that straw. I would be a scared virgin. Beautiful and sacred but scared.

Except, the priestesses would massage me with warm oils for hours in preparation and feed me herbs to relax me. By the time you came to me with

76

your eagle-feather head dress on, I'd be positively somnambulistic. I can picture you standing over me as I lay on that short bed with my legs draped over the end. Your long, hooked beak and red feathers would hold me mesmerized, and underneath the mask I'd spy your face, the face of the man I was meant to love, if only once in a lifetime, before I die. Then I would see the other beak peeking out from under your loincloth. And your broad brown muscled shoulders and arms flashing with golden amulets and bronze snakes. I would be a little frightened but...Fred, do you think we were once Mayans? Say, like in another life?"

"Come here, my little celestial virgin."

"OK. Promise me you won't feed me to the *cenote* god afterwards."

"I promise. But I might have to eat you myself, instead. Give me that bowl for a sec, would you, so I can put it on the bedside table. I love Island Fantasy ice cream, too, but I love you more. Get on over here."

"Oh Fred", she giggles.

Fred pulls her close, leans over her shoulder, and switches off the lamp. "Do you think she's lonely?" Flora asks him.

"Could be. Her daughter's coming home and she sounds like she's a nice girl. That should help."

"It's just that a woman left lonely..."

"Don't worry, dear, I'll be true to you."

"Wasn't you I was worried about, you old fool."

"Aw, I might be a fool and I might be old, but I'm your old fool."

"That you are, Fred. That you are."

11:11

Emily grew accustomed to Luke's absence. Maybe she should think of him as her pen pal, since he lived so far away and she would never see him again. Then she remembered how quickly the coyotes discovered an ice bridge to PEI. But Luke wasn't canny like the coyotes. He was kind of a stunned arse when it came to directions; probably couldn't find PEI or her again, either.

She could try writing to him the old fashioned way: sit down with pen on paper; read the letter twice before sealing the envelope; scratch out the personal stuff; rewrite it; mull it over on the way to the post office; buy a stamp and talk to the post mistress while deciding whether to waste fifty-two cents on it or stash the stamp instead; contemplate some more; drop it in the big red mailbox. Or not. Let the lack of technology be her guide for a change.

Seaglass Cottage
Spruce Lane
Tracadie Bay
Prince Edward Island
June 4, 2005

Dear Luke

This weekend we gave a birthday party for Trudy, who organizes everything. Our card for her showed a Charlie Brown scene on the front with all the characters getting Lucy's party together, smiling as they pinned up her birthday banner and decorated the cake. On the inside of the card, the banner is upside down, the cake's on the floor, the place is a mess, and a dejected Linus says,"We should have had a meeting. We meant well." Well, I meant well. And you and I should have had a meeting.

I better get to work. I have such a shitload left to do. Would you like me to write about the present? Not Trudy's present. Mine. My present is boring and stressful, so the story might not be much fun, and the painting still isn't finished.

As I've mentioned, sometimes I talk to my dead friends. This is how today's coffee break conversation went.

My Boring Stressful Present Life

11:11

Kate: What is missing in the midst of all this chaos that has left your nerves so frayed?

Me: Not men, that's for sure. Too many of them around: carpenters, plumbers, electricians, well-intentioned neighbours, and not a capable one in the whole crowd. Or a painter, either.

Kate: What, then?

Me: Music. I need music. Hey, Kate, did you hear what the brain-mapping scientists discovered? The part of the brain that is reserved for music? Well, it's right next to the one for spirituality.

Kate: God was telling me the other day He arranged it that way. That's why we call God the Grand Conductor.

Me: You do? Thanks for the lovely distracting image. But I'm still overtired. So much work to get the place ready for Erin.

I'm worried about what Erin is getting herself into. Now she's engaged to the rich old geezer with the two kids and all the baggage. She might be the oldest of my girls, but she's still only twenty-seven. Too young to get so settled down.

Kate: How old is the geezer?

Me: Thirty-eight.

Kate: She could always get out of it.

Me: Yeah, but it is a lot harder when he puts a ring on it.

Kate: Me and God talked about marriage the other day, too. He says, yes, 'until death do you part' may have been a good idea when people only lived for forty years. He loves you humans so much He wouldn't want couples to be together if, along the way, they change 'till death do you part' to 'until death do us part or we kill each other.' That would be violating one of the other great Ten Ideas He recommends for you people. He wouldn't want a couple to stay together if they make one another miserable or cause too much pain.

Me: Not even for a million dollars?

Kate: Not even for a million dollars.

And that was it. Short conversation, eh? Just long enough to drink my coffee and get back to work. So goes my life.

Sincerely

Emily

Countdown to Erin

Emily was so worked up from anticipating Erin's visit she had to write a quick note and leave it on the pillow in the guest room. As she counted off the nights until her arrival, she would check in and remind herself if the letter was still there, Erin wasn't. Not yet. Later she considered that by writing, she may have been preparing Erin for the changes Emily had gone through, and herself for this daughter whom she hadn't seen in far too long. She admitted to herself she felt a certain amount of trepidation. She could count on writing, though, to calm the burly beast of family ties.

Seaglass Cottage
Spruce Lane
Tracadie Bay
Prince Edward Island
June 6, 2005

Dear Erin

Can't wait to see you! I want so much to show you this beautiful little community I live in and all the ceaseless wonders of Tracadie Bay! It's not exactly high-rise Vancouver and is sadly lacking a Starbucks, or any coffee shop at all. You have to go to town for a decent brew, or as far as Mount Stewart to the Irving Big Stop. I bought a new coffee-maker and a couple of pounds of fair trade coffee from the Farmer's Market, so we should be able to feed your habit with some degree of satisfaction. At least, I hope so!

I think you'll like Kate's beach cottage/house. She called it Seaglass Cottage, so now I do, too. It is a rare find and morphs with the seasons. In early spring, the ever prolific lupines fill the ditch and the field between the cottage and Jack's house. Today, the peonies and tiger lilies line the little path to my door, but by October, the white sand from the dunes will reclaim my walkway. Fall storm surges will deliver any number of varieties of seaweeds and spread them all over the yard: kelp, Irish Moss, Dragon's Tails, Dead Man's Fingers. Too much sea lettuce chokes the bay now, but that's another story. I'll explain it when you get here.

Remember how you loved to pop the bubbles on the kelp when you were a kid? I have a photo in a frame on the mantel of six-year-old you with two long strands of Dragon's Tail draped like a silk scarf over your shoulders: the rubbery old seaweed with the curly edges turned my saucy child into a sea nymph, for sure. You always were a precocious child, rushing head-long into womanhood.

As you can see from the recent pictures, my little house is now painted yellow. I read somewhere an excess of yellow is bad for you, but I don't believe it for a minute. Winter will be here soon enough and will surround us with more white than we need to see in an entire lifetime.

Your room is on the main floor and doubles as my craft room. You know what I'm like with my craft supplies. Please be patient with me! I stowed most of them away to make room for you the best I could.

I have tons of surprises for you. We've been so busy here working away as we anticipate your visit. The last time we hosted royalty here goes way back to 1945, so we—my Tracadie Cove neighbours and I—have been frantically preparing for you, my Dear Princess!

Behind the house grows the little woods, where you'll see short stubby spruce trees bordering the properties on Spruce Lane. They may disappoint you after your exposure to all those tall trees in Stanley Park, but don't let them fool you. They've lived forever, hardy little guys that they are, and you would see a multitude of narrow tree growth rings, if you cut into them. You West Coasters might be proud of your old growth forests, but these little trees are part of the old growth forest of Prince Edward Island we call the Acadian Boreal Forest. They have survived by planting themselves close to the surface and digging their trunks in every winter, growing stubbier and stubbier, to protect the tender new branches from the salt sea air and the harsh North East winds.

My little buddy, Charlie, managed to break his nose climbing one of the spruce trees last April. He is my neighbour Flora's grandchild and he's only eleven. He knew he wasn't supposed to climb trees in the winter, (and yes, it is still winter here in April) so he sent his friend in to tell his grammy while he put snow on his nose to stop the bleeding. Grammy needed a minute to calm down, so his plan worked. He didn't get yelled at. Apparently, climbing trees and breaking your nose doing things you aren't supposed to when you are eleven is a family tradition. His mom did it, and his grammy, too. Times like these, I realize how much easier it is to be a backseat parent.

How are Maddie and Clair? They must be getting so big. I hope you don't ever feel like a backseat parent to them, though. Step-parenting must be so hard. Pierce better give you plenty of support or he might hear from this Mama Bear. Now, don't get mad. I'm not meaning to criticize him. I'm just saying.

I loved climbing trees when I was a kid—which is kind of funny because, as you know, I get vertigo around heights, especially if there is air beneath my feet, like on a staircase with mesh metal steps or no riser boards. When I'm awake, having 'only air' under me makes me nervous, but I have amazing dreams where I can fly. I love those dreams. I'm not afraid of heights when I'm sleeping. Do you climb trees with your step-kids?

Do you ever dream about flying? Do you still remember your dreams? Things I never think to ask you and should know.

I remember warm afternoons climbing one big tall oak tree at Canoe Cove, sitting way up high and looking out over Hillsborough Bay. I could see all the way to St. Peter's Island, Governor's Island, and the shooting range. (We used to call it Squaw Point. Not very politically correct. Odds are it's not called that anymore.)

It seems to me my parents must have expected us to do things like climb as high as we could and sometimes break parts of ourselves. Maybe they thought it would prepare us for all our future broken hearts. Either that or they were so busy feeding us they didn't know the half of what we got up to. Some of my best memories of childhood came from doing stuff I wasn't supposed to do. But I don't think I climbed spruce trees in winter. Let's do some things we're not supposed to. Soon!

Love you so much my Darlin' Daughter!

Mom
XOXO

Chris

After what seemed like forever, Luke texted Emily he had been unusually busy with his summer job at the fish plant, his music, his wife and his kid. But he didn't want her to think he'd forgotten her. She could accept that; your twenties is a hectic time in life. Over a winter of coffee breaks, lunches and study sessions, Emily had grown to trust Luke. Trust didn't always come easy to Emily, but he seemed too much of a big goof not to. Harmless, it seemed, and he made her laugh.

Thinking about trust reminded her of Chris. She kept seeing pictures of him in her dreams, so she wrote about him. She hoped Luke would understand. Otherwise she might be embarrassed the next time she saw him, whenever that happened. And forever afterwards.

Seaglass Cottage
Spruce Lane
Tracadie Bay
Prince Edward Island
June 10, 2005

Dear Luke

You probably don't remember, but I once mentioned to you I lost a man I loved to an awful accident. I've been thinking about him lately, partly because of what Erin is going through, and because I'm spending too much time wanting what I can't have.

The other night I was half asleep when I thought I could hear him, so I started talking back. But he kind of faded in and out, and I had to make up some of his responses. I think I came close to what he said, or maybe that's just the way I imagined it. Some of his smart-ass responses sound more like something you would say. I can't remember him being quick with the wit. His story needs some humour, so you may hear your voice in it, except for the last part. When I wrote the somewhat witty ending, I didn't think you would ever say any of it, especially the part about making someone's day. But Chris would have.

It was a long time ago.

You must have put a lot of deposits in the trust account for me to share this with you. I hope you don't find it too weird. Or get bored as, for once, it has nothing to do with you—or only peripherally.

This is Chris. It's all true. Except, the last time I spoke to him in his body I was twenty-one. We only got one chance.

Me: Hey, Chris! My heart's in trouble again!

Chris: Emily! I didn't expect to hear from *you* any time soon.

Me: Yeah, well, I don't want to wait till I see you to talk. I'm sick of waiting. I must be meant to be stuck on this earth forever and ever amen. Not like when you died, and everyone said, 'Only the good die young.' Don't know what it says about me, since I seem to have at least fifty years left in me. I'm getting impatient for you, though.

Chris: Well, you're lucky because the Big Kahuna is gonna let us talk just this once. What's going on?

Me: A week ago a couple of stray young people washed up here at the beach house. I nicknamed them Flotsam and Jetsam.

Chris: Which one is which?

Me: The guy would be Flotsam and the girl would be Jetsam. They needed a roof over their heads and money and food. They took the bus all the way from British Columbia for a job in Charlottetown which, allegedly, didn't materialize.

Chris: Why did you decide to take them in and trust they wouldn't rob you blind?

Me: I caved when Jetsam told me her grandma was sending her some money, and she needed to wait and stay put till the cash caught up with her. How could I say no to someone's grandkid, a long way from home, out on the road? Of course, my oldest had something to say about it.

Chris: Did she roll her eyes?

Me: No, she's kind of past that. When we drove into my yard after her long flight from Vancouver, she said, 'Why are there extra people sleeping in your yard?'

So, the guy had a big long scar on his neck, plus a couple of other ones. One day I asked him where he got the scar. He said he had been driving down a mountain in a blinding snow storm and got into a head-on with a truck carrying a load of aluminum siding on back. According to Flotsam, a piece of siding came through his window and almost severed his neck. The doctor was amazed he managed to save him. Or that's how the story goes.

Chris: Did you believe it?

Me: No. But I've come to understand people sometimes need to believe their own stories, whether they are 'true' or not. Doesn't always matter if I believe them.

Chris: When did you ever figure that one out? You always wanted to cut through the bullshit when I knew you.

Me: I don't know—somewhere along the way.

Chris: Did you eventually stop believing things those kids said?

Me: Afraid so. My daughter realized they had gone into the house and all the way up to my bedroom and stole some homemade wine. She went wild, as you can imagine, after me feeding them and giving them a place to stay and all.

Chris: So you have three hot-tempered red-headed girls. Your poor husband.

Me: Possibly that's why Roberto and I are now divorced. To keep Erin happy, I ended up giving the two strays a deadline to move on down the line. Erin cleaned up the mess they made in the tent and she was not impressed. So she told them off. Gave them quite a blast.

Chris: Her mother's daughter.

Me: Shut up.

It turned out they both had a huge capacity for alcohol and whatever else they were using. Users in many ways—but they could work, thanks to some half-way useful skills. So I figured they should at least earn their keep. Lord knows there are lots of chores and repairs need doing around this place. Kate couldn't do much the last few years she lived here.

Chris: So what else did they tell you?

Me: The girl said her mother was a crack addict and her grandma raised her. She was twenty-two, or twenty-three, depending which day you asked. Their addictions made our local addicts look tame by comparison.

Chris: What was the real story?

Me: We'll never know, but it sounds like the five-inch scar didn't come from an accident.

Chris: No?

Me: She took a knife to him.

Chris: Wow. Whose story was that?

Me: Flotsam's.

Chris: You have good street smarts. What do you think?

Me: Who knows? He doesn't have a whole lot of credibility around here. And my street sense has been dulled by all this country living. Erin always had this fear of strangers invading our house, so not good timing on my part. And they stole some movies. They better not have stolen any Johnny Depp, or the two of us will track them down wherever they are.

Chris: Remember how you chased down your *Tommy* album when Frank and Little Stevie stole it? Those two addicts should be worried.

Me: Ha ha.

Chris: How do you feel about helping someone's lost grandchild now?

Me: Mixed feelings. It made me think of you. I still hold a picture in my head of you tying off your arm with the rubber tubing at the seedy motel on the Avenue one summer night. It gave a whole new meaning to the old expression 'tie one on.' I remember you told me, as you stuck the needle in your vein, you didn't want me to ever do speed, or amphetamines of any kind.

Chris: Had to be one of the smarter things I said back then.

Me: The moon reminds me of the night we took my old, rust-coloured Valiant to Canoe Cove, and you wouldn't go in the water, and I made fun of you. You were wearing those big old construction boots, and you wouldn't even take them off and go wading in the little bitty water. I thought you looked hilarious. You weren't afraid of much. Did you get like the two users towards the end? Lying all the time? Making up a life as you went along? Washing up on someone else's shore in your Greb Kodiak boots?

Chris: No. I only ever lied to myself.

It seemed like a good idea to go quiet and admire the moon. So we did. Later:

Chris: Remember how the water did me in at the end?

Me: Thank heavens you didn't die from the speed, of either the drug or the motorbike variety.

Chris: It would have only made their grief harder for Mom and Dad to bear.

Me: And for your beautiful blond sisters, too. You told me one night that when you went out, it would look more like an accident than a blaze of glory. I asked you if you would blow apart on the motorcycle, because that would be so cliché. I was so annoyed with you. I hate clichés. You said you couldn't say how it would end—you just knew it wouldn't be on your bike.

The first night we spent together, you drove me to your attic apartment on your old Kawasaki. I could see the speedometer in the moonlight as we crossed the railroad track. We were doing 100 mph. That's miles, not kilometres! And the seat came up when we hit the tracks. You forgot you hadn't gotten around to bolting it back on.

Chris: No guts no glory!

Me: Hah. Hah. It wasn't only the seat popped up into the air. Left me *clinging* for glory to your back and praying for the best, whilst you, ya bugger, could at least hang onto the handlebars.

I could hear someone singing in the distance, so I asked Chris if he recognized the song.

Me: You used to sing 'we're here for a good time, not a long time'. How right you were. The people I get out with now know a lot of those old songs. Takes me back.

Chris: I'm glad you're getting out. You always liked a fun time.

Me: You, on the other hand, were inclined to be a little serious. Must be your Ontario upbringing.

Chris: You often gave me a good laugh, sometimes at my own expense.

Me: Upper Canadians are such easy targets.

Your folks moved back to Ontario after you died.

Chris: Yeah, the Island felt too sad for them after my death, and they wanted to be closer to my sisters in Kitchener.

This crowd you get out with—what are they like?

Me: Well, they don't ride motorbikes. But quite a few of them can sing and play guitar or piano. They piss me off sometimes.

Chris: Why? I thought you said you like them.

Me: 'Cause they don't always sing and play. My heart is so hungry for music.

Chris: Is that what's going on with your heart?

Me: No.

Chris: People don't always feel like doing what you want them to.

Me: I know. You couldn't have been a more perfect example of that, especially when you died. Doesn't mean it doesn't tick me off.

Chris: I never was much good at singing or playing music.

Me: If you had tried, no doubt you would have been good at music, too. You were good at most things.

These guys even cover Lynyrd Skynyrd.

Chris: Huh.

Me: Too bad they held such a grudge against Neil Young, just because he wrote an anti-KKK song.

Chris: Well, I heard Mr. Young sing about her

      Well, I heard ol' Neil put her down

      Well, I hope Neil Young will remember

      A Southern man don't need him around anyhow.

Me: Whatever that means. You'd have to be an American to get it.

Chris: Or a man from the Deep South. They should have paid attention to Young's lyrics.

Me: : "Simple Kind of Man" is still one of the most powerful songs out there, though. They got that one right.

Chris: Mmm...a song from the heart of a man. Instead of his other part.

Do your friends know any Alice Cooper?

Me: Yeah, him too.

Chris: Eagles?

Me: Yup.

Chris: "Take It to the Limit"?

Me: Yup. Stuck in the eighties.

Chris: About the heart thing—are you ready to talk about it?

Me: No.

Chris: I would have been honoured if you had told me your heart was in trouble, back then.

Me: You mean, as opposed to flaunting my new boyfriend and telling you maybe we could get together if I could ever spare the time, like I did the last time I saw you?

Chris: Yeah, that time. I would have liked to hear about your heart, instead. But other times, too. And it wasn't the very last time I ran into you.

Me: No. The very last time was at the bike show the next day. My sister Nora came with me and you were hanging out with some friends; can't remember who. One must have been Shane, since he was there at the beginning and there at the end. Nora said you were the most handsome man she never met.

Chris: You wouldn't introduce me to her. But you did say to me, 'Looks like you're not speaking.'

Me: And you said, 'I'm not the one who's not speaking.'

Chris: And that was that. You wouldn't even look at me later at the dance. Gawd, you could be pig-headed sometimes.

Me: Don't think I didn't know about the horrible girlfriend you lived with by then, the bitch! Big Boobs and all.

Chris: I was lonely. So was she.

Me: She was a greedy cow. She got to play the grieving widow for the wake and funeral, till she fucked one of your friends at the drunken party afterwards. Can't remember which one.

Chris: We don't need to talk about her. I heard you made such a scene at the graveside they had to haul you away.

Me: Yeah, well...OK. So I deserved that. But she's still a greedy cow.

Chris: Didn't you ever think having her all in your face at my funeral and party could have been a little karmic payback for the time you seduced my friend who came down to PEI to play Biker Tourist with me? You came on to him right in front of me.

Me: And succeeded. A little jealous, Chris?

Chris: No. Well, yes. But you don't need to know. It's not good for your mental health to know how jealous you can make people.

Me: Working on my mental health, are we now?

Chris: I'm *trying!*

Remember how we used to pull that stuff on each other all the time?

Me: Yeah, but I didn't usually get so much satisfaction out of hurting you. That last night, snubbing you felt particularly good. Not so good the next day. Or a couple of months later when I found out you had died in an Ontario hospital.

Chris: You were some stubborn back then.

Me: So were you.

Both of us: We were both so young.

Chris didn't fear words, but I thought I should let him rest for a few minutes. He often played around with writing science fiction and dreamed of becoming a writer, if he lived long enough. Not many people knew that.

Me: If I ever come back as a woman again, I'm finding a man who speaks up and says what he thinks and gets it over with.

Chris: Is that the kind you ended up with?

Me: No. More like the three-day silent treatment type.

Chris: Must be the make-up sex.

Me: I'll pretend you didn't say that. In my next life, if I meet a strong silent type, I'm gonna run as far and as fast as my little legs will take me. What a myth that is! The words 'strong', 'silent' and 'man' in any combination should be declared an oxymoron.

Chris: We *have* been the scourge of your existence, haven't we? The good news is, if you come back at all, you'll come back as a horse.

Me: Oh good! Horses are the most beautiful of God's creatures. Then I could run really fast and really far. My legs wouldn't be uneven with cow hocks for ankles. They'd be long and graceful and let me run away from those strong, silent cowboy types. No cowboy would ever lasso me with any stinky old rope. I'd run like the wind; get rid of this gimpy leg; outrun all their three-day silences.

Chris: How's the heart thing?

Emily: Still hurts, but I'm not ready to talk.

And, to quote the inimitable Porky Pig, that's all folks.

Sincerely

Emily

91

Chris showed up on his own again a few nights later, without being called on. He came in loud and clear, so Emily recognized his dream voice immediately. She wanted to share a little road trip with Chris. She knew he'd be interested:

Emily: Hey, Chris.

Chris: Hey, Em. What's up?

Em: Not much. Erin and I went to a motorcycle show in Moncton last week. This is the first time I've been to a bike show since I lost you.

Chris: How was it?

Em: Good. I wanted to check things out because my middle daughter, Christina, rides a Street Bob, and her father, Roberto, purchased a Fat Bob last week.

Chris: What are they?

Emily: Types of Harleys. So they are planning to go riding together a lot, spend some quality father-daughter time. I wish they'd spent more time together when I was still married to him.

Chris: So, tell me about the bikes.

Emily: First, we checked out some T-shirts. One of them read 'Gas, Grass or Ass No-one Rides for Free'.

Chris: That one's been around a long time.

Em: You're not kidding. That and 'Don't Come a Knockin' if the Van's a Rockin'. Quality quotes for the masses.

There was one I hadn't seen before. The screen print on the front shows a girl dressed in a bra, heels and a thong, leaning over her Harley with her butt sticking up in the air.

Chris: What's a thong?

Em: Basically, three pieces of string and a triangle of fabric. Butt floss.

Chris: What's floss?

Em: Oh, never mind—think of the butt part and you'll get the thong picture. Women wear them as panties.

Chris: Hunh.

Em: Anyway, so the caption on the T reads 'Remember Your First Ride on a Soft Tail?'

Chris: What's a Soft Tail?

Em: A type of Harley.

Chris: Oh. Oh OK. I get it. What did you say when you read that one? Did you do that sarcastic little 'ha ha' thing you do and groan?

Em: I confess. I did.

Chris: Any other good ones?

Emily: A few more T and A ones.

Chris: T and A?

Em: Tits and Ass.

Chris: They have a short form for Tits and Ass?

Em: Yup.

Chris: Wow.

Emily: Another one read 'It's Better to Burn Out Than to Fade Away' from the Neil Young song.

Chris: Neil Young from Crosby, Stills, Nash and Young? He's still writing songs?

Emily: Yeah, he's had a long career on his own. Kurt Cobain quoted that line in his suicide note. The word is Young said he would never perform the song again when he heard about Cobain's note.

Chris: Who's Kurt Cobain?

Emily: A young rock star who burnt out, rather than fade away. You did that too, Chris.

Chris: I sure did.

Em: So which is better?

Chris: I don't know, Em. It was just my time.

Em: I know that...now.

Chris: Did you buy a bike?

Em: No. But I bought a pair of sunglasses. I tried on one with rose coloured lenses—thought it might be better to see the world that way again. But they didn't do anything for me.

Chris: What about the bikes?

Emily: First, we checked out some vintage ones. There was an old red Indian...We're not supposed to say 'red Indian' anymore. But anyhow, it was red and it was an Indian make, almost the mate of the one Billy blew the motor outta.

Once we got to the new bikes, we found a gorgeous factory-made chopper. Made by Honda and called the Fury.

Chris: Wait a minute. What are you talking about—factory-made?

Emily: The motorcycle companies design the bike to look like a chopper. Then they mass produce it for the mass market. And...

Chris: Hang on now. Factory-made and a chopper?! Doesn't make any sense!

Em: No, it doesn't. That would be what we now call an oxymoron.

Chris: Way to take the fun out of it. Now you've got me upset.

Em: Yeah, well, the marketplace has a way of doing that. It's not my fault.

Chris: What do you mean by the marketplace?

Emily: Let me try to explain. You know how a lot of women are riding bikes now?

Chris: I gathered that when you said your daughter rides a Harley. We've seen a big increase of chicks landing their asses up here, because of motorcycle accidents.

Em: Nowadays, it's not only your typical butch who wants to ride a Hog. There are some girlie girls riding, too.

Chris: Like your daughter?

Emily: Yeah, like my Chris. So see, the company spots the women and thinks, 'Oh, would ya look at that, all the pretty girlies into bikes. Could be a whole new market for us and make us big gobs of money.'

So they put together a program exclusively for women. Then they print a promotional pamphlet; call it Garage Party. The caption reads 'You've got the Femme down'. The photo above shows a girl in leathers and a bandana applying her mascara by using the chrome gas cover as a mirror. You open the flap and there's the killer caption 'Now let's work on the Fatale'. Poor choice of words, if you ask me.

Chris: Especially when you consider how many female bikers end up here. Pretty fatal, I'd guess. But I get their point.

Em: Me too. What woman doesn't want to be a femme fatale?

Chris: Including you.

Em: And my Christina. Your namesake.

Chris: I forgot to thank you for naming her after me.

Emily: No problem. The name suits her; so does the femme fatale label.

Chris: This marketing stuff, it sounds complicated. Why don't they just run an ad on TV, or the radio, or something?

Em: They do. All part of their marketing strategy. First, they figure out what motivates women to make a purchase, and then they convince them they have the best toy ever for them. Plus, they are now designing bikes to suit women. I found the one I want today: a Blue Ice Victory Kingpin Low. Fits me like a glove.

Chris: Did you ever want to own a motorbike?

Em: I didn't think I did. Not till today.

Chris: So...this marketing stuff—it works? They mass produce 'choppers' and design bikes for girlie girls? And make big buckets full of money? Would it be fair to say marketing rules the world you live in?

Em: Pretty much.

Chris: Huh.

Em: I should tell you, Joe makes an excellent living doing the real thing—chopping and customizing and rebuilding bikes.

Chris: Black Joe?

Em: No, Red Joe.

Chris: You mean there's still hope?

Emily: Yeah. Even with the marketing, some people still want an authentic chopper. Sometimes I see Joe's ads on TV on the Ontario station.

Chris: Hold on a sec—you get Ontario channels on TV?

Em: Now we live in a five-hundred-channel universe. Bruce Springsteen wrote a great line for a song, 'Fifty-seven channels and there's nothing on'. That about sums up TV these days. Only now, we have five-hundred and fifty-seven channels. And there's *still* nothing on.

Chris, you should see these ugly bikes Harley makes now. Buell, they're called. Their crotch rocket line.

Chris: Crotch rocket? What the hell is that?

Em: It's a name people use for a racy style of bike—kind of a street racer. They have a futuristic, or aerodynamic, or Asian style to them. I don't know how to describe them. But anyway, the Buells are by far the butt-ugliest of an ugly-looking lot.

Chris: Who had the prettiest?

Emily: My pick is the customized Victory Kingpin. V Diamond Cut engine. Tear drop mirrors running horizontal to the handle bars. Wheels cut out like

Viking axe heads. I'd love to take a ride on it. I'd climb on and my chauffeur would say, 'Your chariot awaits you, my dear.'

Chris: Wish I could do that for you. Take you for a ride again. Maybe someday. How did the Kawis fair out?

Em: Hate to say it, but they can't compete in looks with Harley and Victory. But they make way classier T-shirts. They specialize in dirt bikes now.

Chris: OK, so what the fuck is a dirt bike?

Em: Language! I didn't think you talked like that up there, Chris!

Chris: We don't. But you are telling me so much has changed I can't keep up! And I'm disappointed to hear about Kawasaki.

Em: No doubt. You swore by yours. Took a lot of guff for it, too.

Chris: What's a dirt bike?

Emily: It's a bike that's designed for racing around gravel pits and hill trails, and all that shit.

Chris: They have a specific bike for pit racing? Christ, we just drove our regular bikes.

Em: I remember one night when you tore up the footpaths at the Experimental Farm with me on the back.

Chris: Hey, it wasn't that bad. Why on earth would people need a special bike for off-roading? Tearing things up is half the fun.

Em: Well, they didn't know they did till the....

Chris: Wait. Let me guess—till the companies started marketing dirt bikes to the masses.

Em: You got it, Chris.

Chris: What if a person didn't want to be part of this big marketing scheme?

Em: You'd have to go live under a rock in the woods somewhere: no TV, no radio, no computer, no cell phone, and no mail. Even then they would find you.

Chris: Tell me about the other bikes you liked.

Em: I didn't like the Suzukis—too much crotch rot. Or the Ducati, made in Italy. My youngest daughter, Bethany, works in an Italian restaurant in Calgary, and her boss purchased one of those for sixty thousand dollars, to put in the restaurant.

Chris: Like inside?

Em: Yup. In the front window where the display case used to be.

Chris: And not even ride it? What would ever possess him to do that?

Em: There are a lot of Italians and other people who eat at the Piazza who particularly like the Ducati. So, he figured it would be...

Chris: Good marketing! Don't you ever get sick of it?

Em: All the time. Some days I wonder if it's all we think about. Either buying or selling or being sold to.

Chris: Did you get to be a happy participant in the marketplace today?

Em: I bought the sunglasses, filled up a bag with free stuff, and entered all the contests for more free stuff.

One thing I found that I love is called The Back Road Map. I can get excited about those maps. My mom uses them all the time, because she likes to get way off the beaten path on these old logging roads, and she counts on their maps to get her back on track. I should get one for my friend to use when he goes night crawling. So he doesn't get lost.

Chris: Does he ride a Harley?

Em: No, just an ugly old van, a musician's rig. He's not into rigs, other than as a means to get his gear around. Still though, he does go night crawling after his gigs sometimes...

Chris: Still though...

Em: He might want to venture off the beaten path now and then...

Chris: And you'd be just the person to send him there.

Em: Yeah. Or help him find his way back, when the time comes. Give him a Back Road Map.

Chris: Does he have much of a sense of direction?

Em: No. At least I don't think he does. He's not too bright when it comes to knowing where he's going. Not on the road, anyway. I seem to be the one in need of a moral compass these days though, not him.

Chris: Whose magnetic north are you worried about: yours or his?

Em: Mine. I think.

Chris: Which would you prefer, Emily? The moral compass or the Back Road Map?

Em: The Back Road Map.

Chris: Why am I not surprised to hear that?

Em: Was there ever any doubt?

I have three men I talk to lately.

Chris: That must be a pain in the ass.

Em: You, and you're like...well, you're dead. You don't have any human needs now, thanks to God, and all that. There's my ex who is very much alive and has all the basics: food, shelter, sleep, sex. He ain't getting any of them met. Not by me.

Then there's this other guy I talk to in my head.

Chris: Is he the guy you told me about last time we talked? The music guy?

Em: Yeah, that guy. The young fart. The guy who goes night crawling.

Three men: the father, the son, and the holy ghost. The unholy trinity.

Chris: Are you saying you're a polygamist?

Did you just do that 'ha ha' thing and groan?

Em: Yeah.

Chris: You know I'm fine with you talking to me in your head. I'm available anytime you want, since I'm dead. But how does this music guy feel about you yakking away at him in your head all day long? Doesn't it crowd it up?

Em: Not for him, it doesn't. He doesn't say so.

Chris: And he puts up with it.

Emily: I guess. He puts up with it from a distance, since he moved away.

Chris: Well, Emily, putting up with you and your thoughts, even from a distance, is not the worst thing in the world.

Em: I guess not. But it's that human needs thing I wonder about sometimes.

Chris: Does he have any of those? Well, of course he would: you did say he's alive and a man, didn't you?

Em: Yeah, he's alive. He never says about those, either.

Chris: Maybe he's got all the basic stuff covered.

Em: He probably does. He's got a wife.

Chris: What's her name, this wife?

Emily: Shaw-vaughan.

Chris: Weird name!

Em: Celtic.

Chris: How do you spell it?

Emily: S-i-o-b-h-a-n.

Chris: Even weirder.

Em: They're from the Cape. What can I say?

Chris: So what are you worried about?

Em: Nothing, really. But I wonder sometimes. I wonder if he'll even remember me.

Chris: Emily, sometimes people don't appreciate what they get from other people till the person's no longer there, as you well know.

Em: Well, he'll soon find out. I won't be seeing him much. I wonder if he and his little family will be alright.

Chris: I'll keep an eye on them for you.

Em: Could you, Chris?

Canada Day on PEI

Emily loved the time spent with Erin at her beach house. They walked on the sandbars every day and talked about this and that and nothing at all. Erin slept in when she wanted and went out when she wanted and ate when and whatever she wanted. The southwest wind cured her of her constant need to confine her auburn hair in up-dos and braids, and her well-defined muscles and limbs seemed to loosen up somehow, possibly from walking and running on white beach sand instead of black asphalt. It pleased Emily no-end when Erin seemed to glow again, but they didn't talk about her lifestyle and what it must be doing to her. Emily never seemed to find the right moment; she didn't want to ruin what little time they shared by starting a big debate.

Prince Edward Island in the summer guarantees more than a few good parties. On July 1st, Emily did something she didn't often do. She got drunk. Spent too much time in the beer tent at the Canada Day celebrations at Victoria Park. Too much beer led to getting stuck in line at the port-a-potties, so she missed the fireworks. But she didn't miss the all-nighter with Erin's friends. Still half-cut the next morning, Emily cranked up the laptop again:

Sent: July 2, 2005, 7:45 am
To: Luke
Subject: canada day
Went to Jenn's party. Got drunk. Very drunk. Staggering stumbling drunk. Sore throat went away. Spilt Amber's drink. Spilt Trina's drink. Soaked my socks. You weren't there. Thank God.

Slept. Dreamt. Big party. Many people. Huge hotel. Coloured glass beads. Marble floors. You were there. Tried to pick up a scientist. Gorgeous. Thought she could fix your septic tank. Too many big words. From you. And her.

Woke up. Lights hurt. Sore throat back. Head wants off my shoulders. Advil caps. Two. Still drunk.

100

The End

Someone said I called your home phone and yelled at your voice mail last night.
Sorry. Delete that message, OK?

E

Dragons' Tails

The next day Emily and Erin got into it hot and heavy. In her humble opinion, Erin and Pierce were heading towards a heap of trouble, and she forgot to shut her mouth about it. She didn't know if the mutual hangovers set them off, or all the things that had gone unsaid, or the loneliness Emily knew she'd feel once Erin was gone away again. She got so tired of people going away. Gone away. So many ways people could come to the state of gone away, but they all came down to the same thing in the end. You couldn't touch them, even if you Skyped.

Erin flew back to the West Coast, but the hangover fight still hadn't been resolved. The leftover tension hung over Kate's peaceful little house, and Kate wouldn't approve. So one day after a walk on a South Shore beach (for a change), Emily wrote a story for Erin. She called it:

Dragon's Tales

I like the South Shore beaches best. Stuff grows there. Wild mussel spat, umpteen seaweeds, clams, sea urchins, barnacles, even hermit crabs. Next time, when you come home with your new boyfriend and step-kids, I will take you there and show you what I meant to show you when you were little: the beaches of my childhood, the shoreline where I grew up. I'll find some red modeling clay, and you and Pierce and Madison and Clair can make a pot with it and let it dry in the sun. I've told you about the modeling clay, but I don't think you ever played with it like I did.

While I'm at it, I'll make up a story about a man who loved too much. A man who lives in a little clapboard cottage by the sea and wakes up every day to watch the sun rise over the South Shore. Every morning he praises the South Shore, the sea, the sky, and his beautiful wife and thanks her from the bottom of his heart for the two lovely gifts she has given him—a freckle-faced little boy and a blue-eyed girl.

This man's name will be Daniel. And his children will be called Maeve and Peter.

His clapboard cottage by the sea is a magical cottage. It has been protected by sea sprites for generations.

Since he was a wee boy, Daniel watched the sea from the round window of his bedroom, as did his father and his grandfather before him. By the time of this story, the window frame of that round window will have rotted and should be replaced with something more sensible. Maybe a rectangular window next time. But Daniel doesn't have the heart to replace it.

Every day he tells his wife how beautiful she is. And every day he goes out on the Northumberland Strait and works hard to make a living for his family. When he comes in from fishing the Strait, he heads to town and buys her pretty things to adorn her porcelain skin: seed pearls, spun gold, topaz, rose quartz and amethyst.

And the tide rolls in and the tide rolls out, and the days turn into years. He counts himself one of the lucky ones.

One day, he brings his gift from town to his wife at suppertime, as always, and she makes a sour face at him. He asks, "What's wrong?"

She says, "I don't want this. I want true beauty. And I will go to the shore tomorrow and search the seas for it."

So she does. That day and every day. Rain or sun, storm or calm.

Meanwhile, as his wife spends more and more time at the shore, Daniel stops going to town to buy her pretty things and comes home to the kids as soon as he gets in from fishing. His wife takes off the moment he steps in the door, for destinations unknown. He takes the kids to the shore to play, but he never comes across his wife there, even though he knows she has to be somewhere.

He has a lot of fun at the beach with his kids. The little girl, Maeve, often finds a scoop in the rocks and places her foot in it to see if it fits. One day, she finds one that fits just so. Her dad tells her, "The Sea and the rocks made that scoop especially for you. The Sea is telling you that you are perfectly safe in both worlds. She will always give you a foothold to take you back to me."

They spend hours playing with seaweed, wrapping the dragon's tails around their necks like scarves, and making ducks and pots and crabs and fish with the deep red modeling clay.

But sharp things live in the sea too, and sometimes the boy, Peter, complains because he cuts his foot on a cracked clam shell or a barnacle. Living things can hurt us, although Peter doesn't understand that yet. His dad patiently shows him how to curve the soft part of his foot away from the stones and shells and roll his foot in the waves. He tells Peter the story of St. Peter and how St. Peter was a fisher of fishes, even when Jesus was busy fishing for souls. Peter says he wants to grow up to be like St. Peter. And like his dad. But not like Jesus. He figures that would be too hard. So his dad says, "That's OK, Son. Not many of us can grow up to be like Jesus. I didn't. I can only love you like Jesus does."

One day Daniel comes home to find the children all alone, playing quietly by the wood stove. He goes in search of his wife, once again, and finds her at the shore, covering her body with the same modeling clay he and the children played with. So he asks, "What in the world are you doing? You left the kids alone in the house to come out here and sit on a rock?"

She replies, "I am changing the colour of my skin."

What can he—or any man—say to that?

So instead, because he doesn't know what else to say or do, he takes her home. From then on, he strums his guitar and sings her happy country songs whenever she gets that urge to roam. Unless she wants sad country songs, and God knows there are plenty of those. Eventually, she doesn't even make any requests and she no longer sings along.

This goes on and on. All he can think to do is tell her time and again how beautiful she is and how much he loves her. One night, he wakes to find her gone from her side of the bed. Sure enough, she has gone to the beach again. He watches her in the moonlight, as she takes off her fine silk nightie and drapes the Dragon's tails over her breasts. And he doesn't understand. He hopes she will get over it soon. Whatever it is.

He lies awake and waits and waits until finally, at dawn, he hears her slip into bed. Skin soft and cool, salt in her hair, and he thinks, 'I love her more than ever. She smells like the sea and she feels like satin under my skin.' But eventually, her skin starts to feel slippy slidey under his hands, and she turns away from him, more often than not.

Daniel decides he must say something, speak up. He asks her what is wrong. He pleads with her to tell him. He reminds her of all the good times. As he paces around the bedroom under the gable end, he talks about the early days and how they slept in a three-quarter bed with a belly full of baby along side. He talks about how they had graduated from the three-quarter bed to the king-size one when the kids were little, so they could all be together. This bed is so wide sometimes he bumps his head on the sloped wall trying to get in on his side. He's a tall man, not built for such a small cottage, but he doesn't mind taking the odd crack on the head. He wants to know why she doesn't want to do that anymore— cuddle up on the king-size bed, just the four of them. But she won't answer.

Then comes the night she doesn't come home at all. The next morning, he watches from the round window of his little cottage by the sea, as she walks out into the ocean one last time. And the sun comes up over the Northumberland Strait one more time. And the sun goes down again that night, as if nothing has changed.

One day, his little girl Maeve disappears, too. He walks the beaches every day and every night. On a bright sunny day with a clear blue sky, he discovers her little broken body. He picks her up and cradles her in his arms. He can't see her eyes that are as blue as the sky.

A few weeks later, Peter disappears. So Daniel starts another vigil at the shore. Day after day, night after night, hoping and praying he will see those freckles that tell him this is his boy, his fisher of fishes, his own St. Peter, his child who has been kissed by the sun.

In the darkness of night, Daniel finds Peter. And the freckles stand out like a reverse image of the stars in the night sky. Painful black dots on a parched white sky. Daniel stares at the black sky with all those bright pin-hole stars, and he looks at the white sky of his son's face with the dark freckles, and he thinks the night sky has turned itself inside out and is tormenting him, taunting him, laughing at him. He shakes his fist at the big cruel night sky, and screams and screams until his screams become a keen, a never ending keen. His throat hurts, his eyes hurt, every part of him hurts. But his heart hurts most of all.

This carries on for days and days, until Daniel can't stand it anymore. He wades out into the ocean and, as the water gets deeper and deeper, he swims until he can swim no more. Then he finds her. Lounging on a rock only two miles off shore, as it turns out. His beautiful bride. Only now, her skin is sparkling like fish scales in the sun, as she sits on the rocks of an unknown island. At least, the island is unknown to him. He doesn't think it belongs to the Northumberland Strait. Her once golden hair covers her arms, her breasts, and her belly like a fuzzy green moss, and her tail covers the rest of her body.

He whispers in the whisper of a condemned and exhausted man, "How could you?"

"I gave them to you. I will take them away."

"But I gave you everything. Love, a home, pretty things. How could you do this to me?"

"You didn't ask me what I want. I want this life. I want my beauty, not yours. My life, not yours."

"Every day, I told you how much I love you and how grateful I am for the two children you bore for me. Yet, you took them from me."

"I don't want your gratitude. I didn't ask for it and I don't want it. Never did."

"Not much chance of that anymore. You've not only destroyed me, you've destroyed the two most beautiful things you could ever create. Our children. And sealed your legs for good. You won't be able to have children, ever again. You can't create again, not ever."

She tells him, "But my hips are still amazing."

"What do you have to say for yourself?"

"Ooops, I did it again?"

(By this time, freckle-faced Maddie will be staring at me with those big blue eyes. But she won't blink and she won't cry. This kid doesn't get scared watching Monster House, and I can't even do that.)

Daniel looks at his wife and, instead of the beautiful mermaid, he sees the sea hag, the sea hag inside the mermaid, the beast within the beauty, the frog inside the prince. And he is free.

So he goes back to the little cottage and finds a South Shore girl waiting there for his return. They don't worship one another, but they love each other just the way they are. So they get married and have ten kids, and let all the magic of the magical cottage come out to play. And they laugh a lot and play a lot and breed like rabbits.

(Maddie will giggle at the very idea of parents as rabbits. She likes rabbits.)

But the hole in his heart where those first two kids, Maeve and Peter, were supposed to live is always there. And eventually, it kills him.

Clair will start to tear up at this, so I will add: But he lived to be one-hundred-years-old, so not so bad a life.

Pierce will look at my darlin' Erin and say, "Erin is a South Shore girl at heart." And I will look at Madison and say, "And so is Madison". Madison will glare at me and say, "Well if I'm one, so are you." I'll tell her, "It's a good thing to be a South Shore girl", so she doesn't get confused. She's only barely five.

Then we will go back into the warmest waters north of Florida and chase hermit crabs, wild mussels, and barnacles, too. Did you know wild mussels move really slow? Those barnacles aren't too swift, either. And Maddie will tell a fart joke, probably the one about how her Daddy claims his farts sound like the rumble of the Harley, so we don't have to think about children dying anymore. Then we'll all dissolve on the sand in a fit of giggles.

The End

Erin wrote back to say she enjoyed the story, even if it was a thinly disguised morality play, a fable for Erin, the soon-to-be trophy wife to a big-time corporate finance man. This was the first bit of writing Emily shared with anyone but Luke, so she was pleased. She didn't mind that Erin caught the warning. She worried about her and her big city lifestyle. Emily was all over the Diva Darlings thing when they were out playing at a party, but Erin wouldn't be much help around a wood pile if she didn't learn she could break a nail or two, sacrifice one of those Glamour Girl gel-nails every once in awhile. No practical skills, that girl.

At least Erin took it all in stride and didn't get upset with her all over again.

3 am Phone Calls

Luke, on the other hand, was not too impressed with the 3 am post-party call to his landline. The day after the Canada Day call, he sent Emily an email to blast her for waking his wife and kid; nailed her to the wall. He told her never, ever, in no uncertain terms, could she call his home again. Emily resolved to drop it and forget about him. Emily being Emily, and never one to leave well enough alone, called his cell phone instead, late at night. She was, unfortunately, overtired and once again, a little bit drunk from sharing one more attempt-at-reconciliation bottle of wine with Erin. Fortunately, she caught him as he was packing up after a gig. Unfortunately, it didn't go so well. After several minutes of non-stop yelling at him, she took a deep breath and said the inevitable 'L' word. Not a good idea. Fortunately, she didn't remember that part the next day. Or any other day. Luke didn't confront her about her confession of love—chicken shit that he was. So Emily remained oblivious forever.

When she woke the next morning, she wondered why drinking always led to drunk-dialing. Something about her, alcohol, and Luke seemed to lead to the birth of one more conflict. Just as well he moved back to old Cape Breton. Best to forget him.

But all her resolutions to write Luke off didn't keep Emily's dead friends from teasing and tormenting her a little about those 3 am phone calls a few nights later:

Tessa: That was quite a rant you went on, Emily.
Emily: Who, moi? I wouldn't call it a rant, exactly. I didn't yell or anything.
Chris: Yeah, you did. Your screaming banshee cell phone fight was almost as funny as when you accosted the poor guy at the ferry terminal. Hilarious! One of your finer moments.
Emily: Gee thanks, Chris.
Chris: How come you never screeched at me? I'm jealous.
Kate: I can't picture you as a screamer, somehow.

Tessa: He didn't look too cool that day himself, stumbling around under his backpack, with about six beers in him. What a way to go home to the wife and kid.

Emily: He only had three beers, Tessa. But, yeah, he did look pretty geeky.

Chris: What's a geek?

Tessa: Is it like a klutz?

Kate: No, it's a word that started circulating a few years before I died. It's more like someone who spends too much time around computers and, as a result, ends up a little socially challenged. It applies to a lot of people, since we are in the new millennium.

Chris: I worked with computer punch cards in Ottawa, so would you call me a geek?

Emily: Oh, that's a hoot! No worries, Chris, you were way too gutsy and drop dead gorgeous. See, Chris, this is the thing about geeks. Bill Gates notwithstanding, for most women, geeks are a little less sexual.

Chris: So is that how he sees himself?

Emily: No. More like a rock star. He likes that image of himself. In fact, I think it's his favourite. The one he rode in on.

By the way, thanks for not laughing at me when I got drunk with Erin again the night after Jenn's party, Tessa.

Tessa: Don't you worry, I laughed my cutest non-existent derriere in heaven off. At both of you.

Emily: I didn't plan to drink again. The wine hit me a little harder than I thought, thanks to the stress of the blood-on-the-floor match with Erin in the afternoon. She said some things she needed to say, but I didn't want to hear.

Kate: Knowing Erin, she'd win that one.

Emily: I cried a lot more than she did, but I got to kick her out—my house and all—so you could call it a draw. When she came back from Jenn's, we hugged and made up over the bottle of wine. It's one of the rules in our house—we don't leave each other with anger between us. I never forgot that lesson, Chris. Erin made it easy, though. She told me I was the best-est Mommy in the whole wide world. Of course, it was never me as a mother in contention, just her status as arm candy for a stock broker.

Tessa: What did you tell Erin when she called from Jenn's?

Emily: The same thing every time—that I didn't want to fight anymore and I needed some time to clear my head. Once she let go and stopped harassing me about the 'horrific effects of her fucked-up childhood', it didn't take long for me to want her to come back home. I let go, too.

Kate: That old cliché, eh?

Emily: Yup.

Kate: How did you manage to let go?

Emily: I was trying to lose myself in a good movie after Erin stomped out and took off to Jenn's, when I heard a voice in my head telling me: 'if she says she loves you and still needs you, it's because she does'. Thank you, Kate.

Kate: No need to thank me.

Emily: I loved having her back. Her time on the Island was so short; we were foolish to waste any more of it fighting. Blame it on the hangovers.

Chris: Did you tell her you had to spend some time evicting the imaginary boyfriend because he wouldn't leave?

Emily: Yeah, right. Erin doesn't need to know about Luke. She may be twenty-seven, but she's still too young to understand. Besides, Luke's not my boyfriend, imaginary or not.

Chris: It's still so much fun getting you going.

Emily: You'd think I'd know better than to take the bait by now.

Tessa: Why did you evict this imaginary boyfriend?

Emily: He took up too much space in my head. His stuff was everywhere.

Tessa: He didn't seem like such a bad imaginary boyfriend to me. Never bugged you for sex. It can be sooo annoying when men do that, especially when you're trying to get supper on. Did you *have* to kick him out?

Emily: Yes. He didn't pay any rent, either.

Tessa: That's too bad. Where did you get such an awful tenant?

Emily: You guys. Don't you remember?

Kate: Oh. That guy! But I sent you a friend, not a boy friend! What were you thinking?

Emily: Did you just clue in, Kate?

Kate: Why did you let him move in, if he was such an inconsiderate roommate?

Emily: There didn't seem to be enough space left in his head. Too many noisy chords and screaming guitars and incessant groupies. I figured he'd be safer if he came and lived in my head; I would protect him from all that sex, drugs, and rock and roll, and send him home safely to his wife and kid.

Tessa: Did he want to take up residence in your head?

Emily: No. Not at all.

Chris: So, did you kidnap him and hold him for ransom? Hey, this is starting to sound like fun! We could write a murder mystery. Or make up a sci-fi film: *Whatever Happened to Luke the Disappearing Boyfriend?* Subtitled: *Could He Have Been Abducted By Aliens?*

Emily: You guys are too nosy. And weird. Way too weird. Let's just say he's gone and no longer inhabiting my mind. Luke can text me if he wants someday, but to hell with the imaginary boyfriend.

A few days later:

Chris: I've been thinking about your famous long goodbye again, and having a good laugh about all those words. Impressive. And really, really long. What got into you—verbal diarrhoea?

Emily: At least I wasn't cold to him like I was to you.

Chris: As soon as I got here, I knew how sorry you were about the last day we met up on earth. God explained it to me. And you found me again.

Emily: It only took me twenty-five years.

Chris: You know what, Emily? Twenty-five years on the space-time continuum? It's just a speck of dust, a dot in the universe, a bleep on the screen.

Emily: And this guy wonders why I can't simply wait for him to move back to PEI in fifty years!? You and Luke should get together, discuss the artificiality of human constructs of time and the potential for world domination by rock and roll heroes. But leave me out of that conversation!! Please!

Chris: OK. Tell him, 'anytime'.

Emily: Chris, I sat in my old car the other day thinking about the day of my Great Embarrassment when I left him at the ferry. I was clearing my old stuff out so I could sell it, and I sat for a minute on the driver's side, returned to the scene of the crime.

Chris: You don't still think of it as the scene of the crime after all this time, surely?

Emily: No, I was just being sarcastic. The old bomb felt kinda seductive. Sometimes I think I can still smell his cologne in it. Then again, it could have been the music on the CD player causing the little flash of warmth. My old car played CDs and my 'new' old car, which is actually older than my old car but doesn't need near as much work, only plays the radio and cassettes. So, nothing to do with Luke and his leftover cologne at all.

Chris: What did you do about the cheap thrill?

Emily: Called the guy who wanted to buy the car and told him the old shit-box wasn't worth much, except for parts, and dropped the price in half. Sold it to him on the spot. And got on with it.

Chris: Good choice.

Baby Dunes

Emily sat at her kitchen table, watched the waves lap up onto the sand and thought. She often sat and stared out the window and thought. Hard. Emily minded the heat as the dog days of summer wore on, so sitting still seemed as good a way to be as any. She hadn't anyone much to talk to, except the cat, since Erin had long gone back to British Columbia. And she hadn't heard from Christina for quite awhile. Not that it was out of character for her; too independent by halves was that Christina, like her namesake.

Earlier that morning, Emily had taken a long walk on Blooming Point Beach. On the way back the tide had been rising in a hurry, so she went around the long way, cut across the marshy part, and climbed up the wooden stairs. Her jeans got wet from splashing around, even though she was wearing her rubber boots. She didn't mind though, because she knew every big adventure comes with a little discomfort. Which seemed to be the case, even for the adventures where she didn't get to go anywhere, at least not physically, like the ones she'd been having with Kate since she died. Kate might not have been as lively or daring as Christina, but she served as a good cheap substitute when she showed up in Emily's dreams.

Emily loved two things best about the Blooming Point Beach: the woods she walked through to get there, and the way the end of the main dune kept reclaiming land from the sea. What an adventure, to be part of the evolution of a sand dune!

A month before, she found a little shelter under a baby dune at the end of the beach closest to Tracadie Bay. Baby dunes aren't very firmly attached to this earth, she observed, much like the spirits of newborn babes. She curled up on the sand where no one could see her. The little hollow reminded her of a shrine, of all the shrines she had encountered over her lifetime: the little alcoves carved out of a church wall, or hollowed out of a tree, or dug out of the rock face, like in Quebec where supplicants can actually *find* rocks of granite.

Not many carving rocks on PEI, as the Island sits on a base of sandstone, which would only break into a thousand pieces if you chipped too hard. Emily tried once to whittle a sundial for her garden out of one big slab of sandstone, but it broke into a bunch of chunks and made her so cross she threw the chunks at the wall where they stained the shingles with a fine pink dust. In different parts of the world, like Mexico, Emily had seen shrines occur naturally in caves. They might have been called *grottos*, but she wasn't sure.

All those little alcoves were big enough to hold a small statue, usually of the Virgin Mary, at least in Catholic Quebec, where people made offerings to the Virgin with a hope and a prayer. In Costa Rica, worshippers made pilgrimages to the *Basilica de Nuestra Senora de Los Angeles* to visit the Black Madonna, called *La Negrita*. The Costa Ricans believed *La Negrita* possessed exceptional healing powers. They had a special rock there, too. Emily couldn't remember the significance of the stone, but she had seen people kiss it when she visited the Basilica with Christina.

The shrine she once found for Kate grew on the lee side of the dune. No rocks at all, just white sand brought up from the sea, too new to compact into shale.

As Emily tried to find the baby dune, she recalled a childhood friend named Diana, who reminded Emily of Diana Barry from the *Anne of Green Gables* books. When they were little kids, before she met Kate, Emily and her Diana would make shrines in the trees at Canoe Cove. Emily's parents owned a summer place in the Cove, which started as one small cottage but multiplied into a compound for the entire extended family. Emily's family gave it up later when the payments for all those little cabins turned out to be too much for her parents and her aunts and uncles. It seemed to be a common theme in her family: they loved property but couldn't always figure out how to hang onto it.

Diana's cottage sat on a cliff, closer to the ocean. Some sunny summer mornings, she would wait for Emily to finish her chores. Off they'd go through the cow pasture to the woods, picking bouquets of daisies and devil's paint brushes along the way to set in the cracked vase in the sacred space their nine-year-old imaginations had created for the Virgin. Emily wondered whatever became of her old friend Diana.

As Emily shooed the cat off the table, she remembered when she and Kate walked the beaches of PEI together, right up till the time when Kate could manage no farther than the path from the bed to the bathroom. Emily didn't have any luck locating the dune shrine today. She had found many clusters of wild heather by the baby sand dune the day she discovered it. If she could find the heather again, it might lead her to the right dune. She found lots of different wild plants, but no shrine. She decided she should christen her little Blooming Point sand dune: Shrine to Kate and Diana and Beach Heather if she ever found it again.

Emily needed to locate the shrine because the day before her sister-in-law Daniela called her from Mexico to tell her Daniela's sister had been killed in a car accident that morning. Daniela had been crying hard and speaking so fast in Spanish, Emily could barely understand her. Emily promised Daniela she would walk the beach and sing and pray for her and her family. What more could she think to say? And what better place to pray than at a beach shrine? She sang lustily in the wind all morning and, for Emily, to sing is to pray. But she couldn't find the shrine to help out her sister-in-law and her family, either. She picked a bundle of beach heather, twisted it into a wiry bouquet, carried it home, and set it on the windowsill to dry, so she could send it as a gift to Daniela.

Sometimes when we search too hard, we can't find the things we think we have lost. Emily hoped the little baby dune would be there again another day. Unless a sea storm took it out this fall, overpowered it. Then it would be up to the mother dune to form another one and up to Emily to find it. Always something to look forward to when you live by the ever-changing sea.

Emily was frequently on the look-out for beach glass, and the day's pickings turned out to be plentiful, once she cleaned them off and took a good look. She fiddled with some beach glass and various jewellery fittings she had crafted, sorting and fitting till she found a close match. A little twist here, a little twist there, a little polishing of rough edges, and she would have a dozen more pendants to add to the pile. Selling her crafts at the farmer's market on Saturday could bring in a little cash. And a pendant might cheer Daniela up. Or at least let her know Emily cared.

No sacred spaces could be found in the dunes, but many other treasures surfaced for her. A set of bones, that looked like they once belonged to the head of a blue-fin tuna. Irish Moss washed up from the recent sea storm. A dead and dismembered seagull, and a very-much-alive sandpiper who kept six feet of distance between itself and Emily as the two of them walked the beach together.

Plenty of God's creatures. On the walk home, she spotted two squirrels, a blue jay, ten spiders, and three clever foxes, all of whom conspired to spin a web of enchantment over the Blooming Point woods. Beach heather, wood wizards, and beach glass. Not a bad day's catch.

Emily had forgotten to eat lunch so she pushed herself up from the table, stretched, and opened the fridge to retrieve last night's leftovers. As she heated the spaghetti on the stove, she believed when she looked again one day, she would find them: lost shrines, lost sisters, lost daughters, lost summers, lost beach days, old friends, old loves.

The phone rang as she sat down to eat. She hoped it was Luke. She hadn't heard from him for awhile. Or better yet, Christina. But it was neither of them.

Liam and Luke

Luke stared out of the window to the sea. He perched Liam on his knee, but his mind wandered elsewhere. Liam wanted to play and kept pulling at his hair, to the point where it got annoying. Liam needed a nap and he was often hard to put down. At least, when Luke tried. He fussed and kicked up his chubby little legs and would sometimes wail like a scalded cat if Luke dared even try to leave the room. Luke called to Siobhan to come and get the baby and do something to keep him entertained. Siobhan said she was busy baking bread and couldn't he make some time for his own son? Luke heaved an almighty sigh, lifted Liam up into his arms and headed for the door.

As Luke walked along the path by the cliff, Liam grew more interested in his surroundings than in getting in Luke's hair. The baby-distracting sounds of the ocean gave Luke time to fret and puzzle and calculate and fret some more. He couldn't see how this music thing would ever work out if he lived in Cape Breton and the rest of the band stayed on Prince Edward Island. Halifax maybe, because he had lots of reasons to go to Halifax; it wasn't too far from Cape Breton; you don't have to pay the stupid forty-two dollar toll for the Confederation Bridge, either, only the four dollars at the Cobequid Pass. Luke knew enough people if he had to couch surf, and the boys should be able to find day jobs in the restaurants, or whatever. Plus the sizzling eclectic music scene in Halifax gave Luke quite a buzz.

Luke made up his mind he'd have to tell the guys to move off the Island, or he would replace them. PEI was too far away and inconvenient.

The air was fresh and clear. He cuddled Liam close to him, swayed with the breeze, and sang him a little song. While his baby dozed in his arms, Luke contemplated this place he called home. The little house he inherited from his grandfather needed a coat of paint. The driveway could use a load of gravel, or asphalt millings, or even pavement if he could afford it, to keep the dust down. The flowerbed Siobhan planted last spring might amount to something eventually, but she sowed all perennials and none of them showed much sign of bloom so far, other than in June when the peonies performed their brief show of

118

colour. He should fix the slide on Liam's swing set someday. Get on it. Take care of it. Soon.

Luke decided the best thing about the whole two acre property must be the shimmer of sun on water on a day like today. Or, if not, the sound of the ocean crashing on the rocks on a stormy day. There had to be a song he could write in there. Oh yeah, there was. And it had already been written. About a thousand times.

Luke's thoughts and Liam's nap were interrupted by his cell phone playing "Baby I Was Born to Run". He supported a crying Liam in one hand, while he fished out his cell with the other. He sure as hell hoped it was Matt because he wanted to get this conversation over with—now! Move on. Put the boys in the band on notice. Things had to change if they were ever going to have any chance of success.

The Cell Call

But it wasn't Matt. It was Emily, in tears. The call she received hadn't been from Christina. It held very bad news. Emily needed to talk to Luke, even if he wasn't paying attention. She counted on him to make her laugh.

Inconsolable, Emily hung up on Luke and headed to bed so she could continue to cry her eyes out. Even after the lovely walk, all the fresh air, and all her tears, Emily tossed and turned. She was not too impressed with any of her dead friends. One of the few people on the Island she still felt close to and could share her grief with was her old friend Trudy, Tessa's younger sister. It was Trudy who had phoned when Emily sat down to her leftover spaghetti supper. Since she couldn't sleep, Emily vented to her dead friends:

Em: Chris, what the fuck is this?

Chris: You've heard about Trudy?

Emily: Yeah, she called. What the hell is going on here? You're supposed to keep an eye on my people for me.

Chris: That's Tessa's department.

Em: Don't give me any bureaucratic bullshit! This is plain not right and you know it. Fuckin' ridiculous. And don't try to pawn it off on Tessa.

Chris: Well, she is Tessa's sister.

Em: I don't care. Who is supposed to help me sort out all these deaths and cope, if not Trudy? Don't you remember the night you wore your Greb Kodiaks to Canoe Cove, you called me the Memory Keeper, said it would be my job to keep track of you and all the other souls I've lost? For my whole fuckin' entire life! Now you're thinking of adding to the list? As if it's not long enough! Cancer for Trudy? WTF! What is this—some grand game you play to amuse all the dead people who leave Emily behind?

Chris: But...

Emily: Just fuck off, Chris. I don't want to talk to you.

A few hours later

Chris: Emily, have you calmed down?

120

Em: No.

Chris: Do you want to talk?

Em: No.

Chris: Do you want me to go away?

Em: No. Shut up for a few minutes, would ya?

After a few seconds:

Emily: I have been having weird dreams for two weeks! Two weeks, Chris! You couldn't tell me why? I HATE when I dream these prophetic dreams and don't have a clue why. It's not supposed to be about Trudy. Not a freakin' wonder I can't sleep! Put Tessa on.

Tessa: I'm here.

Emily: What's it gonna be, Tessa? After all those years raising the kids as a single parent, she will get diagnosed with cancer, meet the love of her life, marry him, and die—all within two years? Like you, all over again?

Tessa: She won't meet the love of her life.

Emily: Oh, and that makes it so much better?

Tessa: Calm down, Emily.

Emily: Don't tell me to calm down. I'll calm down when I'm good and ready to calm down.

Tessa: Did you figure out what you are going to do?

Emily: No. But Trudy has. As usual, she's away ahead of the rest of us She's flying off to Cuba to play in the sun, then she's making another trip to New York to shop till she drops. She better not drop! Not yet. After the trip that's meant to put her in a New York state of mind, she is getting to visit the daughter she's been missing so much and meet the new grandson.

Tessa: Cathy's coming home?

Em: It's about freakin' time. Cathy hasn't been home since she graduated from university. She should be home right now. She'll live to regret it if she doesn't, I know she will.

Tessa: She may not. Trudy would not expect her to be mad at herself over her choices. She wouldn't ask her to come home, either. She would want her to carry on with her life.

Emily: Guess what? When Cathy gets older and understands more about time, she'll be sorry. She'll regret every minute she missed spending with her mother.

You might think you are all so fucking evolved up there, but I know how things work here on earth. Won't matter what her mother says.

Tessa: Emily, could you cut back on the cursing?

Em: No.

Tessa: Let's get back to Trudy's plans. I heard something about a party.

Em: Because she knows how sad all her girl friends are going to be, she's having a girls-only, pity-pal, potluck party on Sunday afternoon so we can all get together and cry, think up fun things to do and how to cure her.

Tessa: She always has been well organized.

Emily: Not a wonder. When you left, she had to take over all those 'oldest daughter' responsibilities. And, by the way, I'm not ready to talk to you yet, either.

Chris: She's also brave. I've seen her go through fire and back for people she loves. Impressive.

Em: Not a fuckin' wonder! Between you and Tessa and life in general, she hasn't had a lot of choice. I want you to know I'm holding both of you personally responsible for this mess. And don't, *don't* tell me everything will be alright. I'm not buying it!

Chris: Don't take a shit fit, Em. She'd make a good first-round draft pick for our hockey team. Or she could make up the nine we need for our baseball team.

Tessa: Or sing in our choir.

Em: Why would you want her—she's not a bit musical! As you well know, Tessa, she's the only one in your family who isn't gifted musically. She can't sing or even play the kazoo. Not well, anyway. You know that! So if you're trying to be funny, you are not even a little. Chris can't sing, either, so your choir would suck.

Tessa: Trudy could come up here to brush my hair.

Emily: All those months you were in palliative care, you monopolized her. 'Brush my hair, bathe me, feed me.' Until you stopped being able to sit up for even that. Hours and hours she spent with you when you couldn't do anything for yourself. Right till the end when your poor body looked like someone fresh out of Auschwitz. Do you think she had FUN watching you waste away to nothing but a death rattle? Now you are going to let her body go through all that just so you can see her again?! You had your turn.

Tessa: And where were you at the time?

122

Em: I know, I know, I wasn't there enough. I didn't brush your hair for you. Blah blah blah. Give it up already.

So we're going to a party. We'll all fiddle while Rome burns. Of course, she's going to investigate alternative treatments and plan to live a long time.

Tessa: Sometimes it helps.

Em: And sometimes the alternative is just that, an alternate path to the same reality. Doesn't change the final outcome.

Tessa: Prayer works.

Em: I'm sorry. I can't be optimistic enough to pray. On-line it says the cancer could spread to her lungs or liver. Either way, not good. Besides, it's not fair if it gets in her lungs. She went through so much watching and worrying when cancer invaded the lungs of our friend Lisa. With her, it moved so fast we barely had time to breathe and she was gone. Six weeks.

Tessa: But she made sure you got a chance to visit Lisa in the hospital, even though you weren't family. So what are you complaining about?

Em: And I've always been grateful to her. That's the kind of friend she is, to me and Lisa and all her other friends.

Tessa: It's going to be OK.

Em: You two sit up in your ivory cloud and think you're so smart with your 'there are no easy answers', ad nauseam. Your talk is all crap. We're standing in shit here, and all you spirits can do is keep telling us to look up at the blue sky. WHO CARES!

It's not only me you're hurting here. My girls have grown up loving her and her family, too. Stop taking the people I know by heart away from me! There are so few I ever get to know that way, the best way. Not fair, not one bit.

Chris: We're not in charge here.

Emily: Well then, who the fuck is?

Chris: God, of course. But He's tied up in a meeting.

Em: Sounds about right—a God who's too busy and remote to be any good to us. How New Millennium is that?

Chris: It's not like that. He's awfully busy.

Em: Oh yeah, everybody's *awfully* busy these days. Doesn't stop people from dying, does it? Oh no, never too busy for death and destruction!

Chris: What do you want God for?

Emily: I'd like to holler at Him, get Him out of his conference call, and tell Him, 'Why do You keep giving me these amazing girl friends just to turn around and yank them away from me on a whim?'

Chris: You have to admit, He still keeps sending you more loving women friends.

Em: Yeah...well, maybe...not too many lately. Unless you count Betty. Trudy's the closest friend I have here now.

Tessa: How is she coping?

Em: Of course, her attitude is as positive as it could be. You know Trudy. She has even managed to find humour in it. I, being somewhat stunned, said I'd make my pecan squares for the potluck party because they are deadly, they are so good. So she said, 'You sure you want to bring them? I think I would prefer my Death by Chocolate Dessert.'

Tessa: It's not funny, is it, Emily?

Emily: No, it's not funny. Not even a bit.

Around midnight:

Kate: Are you awake?

Em: No, I'm asleep.

Kate: Are you OK, Em?

Em: No.

Kate: Anything I can do?

Em: Just call me on the phone like you used to. 672-32...672-2...I can't even remember your number anymore. And it's not even two years.

Kate: I'm sorry.

Em: Yeah. Me, too.

Crocodile Hunting

Seaglass Cottage
Spruce Lane
Tracadie Bay
Prince Edward Island
August 28, 2005

Dear Luke

I haven't heard from you for so long. Did the last phone call scare you away? It must seem kind of weird listening to me cry on the phone. You hardly know me.

I think we need to talk. I don't like to do this by mail, but it seems to be about the only way, so I hope you'll take a minute when you're not super busy. Usually, when I write to you, you can read between the lines, if you want. I like the idea that you would get a smile out of some of my writing. It's the least a person can do for someone else, make him laugh. I'm also curious as to how subtle your mind is. This letter will be quite straight forward though.

Last night we built a bonfire out by the dunes. (And no, we didn't go skinny dipping. I knew you'd ask.) So peaceful. Remember Trudy McNeill? She's the one I called you about who has cancer now. You met her when you played the SUB in the spring. Long, lean, yoga master's body, glasses? Dark hair, clear white skin: Black Irish colouring. Trudy starts her chemo soon, so we wanted to spend one more day soaking up the sun before she's not allowed to sun bathe anymore.

Trudy and the McNeill kids and I walked back to our cars in the dusk together. The McNeill boys are Trudy's nephews. The lagoon gets quite deep in spots, I guess because of the tides and the bit of a sea-storm. As we waded through the swampy part, we pretended we were crocodile hunters out in the bayou. The kids kept hitting the eel-grass with the switches we had collected on the beach earlier, as if they could scare out a big ole croc, and growling "ROAR, GRRR, GROWL, GROAR." The only thing we caught was mosquitoes. Lots of them, as

125

it was a flat-calm night. The moonlight threw shadows all over the dune grass, and if not for the one and only flashlight, might have turned the night positively scary. Trudy creeped us all when she did that thing where you put the flashlight under your chin and the light makes your face go all weird. We all took turns wiggling it around to see who could make the freakiest face. I won.

It is a big change and a ton of fun for me to be around boys, since I didn't get to raise any myself. Trudy's nephews are such quirky little characters. The three Ps: Patrick, Paul and Philip. Usually I object when parents want to pick names for all their kids that start with the same letter, unless the kids are multiples, but these boys are all Black Irish, like their Auntie, and could be triplets, if not for the age difference. They are seven, ten and twelve, all wonderful ages for adventuring. I wish I had done more of bonfires and beaches and exploring with my girls when they were younger, but I lived with no end of work and worry. I hope you go on grand adventures with your boy.

A few weeks ago you asked me what I want. You surprised me too much for me to come up with an appropriate zinger back to you. Plus, talk about a wide open question: What do I want out of life? From you? At this very minute? The answer to all three is: to play. And trust again. For some reason I trusted you enough to want to include you. People say they work hard and play harder. Well, for a long time I've mostly worked hard.

This summer has been terrific for me. I spent a lot of time singing and dancing and beachcombing. Some of the best times of my life have been with music or the ocean or both. All this change has its side benefits, too: I'm getting back in shape, and I'm writing again, too. Too bad for you 'cause I can get long-winded. Maybe I'll write you some more lyrics, lol. Not.

Here comes the part I wish I could say to you in person, because I might be making assumptions, and you're not here to tell me anything different. When I called your cell the other day, once I stopped sniffling, I felt like you were afraid I was going to say something that might spell trouble, something stupid like, 'I love you', or 'I want to marry you and have your babies'. Or, 'let me talk to your wife.'

If I'm picking up a paranoid tone from you, I question whether you have enough respect for my intelligence to understand I know how to behave myself, even if I am a little loopy, or looped, or whatever. I do know the difference between play and keeping private things private. The last thing I want is to be responsible for anything that might upset your family or mine. Besides, we both know the big 'can't' word is right there—I would love it to be my turn to say that word soon. Also, I don't like to be cast as the Jezebel, even if it is more exotic (and erotic) than my 'oldest lady on campus' role.

Reading this, you might think my worry is an insignificant thing, but from what little I do know of you, I don't think you will. By now, you should know enough about me to realize I am a responsible person and letting go of responsibility and concentrating on playing for a change is a bit of a challenge. The other day when you were walking Liam, I interrupted you and when you first picked up, I felt a little like you were angry with me for simply existing. Meeting you has meant opening up a part of myself that I'm not accustomed to sharing. I wish you respected me more and understood how exposed you can leave me, often without even trying. I wish I could talk to you face to face. I wish I could wish you away.

I just ran out of words.

Emily

Shells and Things

But Emily forgot to put a stamp on the letter before she dropped it in the mailbox and forgot that she forgot. It was just as well because Emily hated when she got all angsty and made stupid comments about their age difference and talked like she was insecure, especially around Luke. Tommy maybe, but not Luke. And she hated being oversensitive and trying too hard. Friggin' hormones.

Days went by and still no response. So she thought she'd try email.

Sent: September 8, 2005 1:11 pm
To: Luke
Subject: shells and things
Hi

When we agreed to be friends we seemed to have an unspoken agreement to try not to hurt each other. Right now it's not working for me; my fault for opening up too much. You seem to be six feet tall and bulletproof when it comes to me. Lucky you.

I think I should crawl back into my shell for awhile. Before I go quiet—I can do that, you know—there is something I need to do. I need to ask you this, and I need you to be honest—what is it you get from me writing to you and including you in my world?

After I've gone away from you, you can think of me as a sea anemone—such a pretty name for a sea creature. If sea anemones don't have a shell—I don't know about that, they live too far under water—you can think of me as a sea urchin. Only without the spines. Don't be smart, you jerk, and use the name the fishermen call them!

It was you who told me once, sometimes all you can do is laugh. But I don't feel much like laughing.

128

I'm going to the beach to catch some sun and some sleep.

˙ˎˏ·ˊ˜˴ˏ·ˊ˜˴···˴><((((º>

Did you notice she's swimming away? Someday I might figure out how to turn her around so she can swim in the other direction. Be patient with me, OK? My technical skills aren't so hot.

;o)

E

Sent: 3:15, September 8, 2005
To: Emily
Subject: Re: shells and things
Hi you

I just got in from a mini tour of the province with the band. You mean Whore's Eggs? Lol. I promise I won't ever think of you as anything but a spineless sea urchin. lol.

I'm not bulletproof when it comes to you. Don't know why you think that. I'm not good at expressing what I think or feel...Guess I find it easier with a guitar in my hands, ha ha.

What do I get out of you writing to me? I guess I thought I got the opportunity to be an outlet for you to get your thoughts out.

I don't think you should crawl back into your shell. Don't know why you would say that.

L

Little Luke

One day in September, Emily received a call from an old boyfriend, someone she hadn't spoken to in years. Jim heard from a friend of a friend that Emily had returned to the Island. She agreed to have dinner with him, more out of curiosity than anything. The curiosity of Islanders is contagious. The dinner date brought back some bitter memories.

She found herself missing Luke when she was supposed to be concentrating on Jim, oddly enough. She had hoped in the spring to stay in touch with Luke. But as the summer wore on, she started to worry about the appropriateness of relying on a young man to ease the loneliness. She grew so tired of having to do everything around the place by herself, with no daughters or man to help her, and it frustrated her no end.

When she got home after her dinner date, she decided to move her desktop computer and clean all the crap off it. Twenty minutes of untangling cords later, she felt all hot and cranky and tired of struggling with the hardware of software. She hit the couch for a minute to calm down and fell asleep. As she dozed in the sun, another phone call, not from Luke, changed her mood dramatically. This time she called up her friends in heaven first:

Emily: You guys wanna hear a good one? You know how I keep meaning to phone Bethany, because I can't get rid of that boomy-hummy, subwoofer sound in my computer speakers? Tonight I moved the computer—for the second time this month—and I took a look at the what-cha-ma-call-it.
Chris: The amplifier?
Emily: Yeah, that box thing on the floor. And I noticed a thin sheet of plastic covering the hole, so I thought, 'The box is already dirty everywhere else now. I might as well take the plastic sheet off.' It peeled off real easy—turns out it wasn't attached in the first place. Lo and behold—no more boomy-hummy subwoofer sound!! No matter how loud I crank it up!
Chris: How long have you owned those speakers now?
Emily: About a year.

Tessa: Sounds like something I would do.

Emily: It is like something you would do, Tessa. I can already hear Bethany's little 'tee hee' when I tell her this one. Then she'll say, 'Oh, Mom'. I can't wait to tell her Trudy's news. I am so excited! And relieved!

Tessa: Yeah, well, we had a little chat with God and asked Him to cut you some slack. We told Him we didn't need her here yet; we'll borrow some Canuck from down below next time we play hockey.

Emily: All I can say is thank you, thank you, thank you!

Tessa: Don't thank us. Thank the devil. He let us draft an amazing *Canadiens'* centre and a big mother of a Russian defenseman—name of Rasputin. Trudy was never much of a hockey player, anyway. We can't create miracles every day, you know, and it would take one to turn her into a Gretzky. She skates like a girl.

Emily: So she doesn't have to work her way through her bucket list all in one year, like her family doctor recommended? And she actually is going to be around for a long time like her oncologist said? Maybe long enough to meet her children's children's children?

Chris: Maybe not that long. But as long as we can play this guy from hell, we're set for quite a while. He plays like a demon. What a rush! Best high since I left earth! We feel like eternal everlasting Stanley Cup winners. All the time!

Emily: So does Trudy. And so do I. You can't even imagine how relieved I am.

Kate: Oh yes we can. We know how you worry, but we've been telling you all along, even if Trudy showed up here in a year she'd be fine; we'd take good care of her. She's Tessa's sister and your friend. What did you think we'd do—let her crawl into a hidey-hole somewhere and die all over again, only of loneliness this time? Do you think we would leave her all on her own to figure this place out? You worry too much.

Emily: So I've heard. That friend you sent tells me that a lot, all the time.

Kate: I meant to ask you—what did he think of the fact that you talk to dead people?

Emily: He wanted to tell me about what he thought when we met up at a dance one night, but I didn't want to listen because I figured we had more important things to discuss.

Kate: Do you remember what he said?

131

Emily: Yeah. He sounded kind of concerned because he didn't know the people in the conversations, so he didn't think he could relate.

Kate: So...how did you explain it to him?

Emily: I don't remember; I wasn't paying a lot of attention. The hall was super noisy. I meant to say, 'That's the whole idea; you will get to know my dead people a little, like you get to know characters in a book a little, and learn about the author too, through the characters.'

Chris: Not much chance he'll get to meet us now, so he needn't think he can sit around all day and wait to catch on. He might as well smarten up and read.

Tessa: Maybe he thought it was weird.

Emily: I don't think so. Maybe he did, but he was too polite to say.

Kate: Did he get the point eventually?

Emily: I'm pretty sure he did. He kept reading anyway.

Tessa: And, once he got to know us, was he awestruck by how amazing we all are?

Emily: I don't know. But I imagine he thinks I'm extra lucky to have friends who stick around even after they are dead.

Kate: Are you disappointed?

Emily: Yeah.

Tessa: About what? That we stick around?

Kate: No. Emily wanted him to understand how important friendship is, and although family, especially kids, can be invaluable, friends can help you survive anything, even family.

Tessa: He didn't get that?

Emily: I don't think so.

Tessa: Oh, that's so sad—for you.

Em: Yeah. I fucked up.

Kate: Remember when you first met him how good and easy it was between you two? I heard you talked to him the other day about shells and sea anemones and the ocean.

Emily: Where'd you hear that?

Kate: Chris.

Em: Figures. When he returned home to Cape Breton after his last tour, he said for me not to stop writing or crawl back into my shell, either. I needed to hear it straight from him. Meant a lot to me.

Kate: And what did you write back?

Emily: I wrote to him about how I wanted him to take his kid to the ocean and go on an adventure with him.

Kate: No, you didn't. That was before. You wrote him a long crazy email and gave him the gears about expressing his feelings, after he had asked you politely two hours before not to expect him to be good at sharing, being a guy and all.

Emily: Are you sure? I remember that one. I was so relieved by his reply I had to give him a little shit for making me worry. Are you sure I didn't send him the one about me and Trudy's nephews finding our way across the dunes one night with our flashlights?

Kate: Sorry, I hate to tell you, but you didn't send it. If you even wrote it down.

Emily: Are you sure you're sure? I meant to tell him to take his son and feel the healing power of the sea, be a crab for awhile, a hermit crab even, if he's not feeling adventurous and that's more comforting for him. Not as pretty as a sea anemone, but still a sea creature. I thought for sure I sent it. He lives by the ocean so he should know. I shouldn't have to tell him everything.

Chris: The water is not always healing, Emily. Look what happened to me.

Emily: But that's different, Chris. That was a stupid little old Ontario lake, not the sea. You are right, though. The sea can be healing, but it can be something fierce, too.

Chris: Sorta like you, Em.

Emily: Thanks, Chris. Well, at least I think it's a compliment. So I didn't teach him anything about the ocean?

Kate: No. You know, Emily, I was thinking. Sometimes you sound more like a teacher than a friend. Well, not at 3 am—then you sound like the proverbial woman scorned—but sometimes, like when you think you should teach him about the ocean and adventures in parenting. Or friendship.

Emily: That's me alright. Professor Emily. And he doesn't like teachers. Well, at least certain ones, the ones who fail him in Early Childhood Development class, for instance.

Tessa: Makes you look like a smart aleck.

Em: Yeah, I know. The Lucy and Charlie Brown Syndrome. So maybe I shouldn't have behaved like Lucy. But he's so much younger than I am, and everyone has a lot to learn in their twenties.

Kate: As they still do in their forties.

Tessa: Do they?

Kate: You and Chris wouldn't know, but trust us, they still do. You two are like him that way—you are only working with the benefit of about a third of an average life span.

Emily: And the biggest difference when you turn forty is: you realize just how much you don't know.

Emily heard from her dead friends once again, after midnight on her birthday, October 12th:

Kate: How did your birthday go?

Em: Great. Last year, I turned forty-eight; this year, I'm forty-nine; next year, I'll be fifty; and the year after I'll be fifteen. See, all you have to do is start reversing the numbers once you turn fifty. I'll be twenty-five, and then thirty-five, and forty-five again, and then fifty-five, and the year after that…oops, sixty-five. When I get to fifty-five, I'll have to stop reversing them.

Tessa: What's on your mind, Girlfriend?

Emily: I've been thinking about age. I'm now twenty-four years older than my friend again. I like it better when there is only a twenty-three year difference. I literally am old enough to be his mother. I have the three daughters you and Kate know and love and Flora's grandson, Charlie, who is starting to feel like a grandson to me, too. More and more, I think of him as one of my own. Besides, he eats my cookies and borrows money from me so he qualifies as a relative. Sometimes, when my male friend was being a bit of an arrogant arsehole, I used to think of him with dismay as my fourth child, the son I never knew. I would think, 'Good Lord, I would have spoiled him worse than he already is if he had been my son.' I also try to think of him as my little brother. If I could imagine him as my little brother, it would all be more appropriate.

Chris: Son, little brother—did you ever think that might be a wee bit emasculating for him?

Emily: That's the point. He would be less of a man to me. Problem solved. I always wanted at least four children. I thought I was meant to raise a boy, too.

Kate: Do you remember you told me you miscarried once?

Emily: Yeah, Jim's baby. I got pregnant a few days before he left for Alberta. He wrote me a 'Dear John' letter after he caught up with the dream he'd been chasing. He told me what a *nice* person I was and, once he got that out of the way, kept going on and on about this wonderful woman he caught up with and how much energy she possessed. I remember being so offended, as if we were cows at the Royal Winter Fair: ten points for beauty, ten points for brains, ten points for humour, ten points for manners, and fifty points for energy. As if I hadn't quite made the grade. The funny thing is now this dream wife can't slow down and is a little insane with all this nervous energy. She drives everyone around her crazy. So he doesn't get to relax a whole lot, even though he wants to. Gives him lots of stress. She's the same age as me and looks about ten years older.

Tessa: A little cosmic revenge?

Em: I'd like to think I'm a bigger person than that. But I'm not.

Tessa: Have you ever seen Jim again?

Emily: Yeah—irony of ironies. About a year ago, he moved back from Fort Mac to live in the same community as I do. Someone told him I was living on the Island, so he called and invited me out to dinner. I didn't have any problem letting him pay.

Tessa: Did he ever know about the baby?

Emily: No. Tessa, do you think it makes me a great big hypocrite because I believe this unborn child's soul transcends his short life, but I won't go to the local church 'cause of their stupid fuckin' anti-abortion sign?

Tessa: No. Stuff like old white men putting up signs in parking lots won't bother you so much when you get up here. Those men all get taught a lesson about judging. One of the first things God does when they get here is sit them down and give them a long, long talking to.

Chris: Then He turns them over to the Goddess and lets Her have a go at them, poor guys. It's not pretty.

Kate: Em, you call the baby 'him'. Did you know it was a boy?

Emily: He felt like one to me when I carried him in my belly. A darlin' little blue-blanketed boy.

Kate: How old would the baby be if he had lived?

Em: I don't know.

Kate: How old were you at the time?

Emily: Fourth-year university. Just turned twenty. It happened the winter before you died, Chris.

Kate: So now you've turned forty-nine. He would be twenty-eight, twenty-nine. Not much older than your 'fourth child'.

Em: No, not much older.

Chris: He's here.

Emily: Luke. Every baby we had we wanted to name him Luke. Our fourth child was supposed to be Luke. We lucked in with an Erin, a Christina, and a Bethany, but no Luke.

Chris: I am telling you he's here. Luke. He's been trying to get through to you all along.

Emily: My lost baby boy?

Chris: Yeah, that Luke.

Emily: So all those 11:11 messages?

Chris: That was Luke.

Emily: Huh. Wow. Can I see him?

Chris: No. Not yet.

Kate: I thought of your unborn child because I have been meaning to tell you— I've been spending a lot of time with my granddaughter. You know? The baby my oldest daughter lost the year before I died?

Emily: When she miscarried at six months?

Kate: Well, up here her baby is a beautiful three-year-old with long wavy blond hair and kiss curls all around her plump little cheeks.

Em: I know.

Kate: You know? How would you know?

Emily: The night you died, Brenda, your palliative care nurse, dreamed you were with a young child and that's exactly the way she described her. So we figured out the little girl in her dream must have been your unborn grandchild.

Kate: Now it's my turn to say, 'Huh'.

Song of Songs

Emily wondered why she could never see her dead friends when they talked. She read somewhere that some people can, but not her. She also thought they should speak with their own voices, but neither Kate nor Tessa nor Chris did. They didn't exactly sound like themselves, or her, either. They simply spoke like thoughts. The article said lots of times the people who live in spirit sound like your own head voice. Emily figured it was hard enough paying attention to who was saying what, and trying to keep Tessa and Chris from arguing. Their own voices might help.

She would like to see them, too. The article said spirit guides send 11:11 messages, though, to reassure people they are still hanging around, watching out for them. Emily had been seeing a lot of 11:11 or 1:11 messages, more than she ever noticed before. Or maybe the switch from analog to digital clocks made it seem so.

Funny thing about Chris. Men were so hairy back then. Like so many of the rebels of the time, Chris wore his beard full and his hair halfway down his back. Her daughters with their buzz-cut boyfriends couldn't understand how anyone could find an attractive man under all the hair, back in the day. For certain guys, though, the long hair and beard brought all the focus to their eyes and mouth and nose. Chris' eyes were deep and almond shaped, evenly spaced, and green. His nose was straight and very Upper Canadian, and his mouth was *très* kissable. He had the right luck wearing a beard. So did the guys with weak chins. Beards provided a handy place to hide all kinds of minor flaws: thin lips for one, acne scars for another.

But Chris didn't need to hide. Emily had never actually seen him without a beard, but she knew his chin and neck and the space between that straight unblemished nose and those sexy lips would have been as perfectly lush as his naked body. Which she had seen. Plenty of times. Long lean muscles, six feet even, and a tush that stood firm. On both sides. 'Oh my,' she groaned, 'I desperately need to get to sleep!' A few hours later, as Emily was still reading herself to sleep:

137

Kate: Emily, you should join a book club. I know you love to read, and it's time for you to make some new female friends. What have you been reading lately?

Emily: Come Away. It's about "The Song of Songs". Apparently, "The Song of Songs" or "The Song of Solomon", as it is sometimes called, has always been a controversial part of the Bible because it never once refers to the one male god and speaks of earthly desire in a way no other part of the Bible does. The author of *Come Away* explores the theory that "The Song of Songs" comes from an earlier time of worship of the female: the goddess of fertility, love, passion, and compassion. She also claims the Church has worked diligently to suppress that interpretation and replace it with one where "The Song of Songs" is 'seen as a description of Christ's relationship to the Church or the Logos (Word).'

The writer believes "The Song of Songs" is no less than 'the poetic fulfilment of a heart's cry for rebirth of ourselves, our religions, our world. It is the reaching out of the feminine divine, the spirit of passion and creativity, to the transformative power of god.'

Kate: Leonard Cohen wrote a song about the feminine divine.

Emily: Yeah, "Hallelujah". I thought so, too. The other day in an interview I heard him say people could stop singing his song now. It's been covered by so many people. Jeff Buckley performed it regularly in New York's East Village clubs, and called it 'a hallelujah to the orgasm...an ode to life and love'. It's even been rewritten—with Cohen's permission—and turned into a church song.

Kate: I can't imagine. That song is sacred to us who grew up with Cohen. There is something mildly sacrilegious about rewriting it, in my humble opinion.

Emily: It is a beautiful version for Christians, though. And it got a million hits on Youtube last Easter.

Kate: I can appreciate the irony of an old Jewish Buddhist providing an Easter song for Christians.

Emily: I thought you might. Anyway, about the book. The explanation of *Come Away* I just read to you may sound quite academic, but the actual story this woman tells is short and fairly simple and involves an imagining of another time and place. The quotes are from the author's notes.

Tessa: I think I love this passage best from "The Song of Songs":

> I am the rose of Sharon
> And the lily of the valleys.

As the lily among thorns
So is my love among the daughters.
As the apple tree among the trees of the wood
So is my beloved among the sons.
I sat down under his shadow with great delight
And his fruit was sweet to my taste.
He brought me to the banqueting house
And his banner over me was love.
Stay me with flagons,
Comfort me with apples;
For I am sick of love.
His left hand is under my head
And his right hand doth embrace me.
I charge you, O ye daughters of Jerusalem,
By the roes and by the hinds of the field
That ye stir not up
Nor awake my love, till he please.
The voice of my beloved!
Behold, he cometh leaping upon the mountains
Skipping upon the hills.
My beloved is like a roe or a young hart:
Behold, he standeth behind our wall
He looketh forth at the windows
Shewing himself through the lattice.
My beloved spake, and said unto me
Rise up, my love, my fair one, and come away.
For, lo, the winter is past, the rain is over and gone.
The flowers appear on the earth;
The time of the singing of birds is come;
And the voice of the turtle is heard in our land.
The fig tree putteth forth her green figs
And the vines with the tender grape give a good smell.
Arise, my love, my fair one, and come away.
Take us the foxes, the little foxes...

Emily: Whoa! Whew! Is it hot in here or is it me? I feel a little flushed!

Kate: Me, too.

Tessa: Me, too. Giggle, giggle.

Em: All of a sudden, I love the Bible.

Chris, Kate and Tessa: See! We told you there was good stuff in it, too!

Em: Think I'll go take a cold shower. That reminds me, do you guys remember shower sex?

Chris, Kate and Tessa: You bet! Our minds are dead, not empty.

Emily: I was thinking about this date I went on when I moved out west after graduating from my first degree. The guy was the younger brother of my first love; my sixteen-year-old self thought it was love, anyway. About seven years later, I caught up with the younger brother in Edmonton. He took me out for a terrific steak dinner at The Keg. The Keg hadn't moved as far as the Maritimes at the time, so the whole concept was new to me. Steak always gives me energy; it must be the iron. After a long, lingering dinner, we went back to a decent hotel, had shower sex, and, after getting all squeaky clean again, bed sex. I slept over and he drove me back to the apartment in a snowstorm the next morning. He got out in the blinding snow and came around and held the door for me; made sure I made it in safe. One of the best times I ever experienced with a man.

Chris: Better than with me?

Emily: No, Chris, just different. Sex with you came to me as naturally as breathing. Anyway, sex with Donnie's younger brother was just sex: no fear, no guilt, no remorse, no recriminations, and no obligations. Two people enjoying the gifts the Goddess gave us poor miserable humans to make up for all the other rotten stuff. The perfect zipless fuck. Do you girls remember that book?

Kate and Tessa: Yes, of course, *Fear of Flying.* Every woman's dream is to indulge in that kind of sex just once in her life. So the theory goes, anyhow.

Me: I was lucky enough to find my 'once' when I was young and free enough to enjoy it. And he wasn't even a big guy—I mean tall.

Chris: Hey! I didn't know you did it with Ethan!

Kate and Tessa: You just caught on, Chris? The male brain...

Emily: Well, it wasn't exactly your business, Chris.

Chris: He's so much younger than you. What did you think you were doing with Donnie's little brother?!

Emily: Like three years, Chris. And it's still none of your business.

Chris: Did you ever see him again?

Emily: No, I think he still lives out West. If I ever do, I'm going to tell him he gave me the experience every woman wants. Just once.

Chris: Lucky bastard. Wish I could say that.

Emily: Ethan was the youngest and the best of the three brothers, and a natural born gentleman.

Chris: And I wasn't?

Emily: No. Well, not the same. He didn't have a dark side. I'm not sure if you can be a natural born gentleman and have a dark side. On a more serious note...

Chris: You mean sex isn't serious?

Lucy/Emily: Gawd, Chris, you must be slipping back to your adolescence. Haven't you learned anything up there? Sex is not all about competition, control, and male dominance, Idiot. Or at least it doesn't always have to be. Neither does the rest of life. I think that's the point of both *Fear of Flying* and *Come Away, the Song of Songs*. Sometimes sex and life can be beautiful. And free. No pain.

Charlie Brown/Chris: Sorry, Lucy, I forgot myself—thought I was seventeen and jealous again.

Kate: Emily, remember Chris never lived past twenty-three. So when he hangs out with you earthbound types, he's likely to forget himself.

Lucy/Emily: You were jealous when you were seventeen? I never knew.

Charlie Brown/Chris: Why do you always want us men to explain our feelings? I thought you were all about trusting your own instincts.

Lucy/Emily: I still like to hear the words spoken. Calms down the Lucy in me. As I was trying to say before you interrupted, did you know the celebration of Easter was originally a pre-Christian festival for the return of spring, renewal, rebirth, and fertility after a long winter? Well, of course, you guys *would* know. Towards the end of our marriage, my husband and I made a vow to start talking again after a long winter of ignoring each other. On Holy Thursday, we tried to renew something. By Easter Sunday, we were into another big fight. Whatever happened to renewal? Maybe Easter came too early that year. The snow still clung to the parking lot outside the church as we stood by the car, arguing.

Chris: Parking lots can't grow anything, anyway.

Emily: You'd be surprised.

Drinking. For Once.

Luke hoists himself out of the car—steady now. It's still dark, but the first shadows of morning sun bring a faint light to the horizon. He didn't have far to drive to get home, he wasn't very drunk, and Siobhan likes to see the car in the driveway when she gets up with Liam in—oh, about an hour. She always leaves the porch light on and the door unlocked. No need to fumble around for a key. He turns the lock after quietly closing the bright red exterior door.

First to the can, then to Liam's room. When he and Siobhan moved into his grandparents' house five years ago, they wondered if it would be big enough for the two or three kids they wanted. The house is small, much like the one he grew up in where he and his brother shared a room until Tommy went off to college. Maybe someday he'll build a piece on for a music studio

He leans on the door as his baby sleeps and is filled up to the brim with the joy this child gives him. Siobhan is such a good mom. Per usual, the toys are neatly stacked on the shelf, but blankets, pillows, arms and legs and little boy are scattered all over the bed—little butt up in the air. This is the way Liam likes to sleep and that's fine with his dad. Perfect in fact.

Maybe one more shot before bed. He fetches the Jack Daniels from the upper cupboard by the kitchen sink. No shot glasses in this house, so he grabs a juice glass out of the dishwasher. Drops it on the new cork floor; watches it bounce. "Shhhh", he says, as he bounces himself off the counter and retrieves it unbroken. Gotta love that cork floor. One more good big shot, one for the road, except he's not on the road. Not anymore. Thank Christ for small blessings.

He stumbles down the hallway and slips into bed, careful not to wake her. He turns his back so she won't smell the night's party on his breath. Spent now from the music and drinking, he's ready to sleep. She stirs in her sleep and he feels the soft edges of her hip. He curls up, wondering again what is wrong with him. He can't seem to shake the morbid thoughts. He thought getting drunk might scare them away but apparently not, because they are still there. For a while he thought it might be all this travelling, the long drives and Maritime road conditions making him nervous. Sometimes he tortures himself with what might be omens of cancer. He is too young for that, but a former classmate had recently been diagnosed with testicular cancer. Cancer in the balls? For shit's sake! How could that happen to a young man? Or any man.

He wants Liam to enjoy a perfect childhood. He doesn't want to die ahead of time. Sometimes, when he and Siobhan manage a night together after Liam has gone to bed and they've curled up with a movie and popcorn, he mentions his fears to Siobhan, casual like, so she won't think he's a wuz. She usually points out that it might be a good idea to stop driving so fast, slow down, and live.

But all the good advice in the world is not enough to ease his mind. He's afraid to think of what would happen to Liam if he got himself killed, too afraid to even name it in his thoughts. What if Siobhan couldn't afford to feed them both? What if Liam got bullied at school? Who is going to teach his little half-orphan child to stand up for himself? Who's going to teach him music? Who's going to help Siobhan discipline him? His sister is too young and Tommy lives too far away. He and Tommy should have talked about his fears when they were both half in the bag the last time he was over on the Island. Maybe he should make Tommy Liam's guardian. But his parents, sister, and brother have their own lives to live. Odds are, if Tommy wanted a kid, he would have had one by now.

He and Siobhan have known one another forever. They are each other's best friends and she needs him. Always has, and he figures she always will. Christ Almighty, he only wants to protect this little, tiny family he has known was for him since he was a young kid.

There was a blond at the bar again tonight. She came onto him in the parking lot as he was getting into his car. He wished she'd just go away. He wishes all the women and thoughts of death would go away. He can feel the last shot of whiskey kick in, so he gives up trying to think. Thinking is too damn difficult.

Running Down the Road

Emily knows nothing about Luke's sense of impending doom, but she does worry about him and his drunk driving and speeding. Kate comes calling again and picks up like close friends do, right where they left off, as if no time has elapsed at all:

Kate: Read any good books lately?

Em: This morning I finished *The Beekeeper's Apprentice*. Once again, the Sherlock Homes story, but the protagonist is a teenage girl who strikes up an intimate friendship with an older man—Holmes.

Hey, THAT'S IT!!

Kate: What's IT?

Emily: That's what we should have called it!

Kate: What the heck are you talking about?

Emily: My friend and I. That woulda worked.

Kate: Do you think it would have made any difference—putting the right label on it?

Emily: Maybe.

Tessa: What are you guys yelling about? I don't get it.

Emily, Chris and Kate: 'Intimate friendship'.

Emily: I googled it one day, but all I could come up with was 'Get intimate with Jesus' and a Melissa Etheridge video on YouTube of two women going from an intimate conversation to...well...just plain intimate. I don't think either is quite what Dr. Phil or Oprah or whoever had in mind when they coined the phrase. By the way, Luke is not the only younger male friend I made lately. As I meet more under-thirty-something guys around campus, I realize he is not the only one who has it rough. I can't understand why I felt so much sympathy for him.

Chris: Neither can I.

Kate: But Emily, these new friends have gone through their tragedies and found a way to make peace when they came out on the other side. He hasn't yet.

145

Emily: He wouldn't know a good tragedy if it turned around and bit him in the ass.

Kate: It might one day. I thought you were finished with being mad at him. So why are you still angry with him, honestly?

Emily: He drives too fast. Probably fall off the Cabot Trail one day soon. Leave his wife a widow and his kid a half-orphan.

Chris: Which half? Top or bottom?

Em: Oh shut up, Chris.

Kate: Don't forget, he promised you he'd die of a heart attack.

Emily: Yeah, well fuck him; I'm not worrying about him anymore. Wasn't so much a promise, anyway—more like a recommendation for his own demise. Wishful thinking for a fast passing. He's not driving my friends home, not if I can help it. He's got a heavy foot; probably die in a car wreck, instead of from a heart attack.

Chris: What about your own driving habits? You've been falling asleep at the wheel a lot this fall.

Emily: Too much stress.

And he runs awfully fast, too.

Chris: Yeah, he kind of proved that last spring. You had a lot to do with it, played a major part with all that clutching and distracting you did. You could have just let him get on the ferry.

Emily: I can't help it if he ran like a scared rabbit.

Chris: I saw him driving to Charlottetown the other night. Man, was he ever flying!

Emily: He thinks he's Mario Andretti since he bought the T-shirt.

Chris: You're lucky he didn't hit that skunk you left for him in the middle of the lane.

Emily: Hey, I didn't leave the skunk for him! It's not my fault I hit him on the head earlier in the night.

Tessa: The skunk or the friend?

Emily: What's the difference? The skunk. I only *wanted* to hit the friend on the head.

I've got to calm down, change the subject. I came across another skunk last night, but this time I swerved so I could drive over the top of him and not kill him and he sprayed my car anyway. Ungrateful Bastard. Just like the friend.

Tessa: Maybe the skunk you killed earlier was that skunk's uncle. They might have been related. Maybe he was still holding a grudge. Skunks do, I hear.

Em: I'll take your word for it.

Chris: Lucky you didn't run over the skunk's uncle all over again when you went speeding down the road that night. You doing a hundred and twenty in your old shit-box—accelerating like crazy, it's a wonder you didn't pop a rod. I'd say your ex-friend's not the only one with a heavy foot. What were you thinking?

Emily: I couldn't believe he wouldn't pick up his phone! And he didn't tell me he was playing on the Island again last weekend. Jerk!

Kate: So you speeding and getting yourself killed would...What? Teach him not to drive so fast? It reminds me of all those high-speed cop-car chases in the movies. They don't make any sense, either.

Emily: Will he ever learn??

Chris: I doubt it. He's a guy. We're kind of slow learners when it comes to fast cars and women. Plus, a lot of this feeling stuff is still a mystery to us. The way we're wired, I guess.

Emily: It's not about the feeling stuff, Chris. The issue here is his irresponsible driving.

Chris: Yours, too?

Em: Shut up, Chris.

I've got another skunk story. Kate, do you remember the song "The Way"?

Kate: Oh yeah. It goes:

> They made up their minds
> And they started packing
> They left before the sun came up that day
> An exit to eternal summer slacking
> But where were they going without ever
> Knowing the way?
> Anyone can see the road that they walk on
> Is paved in gold
> And it's always summer

They'll never get cold
They'll never get hungry
They'll never get old and grey
You can see their shadows
Wandering off somewhere
They won't make it home
But they really don't care
They wanted the highway
They're happier there today, today

Emily: Sing along, you guys.

Tessa and Chris: Don't know it.

Emily: Well, around the time Fastball wrote this song, there was an aging couple in New York City who knew they weren't much longer for this world. So, instead of waiting around for the inevitable, they walked off together into the sunset, never to be seen again. Apparently, the guy who wrote the song didn't know about the old couple. Could be an urban myth, but I heard about the couple a while before the song came out, so who knows? Anyway, I like the story and the song and the image of them walking away hand in hand, no longer worried about control. Doing what they wanted to do.

Tessa: Was I dead or alive when that song came out?

Emily: I don't know. I do know one thing. It's bloody cold out here now, another cold snap. The other night I drove by a very confused and very dead skunk. Poor little fella shoulda stayed at home and kept warm. I wonder if Mr. Skunk was trying to escape, too. Maybe he and Mrs. Skunk were hoping to run away to a warmer place. The dreams of another free-spirited skunk shattered by this fucking climate.

Kate: Interesting story, Emily.

Em: Want to hear another good skunk story?

Kate and Tessa: No.

Emily: My friend, Mark, was driving on a back road a couple of weeks ago and he saw two skunks circling each other in the middle of the road. So he could either pull over or run the risk of getting sprayed. Mark, being a sensible fellow, pulled over and watched the stinky love tango.

148

Chris: Now that's what I call voyeuristic.

Emily: Shut up, Chris. Eventually, one skunk climbed on the other and they started going at it right on the yellow line of the pavement. Quite a dance, I imagine—or no, I don't want to imagine. To quote John Prine, 'They humped each other like they had no shame. Oh yeah.' Anyway, the good news is Mark escaped unscathed. And two skunks went away happy—and still alive—that night.

Chris: I like that story better.

Emily: Knew you would, Chris. Hey, you guys! I just realized if you change one letter, 'mystery' becomes 'my story'.

Kate: When you get here, you will realize each person's life story is all part of the mystery. You have to get here first before you'll truly understand.

Emily: One of those God things?

Kate: Yeah.

Tessa: So, why *do* you drive irresponsibly?

Emily: I'm not off the hook yet, eh, Tessa? You need to understand, when I drive like a maniac, it is not irresponsible; it's stress.

Tessa: Tweedle Dum, Tweedle Dee.

Em: Buzz off, the bunch of ya.

Kate, Tessa and Chris: OK. If you don't need us for your story...

Em: I don't, not now. But I won't forget you, all three of you, are still in my story, my mys-story.

Chris: Go figure.

Liam's Molars

Siobhan came running down the front porch steps as Luke pulled up in the old van. She couldn't believe he got home early from his road trip, for once! The thought of a little 'me' time was enough to make her day. Liam's molar teeth still hadn't cut through, his gums were red raw most days, and his little cheeks had broken out in a rash. His all-night crying sessions had her wrung right out. Poor little tyke. She could leave him with her mom more maybe, but she hated to think of him suffering and missing her at the same time, so she carried the weight on her own.

She didn't spring all her plans on Luke immediately. He'd balk if she asked too much too soon. First on the agenda would be a girls' night out. Then she'd love to treat herself to a spa day at that beautiful spot they had added to the Keltic Lodge up in Ingonish. Afterwards, a little hike in the National Park, something they could all do together. Liam had grown too heavy for Siobhan to carry in her baby carrier for any length of time, but Luke could handle his weight.

The forecast called for clear days and nights for the week Luke was supposed to be home, before he hit the road again. Perhaps they should take in one of the Celtic Colours shows. She read on-line about a good one over in Margaree Forks. Siobhan didn't care much for traditional music and considered this big festival a bit of a scam; something made up to drive the aging boomers further north; hold all the tourists captive for two weeks, till the first of the winter winds came and drove them all back down south again. But she had to admit Cape Breton looked spectacular when the trees turned all brilliant colours with the early frost. No place like home in the autumn. Playing tourist might be fun, for a change. Anything to get out of the house.

Before long, she realized none of her wishful plans would materialize, not this time, anyway. Luke emptied his wallet on the kitchen table, to illustrate how little cash the leader of the band netted out on his road trip. He blamed it on the back-up musicians, their big appetites, the price of gas and hotels, and the poor economy. He could blame it on whatever he liked; either way, Siobhan wouldn't be partying with the girls or getting that massage or attending concerts any time soon.

She asked if he'd at least take her to Walmart, so she could pick up a few supplies. Her own cheque was long gone, but she figured she could borrow from her mom till she got the next one, and Liam needed diapers and sneakers for his little feet.

Aw well, her mother had warned her about musicians. She said they would always love music more than anything or anyone else. As her mom also said, she'd made her bed, nothing to do but lie in it now. And she knew Luke loved her and Liam next best to music. Next best would have to do.

The Moose is Loose

Luke hated Walmart. But Siobhan wanted to go shopping for Liam, so he got roped into driving to Sydney. Siobhan thought it would be fun, a real family day. Shopping—fun? Not likely. The whole way there, Siobhan flicked through the radio channels and turned the volume down every time he turned it up. Liam wouldn't stop wailing in the back seat. Luke tried to drown out his crying with Def Leopard, but Siobhan insisted she could find music to soothe him, if Luke would butt out. Luke mumbled something about the most soothing thing for Liam would be to stay away from Walmart.

Siobhan kept doing the 'hhe' thing he hated, that sharp intake of breath, whenever he passed a car stopped at a gate or a stop sign. Did she think he couldn't see? Even the moose a quarter of a mile away on the ridge prompted another 'hhe'. How fast did she think a moose could move, anyway? Did she think the moose was stupid enough to run right out in front of them? Actually, he had heard moose could be about that stupid, and that fast. So he slowed down.

Oh joy. Now he was stuck in the baby aisle holding Liam and all the other stuff Siobhan piled into his arms. He *told* her she should have grabbed a cart. His cell phone beeped at him. Siobhan fished his cell out of his pocket and handed it to him in exchange for Liam. But not before she read the text 'r u there.'

Siobhan asked who texted him, but Luke wasn't about to tell her. Instead he said he'd had enough of Walmart. The place gave him a headache. Liam needed a nap. Why he didn't nap during the drive remained a mystery to Luke. Other toddlers did all the time, or so he heard. So he took Liam out to put him in the car, once he found it. Walmart parking lots were too big and confusing. So were most parking lots. All the cars looked the same; beige and grey must be the big trend colours for the new millennium. Boring. While Liam snoozed in his car seat, Luke sorted out his texts. Emily.

What do u want

woke up from an awesome dream

I'm busy

o sorry

Call u later k

k

bye

I wrote it down.

Send it

So Emily sent her dream to his iPhone. She went on and on about jewellery and beauty and stuff he couldn't pay much attention to, since Liam woke from his nap and needed tending. Lucky Em, she had time to dream in technicolour. He didn't reply, though he meant to. It's just that Siobhan yelled at him when she got in the car, called him an old crank, said, "What is *wrong* with you, Luke?" Nothing, he wished he could yell right back. There is NOTHING wrong. He hated when people asked him that, even more than he hated Walmart.

Emily was always going on about different beaches where she'd love to live. And she called at the *worst* times.

On the way home as they passed the ridge where they had seen the moose, the car overheated. Three hundred bucks and five hours later, the old bomb boasted a new rad. These old rigs were killing him. Another perfect family day in paradise.

Thanks but no Thanks

Emily waited and waited to hear back from Luke after she shared her dream. She couldn't understand why he hadn't called or sent her a text or an email or something. Anything. She thought the dream was pretty cool, especially the part about living on a beach down south and meeting lots of new people there. And she wanted to explain to him how clearly her dream mind visualized all the colours and materials and designs and everything for these new necklaces. So now she could make them up and sell them for a much bigger price than her seaglass pendants. Make gobs of money. He always asked her how to make money, so he should be able to relate to that part of the dream at least, even if he didn't care how beautiful her work would be.

By Wednesday night she was disgusted with waiting. In fact, she was madder than a wet hen. So she called to yell at him and kick him out of her life. Once again, he wouldn't pick up. Emily swore he'd been put on this earth for one purpose only—to make her crazy. She fumed all evening, as she waited for the phone to ring. But fuming never got her anywhere when she had no-one to fume *at*. So she dialed his cell one last time and fumed all over his voice mail.

Emily enjoyed herself on Thanksgiving weekend. She skipped class on Friday, picked up her mom in Halifax, drove back to the Island to spend time with her, and played in the Annual Thanksgiving Car Rally at the university. She had never participated in a car rally so she got voted designated driver for a van full of old farts, but she didn't mind. Besides, this one gave her team lots of weird clues to work on, and they came in third because, given the average age of the farts, they knew stuff. They might have taken first place if they had been young and observant like the other students and could still see further than two feet in front of them—and didn't need to stop by the side of the road to pee so often.

Once she returned her to Halifax, after serving her a humble little Thanksgiving dinner, the cottage started to feel awful big again. Emily asked Kate for a private conversation:

Emily: Do you think my alone time here on the Island is accomplishing anything? It sure creates a lot of fuss and bother. And I don't get any help with the trash or the plugged toilet or the grass cutting.

Kate: You've discovered how comfortable you can be in your own skin and with your own company. There's that.

Emily: I guess I don't find it that lonely; sometimes, but mostly it's lovely and peaceful. Maybe that's all my Great Embarrassment at the ferry terminal last spring amounted to—fear of being alone.

Kate: Could be, Em. Did Luke ever tease you about your Embarrassment?

Emily: I don't think he noticed. Kate, remember when I was still married and I used to get an unbearable ache in my neck and shoulders sometimes? I am hardly ever in pain now that I live alone.

Kate: Are you suggesting that ex-husband of yours had become a big ole pain in the neck?

Emily: Sounds like it, eh?

Kate: So what's the real story behind the termination of the friend I sent you?

Emily: Luke, you mean?

Kate: Yeah, him. That guy. It would be much more like you to send him to detention. Did he prove to be simply too much work?

Emily: No, I'm not afraid of work. It wasn't that. I dropped Mom off the other night and on the drive back it came to me. Calmed me right down when it hit me. I'm no help to him. So I let go.

Kate: How do you feel now?

Emily: Just sad. Not sorry but sad.

Kate: Yeah, I can see why.

Emily: And some days I just miss him. I don't think of little things to share with him or hold long-winded conversations in my head with him anymore, only with you three.

Kate: I am sure he would be relieved to hear you're talking to dead people again. Further proof of your return to sanity. How did you get the sharing to stop?

Emily: The urge stopped when I let it all go. Besides, I don't want to see him or have any experiences of him. I'm still so embarrassed for hitting 'redial' too many times the other night.

Kate: Is there anything he could do to help you get over your embarrassment?

Chris: Become unobtrusive?

Emily: When did you get here, Chris? Kate and I are having a serious discussion here. And you're being *very* obtrusive.

Chris: A few minutes ago. I promise I won't tease.

Kate: He's not dead, you know.

Emily: Who—Chris?

Kate: No. Your friend. That Luke guy.

Emily: I know. But he's gone.

Kate: That's too bad. I sent you a good, honest, decent guy.

Emily: And he started to make fun of me, so it's a good thing he quit school and went home. One time, he belittled my words and the way I would put extra significance into something I was writing about, stuff most people wouldn't notice or care about. He seemed to think it a good idea to laugh at the way I see the world.

Kate: Uh oh.

Emily: I don't know why he's like that. Immaturity, I guess. I don't judge his music and, in fact, at first, I didn't think he was judging me. I wouldn't have opened up to him if I had. I think he simply wanted to be mean. Ridicule me. Search and destroy. Make me go away.

Kate: He picked a sure fire way to blow you off course.

Emily: That he did. The Little Tornado.

Kate: Did you ever have a laugh at his expense?

Emily: No. Well, only the once.

Kate: And what did you make fun of?

Emily: His stage presence. But he started it.

Kate: Anything else?

Emily: Maybe...his singing voice, a little. He was pissing me off at the time. Not my fault. Besides, he knew I didn't mean what I said about his voice. He should know the voice is the most imperfect instrument of all. I'm sure I taught him that.

Kate: Is that so?

Emily: He should have known. And he shouldn't have moved away.

Chris: You moved away before. Twice. Once when you went out West, and once when you came back to the Island.

Em: None of which counts.

Chris: That doesn't include all the times you moved between Nova Scotia, Alberta and British Columbia.

Em: So? Who's counting?

Kate: Sigh. Sometimes you two are so high school.

Emily: Who? Me and Chris?

Kate: No, you and Luke.

Emily: Were, Kate, were. Trouble is, he'll do the same thing with everything, even the little emails I send him. Belittle them. If he reads them at all.

One good thing—I don't pretend I like heavy metal music anymore.

Chris: Did you ever pretend?

Emily: Nah. Music is still the one sacred thing between us, so I would never pretend. Don't even mention such sacrilege. And I do like the version of Bob Seeger's "Turn the Page" Metallica covered, and a couple of AC/DC songs. I liked when he played grungy guitar one night. More honest than all the cover stuff. But I wouldn't be his groupie, 'cause I'm so mature. Nothing but his number one fan.

Kate: Super-groupie, teacher, mother, big sister, number one fan. Such a lot of ways to think of yourself in terms of him.

Emily: I am not his super-groupie. Or any kind of groupie.

Kate: What if you think of him as your friend? Plain and simple.

Emily: Can't get there yet. You know what else? It's not all me. He can't get there yet, either. He thinks he's ready but what he wants is a *petit* friendship, a petty friendship, a 'petit mal' friendship. And that's not big enough for me. He lives too far away, anyway. How long can I talk to a vacuum, communicate when the line is dead? It's not ever gonna go anywhere.

Kate: Never say never.

Emily: This isn't another one of those stupid lessons about patience God keeps sending me, is it?

Kate: No.

Emily: Good. Let's change the subject.

Chris: How's Christina doing with the cards?

Emily: She wins real big by times, considering she doesn't have any money to work with. I often think she's channelling my neighbour Jack's spirit. As Fred

157

says, she's a deft hand at the cards. She often 'takes one for the ladies', as the headline in Poker News read after her last win.

Kate: Jack would get a kick out of her and her big wins.

Emily: Jack always knew when to hold and when to fold. How's he doing?

Kate: Terrific. No pain.

Emily: I'm so pleased to hear that. Jack was always a favourite of mine. He made me feel so welcome when I first moved here. His poor body had suffered too much by the time he died. Like what Mom is going through now.

Tessa, remember how your family called Mom 'Mama' even though you guys aren't even vaguely related to us? She loves when your brothers and sisters still do. She is so crippled she often feels 'like a two-year-old', as she puts it. I'm amazed she can still play piano. Her hands are so bent and crooked now; they remind me of the wings of a dove. So when your siblings call her 'Mama' she feels wonderful, like the matriarch she's always been, and not so much like a two-year-old.

I took a run over to Halifax last week and picked Mom up for a weekend visit. We were driving through the Cobequid pass and she said something to me that I had to write down. She said, 'Addicts spend a lot of time trying to find a way to be comfortable with themselves.' The things you learn on the Cobequid Pass. Wish I'd thought of that when I met Roberto. Then again, if I hadn't married him, these three beautiful, intelligent daughters wouldn't be in my life. No doubt Mom recognizes that.

Tessa: When I lived on earth, I used to be in awe of Mama's wise counsel. Since I got here, I realize she listens to several wise counsellors of her own, both worldly and other worldly.

Emily: And the wise part is—she is wise enough to listen.

Tessa: You know, Emily, you thought about your friend an awful lot over the short time you allowed him to live in your head.

Emily: Not this again! Just so you know, Tessa, it comes with that unfortunate little state of being alone. Too much time wasted thinking about what you're missing. Did you guys forget how things work down here? Now, I think about how the rain sounds on the roof. Or whether the sheets need changing. Or wondering if it's time to give my own single solitary space an overhaul; redecorate my mind.

Now I have lots of time to think since I can't write to him. I promised myself I wouldn't. Because my words suck.

Tessa: You could always say you aren't writing *to* him, only *about* him. Rationalize it. Like you did before.

Emily: I can't believe you angels are advising me to make excuses. Whatever happened to accountability? Anyway, I hate when I make promises I can't keep. He'll think he's right about the whole writing thing and tell me I'm too sensitive, get on his moral high horse and start acting all superior. I hate when he does that!

Chris: Screaming matches. Moral high horses. High-speed chases. What were you two thinking?

Emily: I can't speak for him—God forbid—but the other night, I wanted to tell him to go fuck himself. Fortunately, that's not physically possible. I've never actually seen any man fuck himself. So it's kind of an empty curse. He didn't pick up, anyway. I got his fuckin' voice mail, instead. He has to do everything electronically now that he lives in Cape Breton. Probably for the best, or it could have been a real bare-knuckle round.

Kate: So one of you had enough sense to stay off the phone.

Chris: I don't agree, Kate, that Luke was the sensible one. I'm surprised Emily found the courage to tell him at all. The one bad thing about the lesson she learned from my death is she's a little afraid to speak her mind, tell it like it is, even when the person deserves to be told.

Emily: Hey, you guys, I'm still here!

Chris: Whoops! Sorry, Emily. I think it's hard for you to trust that, if you are honest about your feelings, the person won't disappear off the face of the earth, like I did, and leave you hanging around the parking lot, apology in hand. Waiting. That's all I'm saying.

Emily: The way I feel right now, if he moved to China, it still wouldn't be far enough.

Chris: He certainly does make you crazy.

Emily: Yup. More than anyone I've ever met.

Chris: Even more than me?

Emily: Yup. Even more than you.

Chris: Even after you evicted him?

Emily: Yup. Even after I evicted him. Thank God I'm not married to him.

God: You're welcome. It's good to show gratitude on this week of Thanksgiving.

Emily: Unlike him, I am not an Ungrateful Bastard.

God: That's a good thing, Emily. Here's another thing you could be grateful for: he did tick you off enough to make you put all these scribbles into the computer and tell him how you feel, get it out there, even if he never reads it. Works like a charm every time, eh?

Emily: Yup.

God: And what do you say?

Emily: Thank you. I guess.

God: You're welcome.

Emily: Now that I have you on the line, what the heck did the Goddess think She was up to with all this uproar?

God: The Goddess is here. You can ask Her yourself.

Emily: Goddess, I'd like a word with you. Why did you set me up like this?

Goddess: Oh, I don't know. Guess I was bored. And you two needed an adventure. Didn't you have a good time?

Emily: Once again, I won't speak for my friend, God or Goddess forbid, but for me it proved to be exhausting. Exhilarating maybe, but...

Chris: Don't you mean accelerating?

Emily: Yeah, that too. Now this great big pile of illusions is falling down all around me.

Goddess: Too bad, kiddo. You wanna play the Diva and channel Mae West, you gotta pay the piper. Anyway, I'm bored again, so I'm outta here.

Chris: Mae West—'Hey Big Boy! Is that a gun in your pocket or are you happy to see me?' What an awesome line! I always loved her. Madonna's inspiration—the rock star that is, not the virgin. 'Come on up and see me some time.'

Emily: You can leave now, Chris.

God: Now that the Goddess and Chris, Mae and company have left the room, can we spend a moment together? I would like you to search your heart and see if you can find any love left for this person.

Emily: I don't want to. Please don't make me. I've been working real hard on hardening my heart. I chucked what love I had left into the room I kept for him there, built a concrete wall around it, locked the door up tight. He wasn't using the room anyway, so I figured what the fuck...oops...I mean, what the hey...I'll throw away the key. So I don't know, God, if I have any love left. Sorry.

God: See if you can break through again one more time, for old times' sake. Please.

Emily: Ooo...kay.

A few minutes later:

Emily: Sorry, but I can't go back into that room. I just can't.

God: Will you check around in the other rooms where you keep your love and see what you can find? Maybe some recycled stuff. Recycling is good. I recommend it for all you folks.

Emily: OK, but you'll have to be patient.

God: I've got all of eternity.

In a lot less time than eternity takes, Emily came back to carry on talking with God:

Em: Afraid I found some. A wee, little, tiny bit.

God: Can you do me a favour? Can you hold onto that wee, little, tiny bit?

Emily: I suppose so. Sigh.

God: Thank you, Emily.

Emily: You're welcome, God. But if you insist I keep loving him, you should make people stop moving away and dying on me.

God: I'll see what I can do.

Little Red Hens

Practise teaching time arrived in early October, and Emily's assignment set her up in a classroom of five and six-year-old boys and girls. Being with kids filled Emily with hope. She didn't recognize it at the time, but the little kid years with Bethany, Christina, and Erin had been some of her best. Busy yes, but filled with optimism, humour and joy. Children do make every Christmas, every Easter, every everything livelier and more exciting. Except Remembrance Day. Nothing much could turn Remembrance Day into a cheerful holiday.

One little girl in her Grade One class possessed a fashionista's heart and a wardrobe full of the liveliest clothing, all complimented by her big wide smile. Chloe declared that her mom picked out most of her sparkly outfits, but one day, during outdoor recess, she wore a pair of rubber boots Emily was quite certain Chloe chose for herself.

Chloe's boots had floral shafts, purple uppers, and soles with strong grips for slip-sliding around on ice and slush and snow. What Chloe liked best, as she explained to Emily while splashing in a puddle, were the oblong vents at the top of the mesh shaft where she could stick her fingers to help pull them on. Only Chloe called them, "the holes on top of the stretchy part". Chloe told Emily you could buy them for big girls, too, so Emily invested in her own pair, which were henceforth and forever known as 'Chloe Boots'.

For her long workout in the garden on Remembrance Day, Emily donned her wool lumberjack sox, her old barn jacket, and her best pair of dress-up rubber boots, her Chloe boots. The red-tailed hawk that had been hanging around seemed quite entertained by all her labour. After three hours of raking up leaves and seaweed to build up the winter mulch for her plants, she could barely creep back into the house. She stretched the muscles of her back against the wall, pushed one foot on the little kick-plate at the back of the other boot, and heaved her boot across the kitchen, where it came to rest by the woodpile. That kick felt good. She didn't want practise teaching to come to an end yet, or autumn to end, either. She collapsed on the floor and thought about little girls she had known, including her own, no-longer-little, sparkling daughters.

Emily kept a picture on the counter of Christina snowboarding on Whistler Mountain, one taken before Chris broke her wrist showing off her moves. Christina was always breaking something: noses, wrists, thumbs and toes, and, all too often, hearts. All the breaking in the world could not compete with her lively spirit and hell-to-pay attitude, much like Chris Senior's, and all the action enhanced her bright blue eyes, clear skin and long straight strawberry blonde hair. Chris wore his hair long and straight, too, but it shone like pure flax, almost too pretty for a boy. But not quite. Christina *looked* a lot like Chris, too. Tall with long strong limbs, only not as hairy.

Emily's youngest daughter, Bethany, provided quite a contrast to Christina: tiny-boned, dark auburn hair, and chirpy like a chickadee. She took after her father's side: his Italian genes revealed themselves most in Bethany. Beth called often when she needed something: advice, money, a shoulder to cry on, a pep talk—or a griping session, some of which was directed at Emily for past offences. Too often, in Emily's opinion. Sometimes, Bethany called when she didn't need anything at all. Chris and Bethany were born two years apart, fought constantly growing up, but were good friends now. If she didn't hear from Christina soon, she would call Bethany to get an update on both of them. Emily was grateful the girls lived a few blocks from each other out West. So, with Erin safely back in British Columbia, and Luke ensconced in Cape Breton, safely out of her way, all Emily's chicks were accounted for.

The joy of working with Chloe and her little friends reassured Emily that her middle age career change was not so crazy and not just a case of Emily following a whim. But practicum was only six weeks and, without little kids to cheer her up on the grey short days of November, Emily struggled to keep her courage up. TS Eliot may have called April the cruellest month, but PEI in November would give April a run for the money anytime. Emily still wanted to trust in Luke and thought about sharing her stories one more time, giving him one more chance. Chris, on the other hand, she trusted implicitly. Chris was one man who could never hurt her again. Not from his current address, at any rate:

Chris: How are things this fall?
Emily: Not as much fun since I finished my practicum. But some of my old girl friends from my school days are getting together on Facebook and we're having a

grand time sharing stories and pictures from our childhood. None of them are dead, yet. Well, obviously, or they wouldn't be on Facebook.

Chris: You can't be dead and be on Facebook?

Emily: No, Chris. Sorry.

Chris: Maybe we'll start up our own Facebook, if that's the case.

Emily: Fill your boots, Chris. But don't say I didn't warn you. You would have to figure out how to add people and 'like' and 'share'.

Chris: I already like everybody.

Emily: Not like that. It's like you 'like'...Oh never mind. Just start with Little Stevie. He'll help you figure it out. Remember the winter Stevie camped out in Frank's back yard and slept in a tent all winter? What a tough little bugger! During one of those famous ice-cold PEI winters.

Chris: I hang out with Little Stevie here sometimes. He's doing good. We listen to the album by The Who he stole from you at your party.

Emily: Haha. Very funny. Tell him I still want "Tommy" back.

I attended the Remembrance Day service at the cenotaph the other day. Our parents' generation prided themselves on remembering the war dead, the heroes. The people I remember never did anything heroic, so what does it matter?

Chris: Emily, your friends and neighbours lived and died with their own personal kind of war. And trust me, it matters.

Emily: Seems to me you used that 'trust me' line on me before, back in the day.

Chris: Besides, if you were the only person left in the world who remembered your people, would you want to forget them?

Emily: No. And yeah, yeah, I know all that stuff, Chris, but people shouldn't be so self-destructive. They leave such a pile of pain behind.

Chris: There are no easy answers for that one. Not even up here.

Emily: I remember when we were in our teens and one of us, either me or Nora, was crying because she had to attend another funeral, and Mom said, 'This is almost like a war. So many young people dying.'

Chris: It's true though. Too many of us drove drunk or stoned. Motorbikes, big ole Chevys with those monstrous V8 engines. Roaring down the road at one-hundred miles an hour. Not a wonder there was so much roadkill.

Emily: And people say the seventies were all about sex, drugs and rock and roll. Come to think of it, they were. But they were about a lot of sad things, too.

Chris: So you get to keep track. Someone has to do it. Might as well be you.

Emily: Gee, thanks, Chris. Let me know if you find a replacement for me real soon, will you?

Chris: I'll take it up with the Big Guy. But I don't think he'll change his mind. You always did have Little Red Hen Syndrome anyway, so why not?

Emily: Even the little red hen got sick of growing the wheat and taking it to the mill and baking the bread with no-one willing to help. Chris, I'm worn out from all this.

Chris: Too bad.

Emily: And I suppose I have to do this one all by myself, too?

Chris: Quit complaining. So what's the good news?

Emily: The good news is I still haven't lost a sibling, a mother, or a child. Which is surprising, because I'm getting older. So are we all.

Chris: Not me. What's the other good news?

Emily: I saw an eclipse of the moon last night.

Chris: By request from me to you.

Emily: And I get to talk to you again.

Chris: Mmmm. Good Night, Em.

Emily: Night, Chris.

Back Roads and Break Downs

Luke stood by the side of Highway 15, several miles north of Buctouche, and glared at the flat back tire of the van. He roared to Perry to get the drums out and dig out the tire iron and the spare. Perry wasn't moving too fast. When Luke yelled at him to get the lead out, Perry fired right back, "I'm not putting my drums out in the rain."

As far as Luke was concerned it wasn't raining, just sprinkling, and they couldn't afford to waste any time if they expected to make their Moncton gig. Set-up time was eight with the dance starting at nine-thirty, but the boys in the band had slept in after their late night gig in Bathurst. Then they dawdled away the day like a bunch of tourists. Perry had heard good things about a Chinese restaurant in Miramichi, so they waited till noon to check it out. The service was slow and the food tasted way too good. Luke couldn't get the boys to stop ordering. It was like herding cats with this bunch of Islanders. And people complained about Capers being too laid back for their own good! If Islanders were any more laid back, they'd be dead.

At least the tire hadn't blown into a million pieces, like Emily said the pre-radial-tires did if the sidewall blew out on you. Emily told him once she had a blowout doing one-twenty in the Rockies and still managed to pull over to the side of the road. A cop saw it all happen and came back to check on her and congratulate her on controlling the car so well. The only signs of stress Luke had ever seen Emily show during a crisis were chattering teeth and a bad case of the shakes about thirty minutes later. So he wasn't surprised when she said she had controlled the car and kept it from ramming into the face of the mountain. Or off the edge. Scary stuff.

By the time Bob and Matt moved all the equipment around and dug out the tire iron and the spare, all hopes of the Moncton gig faded into the mist. Or the rain, more like. Someone, and Luke wasn't saying who, but he turned his glare on Perry again, had forgotten to patch the spare tire. He wondered what Em would do in a situation like this. One thing he knew she wouldn't do was lose it. Emily held this theory about the way people react in a crisis. She said some people stand and some people lean. Luke was pretty sure the temper tantrum ones would have been placed squarely in the leaning camp. Emily would be in the standing one. Except for one time...Come to think of it, Em did have quite a temper. Or maybe, just around him. No accounting for that.

Luke wondered why he was thinking of Emily when the only thing in the whole wide world he wanted was to go back home to Cape Breton and curl up next to his wife in his warm comfortable bed. He hadn't thought of Emily for months. Or weeks. Well, days at least.

The previous day's trip to Bathurst had hardly been worth it. By the time he deducted the gas, meals, and hotel from the base rate and the shared gate, it didn't leave much to split with the guys. Not a big crowd at all, but those who did show wouldn't go home, even though they didn't seem overly enthusiastic about Luke's band. Not enough French songs or fiddles, Luke figured. Or they hated the sound of Luke's voice. It happens. Luke realized he must be getting bagged out, because he never worried about the crowd's opinion of his voice unless he was about to crash. Luke remembered what Emily said about the voice being the most unreliable of all the instruments. Based on last night's performance, he'd have to agree with her.

Now they were bound to miss the gig at U of Moncton, which could have covered the trip home for everyone and actually left some money in their pockets.

What would Emily do? Luke wondered. Her voice in his ear told him to get on his cell, call a tow truck, and then call the university. He could hear her saying, 'Convince them a postponement to Friday night will be much better for everybody, because the rain has been teeming down all evening, it's not much of a night to go out, and the freezing rain is due to start any minute. The students can drink more if they wait till Friday night, too.'

Her voice told him she heard the U of M students were still writing mid-terms, but would be finished tomorrow. 'Charm them, Luke,' she said. 'The students will be way more pumped if you all wait.' But Emily didn't understand how these things worked. By the way the boys were screwing around, neither did they.

Luke wasn't having much luck raising anyone at the local garage. Times like this, he wished he could afford CAA so he could call a tow truck for free. Or owned a newer rig with better tires. Luke was soaked to the skin by the time a beat-up old quarter ton pulled over by the side of the road. A hunched old guy climbed out, asked what he could do to help. He offered to drive them to the closest garage, so Luke and Matt squished into the cab of the old truck and stuck Bob and Perry in back in the open box. When they found the garage a half hour later, it was closed up tight for the night. Bob and Perry were drenched from riding in the back, and getting cranky and hungry. Now 8:30, they hadn't eaten since mid-afternoon, and everyone knows Chinese food doesn't stick with you. The old fella invited them to his house for supper. They were too hungry to decline the invite.

So the little man drove down a little back road and pulled up in front of an old farmhouse with a crooked porch held up by crooked posts, and a crooked chimney that spewed toxic black soot. As they huddled in the hallway to remove their wet coats, Luke took a good look at the kitchen. A pile of tar-covered boards with nails sticking out all over the place stood stacked neatly by the wood stove. The little man explained how he had taken down one of his old sheds and burnt every bit of it, down to the roof boards. He hoped the wood from the roof would get them through till January. When it ran out, he couldn't fathom what he would do to heat the place. But he wasn't complaining.

Meantime, the Missus cooked up some sausages and a rash of eggs collected fresh from their henhouse. As the boys in the band sat down to share the little these folks had on offer, Luke spied two tiny towheads peeking around the door frame.

"Grandkids," said the man. "Raising them, too. Their mom took off for Fort Mac. Haven't heard from her since."

When Luke offered to give up his beat-up chair for the kids, the Missus said, "They'll be alright; I fed them at supper time. Eggs and sausages and homemade bread. Should keep them for the night. And it's past their bedtime."

The kids were too scared to come into the kitchen, but they giggled when the old fella chased them up the stairs to bed.

After a hot meal and several cups of tea from the pot sitting on the back of the woodstove that had boiled away all day long, the little man offered them the use of whatever beds or couches they could find. Luke declined as it would have left the old couple sleeping on the floor, by Luke's calculations. The old

168

man told them about a nice Bed and Breakfast in Buctouche; he would happily run them over.

By ten o'clock, they were checked into a comfortable and warm B&B and enjoying a night cap with the German proprietress. When they mentioned the purpose of their travels, she urged them to get out their guitars to sing a few tunes for her and her four blonde children. It was a slow night at the inn, and the kids didn't have school the next day, thanks to parent/teacher interviews, so they could stay up a little longer. Matt and Bob and Perry couldn't resist the invitation. The innkeeper played the accordion, and her kids moved like hell on wheels with the clackers. By the time Luke finished his complimentary cookies and green tea, the music originating from the dining room sounded like a cross between the Von Trapp Family and Def Leppard.

Luke made his apologies and hoofed it upstairs to the room with the double bed he would be sharing with Matt. He was determined to beat Matt to sleep so if anyone was keeping anyone awake with his snores tonight, it would be he, and not Matt. Luke closed his eyes and dreamt of Emily all night long. To his surprise.

Keep on Rockin'

After all this talking to the wall and a couple of unsatisfactory phone calls, Emily decided it would be best to forget about Luke and concentrate on her school work. Let God take care of it, for now anyway, if He felt so damn impassioned about it.

Emily's friend Trudy called to invite Emily to join her for a road trip to Halifax for the Neil Young concert; offered to let her ride shotgun for free, since Trudy had to pay for the gas, either way. She would not allow Emily to 'excuse' her way out. Trips off the Island could get expensive, but sometimes Emily needed to escape, beat the claustrophobia—before winter and all the short days of depression hit the Island. The previous day, Emily finished her mid-terms and she hankered for a break, so no excuses were required. And she loved writing music reviews. Since she knew so little about music, she could have fun with it and not pretend to have a sweet clue. She thought she should send Luke a copy, even though she wasn't speaking to him anymore. She didn't realize, while she was warm and dry and enjoying a Neil Young concert, Luke was eating sausages and eggs in a little farmhouse way back of beyond, even further than the Back Road maps would have carried him.

Keep on Rockin' in the Free World

Thursday night, I'm sitting at the Metro Centre listening to Neil Young, thinking about passion and creativity and emotional honesty and spiritual growth, and how some people dedicate their lives to the artist's way. Then there are the rest of us. I get to thinking about how we don't all get to live that way, not me and not likely you, either. My next thought is, 'What are you doing here, Luke? Will you get the fuck out of my head? I'm trying to listen to Neil Young and this is plain annoying. Go away.'

But of course you won't go away till I think a little more, and I realize I'm mad about something to do with you. So I think, 'Christ Almighty! What Now?' And this is it—as usual with you, three things.

Have you heard about the cosmic rule governing threes? You'll have to Google it some time.

Thing number one: I can't pretend I don't know you. Sure, maybe I don't know all the gory details of your life (you don't know all mine, either—too many, but not all), but on some level I've known you since the day we met. You must know me by now, too, or you wouldn't be gally enough to call me Em. God only knows why, but for some reason you are in my life, and I'm not good at pretending with you. It never works. I do it enough with other people.

I wish you would write back more often. That's the second thing.

If I can speak on behalf of your kid: when he's grown up and moved on, he won't thank you for sacrificing so much of your Daddy time to music. This is not your mother or your big sister talking, just your friend. So that's thing three, and you need the demands of the dance to change somehow. I trust you'll figure out some new steps when the time comes. And you know how I love to dance, so if you ever need help...metaphorically speaking, of course.

Hope you don't take those three things as a lecture. You can yell at me if you do.

As for Neil Young—thank heavens some of us get to live our lives with artistic legitimacy—a gift from the gods. As for the rest of us, at least if we try to live as authentically as possible, the gods may smile on us, too.

The cold I mentioned to your voice mail? I fretted about it all day Friday, thinking it would ruin the show for me. It disappeared ten minutes into the show when my sinuses register, 'Holy Crap! I'm at a live Neil Young concert and, Man, he still rocks! How amazing is that?!'

I keep noticing this guy painting on stage—can't quite figure why. (Young doesn't stop to do those songwriter circle explanations I love and he only comments on one song—the rest of the time he rolls from one song right into the next.) I read later about the artist, by the name of Eric Johnson, and how Young hired him to join the tour and spend his nights painting images, which the techs immediately project onto the huge overhead screens, so you feel like you are part of his painting process. What a fun way to make a living!

Did I mention I never have much luck with the people who sit next to me in a theatre? Well, tonight I comment to Trudy on how we are surrounded by quiet people, even the four adolescent males behind us. Neil Young and band come out to a standing ovation, and the next thing you know a screaming, shoving match breaks out between the guy sitting next to me and two other guys—because Buddy three rows down doesn't sit back down again quick enough. One guy jumps over someone's shoulder to get at Buddy who committed the big crime. So then Buddy's friends line up behind him, in case he needs them to back him up. Fortunately, Buddy's girlfriend inserts herself between the two of them and female wisdom prevails. At one point, about six guys are all ready to jump in. All this action in the bleachers while the operator of the wall-to-wall video screen zooms in on Neil Young's peace symbol covered guitar strap and Young singing "Love and Only Love". None too loving, this bunch.

My other worry when I spend big money to go to a concert in an ice rink is the quality of the sound. The soundman took care of that little irritation and created excellent sound for the ungainly space. As Trudy said, Young's used to performing in these big steel-beamed arenas, and has the crew and equipment to do the job.

I don't usually worry about losing someone in the crowd, but I did manage to lose Trudy for half an hour; both of us standing under a sign a hundred feet from each other—might as well have been a thousand for all we could see. I couldn't handle the congestion around the beer booth either, and I'm not usually claustrophobic. I must be turning into a real country bumpkin.

Young's voice has mellowed with age (Jesus, he's sixty-three! Makes me look like a babe.) and sounds richer and less nasal, so even better. But he still sings a great falsetto. One of my favourites he didn't play is "Long May You Run"—a perfect tune for a campfire on the beach at dawn. I think maybe some of us have been there at least once? The song is a tribute to his car—the man likes his automobiles—but I never thought of it that way. I thought it was more like something you might sing to Liam.

Most of the show sounded a lot more hard-hitting than "Long May You Run" and gave him a chance to show off his skills on the electric guitar. He played a solid two hours and twenty minutes, including a tune called "Sea Change", which I wasn't familiar with. Clive from Back Corner Music thought it must be a Beck song. I You-Tubed it. I'm not familiar with Beck at all but you probably are, since he plays a terrific guitar. The video didn't go anywhere except to the beach, so you can listen and work at the same time. Turns out this "Sea Change" is a new song by Young, not released yet. I guess that explains why I don't know it. Duh.

Young also played "Heart of Gold" on a well-worn church organ. Picture the pain that instrument goes through being dragged all over North America. Its poor bellows! A few songs featured some tremendous pedal steel guitar—it's getting to be Trudy's favourite instrument—that and the harmonica. She's been trying to decide which one to study; I suggested she start with the harmonica.

For his one encore tune he sang the classic Beatles song "A Day in the Life" which, oddly enough for his encore, was the only song he didn't write. As you may know, it's also been covered by Jeff Beck, not to be mixed up with Beck who is just Beck. Or Jeff Buckley. Confusing! It's almost as bad as the way Hollywood makes those action movies where all the men look the same, unless they are black and the bad guys. Very confusing. And they somehow manage to make all the black bad guys look the same, too, except for the varying degrees of bling. But Hollywood doesn't stereotype. Right?

I'm quite sure you would like Jeff Beck's guitar style—good guess? A musician to emulate. Then I thought of the song you wrote last winter. I've never been able to figure out what the keyboard part after the guitar solo has to do with the main song musically, but I like it. Anyway, this is starting to sound like a pissing contest for guitar players, so enough already.

As we poured out onto those narrow downtown Halifax streets—all ten thousand of us—we passed by a street musician singing "Keep on Rocking in the Free World". So we all sang along. Our own encore tune for Neil Young. We caught some Hali-fever tonight and it wasn't the flu. My musical education continues.

Bucket Lists and Bras

Luke's response was...well, nothing. Emily forgot about her promise and God's big expectations of her and continued to wonder why she put energy into writing to Luke at all.

She was still lonely. She missed her daughters too much, especially with Christmas coming, but she knew she couldn't have them. They were too far away. But Luke wasn't—just a few hours' drive. She couldn't have him for Christmas, either.

He did show up with the band over the holidays at the local pick-up bar, however. She decided to see what he was up to and then sleep over at Trudy's, so she banked the woodstove, packed her high-heeled sneakers and her best red dress, and bummed a ride to town with Fred.

She reminded herself she had made some new friends at the university: old single people like her and married people who still liked to party. So she invited them to go with her and keep her company while she waited for her fifty seconds of Luke at the end of the night. These were good people, people to go dancing with, people like Luke's brother Tommy, her friend Trudy, and Doug and Betty. People who were old enough to help her write a bucket list and slide hers onto the stage and into the pile of song requests:

Emily's Appropriate Bucket List:

1) Go to the cougar bar with Tommy and Trudy and learn how to pick up. But I can't be a cougar. I should be a jackal so I can rip a man's heart out.

2) Do a woman. But not Betty.

3) Kiss Tommy's ass.

4) Fly to Europe. Done.

5) Sing in Luke's band.

6) Buy Tommy a Blue. Done.

7) Should know "what the fuck is going on". I'm not sure what that means—Tommy wrote it so you'll have to ask him. I don't know what the fuck is going on.

Tommy claims Doug wrote it. I must have a word with that boy. Hands off the bucket list.

8) Strip off my bra on the dance floor. But not when Luke is playing.

9) Ask guys how big and how many eggs they have. That's shaker eggs, you fool! You know, like in a band?! Sheesh.

10) Kiss a croc. Kiss Tommy. Find a turtle. Doug added that. We're working on his list next week.

11) Find out who the fuck Alice is.

12) Sing at the top of my lungs. Yup. Last night.

13) Howl at the moon. Already did. A few times.

14) Dance naked in the moonlight. All alone. Done.

15) Chase a poisonous snake through the jungle. Done.

16)

17)

This is hard. We need suggestions. But remember, you have to come up with something I've never done before.

     Emily did have a talk with Luke at the end of the night, or a confrontation (or whatever you want to call it.) She might have pushed too hard, because he pushed her right back, shoved her and a couple of people out of the way, so he could get through with his gear. The heat and press of people tested his nerves, and the woman in the stilettos who stepped on his toes didn't help. Emily could tell he was starting to lose it with all the drunks crowding him and the instruments, but still, he didn't need to be rough. She had never seen him get physical with anyone, let alone a woman. She wasn't hurt though, other than her pride. As he shoved her aside, he asked that question again, the one she had been trying to avoid. He had a way of doing that. She got back at him later, left a ten minute message on his voice mail at 3 am. That should fix 'im. She didn't answer the question he shouted at her, but it haunted her. And around about dawn the blues came a-callin'. Since he wasn't much more present than her dead friends, she took up her pen and imagined she and Luke could have a proper conversation. Or tried to:

December 17, 2005

I am writing this early this morning after eating too much rich food and drinking too many of Betty's fancy coffees last night, and running out of sleeping pills, all of which woke me up again. For the umpteenth time. I made your part up:

Luke: WHAT THE FUCK DO YOU WANT FROM ME???

Me: I DON'T FUCKING KNOW WHAT I WANT!!!! WHAT THE FUCK DO YOU WANT???

Luke:

Me: I thought when my life got happier again you would fade away for me—it would be like you promised—I would discover you are just a product of my own unhappiness, I would stop being curious about your world, and stop memorising all the lines. Instead this is my world now:

I want you to not read anything I've written you in the last three weeks, for at least one of us to live up to our agreement not to do this anymore. I want to stop first so I can be the honourable one for a change. I want you to reply so I know you're still listening. I want to write and write and write to you for as long as I need to.

I want to play piano all night and go stark raving mad like Beethoven so I can pretend I have a talent for something other than dressing up.

I want a new belt so my pants won't fall down.

I want to stop writing ridiculous drivel like this at 5 in the morning. I want to stop hitting 'send' when I do.

I want to meet a new man. I want to be able to talk to him about things I talk to you about. I want to trust him that much. I don't want to think he's sick of the sound of my voice, like my ex at the end of my marriage. I want the honeymoon stage back. I want to sleep curled up next to a sweet, kind, nice man so I feel better and less alone. Sometimes.

I don't want to give up my sleeping space. Or share it with any man, even if he is nice.

I want to change my writing style.

I want to find a pair of high heels that won't put me in so much pain after standing at a skanky pick-up bar for two hours. Then I wouldn't have to ask you to run me over to Trudy's so I can get my Chloe boots, even though I know you're not here for me anymore. I want to have enough sense to take off my high-heeled sneakers and walk barefoot in the snow and ice, instead of asking you for anything, ever again. Or better yet, call a cab. I want to stay out of pick-up bars.

I want you to be my prodigy, little brother, prodigal son, friend, anything but my lover. I want you to go away. I want you to bury yourself so deep in me all your worries disappear, if only for a few seconds. I want to be the one to stop you from ever doing that. I want to be the one to say 'no' this time. I want to write you erotic poetry instead, except I can't write poetry. I want to know if it would have been good between us skin to skin. If we could have gone under the sheets and not needed or wanted anything or anyone else. Just once. I don't ever want to do that. If I am right about you and me, I would be, in the worse sense of the word, fucked. And you would be—well—you would be whatever you wanted to be.

I want a new winter coat but I can't afford one, so you'll have to put up with seeing me in my old blue one, if you ever see me again. I want a new car, but I can't afford that either, so the drunks will still have to drive home with me in my old bomb.

For a few minutes one night, I thought I wanted a man for a zip-less fuck. I don't want you to be mine. Ever.

I want to go out to a party and drink too much and pass out when I get to bed so I don't think about you. I want to start drinking right now.

I want my brain to shut you out so it doesn't talk to you and make me write stuff. I want to rinse you and the night out of my hair so I can get some sleep. I don't ever want to stop writing to you or talking to you about how I see the world. I want to trust again that you won't judge me when I do.

I want my three girls home for Christmas Day and my mom here with us and my two step-grand-children, too. And I won't have any of them. You neither. I want to not have my period at Christmas, for once.

I want to get to know my step-grandchildren well enough to love them like my own. I'm already halfway home with the little girl, Maddie. She talks too much, like Erin. And when she's not talking, she's singing. Like me.

I want to be wise and determined and unselfish like Mom. I want to make a big impact on the world like she has. I want to serve and do something worthwhile with my life, instead of studying and talking to you, especially if you don't want to listen anymore. I want to take Mom down off the pedestal sometime before she dies so I'm not intimidated by the very idea of being her kind of woman. I don't want to knock her down, like my sister Nora does. I want to take her down gently. I don't want to break her heart on the way down—she's so frail.

I want to play fair. I don't want to give a fuck about fair.

I want to go away long enough so you'll actually have time to miss me for a change. I don't want either of us to find out you don't.

I want to give you your Christmas present without any fuss.

I want to not have to make up your replies.

I want you to talk to me sometimes.

I want I want I want.

Luke: Well, now that you got that off your chest, Em...

Me: Thanks, I feel a lot better.

Luke: No problem. Glad I could take care of it. What would you like to do now?

Me: I want to stop talking. OK?

Luke: OK.

Emily didn't share her journal entry with Luke, but she did send him his Christmas gift and a little note on his card that read "What do you want from me?"

Breakfast at Not Quite Tiffany's

Luke gave them both a couple of days to calm down after the slightly shoving match, before he called and invited her to Cora's for breakfast. Emily ordered the gigantic crepes with bananas, hazelnut chocolate sauce and whipped cream. She figured she might as well get one of her appetites satisfied, at least. His dime this time, so why not?

Luke apologized for the way he behaved Saturday night. He blamed his shitty behaviour on frustration, and he talked to her about his disappointment with the band's progress and his troubles at home. He explained that his wife was starting to complain and he hated complaining. He missed them both, Siobhan and Liam, and he knew Siobhan didn't have it easy, but he needed this music life. Emily understood. Why couldn't his wife? Emily wasn't so sure she did understand, but she kept her thoughts to herself and her mouth shut, other than to shovel bananas and chocolate sauce into it.

All this talk as he tossed his blonde hair, a gesture of his that always reminded her of Chris. Except, unlike Chris' classic move which was all smooth and unaffected and usually had to do with fitting his long hair under his bike helmet, Luke's hair fussing was starting to look all girly.

As Luke rambled on about his family life, Emily thought about coming to Siobhan's defence and reminding Luke she had a few more years of living under her belt, which had given her more time to accumulate some wisdom and acceptance. However, she didn't know Siobhan from Adam; she seemed no more tangible than Emily's dead friends. But Luke was real and he was sitting right across from her chewing on some bacon rind. She had waited so long for this. Why spoil it?

Luke offered to share his bacon, since Emily couldn't stop staring at it, but she respectfully declined. All thoughts of Siobhan scattered when Luke said something unexpected, "There's something coming my way. I don't feel right inside." She thought, 'Oh goodie. One more obscure comment from Luke. At least this time I can ask him what the hell he means in person.' But when she

180

pressed him on it, he shook his head and looked away, and she couldn't see his sea-green eyes. No point pursuing it if she couldn't see those eyes.

Eventually Luke got around to Emily. He said he missed her. He missed their little talks, her humour, and the way she made him think he could do anything. He said he was sorry for all the times he didn't return her calls or respond to her emails. He told her, "I can try to reply, but I'll warn you my replies are pretty empty most times. I don't do the reply thing a whole bunch. It may drive you a little crazy but that's the way I am. Always have been and always will be."

Well, duh! Emily didn't find his explanation satisfactory, considering he was supposed to be trying to make amends. She told him so. The best he could come up with was, "Usually my replies consist of a forwarded joke I think most people haven't seen or heard. And I don't reply or send hello notes to most people. So don't take it personally. Don't be so sensitive."

There wasn't anything Emily hated more than being told she was too sensitive. However, in the interest of peace and reconciliation, she bit her tongue and listened. She would get to have her say eventually; she was pretty sure of that.

Luke paid the bill, bought her a piece of fudge they found by the cash register (since Emily hadn't inhaled enough sugar yet). The sun split the trees as he walked her to her car. When she opened her door he caught hold of her—out of nowhere—and wrapped himself around her shoulders. He gave her the biggest bear hug and buried his chin in her hair. She was some glad she had showered and washed her hair before she left Trudy's that morning. She felt him trembling, but she didn't ask why. She didn't want to break the spell with words. Her cheek fit perfectly between his ear and his collar bone and she thought she could feel the tears behind his sunglasses. Her heart went out to him, as it always did when it got even the least little bit of a chance. Foolish heart.

When the second half of Emily's student loan showed up after Christmas, she headed off to Halifax to see Luke's band for their first big gig at The Misty Moon. Emily hoped to cheer him on as he hit the big time, be nice about it. She thought she should warn him she might show up. She tried calling from her sister Nora's place first, but he didn't pick up and that just pissed her off, after all the courage it took for her to call. So she yelled and cursed and lost her temper to his voice mail. Again.

She drove down Spring Garden Rd. to Barrington St. and parked, then walked the wrong way down Barrington, into the area where the snakes crawl at night. She called Luke again to get directions, as she couldn't remember which way to go to get to the Misty Moon. He didn't answer, again, so she had to ask a hooker, who got her turned around and going the right way on Barrington, once Em convinced her she wasn't gay and she couldn't do her for money. Leave it to Luke to leave her stuck on a street corner relying on the kindness of strange hookers. Idiot. Stupid Idiot.

It seemed that neglect and rejection had released a whole flood of thoughts and stories, as she sat in the bar, all alone with her iPad. Funny how that happened.

Sent: January 13, 2006 9:45 pm
To: Luke
Subject: me talking again yap yippity yap yap
Dear Sir

I might be sending a story someday about all the things one person could do on a trip to Halifax that have nothing to do with sex. Well, not one person. Two. I wrote it when I was waiting to hear from you. You know what waiting does to me. I have to have something to do! And it helped me get over all that rejection.

If you think reading the travel story might make you uncomfortable or might make you think I'm mad (I'm not. Now.) or make you think I'm going down a certain road, don't read it. Simple. It's called *unforgiven*. But I'm not sending it till after the weekend. In case *I* feel uncomfortable.

It might be funny. Or I might have been angry when I wrote it. You decide.

You can disregard the begging part at the end since you've already answered that. I left it in 'cause I like to think of myself as ninety years old.

Want to know how I've thought of you the last few months? Like a big ole freeloader. Wouldn't you if you were in my shoes? So you better do a goddamn good job tonight. Start contributing something. I don't want to hear any sour notes outta ya either. Smile. Loosen up your jaw and throat. Hit the notes pitch perfect. Otherwise, I'll have to teach you choir warm-up exercises. It would only make more work for me and I need to write a story for Creative Writing. That you're not in, you bastard. Writing a story is a lot of hard work, you know, and you've been distracting me too much lately. It takes a long time to write a hundred and fifty pages. Especially when most of them are boring: ten thousand sentences that go like this 'she walked down the street to the bus stop.' Blagh!

Maybe I should start with a hundred pages. I've already got about twenty so that would be five times twenty. That sounds much more manageable: a mini-book, un petit livre, a novella, a vignette; no, not a vignette. That's what I've been writing to you all along. Or that's as close as I could come to describing these little missives you make me write to entertain you. And they ain't sellin'. Or goin' nowhere. So I gotta do better than that, 'cause this baby is one that has to be read by millions, make me millions. It could be the answer to all my financial woes. Could be? Has to be. 'Cause you'd be ecstatic if that happened. Think about it: no more temper tantrums, no more reading assignments for you, no more indecisions, no more tears. I'd be Rich. Ridiculously, Stupendously, Enormously, Gorgeously RICH!!! Filthy, Filthy, Filthy RICH!!! Allelujah!

So I got no time for voice lessons. Go talk to your fans the best way you can: make music. Smile and have fun, for fuck's sake.

Think I should get a pen name? What do you think of Emily Lemieux? Or Aristotle Bonaparte? Or Trilby Orion? Or Tearie O'Brine? Or Toulouse la Tricky? Or Tory Delaney? Except I think that one's taken by a Harlequin Romance writer. Hey, I could be one of those...

But enough about me, the famous authoress. Back to the more immediate problem. How to break the ice tonight. I know! I'll go first. Here's what we should do. You'll finish your first set and I'll go up to the stage (what stage? he asks), and I'll ask you for a request. K? Hmmm, what song should I request....gotta think about that. Wanna rehearse first? How's this for my line, "Hi, Mr. Music Man. Giggle Giggle." And you could say, "Hello, Doll." That's what Johnny Cash always said, wasn't it? Or was it Darlin'? Yeah, that's it. OK, OK so I say, "Hi, Mr. Music Man." And you say, "Hello, Darlin'." And I hit the floor with a thump and Matt and Bob have to come and scoop me up. No, that wouldn't work. No fainting allowed. I'd look so silly then.

So I'd stand there gawking and feeling terribly shy, and you'd have to come to my aid; rescue me. You could say something like, "What can I do for ya, little girlie?" And tip your hat. And I'd push my glasses up—you know, the ones with the band-aid around the nose piece?—and I'd hitch up my bobby sox and my bloomers and I'd say, "Ummmm". And you'd be swamped by all your other fans and I'd be pushed aside, but you'd be my big strong gentleman cowboy and you'd push back on all those gorgeous little girlies and you'd say, "Come on, Sugah, spit it out. I ain't got all day, ya know." Then I'd say, "Could you play 'The Mountain of Love' by Charlie Pride. Please, please, please? Please please me oh yeah, like I please you." And once I got started talking I wouldn't be able to stop.

Or is that too unbelievable for my character—that I wouldn't be able to stop? Yeah, you're right. I agree—too much of a stretch. So instead, I'd beg for your autograph. And you'd try to escape to the bar, but I'd wrap my arms around your leg and you'd have to haul me with you, drag my plaid skirt and white blouse and glasses and bloomers and bobby sox all over that barroom floor. Sweep the floor with me. Get me full of dirt and beer and broken glass. Think it would get the job done? Break the proverbial ice? Or should we change your lines? Give me your take on it. K?

Till later I remain

Your Biggest Fan,

Exotic Emily
(My pseudonym. Like it?)
Tory Delorey (Better?)

PS On the drive over today, I was thinking about how inconsistent I am with you. One minute I totally give you the benefit of the doubt and call you 'my sweet boy', and the next I'm tearing a strip off you and calling you everything but. Seems to me one of the first things they teach you about parenting is to be consistent. Trouble is, I'm not your parent. Or would you prefer to think of me that way? Maybe the Auntie Mom character in your life since you already have a perfectly good mom. Since it's one of those questions you don't answer (because it's foolish. Your mom? I don't think so!) I'm going to remind myself I wasn't all that consistent with my kids and they turned out fine. Perfect, in fact. And I'm not going to think about it anymore. K?

PPS Did you notice the new internet word I learned? K? Now I've got lol, and lmao, and btw and :o) and wtf, and bff and...I guess that's it. I'm a long ways from being text-ready yet.

PPPS Oh good. The band's about to start. I hope, as you always say when you are about to go on, you don't suck too bad.

Emily did get to see him. He didn't have time till the end of the night, when he was packing up the gear again. She wrote him a review just for the hell of it.

Sent: January 14, 2006 2:00 am
To: Luke
Subject: musical review
Ya done good.

I wore my leaf necklace—you know the one I bought in September? I thought you should see it in case you want to borrow it. But I don't think you looked long enough. Oh well, next time. And I'll let you try it on, too.

A gorgeous girl in the washroom told me I'm a beautiful woman and have amazing eyes. I have no idea who she is, but I like her already. She also told me teal is a great colour on me. Maybe she was thinking the teal must be creating a trick of the eyes, but I don't think so. Do you? I wear teal and all its variations a lot around you. Me, the great illusionist. You could borrow the teal top I wore, too. See if it works for you. That way you'd actually see the colour and know what teal looks like.

I haven't heard you relaxed when you sing for quite a while. You sounded great. (Did I say that already?)

E

Lukey's in Love

Luke closes his laptop and leans back on the one and only chair in his hotel room. Luke wishes she would stop. Emily doesn't need to talk about herself as old, or fish for compliments, or act all insecure around him. She just needs to be who she is, plain and simple. She doesn't ever have to apologize, least of all to him. Why does she do that stuff? Makes no sense.

Her resilience amazes him. It doesn't matter how many times she gets knocked down, and he knows he is responsible for more than a few of the knocks, she gets back up again and again, like an old Bobo doll. No matter what, she won't stay down.

He can't understand why she doesn't feel his eyes on her when she comes to hear him play. He can always tell when she is watching him, even though she looks away the instant he looks back. He wants her to show up more, he loves to watch her dance, and he's more in his zone with her in the room, listening. His voice, imperfect instrument that it is, needs her there. He shouldn't be thinking about her, but he can't help himself. She makes him laugh with her ridiculous imagination, almost as much as Liam does, and she gets him thinking about the world beyond music and family and the Maritimes, stuff he never thought of before. Plus she asks him the weirdest and most bizarre questions sometimes.

Why couldn't he dance with her, one more time? She'd like that and what harm would it do? But, he always has to play for money and, as the old saying goes, the fiddler never gets to dance. Neither does the lead singer. So instead, he keeps letting her down, leaving her out. Like tonight.

It's late, and the hotel room stinks of stale cigarettes and beer. Next time he'll order a non-smoking room, if this old hotel has such a thing, or they even get a 'next time' for a Halifax gig.

Luke would have preferred lavender, the sweet scent of Emily, as he experienced her the morning he held her after breakfast at Cora's. Even the mix of fresh cut wood and fishcakes from that day at her cottage would do. He shouldn't have walked away that night, when she caught him up and danced with him, because now he is craving the sensation of her head tucked up under his chin, nestled there like she has just come home. But she will never come home. Not to him, anyway. Some other man, maybe.

And he has a home of his own to come home to. Luke wonders what would happen to him if he became totally overwhelmed by guilt, succumbed to it. Would he crash and burn, vaporize into a puddle of brown sludge like the Sydney Tar Sands? So much guilt. Over Emily, over Siobhan. Over Liam, most of all, when he leaves him behind to go out on the road. But the stuff that causes the guilt is also the stuff that cures it, keeps him from drifting so far away he'd never make it back.

He picks his old Yamaha up out of the case and fiddles around with it, tunes it, tries a few chords of the April Wine song he and Emily once danced to, "You Won't Dance with Me", but he is too cold and tired to play. The hotel room is fuckin' freezing. Thoughts of Emily make him want to crawl into the bumpy, creaky bed and curl up into a ball, partly to protect himself from the hunger and partly to protect his body from the cold draft creeping in around the ratty old window. If he could have one more rumply, fresh-cut-wood-pile night with her, he might find some comfort.

One night, when he and Tommy had both had too much to drink, he spilled about Emily. Tommy said it came as no surprise to him, you'd have to be blind not to notice there was something going on. Then he told Luke, "You know what your problem is? Pedestal, Man, you got her on a big high pedestal and you need to let her down. She should take you down off hers, too. Best thing for the two of you, so you can both face reality. You'll figure out that, sweet as Emily is, she's not meant for you. Otherwise, no good will come of it."

Then Tommy started teasing him, like he would in the backyard when they were growing up, and singing to the tune of "Chuckie's in Love", "Lukey's in love, Lukey's in love." So Luke had to tell Tommy to shut up and push Tommy off the bar stool, and in turn Tommy had to grab him and put him in a choke hold, so they would get kicked out of the bar. Thus ended one more night with Tommy.

Tommy is right; no good will ever come of it. It isn't right. None of this is, and he has to stop thinking of her. Tomorrow. Tomorrow will be soon enough. He plugs in his ear buds and listens to that old Dan Seals song that always brings Emily to mind. Shiny, sparkly, copper-penny Emily. Copper pennies are supposed to make you lucky, but all he feels is lonely. He sets his iPod on repeat and falls asleep to "You Still Move Me".

I've often wondered what would I do
If I found you alone like this
Would I remember
What I've got at home
Or forget it all with your kiss
'Cause when you left me
I was hurtin' so
She picked me up off the ground
And I do love her, I want you to know
That I never want to let her down
But you still move me
Though I'd never let her know
There's a place inside of me that just won't let you go
And every time I hold her in my arms
Or look into her eyes
I wonder this time, does it show
'Cause you still move me

Big Bounce

The next morning, Luke turned on the laptop and sent Emily another one of his pithy emails. This time he didn't type anything but the subject line: 'STOP', the one four-letter word Emily had always told him would be his ticket out. Emily also recognized how much all this cognitive dissonance was taking out of Luke, poor unlikely hero that he was, so she agreed. If that's what he wanted, she would just stop writing. He seldom answered, anyway, so why bother writing to someone who hardly ever replied. But her resolution didn't last long, less than twenty-four hours.

Sent: January 15, 2006 8:00 pm

To: Luke

Subject: the end of the review. thought i should write it before the weekend buzz is over

Dear you

Me and my niece, Fiona, had our own little gig today. You know the little bouncy balls that are about the size of a bull's eye marble? Well, we started out with twelve of them in the basement and ended up with—oh, I don't know—two? Have you ever played Big Bounce? It goes like this (Fiona's instructions): "Take all the balls and throw them at the other kid (that being me) one at a time, but really, really fast. And really, really close together. Till it hurts."

It hurt after the first six disappeared—I can't get out of the way nearly as fast as a six-year-old so I took all the punishment. After we lost most of the balls—and this is where the performance started—Fee Fee taught me to sing, "Come out, come out wherever you are, Little Bouncy Ball", while dancing and making ballet leaps. She made the ballet leaps. I'm too old for that. But not too old to be the boy ballerina and catch her in my arms. The kid's getting heavy!

Then I chased her up the stairs so we could play hide and go seek. Which we did. This time I was performing with my best rendition of "Fee Fie Foo Fum I smell Fee Fee's Stinky Bum". And she played dead—that was scary—eyes wide open and not a blink or wiggle out of this very wiggly friend. After we wore ourselves out with 'Bouncy Balls' and 'Dead' and 'Tag You're It' and 'Hide and Go Seek'—that was fun—we played dolls and ponies and zombies and she taught me this song:

My Little Pony skinny and bony
Went to the circus one day
Farted on purpose and blew up the circus
And that was the end of the day

Think you can top that one for lyrics, Luke? I doubt it.

But back to the main event. When you played "Fat Bottomed Girls" did you play it for me? Phew! Now I feel so much better about all the weight I've gained while you were away.

I just thought of something. Maybe the woman in the washroom who loved me in teal was gay. It's amazing what people will say to get into someone else's pants. Rats!

Hey, I thought of a good new name for the band! What would you think of Armageddon? Like it?

And thus ends the latest musical review! I hope you liked it, even though Fee Fee and I were the stars of the show today.

Respectfully submitted,

Me

The Trip

Seaglass Cottage
Spruce Lane
Tracadie Bay
Prince Edward Island
January 18, 2006

Hey Lukey,

Remember how, after the big cell phone fight with your voice mail back at Christmas, you treated me to breakfast, and I said I would like to think I could be more mature? On second thought, not too mature. This is the story I wrote and promised I'd send. And I know the forgiving part is old. But I'm too lazy to rewrite it. Btw the imaginary trip's over.

unforgiven

I'm off to Halifax again and you haven't told me what I should do to make up for being a stupid heartless selfish insensitive bitch. So I was thinking...if you hitched a ride with me, you could tell me all about it. What would be an appropriate punishment? Or an excellent vindication for you? You could describe it all the way to Hali and then...well, it couldn't involve sex because I can't do sex with you...or at least not with my clothes off...so you would have to poke at me through my pink silk pajamas that I always take on a trip...pink is a good colour for me...enhances my skin tones...but then my pjs would get wedged up my arse and we'd just end up laughing hard enough to make ourselves throw up and you're probably one of those people who thinks sex is a serious business and doesn't want any vomit showing up just as you're about to...I wonder what that would be like...a serious man in the sack...don't think I've ever had one of those. So no sex, at least not the first night. I have work to do the next day.

I know!!! We could do like we did when Trudy took me to Halifax last fall and stay up till 3 am talking and eating and laughing. But I've offered you that before and you turned me down. Besides, there wouldn't be much punishment for me in hanging out on your side of the bed till 3 am. There'd be more punishment in sex with a serious man. Are you serious when it comes to sex?

So what else could you do in a hotel room to punish me? You could take your pound of flesh—I gained at least ten pounds I can spare. Another reason you won't ever see me naked. But I can't picture any way you could take ten pounds without it turning gross and grisly, and I'd have to pay for the room repair. Or clean it, even worse. Out damn spot! Wouldn't want it to be like that woman in the hotel in Moncton who cut up her husband and put all his cut-up bits in the box-spring mattress...Whoa! No bloody thoughts allowed. Out damn thought! It would be a lot more fun—and cleaner—to go to the hot tub and sweat it off. Would that count—me coming back from the hotel pool room ten pounds lighter? Not much of a punishment, I guess. Especially if I had too much fun sweating it off. In the hot tub, I mean. Where did you think I meant?

Maybe I got this all wrong. Maybe it's not about punishment so much as me being extra sweet...like super submissive...rubbing your calves for you...as I recall I used to have a real thing for your calves so it wouldn't be a punishment. More like a pleasure. Or I could give your shoulders an extra good massage...ease all the tension away...I used to have a thing for your hairy shoulders, too. No, wait—I got it! I have a rose and blue kimono so if I laid you down on the big fluffy white hotel duvet on the floor and walked all over your back like a Japanese masseuse...but I'm too heavy and would break your back...and my

193

kimono is pretty short so you'd see my thighs and whatever, if you were looking up from below...except you'd be on your belly so you wouldn't be able to see much...unless you stretched your neck up, and I could give you a good kick in the head, flatten you out in a hurry...But that wouldn't do, 'cause then we'd be punishing you, and I promise never ever to do that again. Ever.

On second thought I could be a Geisha Girl, and both of us could stay perpendicular instead of horizontal...but not a Girl, a Geisha Woman, and I could introduce you to the sensual pleasures of the Japanese Tea Service...but I think you're a coffee man, aren't you? Oh, what the hell, I'll convert you to tea...and engage you in the art of conversation...and I could play the Shamisen and teach you some chords...contrary to popular belief Geishas don't have sex...or not indiscriminately and not with just any old one, so it would be OK. And I could wear a long silk kimono so you wouldn't be able to see up it...you could buy it for me, instill a little dignity to the proceedings, your treat to prove you aren't cheap...me neither. But you'd have to pay for your own breakfast. Mine's included. Oh hey, that's what I could do! Bring you breakfast in bed! Not!

Or we could sing "Dashboard Light" and we could pretend we are in *Rocky Horror Picture Show* and I could be Janet and you could be her dorky boyfriend and sing, "Let me sleep on it Baby baby let me sleep on it." And I could sing, "What's it gonna be boy? What's it gonna be Boy? Yes Or NOOOOOOO." "Baby baby let me sleep on you. Baby Baby let me sleep on you, I'll give you the answer in the morning." Oh yeah, but Janet wasn't submissive at that point. More feisty than anything. And I promise never to be feisty again. Only sweet. Sweetie me.

Or you could sing "You Bring Out the Wild Side of Me" to me. Oops, that would be backwards. More likely I'd be singing it to you. Shit, you're so young you wouldn't even know that song. Probably never

194

even heard tell of poor old deceased Dan Seals and his steel guitars. (Just don't sing "They Rage On" to me. It would make me feel old. Or "Addicted". Too sad. And this hotel room fantasy is not allowed to be about sad. Ever!)

My, oh my, we could figure out all kinds of ways to not have sex. While you're punishing me. We could go to the Keg next door and have steak, instead. I hear steak is good for your virility. And I love mushrooms. I think they are some kind of aphrodisiac. Aren't they? After, we could go back to the room and...oh, I dunno...play dominoes?

Eureka!! We could pretend you're my bff and read *Cosmo* together, and untangle the mysteries of male sexuality. You lying on your belly on one bed with your chin on your hands and me lying on my back on the other bed with my head on the pillow and my hands crossed behind my head. Classic girlfriend pose. We could read the article "How to Know if He's Amazing in Bed". Or you read. And make me guess what the number one clue is—Taa Daa!

"...he knows his way around a guitar. Guitarists have a multitasking knack of doing one thing with one hand while doing something completely different with the other, which is pretty useful when it comes to sex."

And then you tell me if it's true and maybe recommend a good guitarist to me, like a true bff would do. But not an ugly one. Or one of your castoffs. And I read you the good advice part:

"...to look for geeks. You'll often find more sensual qualities in people who indulge in so-called 'nerdy' activities. It might not be seen as macho but they have a more erotic outlook on life."

This could be valuable information you might need some day, my bff. And I'd be happy to share it with you.

Then we could pretend we look like the girl in the picture who is wearing a bikini and hanging with the guitar player above the caption which reads "So, you're pretty handy with a G-string"...and we could argue about which one looks more like her—me or you. In a bikini, that is. And discuss where exactly that G spot got to. Do you know? I don't.

I'd also like to practise Cosmosutra's three sex positions to make you body confident. Me I mean, not you. Body confident, that is. You're already body confident enough. They are called:
The Straddle'n'Slide: to flatten your tum.
The High Rider: to lengthen your legs.
The Lap Grind: to hide your bum.

I could show you how to do them in case you want to practise at home. It would be like teaching each other dance steps. You know—like back in high school? Good times! Oh shit, that won't work because, by the sounds of it, all the guy has to do is sit there as she does her therapeutic exercises. Or lie there. Or stand there, as the case may be. Oh yeah, you're a guy. Right? I almost forgot. A serious guy. So you can't be my bff and I can't practise with you. Know anyone I can practise with? Who can also play dominoes? And guitar?

Well, it's OK if he doesn't remember how to play dominoes. Neither do I. But we could have fun trying. Even if none of the other stuff worked out. He could be my hero instead of my bff. Even heroes have the right to breathe. And I'd let him. Breathe that is. Other than when I'd be whupping his ass at dominoes.

If finding my new bff didn't take all night, we could order room service and get the gay waiter to talk movies with us. He's nice and can tell us a lot about movies. He'd keep us away from any thoughts of doing the nasty nasty for...oh, at least an hour. Or we could try watching a movie. But you'd want to watch an 'adult' one and I wouldn't—yechy—so we'd end up in a fight again...a pillow fight this time. Those are fun, especially if you win. But I wouldn't be allowed to win 'cause I have to be submissive. Oh shit, that won't work EITHER!

Hey, I'm running out of steam here. I've given you lots of ideas. Just pick one. It's easy. Make the call, Luke.

Am I forgiven yet? God, I hope so. All that activity would be an awful lot of work. Or fun. Depending on you. If you would be an active participant or a passive observer. A happy man or a sad sack. A man who doesn't take himself too seriously—like me—or a serious man—not like me. But I could be. With the right man. Serious that is. Hmmm...

But the sad sack guy's got me thinking. Where could we go in the little hotel room to avoid the sack? The bar fridge? Too small. The dresser? Too narrow. The desk? Too slippy. And glassy. The closet? Hmmm. Closet dwellers. Another dark corner. Let me think. Might be interesting, if a little congested. Or I could go sleep in the closet and you could sleep in the bar fridge. Does that work for you?

Of course, if we bypassed all the harsh hotel edges and corners and went directly to 'Go'...Whatever you want, if you'll forgive. And you know me well enough to know I won't shut up till you do. Are you sure you want a ninety-year-old me screaming in your deaf ear, "Forgive me. Forgive me, for fuck's sake. You're killing me here!"? And you know I'd do it, because I'm just that stubborn. I wouldn't want to go to my grave unforgiven by you. By other people, maybe—and I think there may be a long line-up of people with something to forgive me for by then. But not by you.

Emily

PS You hand me lemons, Luke, and I keep making lemonade.

PPS You are impossible.

PPPS But I'm not angry.

PPPPS And, since you used your safe word, this is the last you will hear from me.

Digging Up Bones

Winters can be brutal long on PEI and leave a lot of time to brood, even for those who aren't yet in the habit, like Emily. Relatively new to the Island, she thought she could cope, but—Man! Those dark days, depressed air systems, accompanying overcast skies, and banks of smothering snow can get to even the most resilient. Emily struggled to respect Luke's wish that she stop writing to him. She craved light. Of any kind, but especially of the spiritual variety. She called for Kate or Tessa to crash through the dark clouds and enlighten her, but the best they could send on a moment's notice was Chris:

Emily: Chris, why can't I just forget him? Why can't I stop doing this big post-mortem?

Chris: You just have to, Em. Don't worry about it. You did that after I died, too.

Emily: Yeah, but you died. He didn't.

Chris: You cried longer when I died.

Em: That's different. He's still on this planet. Not sure where, but somewhere. So it's time to get over it.

When I was grieving you, I didn't share it with you.

Chris: Because you couldn't. I was irresponsible and left. Hopped the first Glory bound train I could track down. I wasn't there. But I can handle it now.

Em: I hope so. It's not a tough job. All you have to do is listen and whistle Dixie, if you want.

Chris: I don't want you to do this one alone, so go ahead and talk away. Who cares? You're the one who is hurting. Besides, you're still living with the repercussions. You've got a daughter who wishes you'd been there for her instead, is pissed 'cause you haven't listened to her problems this last two years, taken the time to...

Emily: Bethany, you mean? That one's not my fuckin' fault! All she had to do was ask for my time, pick up the phone, stop sending those meaningless texts I'm supposed to interpret. I offered her my help many times. She kept telling me to take care of Erin and the kids, and not worry about her. Now she tells me she's not doing so good, feels sad, wonders what life is all about, and thinks she should quit university. First I heard tell of it.

Tessa: I'm here! Sorry you had to wait. My last travel conference went over time.

Emily: Where do you go to travel?

Tessa: Our next trip will be to the twenty-fifth dimension. Can't wait!

I heard what you said about Bethany. I know Bethany, Emily, and she will be OK. Her mama never raised no quitters. Chris, you can leave. I'll take it from here.

Emily: I can't freakin' read minds, you know!

Tessa: Even though a lot of people expect you to. You can't blame yourself.

Emily: Luke expected me to read his mind all the time.

Chris: And if you asked questions to understand him better, much of the time he didn't answer, so you didn't even know if he heard you or not.

Emily: Snort. Just like Bethany. And my ex. And you sometimes, Chris. You were bad for that. My Chris, too. Another thing you and my daughter share, besides your name. And the list goes on. There is only one word for people who don't answer civilized questions, and it's 'rude'. Rude or 'care less.' Two words, actually.

Chris: Didn't that man tell you at Cora's one morning he realized not dealing with you when you are upset only makes matters worse?

Emily: Eavesdropping, were you, Chris? I can't remember exactly what he said. It's so long ago, a whole two months, but I thought that was what he meant, too.

Chris: You have my permission to do whatever it takes. You'll stop digging up bones eventually. The next conversation with me will be happier.

Emily: I look back over the time he knew me and wonder how he stayed with me through a lot of stuff.

Chris: You weren't always easy on the head.

Emily: I can see why, now.

Tessa: It's my turn, Chris! He must have found enough to hold his interest to put up with the 'hard on the head' stuff.

Emily: Or maybe he liked the part where I became his personal cheerleader.

Chris: You did what? You as some man's cheerleader? Can't see it.

Emily: Yup.

Chris: Sheesh. I gotta think about that one...Musicians are the kind of men who attract women easily. Or so goes the theory. I read it in *Cosmo*, so it must be true.

Emily: You read that article too?

Chris: Yeah, when you did. I was looking over your shoulder.

Emily: Eeew. Creepy.

I wouldn't ever throw myself at him. Ergo, no sex.

Tessa: So that can't explain his interest. Could be he just liked you.

Emily: Well, I wish he'd said it. Even once. Maybe he was waiting for me to spill and tell him those three little words, over and over. Every time I thought them. Talk about repetitive.

Chris: I wish I had stuck around for more of that.

Emily: What, the 'I love you' part? The part I never gave you, Chris?

Chris: No, the 'hard on the head' part. You always were a hard-headed woman. I liked that about you, showed you had balls.

Emily: Not balls, Chris.

Chris: OK, then: spleen, guts, intestinal fortitude, chutzpah. Call it what you want, I liked it. Did he?

Emily: I don't know.

To tell you the truth, I'm not very brave. I am such a frickin' coward I'm like the mouse that roared, most of the time. If I wasn't such a chicken, I would date a real boyfriend and forget about the imaginary one. But I sure liked that he had patience for me. Stuck around. Period. For a while, till he got too busy.

Tessa: You know, you two were in an almost impossible situation.

Emily: We sure were.

Chris: Sometimes people meet each other at the wrong time. Like you and me. God doesn't always give you what you want, but eventually he gives you what you need.

Emily: Yeah, yeah, yeah. Platitudes from heaven. So, what? I don't get to have one last grand passion before I grow too old to care?

Tessa: Didn't you already have one with your ex?

Emily: If you could call it passion. It wasn't so grand. I have no idea what Roberto would call it.

Tessa: Nothing is ever impossible, not if Love is involved. Didn't your mother ever tell you when you love someone, you're looking at the Female Heart of God? She's not mean, you know.

Emily: God or my mom?

Tessa: Both. Moms always want to give their kids what they want, even if it spoils them.

Emily: The Goddess struggles with spoiling us, too?

Tessa: Yup. But She has a lot more experience. She knows sometimes people have a passion for each other that must remain unexplored because of everyone else involved. There's always the possibility another time will be different.

Emily: Gawd, you want me to wait a hell of a long time. Now you want us to wait till his wife is dead, and I'm ninety so he can call me 'toothless', and he's sixty-six and lost his hair all over so I won't be able to call him 'hairy butt'. To think, I was totally looking forward to that.

Tessa: Girl, the things you worry about! You could look at it another way. Imagine how wonderful it would be to be ninety, kids on their own or departed, grandkids too busy to care, and there you are falling in love all over again.

Emily: Bring on the Viagra.

Chris: What's Viagra?

Emily: It's this little pill they've come up with to take care of one of a man's inadequacies. It only works on one of them, however. More's the pity.

Chris: Glad I never needed any help in the sack.

Tessa: Chris, we have to take off now or we'll get stuck back in the sixth dimension, and you know how boring that one was. See ya, Em!

Emily: How much do I owe you? Sixty Hail Marys?

Tessa: The first session is free, so we're all good. But you could sing my favourite hymn "How Great Thou Art". I like the line that goes, 'Then sings my soul.' Mine sings all the time. Your soul can too. Just try it. It could be your best therapy, ever. Gotta go. Love ya, Babe.

Fred and Flora Go Under

Back home on Tracadie Bay, Fred and Flora continue to keep an eye on Emily. Since Jack died, only three homes are occupied year-round on Spruce Lane, so best to be vigilant. Flora sometimes worries it isn't safe for a woman living alone, even on good old PEI. Break-ins have become much more common since so many rich folks decided to build summer homes here. She invites Emily for supper several times over the winter and listens to many stories about university life, the impossible young male friend, and Emily's trip to Mexico, which Emily would love to repeat some time soon.

Late one night, Flora wakes Fred up so she can share her dream and a few other things under the sheets. "Guess what I was dreaming about, Fred. While you were doing whatever it is you do under there, I was imagining we were on a beach in the Caribbean. Just you and me. We went skinny dipping in the moonlight; then we made love on the sand."

"You mean like this?" said Fred, as he snuggled in closer.

"Yeah, kind of like that. You were a gentleman and spread the towels out good and thick so I wouldn't get bit by sand fleas. The water was shimmering with that stuff. You know. What-cha-ma-call-it."

"Phosphorescence?"

"Yeah. The opalescent glow those fish and plants make."

"Did you like it on the sand as much as you like it right now in our bed?"

"Yeah. But get off me a minute. You're smothering me. And I gotta finish the story."

"Can't I get in just a little bit? Turn over on your side. I won't bother you. Much."

"OK. But not so hard. I can't talk when you're pumping away like a jack hammer. And I need to remember this dream so I can ask my Bible Study group to help me interpret it tomorrow.

Anyhow, after the little adventure on the beach, we went back to our hotel room and you went into the bathroom to get cleaned up, wash the sand out of your crack. You were about to hop in the shower after dropping your trunks, you looked up and—lo and behold—a young woman had beaten you into it. You didn't know this, but her boyfriend was in the bedroom with me. Talking. We were just talking, Fred. Front desk had given both couples, the young one and the old one, the same room key. Confusing. Anyhow, in the bathroom the young lady was soaping herself all over with her eyes closed. You thought about looking away. You thought real hard about it. Not that hard, Fred. Take it easy, for Christ's sake!

As she was running her soapy sponge across her brown breasts, she opened her eyes a little slit, caught you looking. She watched you with invitation in her eyes and..."

"Oh shit."

"What Fred? Don't tell me! You didn't come already?!"

"Not much good to *her* now, was I?"

"Oh My God, Fred! Stop tickling me! Let me catch my breath! There's nothing I love better than a man who makes me laugh in bed."

"Even more than those hot young Caribbean men who show up unexpectedly in our hotel room?"

"Ooh, yeah."

What Happens in Mexico

After much negotiating and gathering together of pennies, Emily's three daughters agreed to meet her in Mexico to celebrate her graduation, rather than make the long flight to the East Coast and get sore butts listening to all the addresses at Emily's Convocation ceremony. They decided to return to Huatulco, because they loved the town and the nine bays, and Emily's brother still lived there and enjoyed company. Emily was determined to make some progress on her bucket list and had some success, as she wrote to her friend Trudy:

Sent: April 21, 2006
To: Trudy
Subject: emily's list
Hey there Trudy

I'm sitting in an internet cafe in Huatulco in thirty-degree heat and my arms are sticking to the plastic chair. But I thought I'd send a quick update, since this is a good bilingual keyboard with all the keys working.

Emily's Bucket List:

17) Take a mud bath on La Bocana beach courtesy of the Zapoteca ladies.

18) Drape a three-foot-long Iguana over my shoulder. Hold his chest in my hand. Feel his tiny beating heart.

19) Swim in behind a waterfall. Look at the world through a curtain of water. Live part of my fantasy life at least.

20) Push my back up against a shorter waterfall for a perfect hydro massage.

21) Eat wild boar and stir-fried cactus under a palapa in the rain forest. (I passed over the fried grasshoppers.)

22) Find the cure for breast cancer: Visit a Zapoteca herbalist and buy ten cat's fingernail plants for two hundred and fifty pesos (about twenty-five dollars). Take daily as a tea, with a piece of rattlesnake.

23) Treat myself to a back massage on the beach by a half-naked Chico (young man) after being knocked arse over teakettle several times by breakers, while standing in eight inches of water.

24) Go snorkelling! I can see underwater! All the colours!

25) Get squirted in the eye by a blowfish. Underwater.

26) Go whitewater rafting. (Well, the water wasn't very white. But I did get tipped out of the raft to go swimming in the current. That may be as close as I get to white rapids.)

27) Commune with a fifty-year-old sea turtle from Costa Rica as he floats in the breakers. (Till I realize he's dead. Ooops.)

I have to confess I didn't know some of these were on the bucket list till thirty seconds before I did them. Bethany and Erin think that's cheating. But I don't care. I'll be thinking of you as I sit on a bus for nine hours going up switchbacks in the middle of the night.

Hasta luego!!

Emily

PS I'll send my trip notes once I've finished them.

Setting Day

Charlie can't wait to tell Emily he is allowed to fish on the weekends this spring, now that he has turned twelve, as long as he keeps his grades up. Granddad says you need a college degree to know how to do the paper work if you want to make a career of fishing these days, so he better be smart. Charlie knows he is. He explains all this to Emily, after he convinces his grammy they should invite her over for supper, given today is Setting Day.

Charlie's granddad likes to haul a few traps on the first day of the lobster season, even though the traps are barely in the water and won't have sunk to the bottom of the ocean yet. Granddad can't wait to see if it looks like a good season, and neither can Charlie. Charlie loves the thinking of the North Shore lobster fishermen like his granddad, because it means he will get his first feed fresh out of the boat today. Other poor suffering Islanders have to wait till tomorrow, Opening Day, to go down to the wharf and buy some if they are craving their first taste of lobster. As far as Charlie is concerned, no more tasty lobster can be found anywhere in the whole world than the lobster fished during the spring season off the North Shore of Prince Edward Island. Emily agrees with him, as they walk through the spruce grove.

Emily says she thinks he's grown a foot while she was away. Charlie almost comes up to her shoulder now, and he shows her his new muscles. She reaches over and he thinks for one awful moment, she might ruffle his hair. In the nick of time, her hand veers off, turns into a fist and punches him in the arm, instead. He bet he won't even bruise. One of the girls at school is always punching him there. So annoying! And she doesn't look like Emily. Emily is beautiful.

When they get to Grammy's, Emily offers to help with the crunching and cracking of the lobster tails and claws, but Grandda tells her they're fine; he and Charlie will handle it. Which works for Charlie, as it gives him one more chance to show Emily how strong he is. She's left standing around looking kind of useless, though, so he is relieved when Grammy asks her, "Why don't you help me shred the greens for the salad and, if you really want to be helpful, you could cut the lemon pie. I've never been able to figure out how to make perfect sixths out of it. You're so young and smart. You'll get it just right. I know you will."

Before long, the plastic tablecloth covers the table, lobster meat fills the big bowl to the brim, salad greens tumble out of Great Grammy's Limoges serving dish, and fresh rolls spill out of the bread basket. Time to eat. Emily favours the little claws, or puts, as they call them on the North Shore. Charlie tries not to stare at her lips as she sucks the juice and the meat out of the skinny shell. She isn't a big fan of the mushy green tamale hidden deep inside the body, so Charlie offers to trade her some of the tender white meat you can find in the body if you push the soft inner shell back to expose it. He is happy to show her how it's done and explain that, while the tamale, which is the liver, is fine to eat, you have to be careful not to eat the black mush behind those beady lobster eyes right up against the tamale, as it is the brain and full of poison.

"The lobster's last revenge," Emily calls it, whatever she means by that.

Then he shows her the red roe on a female and she starts singing, "Row, row, row your boat gently down the stream."

Well, not exactly the same kind of roe.

Grandda says, "Close, but no cigar, eh Charlie?"

"What does that expression mean, Fred?" asks Emily. "I've heard it before and often wondered."

"Like when the midway comes to town during Old Home Week and you throw the ball at the target in one of those booths, and it's always close. But no cigar. Well, we used to win cigars when I was a boy and sneak out back and smoke them behind the tents. Never heard tell of that?"

Emily brushes her hair back and laughs, as lobster juice flies everywhere. This time Charlie can't help but stare, and wishes he could make her laugh like Granddad can. If he ever married Emily, he would make her happy all the time. Instead, he laughs right along at Granddad and his funny expressions and the faces he makes. As he snorts along with Emily and Grammy, Charlie drops a big chunk of lobster tail on the floor. Emily crawls under the table to see if she can fetch it, before someone squishes it with their bare feet.

Granddad quips, "What you looking for down there—toe jam?"

"What's toe jam?" asks Emily.

"You never heard of toe jam?" Charlie chimes in.

"No."

"You grew up on the Island and you never heard of toe jam?" says his granddad.

"No. What's toe jam?"

Grandda picks Emily up from under the table, while Charlie giggles and snorts some more. "What do you think? It's what it sounds like. The stuff that gets jammed up between your toes."

"Tastes great on toast," Charlie snickers.

"Oh, gross," Emily mutters, only loud enough for Charlie to hear. She wouldn't want to question the eating habits of the North Shore, not when a good feed is on the table. She says, "Thanks so much for inviting me, Charlie. This is a much better welcome than I received from the Canadian customs officer in Toronto yesterday. You are so kind to think of me." Charlie blushes with pride and pleasure.

Later in the evening, after Charlie returns from walking Emily home, Grandda says, "Not the sharpest knife in the drawer, is she?"

"Maybe not," says Charlie, "but she sure is pretty." Which earns him one more punch on the arm, from Granddad this time.

Dear Kate

Seaglass Cottage
Spruce Lane
Tracadie Bay
Prince Edward Island
May 14, 2006

Dear Kate

I wonder where you've got off to. It's that time of year again. Our favorite dance recital fell on May 6th this spring. Remember when you, Kara, Trudy, and I would all go for dinner and the show together? This year it was down to me and Trudy. We changed the traditional pre-show dinner venue, too. We skipped the Canton and went to the sushi place across from the old post office, instead. With the Asian Invasion, as small as it is, Charlottetown is developing a more sophisticated palate, and so, happily, are we.

It's hard to believe that I am writing to you and not hearing your reply. But your voice is fading. When you don't stop by for a midnight cuppa, it's not so easy to remember what you would have said or how you would have said it. And time has a way of erasing some of my best memories.

But I do remember the night you died. Trudy, Kara and I were on our way to the dance show without you. May 1st. You already know that, as you were in Charlottetown at the time, stuck at the QEH. Wouldn't it have been more fun that night if we'd just hauled your sorry ass out of that hospital bed, taken you along with us, and let you dance and die to Dvorak or Michael Jackson's "Beat It"? Instead of leaving you behind, waiting for your heart to finally say, "Enough is enough. Cancer is making me too tired, so I think I'll quit now." I wonder why I didn't think to take you with us. Too late now.

Which reminds me—I intend to have that talk with my girls soon. You know the one, Kate? The one about what to do with me when I get old and sick and weak. I think I understand better now the choices you made at the end of your life, when you insisted Sam take that detour trip to Cuba on his way back from university and Lori stay put in Toronto, till you reached the bitter end. I always thought that was a little unfair of you, because Sam got home in time to see you buried and Lori only had a week with you. But now I understand your motivation better. You didn't want them to 'attend' you. You didn't want to go out like Cleopatra with countless thousands of slaves in waiting. On the other hand—four handsome chariot riders by my side as I fade away, into the light? I must tell Erin to add that to my funeral directive.

This year Kara had made other plans for the 6th but she lent us her angel cards so Trudy and I could play with them at the Korean restaurant. Her diagnosis has Trudy considering some big changes in her life and she's been wondering what the angels would think of her plans. Her angel reading was, as is always the case with angel messages, all good. Kara's set of cards has a little book that comes with it, which offers more explanation than what is written on the cards. I found something quite interesting in the booklet. It described worry as a form of prayer and said that, like most prayer, it is also a way of wishing. The trouble is, according to the angels, worrying just draws negative energy and experiences to us. Instead of getting the thing you hope for, worry brings you more hardship, instead. So I should probably quit worrying about money, eh?

Actually, there is some good news on the financial front which, as you know, has been pretty worrisome. It took six months of 'mounting tension' (like in an espionage novel), and pressure-cooker winter days and nights (like a bad marriage), but, finally! I've been able to come up with some income relief. Fred says I can help out on the boat this summer. When Fred and Charlie and his crew are done hauling lobster traps, they'll start hauling tourists for the summer months. So he wants to hire me to take the deep-sea-fishing bookings from the booth and run around doing errands for him. Then he can concentrate on charming the tourists with all that Bearded Skipper of the North talk. I agreed, as long as he doesn't ever ask me to clean the boat after the tourists lose their lunch all over the washboard.

Even though some of the local fishermen think women are Jonahs on a boat (superstitious old buggers), I even get to board the boat sometimes! No more money worries.

I want to tell you about today, Mother's Day. I was driving down the wharf road when I noticed these weird looking birds in the plowed field. That's the same field where we saw the red-tailed hawk hanging suspended in the sky a couple of years ago. Remember? We stopped the car and both agreed we had never seen a hawk standing upright, like an angel who has just earned his wings. It just stood still in the sky, like it was standing on an invisible branch, with its wings half open and half tucked in at the bottom. Like a beginner ballet dancer in first position who hasn't learned to drop her shoulders yet. The image of that red-tailed hawk and the pleasure it gave us both are a couple of the best memories I have of your last days.

So this morning, I turned in the little red heritage lane by the old house, the road leading back to the Smith farm that was once Fred's family farm, the lane Trudy calls Clifford's Lane. The school board built a new school right across from that field. Whenever I drive by at night, the school is lit up like a Christmas tree. The new school is not much of a leader in energy conservation, by the looks of it, even though we constantly preach conservation's importance to every school child. I wonder what the neighbours think of all those bright lights shining in their bedroom window every night. They'll get used to it, I guess. And so will I.

Anyway, I pulled into the heritage lane so I could see the birds more clearly and try to identify them. Summer's coming, but I don't have to rush everywhere yet, so I figured, what the hay, why not take a couple of minutes to satisfy my curiosity. The two birds were so still, and I was sneaking up on them so as not to startle them, when I came across a perfect cluster of daffodils. Right there, basically in the middle of nowhere. A brilliant splash of yellow against the newly sprouted grass, fresh shoots of purple clover, and ancient evergreens that stand by the red dirt road. The patch looked to hold an even dozen daffodils, but I didn't count them. I was kind of thinking the daffodil bouquet might have been my Mother's Day gift from you.

I still haven't figured out what make and model the birds were. They sat so still I thought they might be some kind of decoy. But then one of them moved. The Island farmers are now using peregrine falcons to scare the crows and

212

seagulls away from their fields. I saw one just off the Blueshank Road one day, sitting on a post with its hood on. But these two didn't look like falcons. More like undersize eagles. Not ospreys, either. For a minute I thought, by the way they were crouched over, they must be turkey vultures. I don't think vultures visit the Island, do they, Kate? In the end of it, I had to conclude they were just common gulls, even though each one had black lines running over the cap of its head, and I've never seen markings quite like that on a seagull.

My other present, probably courtesy of the Smiths, was the extra fill they dumped on all the puddles and holes in the lane, so I didn't get stuck or hung up in the mud. The Island smells delicious lately—eau d'manure. The Smiths were spreading manure on the field as I watched the birds. The liquid stuff. The most pungent. It drove me away from any further investigation.

Funny thing though, I did smell something very sweet the other morning by the cottage, almost as sweet as mayflowers. On the way home from my bird watch, I pulled over to talk to my new neighbour as she was hauling her wet laundry off the clothesline so her clothes wouldn't absorb the manure odour. We talked about country aromas. She said that daffodils smell very sweet. So I figure it's the daffodils Fred planted for you when you were diagnosed that are perfuming the air at the cottage. I've never noticed the scent of daffodils before. They didn't smell that sweet when I was selling them for the Cancer Society fundraiser that April, just before you died. But then, neither did cancer.

You should see the land this May. Oh yeah, I guess you can. It's absolutely beautiful. Lots of colour already. The tulip lovers must be in ecstasy. All the money they spent on bulbs is finally paying off in brilliant colour and, since it hasn't been that windy, the petals are actually staying on the tulips for a change. Harsh winds and late frosts have made for some pretty short tulip seasons the past couple of springs. The lupines and lilacs will be out in no time. Everything seems to be two weeks ahead of season. And the red-tailed hawks are back. Oh yeah, I guess you sent them. Thanks for them, too.

Mother's Day was looking like another day of missing the people I love— like too many of my holidays—and spending time with people who give me a headache. Till Charlie stepped in, brought me a bouquet of mayflowers he picked in our borderless woods, and invited me over to his grammy's house for the Mother's Day feast he and Fred rustled up for Flora. Your kids would do the same

213

for you if you were here, Kate. We done good, didn't we? In spite of all that worrying and negative praying we did together as we were raising our kids, they all turned out darn good. All five of them.

I wonder what the colours of spring are like in heaven, and what scents you and everyone I love can smell. Man, I've said that a lot. This letter should be called "I wonder"! And to think, I'm trying to teach Charlie not to repeat the same words over and over again. Can't seem to help myself, though; it's been that kind of spring here on the Island. A spring of wonder.

Well, this is getting to be a long rambly letter. I guess you have all the time in the world, so I don't suppose you will mind. And if you want to talk, I'd love to know about spring where you live. Even if God says I'm not ready, yet. Just neglect to tell Him you told me, OK?

Miss you

Emily
XOXO

PS I wonder if God has put you in charge of garden scents. If so, I have a suggestion for you. Wouldn't wild roses be lovely?

Who Was That Masked Man

Emily didn't totally escape graduation or campus life, even though she dodged the cap and gown ceremony with her Mexican get-a-way. She heard from a friend of a friend of a friend that the Don of Monty House had delivered her baby prematurely and wouldn't be able to cover her shifts for at least a year. So Emily filled out a job application.

She returned from Mexico feeling more self-assured and attractive than she had since her marriage fell apart. All that time in the sun and appreciative glances from the Chicos helped. She decided it was time to forget Luke, let him get on with his life while she got on with hers. She stayed in touch with Tommy, though. Tommy was generous and kind and funny as fuck, and with Tommy what you see is what you get. He didn't seem to possess much in the way of dark places. She liked that. Not so confusing. Of course, the better brother is always the unmarried one, and not the one she wants.

Emily knew there wouldn't be much work in teaching that fall, but she applied anyway. Her first job application went into the pile with a hundred and five others; she didn't even get a call for an interview. She knew her age would make it be harder for her to get a teaching job, but she didn't realize the competition for the few jobs on the Island would be so brutal. She did get the part-time job as Don of Monty House, though, and expected she would be able to manage if she landed some substitute teaching gigs as well.

In late fall, Emily took in a conference on special needs kids. It gave her a good excuse to get over to Halifax and visit her family, go dancing with Nora and the other delegates. It turned into one of those Teachers Gone Wild nights.

Much too late that night, she crawled into bed in the hotel room and let her imagination go, as if she was talking to Luke. Because he was still the one she told her stories to. Even though she hadn't spoken to him or written to him for over six months.

A woman checks into a Halifax hotel, as she does every year at this time. She asks front desk for two keys, as she always does, even when she's travelling alone, as she usually is.

After an evening filled with Christmas parties, coloured lights, rock and roll, and Santa, she's had her fill for the night and settles into sleep. She could be singing Handel's Messiah in her dreams. Or Jingle Bells. In major key or minor key. Two keys. We can't know—she's sleeping.

Two keys, one for her and one for someone who hides in the shadows at the late night entrance, a familiar silhouette as the security light gives him up. He slips the key in the lock, steals up the back stairs. Slips it in another lock, gains entry. Slides under the sheets...no one would have to know who he is, not even the woman. She could pretend she doesn't recognize his scent...or taste...clothes wouldn't be a problem since she doesn't wear any...she likes the feel of her skin against her skin, tiny silky hairs, arm against breast, hand tucked under chin, she sleeps better that way. She could roll over in her sleep, give one small moan, and make believe it's all a dream—a lovely dream, but only a dream. And he could leave the second key on the bedside table to remind her of her beautiful exotic dream when she wakes in the morning. It could be that easy.

She does wake in the morning, stretches and purrs. Thinks about him. No, it couldn't possibly be that man. Doesn't matter if the kids and spouses are grown up now and moved away, he wouldn't be sneaking up fire exits. Too undignified. And there are a million beautiful women out there, and they notice him now since he has that hungry, haunted look. They've detected it for a while, at least the past year, when he has carried it in his eyes. Now *he* knows he has the look, too. So he spends his time hunting for a coyote. But not an ugly one. More like someone from the movie *Coyote Ugly*. No cougars for him, either—he's too raw. They'd eat him alive.

She doesn't paint her toenails anymore, so no, it couldn't be him. He wouldn't like bare naked toenails, even if the rest of her was. He's finicky. Of course, he wouldn't have known in the dark, except they don't feel the same. Not slippy slidey, like the rest of her feels this morning.

Her feet are always cold. She started out the night with her toes wrapped around her flannelette nightgown. But they aren't cold now. And they weren't cold last night; not for a while anyway, even without the nightie. Every part of her felt warm, right down to the tips of her toes. She can't think where her flannelette nightie disappeared to. She digs around under the covers with her plain, bare, non-slippy toes until she slips into a special kind of coma, one only induced by semi-conscious sex.

Later, at the hour when the November morning light is bright and grey and evil all at the same time, she wakes from her coma, catches a glimpse of herself in the mirror, and groans. 'I'm too old for this,' she thinks, 'and who was that masked man who breached my security anyway? Zorro? The Ghost of Christmas Past? The Easter Bunny? James Dean? Some Punk Kid off the street?'

But a Punk Kid wouldn't know his way around a woman's body. He wouldn't have the required imagination. Neither would the Easter Bunny. That man did.

The End

I didn't tell you her name. Or his either. It could be Johnny Depp, long silky hair tickling my...BUT I would never be the woman in this story. I am sooo glad I'm such a happy divorcee now I couldn't even imagine such a possibility, not even in a hotel room by myself. Not even in my dreams. Oh, I forgot the ending:

She decides it must have been a dream, and promises never to torture herself with fantasies of random men again. Ever. For now.

The End

Black Ice

Erin called Emily in desperation one night. Her fiancé, Pierce, had to move overseas for a year and couldn't take the kids with him without his ex-wife's permission, which she refused to give. Neither did the ex want to take the kids on full time. They didn't want to go with their mother full time, either. Maddie and Clair called Erin one night and begged her to take them home with her. Erin drove over to the ex's house and observed a full-blown meltdown. Not from Maddie or Clair, though. The ex told her to take the kids and get the hell out; she didn't want to do this anymore. Pierce assured Erin he would be making hordes of money in Asia and would send bags of it to her, if she'd take care of the kids till he got home in a few months. Except, he got caught for insider trading and landed himself in a Japanese jail for much longer than a few months.

Emily told Erin what moms tell their kids during a crisis, "Come home to me." So she did. She moved in with Mom and started hunting for work and draining the bank account. With her first Island purchase, she joined the land of beat-up old rigs.

Sent: December 14, 2006 5:55 pm
To: Christina
Subject: oh yeah and thanks to trudy and erin and me and probably old joe the bootlegger i just had a little adrenaline rush

I just drove home from a bill paying trip to town and came across a little bit of black ice and the arse end of the old car went into the other lane because of course the all seasons on the back are shot and I don't have any money to replace them. And last Thursday I drove the big boat to the dentist to get a $165 filling replaced that fell out the night before and braked on the ice at Murray's Corner and the whole car went sideways right across both lanes. 'Cause it's a big mother. And a truck was coming the other way but he had lots of time to stop. When I got to the dentist's office the car door hit me right in the jaw because it needs the plate that holds the door open fixed and I don't have any money to replace it,

218

either. I hate it when my car attacks me. On the same day I discovered my laptop hard drive is fried—another $220. I had to go to another wake, too.

And today I paid a whole shitload of money out on payments and there is no money left for Christmas. I should be working on the Residence Christmas Party budget instead but it's not going well and I don't think I like it. It's not taking shape. Not worth submitting, will just get me an 'f' for fired. But today is Monday and I have a headache and I miss you and Bethany. I should be grateful to have Erin and the kids here, but it's been so long since we were all together at Christmas. And don't say, "Ah Mom, you're never satisfied." Or, "You could fly out here." Because you know I can't. Your lucky dad gets you for Christmas all the time.

So I'm going to hit 'send' and get in the tub and see if I can get rid of this frigging headache. No I'm not. Trudy called to say Erin got in an accident and I'm trying to find out wtf's going on.

False alarm. Thank the technology gods for cell phones—when she answers, that is. It wasn't her but apparently there was a bad crash in Corran Ban with a car that looked like hers. Old Joe the bootlegger drives the mate of her old beater, so I hope it wasn't him. Fuck I hate winter.

Call me. Please.

Luke's Gift

Emily wanted to do something for Christmas for Luke, or to him, after she ran into him at one more dance at another skanky downtown bar. Maritime Canada can be an awful small bubble sometimes. She didn't recognize him at first, it had been so long. Luke seemed to be going for the lumberjack grunge look with his plaid flannel shirt, denims, and full beard. The beard didn't really work for him; it hid his best features. Emily's reaction was to start writing again. She could out-word him any day. So she wrote him a story. Old habits die hard.

Sent: December 20, 2006 5:55 pm

To: Luke

Subject: womanizer

You know how at Christmas you are supposed to give or do something for the person he wouldn't give or do for himself? Since 'tis the season and you're probably overtired and taking yourself too seriously and would never find the time to write a story for yourself, I thought I would do one for you. I'm in it too much, but that's OK. In my Creative Writing class, the Prof said you should write about what you know and what I know about is ME! If you find too much of me in it, you can add chapters with more of you and less of me, if you want. You could become a famous author, write reams and reams of chapters on your magical life, and this could be the gift that keeps on giving, into infinity.

Luke's ~~Christmas~~ Story

First Chapter: Sammy and Me by the Sea

(This is me talking at first. I didn't tell you, you don't get to talk in your own story? Ooops. Sorry.)

I've been thinking about Saturday night's impulsive request for you to call me. Could you disregard it? I just came from a cuddle and a nap with Sammy, my cat, and now I don't need you to talk to, after all. I want to be happy, and waiting to hear from you doesn't make me happy. I just remembered that. I think Sammy might have reminded me when we were cat-napping. He also said something about your one reply last January being a tad snarky. And abrupt. 'STOP'. What kind of reply is that? I was feeling a bit nostalgic for a time when your replies weren't like that. I'd have to go back a lot further than last winter to find one.

I know how busy you are with the Christmas season, so it wouldn't be a good time to talk, anyway. You'd resent one more person making demands on your time. Sammy thinks I would have way more fun lying on the couch in the sun all day. I don't remember the part where we agreed that you would take exception to everything I say or do. Of course, you probably don't remember the part where I had my fingers crossed behind my back when we agreed we would stop writing. Or the part where I would have to curse the ground you walk on a couple of million times, just to get over you.

Sammy has been with me for over ten years, and he knows when I get totally stressed about money I want to talk to you. So he said—this is all cat talk—that I should talk to him instead, since you wouldn't have a clue what to say, being neither poor nor a cat. So I asked him what I should do about the money thing. Sammy said, "Meow. I'm hungry. Feed me first while I think on it."

Sammy was one day away from the needle when we snatched him up from the jaws of the Humane Society. Since then, he has disgorged himself out of the jaws of feral tomcats, foolish clumsy cars, black dogs, and ugly coyotes at least nine times. Wish I'd seen the coyote after he dragged Sammy through the ploughed field. Bet he won't try that one on again. The only part of Sammy that wasn't mud was the top of his very kissable head. Sammy says the most evil things in this world are: dogs, coyotes, dog pounds and—well, you get the picture.

Sammy looks a bit like my neighbour Fred's orange cat, but he's more of a strawberry blond and much, much prettier. Sammy's heart is like Sammy's favourite butcher Heath's and doesn't always keep the rhythm. He's a desperado kitty cat, and he knows of which he speaks. I would take his advice unequivocally on anything, especially financial matters;

whereas you are a neophyte and doubtless on one of those despicable freedom fifty-five plans. Thanks to your sensible wife.

Anyhow, after he polished off his fifth snack of the day, Sammy gave me his hard-nosed stare and said, "This is what you need to do, Emily. Buy Jack's piece of land next door and the cheap mobile home and set it up for Erin and the kids. I know, I know, you don't want to acquire more debt. However, you can also roll the credit card debt in with a mortgage on the mobile home and reduce your total payments by two or three hundred bucks a month. Take the money and run. You've been dragging the debt around your neck since forever."

After a stretch and a cuddle, he continued: "Much as I love Erin, I'll thank God when she moves out. The kids are getting on my nerves, always stepping on my tail. Only a matter of time before one of the little bastards steps on my broken hip. Besides, I get sick of pretending I'm a stuffed toy and scaring them when I twitch my tail. That joke got old real quick. So did the debt. And, yes, the credit card debt is unsecured, and now it would be secured, and you wouldn't be able to renege on it if you needed to. You never renege on anything anyway, so it's a moot point."

Then he lost his train of thought, because the word 'moot' made him think of the dust mite he had been chasing out of my belly button during our nap. He likes sharing. I don't mind a little symbiosis with the creatures I live with myself, sometimes, as long as they are dust mites and not fleas. The thought of dust mites got him thinking of dust in the sunlight, so he had to go chase some. Can you tell whose cat he is?

You know the old saw about curiosity killing the cat? Sammy claims that may be true for humans, but it is certainly not true for cats. Otherwise, how would they find the empty can with the last little bit of tuna juice or the leftover mouse George Double-Yah buried or the butter some irresponsible daughter left out on the counter? They'd die of boredom from being hand-fed yucky cat food all day. That stuff's the equivalent of rabbit food for humans. No gustatory pleasure at all. Now a big juicy steak...

But I digress. Sammy says I should take a look at Erin's cat, George W. "Now there's a cat that never lets curiosity get the better of her, and look how fat and lazy she is—big black blob."

You'll have to excuse Sammy's manners. He gets a little rude when it comes to George W. Don't we all. Good lord, I'm glad the reign of Bush-isms is over! Sammy's personal favourite: 'I know how hard it is for you to put food on your family.' Or one of my mine: 'You teach a child to read, and he or her will be able to pass a literacy test.'

What a name to stick on a cat! You can blame that one on Pierce, Erin's fiancé. We do. Another good Bush-ism: 'Do you have blacks, too?' to Brazilian President Fernando Cardoso. How appropriate Erin's George Double-Yah is black. Pierce got that part right. Poor little kitten didn't stand a chance. She had such a lousy start during her formative years with Pierce and his clingy kids around, and now she's got the personality to match. She's spoiled, demanding, infantile, aggressive, and self-absorbed. Whereas Sammy is voluptuous, warm, independent, loving, and noble. Like me.

So to end this Chapter: 'In conclusivity, never misunderestimate my self-control of me.' The comics are going to miss that man after eight long years. Did you hear about the letter Bush left for Obama when he left the Oval Office? This is how it read: 'X'.

Chapter Two: Womanizer, Womanizer, Baby You're a Womanizer

(Now who sang that song???? Oh yeah—BRIT!)
If you are wondering how all this came up, I was lamenting to Sammy that if you don't write, I'll never learn the name of the blonde who came looking for you at closing time, or why you always seem to have your hand on some blonde's back or arm. Or ass.

Oh yeah again—the boyfriend of the blond singer with the tattoos you flung your arm around at the bar? He scolded me for taking the piss. He told me in no uncertain terms you are one of the nice guys, the decent ones. He seemed a bit offended that I would create an awkward moment, tease an innocent like you about a threesome, just because you draped yourself over his girlfriend. (Hey, I didn't know what else to say! I'm socially backward. Even at skanky bars) Or...oh ooh, maybe it had nothing to do with me. Maybe he was trying to remind himself you are one of the nice guys so he wouldn't start thinking he should punch your lights out. Guys are nothing if not territorial. Kind of funny he said it to me of all people, because if anyone knows how decent you can be—when you want to—it's me.

I'm still curious about the blonde thing. The singer, the girl at closing time, and Barbie Doll—ooops I mean Becky, Saturday night. All blondes and what else...let me think...they all had bare arms. Hmmm...maybe you like the feel of fair, freckle-less skin. I'll have to ask Tommy if he recognized the closing time girl. That conversation should go well.

The singer's boyfriend. The guy in the suede coat. What is it about you? They say men can sniff out the competition, like a coyote. Could it be your scent that gets you in so much trouble? It is rather a pungent mix of testosterone, male sweat and dirty socks by the end of a gig. Lovely.

Chapter Three: My Happy Ending

Of course, instead of writing to you, I could simplify things from now on and say, "I knew him when"...Hey, I like it! "A simple choice is a happy choice." A direct quote from Sammy.

So I think I'll buy a mobile home, move it to the lot and give us all a summer enclave by the beach; me, my three kids and my step-grandkids. But then, who takes financial advice from a cat, anyhow?

Chapter Four:

Now you can write your own happy ending. Or beginning. I'll help you with a title if you need me to. You can even talk this time.

Unhappy Endings

Emily thought she had buried all the anger, but not quite. If anger can burn slowly, Emily's had been simmering a long time, and if tempers can boil over, the lid was just barely holding hers down. She calmed down enough to give this failed communication with a former fellow student one more shot, the old college try.

To: Luke
Sent: December 21, 2006 9:15 am
Subject: ?
Hi

Could you answer a couple of civilized questions for me? They don't have anything to do with me. I promise I'll never ask you another question as long as I live—maybe.

Do you like kids generally or just your own?

Who was the girl who was looking for you at the end of the night? I figure with me and Tommy's eye witness accounts you must have figured it out by now. What did she want from you that she would hang around waiting and make her friend/boyfriend (?) in the suede jacket wait, too? What did you have that she wanted? Drugs, porn, pirated music—what were you selling? Me and Tommy did a lot of detecting and we're still stumped.

The way I see it, you should answer this one for me. She started all that last run of writing and it was hard work. So could you give in a little? For once?

E

    To: Emily

Sent: December 21, 2006 10:01 am

Subject: Re: ?

Yes, I like kids. Otherwise I wouldn't have had one of my own. I like to talk to all Liam's little friends at the daycare.

Hate to tell you, but I have no idea who she was. Never did track her down. I never thought anything of it.

What difference does any of that make?

To: Luke

Sent: December 21, 2006 10:03 am

Subject: Re: ?

Thanks. Did my taking the piss and teasing you in your ~~Christmas~~ Story bother you, or did you find it funny? If I never ask, I'll never know.

Believe it or not, I try not to judge. But I know I haven't done much of a job on that.

To: Emily

Sent: December 21, 11:01 am

Subject: Re: ?

You try not to judge??? What would you call it when you were asking me why I was always touching blondes? (or something like that)

To answer your *third* question, I didn't let it bother me, but I don't think you were teasing. I already told you I can't do this anymore. Emily, you have to stop.

To: Luke

Sent: December 21, 11:13 am

Subject: Re: ?

Of course I judge people—everyone does—but not about fooling around. And I judge you least of all. I thought you would have got that by now. This is me you're talking to. Emily.

Sorry.

E

To: Luke
Sent: December 21, 2006 11:03 am
Subject: Re: ?
Thanks for answering about kids. Not exactly what I was getting at, but...

E

To: Luke
Sent: December 21, 2006 11:11 am
Subject: Re: ?
Are you there? Luke?

˙·.¸.·´¯`·.¸.·´¯`·...¸><((((º

'Twas a few nights before Christmas, December 23rd to be exact, and Emily couldn't stop tossing and turning, so she called on her friend Chris. Luke might be gone again, but Chris was still hanging around, and Emily knew he didn't like anyone to be sad at Christmas:

Emily: Hey, Chris, I just fell off the stool and broke the light shade.
Chris: Ow. Did you get hurt?
Em: Yup.
Chris: Where?

227

Em: Thumb, elbow, hip, both knees, foot and three toes.

Chris: Your bad foot?

Em: No, my good one. Good thing I didn't puck my head.

Chris: What's that mean: puck your head?

Em: Oh, it's a North Shore expression. Means pretty much what it sounds like.

Chris: Did you pick up any glass splinters with your foot this time?

Em: Nope. For once.

Chris: Any bruises show up yet?

Em: It just happened. But yeah, I got one on my knee. Lovely. It goes from indigo blue to puce to moss green to deep purple. Very artistic, as bruises go.

Chris: What happened to the stool?

Em: Oh, the stool's OK.

Chris: No, I mean, how come you fell off it?

Em: It's a little vanity stool with gold balls on the feet, and I guess they slipped on the tile. Usually Erin is with me if I get up on it. No one home today, though. I'm lucky I wasn't changing the light fixture at the top of the stairs. I don't think I'll climb up on that stool again.

Chris: Are you crying?

Emily: Of course not. Who do you think I am—a big baby? It's only a few bruises. It knocked the wind out of me, that's all.

Chris: Cheer up, kid. Good news is a-comin'.

Emily: You mean Jesus' birth?

Chris: No. Well, that's good news for the Christians. Not so good for the Jews. But no, I mean something else.

Emily: What is it, Chris?

Chris: I can't tell you or it wouldn't be coming; it would already be here.

Emily: So you won't tell me something to cheer me up or make me laugh, either? You're worse than that man or Erin. Can you at least tell me what it's about?

Chris: ME!!

Emily: Gee, I think I can wait.

Chris: I can't believe that. You were never very patient.

Emily: I got good at waiting. Thanks to that man.

Chris: You didn't like him much this fall, did you?

Emily: No. There was a time I didn't think I could even manage to like his chubby little privileged kid. But when I met Liam at Tommy's at Thanksgiving, we had a little chat and talked about honey bees and his old dinkie toys. I could see he was a sweet innocent little boy, just like sweet innocent little boys all over the world, privileged or poor. I decided I could like him well enough, even if his father is a big ass...

Chris: Hush now. You promised you wouldn't call him names again.

Emily: But that was quite a while ago.

Chris: Still. A promise is a promise.

Emily: You're talking to a good one here, Chris. You know how many promises I've made to myself and how much trouble I've had keeping any of them. Promises made, promises broken.

Chris: Emily, I think most promises fall into the category of wishful thinking. You only ever made one promise that counts and you've kept that one.

Emily: Oh, yeah. I forgot. Fuck.

Chris: Here—I'll remind you. To be a memory keeper, for me and for Kate and Tessa and all the friends you've lost. Not so bad. Why don't you stop thinking about what's been lost for a change and focus on what you will have this Christmas—one daughter at home, two little kids, and a play-dough-spaghetti Christmas dinner, brought to you by Maddie.

Emily: I love her already. Speaking of kids who aren't of our own blood, I asked that man if he loves kids generally, or if his love is all reserved for his own.

Chris: What difference does that make?

Emily: When I visit Mexico, I see people so engaged with kids, like one big extended family, whether they are related or not. Here in Canada, I often meet parents who seem to think of their children as extensions of their own egos and are mostly interested in them for their achievements. Ergo, only their own kids count. I'd like to think he is the other kind, the type of man who has room for all kids in his heart of hearts.

Chris: Like—'Jesus loves the little children, all the little children of the world'?

Emily: Yeah, like that.

Chris: Searching for his one redeeming quality, were you? The way you and Kate used to do?

Emily: Or trying to elevate our late night on-line conversation and reclaim some self-respect for ever getting attached to a married father in the first place.

Chris: Kate would approve.

Emily: Kate always liked to keep conversations on a higher plain, even before she moved there herself.

Anyhow, he never answered, or not in a way I can make sense of. I guess I can add it to the long list of things I'll never know about this unfulfilled passion of mine.

One good thing about waiting all that time: any curiosity I had about sex will be long gone.

Chris: You are quite curious about him and sex, for an old lady who doesn't care anymore.

Emily: I could write a funny story about a jealous old lady and a young, stud muffin musician. Oh yeah, I forgot—I already made one up and sent it to him for Christmas. I gave him permission to write his own version, but I would be very, very surprised if he ever does.

Another thing about my Mexico trip. As I waited in the Mexico City airport for my midnight flight, I watched a Mexican father twirl his two-year-old in the air and entertain him so his pregnant mom could get a break. Or, much more likely—because Dad just wanted to. Then he took the kid off to the men's room for a diaper change. The two-year-old was delighted, of course.

I want him to be that kind of dad, a good dad for Liam. And he can't be that if he keeps running the roads all hours of the night and touching women in bars—with his hands *or* his songs.

Chris: Was that what all the bullshit about blondes and backs and bare skin was about?

Emily: So you read 'Luke's ~~Christmas~~ Story' did you?

Chris: Yeah.

Emily: Did you think it was funny?

Chris: In places.

Emily: Only places?

Chris: I liked the part about the cats. But you need to quit picking on blondes.

Tell me something. In an affair, there really are more than two people in the bed? I never lived long enough to experience affairs. They sound like fun. Especially if we're all blonde.

Emily: Simmer down, Chris. It's more like two in the bed, one in the head, and none of them end up happy.

One good thing—only one of the books I read over the holidays was about affairs. Over the last two years, I've read books and watched tons of movies about affairs, and the clandestine relationship always implodes by the ending.

Chris: Do you think the Universe is trying to tell you something?

Emily: Ha ha. Very funny. I apparently picked the wrong affair. I think I can hear the Universe screaming, 'Pick me. Pick ME, instead!' An affair with the Universe. Isn't that what we are all supposed to have? It would be more fun than what I didn't have with that man.

It's funny, no one ever hears about the affairs that work. You know why, Chris?

Chris: Why?

Emily: Because the happy people keep it quiet, protect it from the world; let it be their secret place, only for the two of them. No one else allowed.

Chris: One time when I was eavesdropping on a conference, I heard one of the earth therapists say, 'You can tell how sick a family is by the secrets it keeps.'

Emily: Another platitude.

Chris: A platitude—is that like bullshit?

Emily: Yeah. Chris, we don't say 'bullshit' much anymore, either. You're dating yourself. Now, instead of bullshit, we say 'fucked' or 'fucked up', and instead of bull-shitter, we say 'fucker' or 'asshole' or 'motherfucker' or 'mofo' or countless other insulting names. We're good at them.

Chris: It sounds like 'fuck' is getting overworked.

Emily: Ask George Carlin.

Chris: Who?

Emily: Forget it.

I took the shortcut through the People's Cemetery the other day. Remember the promise I made you? About the roses? Pretty bad when you have to steal the lines of a song for a graveside promise, eh? Do you think the Stones would have minded?

Chris: Naah. Not at all. 'And I won't forget to put roses on your grave.' A lot of people steal those lines now when they bury their dead. I think Mick Jagger and the boys like it that way.

Emily: I guess stealing lyrics isn't as bad as stealing husbands.

Chris: Not in the same league at all.

Emily: You know why I never kept the promise I made to you? Because for years I couldn't find your grave, not till after Kate died. I had the roses, but nothing else. You left no forwarding address or much of anything behind.

I just thought of something. I should Google you! Check you out online.

Chris: You can look up dead people on the internet? Wow.

Emily: And lots of other stuff, too.

Chris: So what does that man think about the fact that he won't ever get to have sex with you, either?

Emily: He seems to be fine with it. I can't for the life of me imagine why!

Chris: Me, neither. Remember the first night when I took you up to my bed in the attic of my friend Samantha's beauty shop? I wouldn't have missed it for the world.

Emily: Rafters, candles, and all. Thank heaven it was summer. It would have been some cold in December.

One other night, you drove me home and we tipped the Davenport over and spilt hot candle wax all over it. And you snuck the bike four blocks away before you started it up, so you wouldn't wake the neighbours. Mom woke up anyway, and wanted to know who was rattling around downstairs.

Chris: I remember us whispering, as I tried to sneak out the door and pretend I wasn't there.

Emily: I got in trouble for that one. Mom didn't notice, but I never could figure out how to get all the wax out, so I kept it as a souvenir of you. Whenever I missed you, I would find the spot, touch the waxy cover over the rough old weave, imagine touching the smoothness of your skin again. I wonder whatever became of that old brown Davenport. Maybe Mom left it on the Island when she moved to Halifax. Or maybe we threw it out when it got too ratty.

Chris: I don't remember the Davenport, but I do remember how warm you felt. See, that's what I mean—I wouldn't have missed it for the world.

Emily: Giggle. We were some compatible, weren't we?

Chris: We sure were.

A few minutes later:

Emily: CHRIS!! GET YOUR HEAD OUT OF THE CLOUDS!!

Chris: Oh, is that where I am?

Emily: I have a civilized question I wanna ask you. You were happy the summer you lived in Samantha's attic, weren't you, Chris?

Chris: Yeah.

Emily: Yeah, me too. Till I realized how stubborn you are.

Chris: Me, stubborn?! You're the stubborn one.

Emily: Aw, never mind, Chris, I'm too tired to argue. Besides, no one is as stubborn as that man, once he digs his heels in.
You know what I wish? I wish I had something to remind me of the greatest Affair That Never Was. A little souvenir. Remember those little plastic rings from the Cracker Jack box, and how lucky you felt if you found one in the bottom of the box in amongst the popcorn and peanut skins and left over flakes of caramel? I want one of those. If that man couldn't find one with a ring in it, a Cracker Jack box itself would do.

Chris: How about a pop can ring? I hear you finally got canned pop on PEI. Thirty years after Ontario.

Emily: I hate canned pop. And pop cans.

Chris: Are you OK? You look like you're crying. Do you hate canned pop that much?

Emily: God, you're a Nosy Parker. I'm not crying, but I am tired and I'm going to sleep now, Chris.

Chris: Sweet dreams.

Little Boys Can Break Your Heart

But Chris wasn't done with Emily yet. The next night as the moon breeched the horizon, he poked her in the nose to get her attention. For some reason, he loved to watch her cry. Maybe because she never cried over him when he was alive:

Emily: Chris, I just punched myself in the nose.

Chris: How did you do that?

Emily: I was pulling the blanket up around me, and it got stuck, and my fist flew up and punched me in the nose. Ow! My eyes are red from crying over that stupid movie. Now my nose is red, too.

Chris: What movie?

Em: You know the one. Weren't you watching me at the time?

Chris: Was it a good cry?

Emily: You men are so nosy about crying. I hate it when people watch me cry. Why don't you try crying for yourself sometime, see what it feels like?

Chris: Why so glum, Chum?

Emily: I don't want to go into it. Some days I'm just not as hopeful about the home front. And now, I'm reading a book called *What is the What* about the Lost Boys of Sudan, and it's incredibly sad. Little boys caught up in a horrible civil war, blood and murder all around them in their tiny villages, walking for days in the blistering sun, and for those few who survive, ending up in an overcrowded refugee camp on a barren piece of land no one else wants. Kids no older than the Grade Three class I taught last week.

Chris: What's behind the conflict?

Em: Oil. But it could as easily be diamonds or gold or slavery. In a word: greed.

Chris: What's 'greed'?

Em: It means someone takes something that isn't his to take.

Chris: Oh yeah, greed. I forgot. Is that what you wanted to do the last couple of years—take someone who isn't yours?

Emily: No. No one can own someone else—at least not in Canada—so no, no one owns Luke, and that's not what I was doing.

234

Oh fuck, Chris, I don't know. Guilty as charged, I guess.

Anyway, the greed in this book is about the rich and powerful taking from those who have so little.

Chris: So, if they don't have much, what is there for the powerful people to take?

Em: The country's resources, which might help the people out. But no one calls it 'greed' any more. The word 'greed' is now passé. They use words like 'globalization', or 'securing the energy supply', or 'geo politics', or 'international development via the International Monetary Fund'.

Chris: Man! Sounds complicated! I'm glad I don't have to think about those great big long words. You better hurry up and finish the book before Christmas. Why are you reading it at this time of year?

Em: Because Bethany sent it home to me last spring and I told her I'd talk to her about it next time she calls. The author who helped the refugee write his story is Dave Eggers, one of her favourites.

Chris: So, this is based on a true story?

Emily: Right, and it's hard to believe one little boy could endure so much. It makes Jesus' life look like a cakewalk. My life even more so. The world is so cruel. Rwanda, Darfur, Southern Sudan—the massacres and genocides are as bad as any in the Second World War. The only difference is the deaths came more quickly—head lopped off by a machete, bullet in the back of a fleeing child, or, unfortunately for some, a slower death of starvation in some godforsaken desert. And the dead are black, not Jewish. No one cares, Chris. And I don't understand. Poor old Romeo Dallaire cried out to the world, and no one listened.

Chris: I know, Emily. On the bright side, it must make you feel better about your life.

Em: Knowing other people's lives are shittier than mine doesn't often cheer me up. It's more likely to make me feel worse and remind me of what a sad old world we live in.

Chris: Why are you thinking such morbid thoughts?

Em: I don't have anyone to tell me to get over myself and shake it off. That man could, but he won't. And Bethany and Christina told me they aren't coming home for at least another year. They say they can't afford it. I try to tell them they don't know what they are missing, especially in the summer.

235

Chris: Erin can't cheer you up, either?

Em: No, not this year. She's too preoccupied with the step-kids and her fiancé's international court battles.

Lots of people get a little sad at Christmas, you know.

Chris: I find that hard to believe. We celebrate like crazy up here. My sisters and I always had a ball with our parents when we were kids and got hopelessly spoiled. Christmas at our house was the best.

Emily: Not anymore. Not since you died. Things got even worse for your parents when Jana died.

Chris: Oh.

Em: How is Jana?

Chris: She's wonderful, and still full of wonder. She hasn't been here that long, so the novelty hasn't worn off. Lately, we've been talking about our childhood Christmases and how Mom and Dad spoiled us. It feels so right to keep her close to me now. She and Tessa talk Baha'i talk a lot. Talking religion is like a parlour game here, something we do for fun and to pass away a Saturday night.

Emily: Comparative Religion for the Young and Reckless. Wow, you guys sure know how to have a good time.

Chris: We're not allowed drinking and fighting, so we do the best we can.

Em: Tessa would have liked this Eggers book. But she would have cried.

Chris: You too? Your eyes are red.

Emily: That's from punching myself in the nose. Go away, Chris.

Big Boys Even More So

Luke told the girl to meet him in the alleyway after he finished packing the van. The boys had gone off to catch the Golden Star before it closed at 3 am. Luke wasn't hungry, not for Chinese food, anyway. He seldom was after a gig. Besides, she might show up if he hung around long enough.

She had a beautifully provocative way of dancing and she'd shown it to him all night long. She must be in her late teens. Barely legal. Tight little body on her. As she kept dancing around him, darting in front of his mike, twirling away from him, he entertained himself with images of what it would be like to grab her long blonde hair and take her caveman style into the back room. Distracting. In a good way.

She came running down the alley to him. Luke pushed her up against the brick wall of the nightclub. She was laughing at him, and he couldn't handle that. He wanted her to take him seriously, whatever her name was. So he pressed harder and moved faster, until he had her where he wanted her— breathless under his fingers. He could taste her so bad. So he slid his fingers inside her, dipped deep, and came up with juices to lick off. Young and sweet like honey. Then he shared the taste of her with her, slipped his fingers into her warm soft mouth. Shared her honey pot with her.

Too cold to do any more in an alleyway, though. He had rented a room in Halifax which gave him the privacy he craved, a room he used to write his songs in peace, a room his band mates and family knew nothing about. He'd have to try out a different kind of piece in his secret room tonight.

She pulled away, blew on her fingers for a sec, stuck them in her mitts, said, "Slow down."

"Relax, why don't ya? I'd like to teach you to relax."

"Well, I'd like to teach you to slow down. It's too friggin' cold out."

"Let me take you somewhere warm."

"I need to go home. My mom will be wondering if I don't get home by three. She's likely to send out a posse after me."

'Her Mom?' Luke thought, 'She still lives with her mom? How old is she, anyway? Man, she should be more careful where she hangs out at 3 am.' Then he said, "Oh, for fuck's sake, get in the van, and I'll run you home." So much for that. His nuts were freezing, anyhow. The night air was cold enough to freeze the balls off a brass monkey. As he tucked her into the back of the van with the gear, he thought he should maybe ask her name.

Krissy. Her name was Krissy.

Luke forgot for one night he had a son named Liam, whose only knowledge of honey pots came from Winnie the Pooh. Forgot he had a friend named Emily, too.

When Trudy stopped in to see Emily on Valentine's Day, she mentioned a compromise that might control Emily's reoccurring yen to talk to Luke. What if Emily wrote to Luke but only when she wrote in her journal; turned him into her Journal Man. Then she wouldn't have to send her thoughts to him, as everyone knows journals are private. Since he was the one she talked to in her head who motivated her to do her best thinking and writing, it should work.

Emily tore into her Valentine's treat from Trudy and found a gold-embossed diary and a shiny pen to match. Trudy reminded Emily no-one ever said she had to share everything with Luke, not Chris, not Trudy's sister Tessa, not Kate, and the Higher Power, least of all. She could even store her conversations with Tessa in her new journal if she wanted to.

So Emily set herself up with all the shimmery gold and waited for the happy thoughts to flow. It was winter on PEI. What more can we say?

Emily did discover she didn't need Luke to write anymore, just a pretty pen and journal and a wonderful friend named Trudy. Trudy's illness had drawn them closer. Emily had lots of experience with cancer and made herself available for Trudy, as she had for Tessa. And she still had her dead friends when she needed company in the middle of the night:

Emily: Chris, I never told you everything about the ill-fated trip to Ottawa. Not when you were living, anyway. Did God?
Chris: He did. But go ahead and tell me; I'd like to hear your version, too.

238

Em: Remember the first night I thought I would do something nice for you, your biker roommates, and your sophisticated sister? So I cooked a traditional chicken dinner with PEI potatoes. You sulked because I didn't make gravy.

Chris: I couldn't help it! I like gravy! But He made me do an extra big penance for that one before He would let me in here.

Em: Yeah right. You left me with your So Called Best Friend, while you went to buy drugs or sell drugs or something.

Chris: I didn't know, Em. I'm so sorry. I didn't learn about what happened that night until I got up here. You were always so street smart, I assumed you could take care of yourself or I wouldn't have left you behind.

Emily: I didn't think I was too street smart with his body crushing down on me. I wish I had fought harder.

Chris: It would have gone a lot worse for you if you handled it any other way. You kept yourself safe from his violent streak. And he still would have taken what he wanted.

Emily: The next day, when I decided I better boot my ass out of your house if I wanted to save it, you got him to drive me and my luggage to my friend's place in his ugly old Chevy half ton because you didn't own a car at the time, only your motorbike. Me, the monkey in the middle. Him, smirking away with a disgusting gleeful expression on his face, once he figured out he was about to have you to himself again. I wish you'd smacked him. You couldn't tell he was gloating?

Chris: Not for one minute did I think him capable of hurting you. I thought he understood what would happen if he ever touched you. If I had known...

Em: He knew I would never tell you. He counted on it. I can't believe you didn't sense something was off. How could you not know?

Chris: Maybe I felt too frustrated with you to notice him. I didn't want you to see me in Ottawa.

Em: Why not?

Chris: I was afraid you'd be disillusioned. Things always went better for me on the Island.

Emily: You are so right. Didn't mean I didn't still love you though, in spite of what I said in the letter I left you on the couch where we slept. I can still feel you, squished up behind me, your smooth lean arms around me, only because they had no place else to go. We weren't very happy with each other that night.

239

I left my friend's the morning after you dropped me off and took a cab out to the airport. The city felt so peaceful and quiet in the dawn light. I love a city at that time of day. I can still picture the street sweepers surrounded by the swirling dust in the early morning light. The street sweepers, the paperboys and me. I was glad to be going home.

Chris: I should have been more careful with your life.

Emily: I had fun on the Kawi that time you forgot to bolt down the seat, even when my arse flew off the bike. But yeah, in the big city you should have been more careful. With your own life, too.

Chris: I wasn't very smart then. I thought I was, but no, I wasn't.

Emily: I always thought you were smart.

Your So Called Best Friend lives on the Island now.

Chris: The word here is he still struggles with life.

Emily: How terrible for him when you went under after you dove onto the hidden rocks, and he tried to pull you out, and no one would help him.

Chris: I'm impressed you can feel some sympathy for him, after what he did.

Em: I would never have wanted to go through what he did—trying to haul you out of the lake and screaming for someone to help. To rescue you and watch you die anyway. I didn't even hear about your accident until three days after he tried to save you.

Chris: How could you? I was in an Ottawa hospital, eight hundred miles away. And I didn't last that long. The broken back would have been impossible for me to live with so, in a way, I was lucky I couldn't fight off the water in my lungs.

Emily: Why was it different when Steve died? I was partying with some friends and at 3 a.m. I sensed he was gone, and he lived all the way out in British Columbia at the time.

Chris: Steve needed to feel your presence around him when he perished from the carbon monoxide poisoning. I had my family with me. Steve had no one, all alone on a mountain top.

Emily: For a long time, Chris, I missed your scent and wished I could get it back, the way my body remembered yours when you would come back home and hold me. They claim some people can smell the scent of the one they loved, even after they have passed on to the next world.

Chris: Someday it might happen for you.

Em: Maybe. That would be lovely.

It's funny, you always acted so calm and in control, most people had no idea you did speed. The ultimate cool man. But you blew through your life so fast. Didn't even make it to twenty-five.

Chris: I never promised you I would stick around till then, just that I knew I wouldn't make it *past* twenty-five. You can't accuse me of lying.

Emily: Still, the way I do the math, you cheated me out of two years.

Chris needed to take a few minutes to do the math himself.

Chris: Guess you're right. Otherwise, how'd your day go?

Em: On the way into the hair salon, I gave a panhandler some change. I told him to feed himself. When I came out, he stood up and rewarded me with a big wide smile. So I gave him a big wide one back. And a toonie.

Chris: Bet you made his day.

Em: Well, I did just come from the hairdresser's...

Chris: Oh, well then, for sure you did.

So, you're OK?

Em: Yeah, I'm OK.

Chris: These things are hard to talk about.

Em: Tell me about it. Even twenty some years later.

Chris: Sorry Em, but I gotta go. God's having another one of those family meetings.

Emily: Like the ones Christina always hated?

Chris: A bit like them. Only here we never discuss anything serious. I'll have to wait to send you your gift, OK? God thinks it's too soon; you're not ready.

Em: What would God know? But OK.

Siobhan

Siobhan put Liam down and picked up the phone. "Siobhan you have to do it. You have to go."

"Oh come on, Mom. Someone else must be able to. Why me?"

"You know why. Your dad and I have to work."

"And I need to take care of Liam. Why don't you send Chad?"

"He can't miss school."

"Why not? He could take his laptop with him and work from the hospital. It wouldn't kill him to miss a few days."

"He doesn't like hospitals. He's no good with Granny. It's going to be longer than a few days, so he can't go."

"Oh great. That makes it so much better. How long will it be, anyway?"

"I don't know. Longer than a few days. What's more, you're terrific with Granny."

"I can't, Mom. Luke's always on the road and I can't..."

"Quit your whining. You're finished university, you're laid off for the winter, you're available, you're family, and you're going."

"What am I supposed to do with Liam?"

"It wouldn't hurt Luke to spend time with his own kid."

"Mom! He has to play."

"Sometimes I think all he does is play."

"It's his living, Mother."

"Let Luke's family take a turn babysitting; wouldn't be before time. Granny likes you. She likes your company."

"But I don't have one sweet clue about nursing. In fact, I'd be a terrible nurse. I can't even wipe up Liam's spit-up without gagging."

"You don't have to clean up. That's why they have staff. All you need to do is be there and keep her company. You don't have to stay all day, only for visiting hours."

"Oh yeah, visiting hours. Nine till nine with an hour off for lunch. Whoopee."

"Siobhan, you're going. No more arguing."

Siobhan took the bus to Halifax, located the key for Granny's big old house in the mailbox, and dumped her backpack in the front hall. The house felt cold, so she cranked up the heat and began the inspection of every room, checking in the closets and under the beds. She hated checking the bathrooms, especially the bathtub. So she ripped the shower curtain back, like tearing off a band-aid. No one lurking inside. What a relief.

She picked the pink room for herself this time. Granny always offered her this bedroom when she came to visit. Thanks to Siobhan, the room was now pink. Pink everywhere. Chad never stopped griping about the bopper decor when his turn came to visit and Granny insisted he sleep there. By her late teens, Siobhan minded all the frills and variations on the pink theme, but now she kind of liked it, again.

She grabbed a quick shower, dressed in her Saturday clothes, locked the house, and hopped on a bus to the Queen Elizabeth II Hospital. Siobhan had only visited there once before, when she was staying with Granny and Grampy on her school vacation and Granny took a gall bladder attack.

Siobhan found Granny in room 402. She appeared to be well enough when Siobhan first spotted her in the back left-hand corner of the ward. She smiled and said, "Siobhan! It's so good to see you, dear. You're so sweet to offer to come and mind the house and keep me company. Now that Grampy's no longer around, I could use a little help."

"No problem, Granny, I couldn't wait to get here. How are you feeling?"

"Not too bad, dear. The nurses take pretty good care of me."

"Do you have much pain, Granny?"

"No, not much, dear. They put me on pain killers."

"What are you on?"

"I'm not sure, Siobhan. I can't quite remember the name."

"Advil?"

"No, it's stronger than that."

"Percocet? OxyContin?"

"No, that doesn't sound right."

"Dilaudid?"

243

"No. My, Siobhan, you know a lot about painkillers. Where did you ever come by all that knowledge? You could work at the pharmacy."

"Not really, Gran. Is it morphine?"

"Yes. morphine. That's what the nurse called it."

Siobhan made a note to check with her mother. As far as she knew, morphine is what they gave when you aren't going to get better.

A couple of days later, she talked to her nurse about Granny's cancer. The nurse wouldn't tell her much, said she should talk to the doctor when he came to visit her granny. She explained to Siobhan, since Mary was still well enough to understand her own diagnosis, the doctor would only share with her what her granny wanted her to know. Siobhan decided she might as well get the facts from Granny. Simpler.

Granny was sleeping when she got back to the ward, so she waited and played with her iPhone. She had lots of messages from her friends, family, and Luke, wondering how much longer she would be stuck in Halifax. Granny slept and slept.

Granny's supper tray arrived, so Siobhan woke her to see if she would try to eat. Her granny squinted up at her, a little confused, and said, "Is that you, Monica?"

"No, Granny, it's me, Siobhan."

"Oh. Is Monica coming soon?"

"No, Gran, Mom's still in Cape Breton."

"Oh. So far away." Granny sighed.

"She'll be here as soon as she can get away, Granny."

"When, dear?"

"I don't know."

"You should tell her to come. Soon."

All of a sudden, Siobhan didn't want to know anymore. She didn't want to ask, even though she had waited all day for Granny, or the doctor, or the nurse, or someone to tell her. Luckily, Granny had a better story in mind.

Emily's Favour

Tommy gave Emily a call and asked for a favour. Luke was coming over to play on the Island on the weekend, and he needed a babysitter for Liam. Siobhan had gone to Halifax to care for her granny, and no one else in Luke's family was available, since his parents made like the snowbirds and flew south this time of year. But Tommy forgot about his buddy's stag party that was taking place on the same Saturday he offered to help out with Liam. Tommy figured Liam would be fine with her for the night, since he had taken to her the first time they met. In many ways, Emily found Tommy the better brother and she didn't want Tommy to miss the party, so she agreed.

Well, Liam wasn't fine. He 'made strange', got scratched by the cat after he pulled Sammy's tail, and whacked Maddie on the arm when she wouldn't do what he wanted. He couldn't settle on any one thing when what he really wanted was his dad or his mom. Around midnight, Emily convinced him to go to sleep by singing lullabies she didn't realize she remembered. Musical recall was a wonderful thing and a life saver, by times.

Luke had a great night. Nothing to worry about, now that Liam was in good hands. So was he. The hands belonged to a fine Jamaican woman who had moved to PEI to make a good life for herself. She crafted beautiful jewellery for a living, and slipped a pendant into his hand as he stepped off the stage. He tucked it away in his pocket, without looking. He hoped she had given him a man pendant, at least.

She agreed to meet him at Tommy's after he dropped the boys in the band off at the hotel. He hadn't exactly planned to go to bed with her, just thought he'd get to know her better, try a little taste of something more exotic. He craved variety late at night when the rest of the guys seemed to be satisfied with beer and Chinese food. And that Stones' song the band covered wouldn't stop running through his head: 'Brown Sugar, how come you taste so good, Brown Sugar, just like a black girl should.' A little bitty taste of Brown Sugar held more appeal than the Canton's eggrolls for Luke. If it was good enough for Mick Jagger, it was good enough for him. Tommy didn't come home from the stag that night which left his bed free, and one thing led to another, and well, you know how these things go.

Emily burst through the door early the next morning, calling desperately for Tommy, one wailing kid in her arms. She dropped Liam on the floor, barged right into Tommy's bedroom and said, "Oh."

Luke scrambled for his clothes and called, "Emily!", as she backed out of the house. He chased her down Tommy's driveway. "Emily, come back! I'll take care of it! I promise I will."

Emily was the last person he would want to find him in bed with another woman. The shame crept up his body from the tips of his toes. As he scooped up his crying boy and tossed her clothes to the Jamaican girl, he wondered why it mattered so much—why Emily's opinion mattered most of all.

Chris' Gift

Emily didn't want to talk to Luke ever again and she didn't want to talk about him, either. She had been busy minding Maddie and Clair at the trailer, as Erin had flown away, once again, to Japan to tend to that feckless, luckless fiancé of hers. Pierce's promise of financial support for Erin and the kids was quickly being sucked up by lawyers, international flights, and his ex's alimony.

Emily missed the creature comforts of the cottage, especially her big tub, and felt like she was on the edge of exhaustion from working at the university, caring for two young kids, and then, to top it off, her late night with Liam. She needed some good news. She sang out an "Alleluia" when Chris showed up late one night to talk about her gift:

Chris: How'd you like the good news?

Emily: Loved it! You couldn't have given me anything better!

Chris: Yeah, well, I'm kind of a stand-up, generous, awesome guy.

Emily: You're OK. But meeting up with Shane was amazing!

Chris: My old friend Shane.

Em: Yeah, and now he's a professional courier company owner and operator. He's all grown up and everything.

Chris: You almost missed your present, you silly fool.

Emily: Good thing I had to call Erin at work about the parcel as he stood in the sun-porch waiting for me to sign, so I had another minute to notice his eyes and mouth and teeth and think about why he looked familiar...

Chris: His hand was on the doorknob before you clued in. Lucky I nudged you and made you speak up, or he would have been long gone down the lane. A little late then, I'd say.

Emily: Thanks to that nudge, which by the way, was more like a hammer on a gong inside my head, I spoke up and asked him if we had ever met. Even better—guess what he said?

Chris:...And of course, once you said your name, he said you haven't changed a bit. 'You look the same as you did the last time I saw you.'

Em: How would you know?

Chris: Why wouldn't I? I made up this present for you.

Emily: You even arranged the nice compliment? At least I took it as a compliment, given I haven't seen him since I was a lot younger. I loved that part of the present best.

Chris: You would. You always were so vain.

Em: Yeah, yeah. You're so vain, too, and I bet you think this story is about you. Guess what? It is. The story of me and Shane talking about you in your absence. After all these years, we got to say so many things we both needed to say, so many things we needed to ask each other. Plus, catch up on our own lives and families and people we used to know, or know in common. You remember Ian Brewer?

Chris: Yes, of course.

Emily: Shane lives in the same subdivision as Ian and Melanie, whose dog mated with my neighbour Fred's Border Collie and whose kid is named Christopher. Melanie and Ian's kid, I mean, not the dog's kid.

Chris: Enough about mating dogs. Let's get back to you and Shane and Christopher—me Christopher, I mean.

Emily: OK, you impatient dead person. Yes, we did talk about you a lot. And we were remembering how he set us up and how he always said you and I would have made a perfect couple. Guess what Shane said?

Chris: He said he still believes we would have.

Em: Ah, you suck! I can't surprise you at all. How come?

Chris: I'm blessed with superior knowledge of the Universe, I guess.

Emily: Lucky you. I'm sorry I didn't stay in touch with Shane.

Chris: Yeah, he's one of the good ones. But I can understand why you couldn't hang around our mutual friends after I died.

Emily: There was one for sure I didn't care to ever see again. Did I tell you the latest on your So Called Best Friend? Stop me if I did. I haven't seen him in years, but the word around the bars in town is he has been cruel to a lot of good women and has pretty much fucked up his life. Not that I'm looking for any kind of cosmic revenge.

Chris: Of course not.

Em: Chris, I think you better arrange some big redemptive adventure for your old So Called Best Friend. I know! Something like rescuing a child from drowning.

Chris: Don't you remember he already tried that?

Emily: Oh yeah. With you. And he failed. Or he thought he failed. That didn't go so well. Maybe we should try a burning building and a favourite family pet. Hey, Ian and Melanie's beloved Border Collie would do.

Chris: Em, are you sure you want Ian and Melanie to have a house fire? Just to save his wretched soul?

Emily: Your So Called Best Friend's pathetic soul. Maybe not. Someone in Ian's family could get hurt while he tried to get his shit together. Or the dog could die. Not good. OK. So we should arrange a bike accident like Apple had.

Chris: Apple who?

Em: Connolly. His real name is Adam. He's our friend and neighbour. He was riding his Harley on the All Weather Highway and ran into Mary Simpson's dog. He killed the dog but didn't crash, which he could quite easily have done, in which case he would have got killed since he was going ninety-eight kilometers an hour. Same road as the high-speed skunk chase. Mary told Erin, when she met her at the grocery store, the dog was named Apple when they picked it out at the pound. So Erin said, 'At least big Apple didn't die, just little Apple.' Not that little Apple isn't important, too. But if big Apple died, they would have to hold a long funeral, and his mom would be very sad; whereas little Apple's mother didn't even know anything about him anymore, whereabouts or anything. And if big Apple died, I would have to take pecan squares over to his mom's, because I made them when his dad died, and they all liked them. The recipe calls them 'funeral squares' for a reason.

They are all such smart people, those Connollys. Those boys can do anything when it comes to building and fix anything when it comes to buildings. Now, *there's* the fella who could teach that man carpentry if he ever decided to get out of music and do something useful for a change. Or at least help him fix up his old house. Adam. But then, if Adam had been killed, he would never be able to teach anybody anything.

Chris: Hang on, hang on. What does this have to do with my So Called Best Friend?

Emily: You could arrange it so *he* could be the one about to hit little Apple doing ninety-eight, instead of big Apple. He could be a hero and swerve to avoid the dog, and then Mary and everyone else in their house wouldn't be sad. Because little Apple wouldn't have died.

Chris: But then my Friend would wipe out and probably die.˙

Em: Not die, necessarily. Permanently crippled. So he would experience what it is like to be the victim; to feel what it's like to have his power taken from him; to trust other people to care for him even though he hasn't done a whole lot in his life to deserve their care; to rely on the kindness of strangers.

Chris: Whoa, whoa, I think you're getting carried away. Hang on before you dream up anything else, and I will take it up with the Boss. A little redemption might be in order for our boy, after all.

Emily: Your boy. Not mine. Anyway, Shane was always a better friend to you. He introduced us. Never once did he set out to hurt me.

Chris: That's true. We had a lot of fun. He was the first kid I met on our block when we moved down from Ontario. The good times rolled for me and Shane.

Em: He told me he got himself a good wife, but he lost her briefly, for a year. So he took a long hard look and did what he had to do to get her back, and they've been together over thirty years now. According to him, she is the best woman in the world. She was with him the last night I saw you. He was worried about you at the end, Chris.

Chris: I didn't mean to worry anyone. I'm afraid I got too wrapped up in the whole tough biker image.

Emily: Another thing for me to thank your So Called Best Friend for. Chris, you were so smart. Why didn't you see through the bullshit?

Chris: I did. I was just living on the edge and waiting to die. I have learned something up here that never occurred to me when I was twenty-one. Knowing your time is short can make you do some desperate shit. Especially when you are too young to have had time to build up a philosophy of life—or death—to help you deal with it.

Em: I wouldn't know. None of my other friends died that young or knew much about it ahead of time.

I told Shane about the time you told me you didn't think you would ever make it to twenty-five.

Chris: How did he take that? Did it hurt him?

Emily: I think it helped, put a piece of the puzzle together for him. I think he felt less like he should have done something more to get you out of Ottawa and away from the drugs and bike gangs. At least, I hope it gave him some peace. Talking to him certainly gave me a lot of peace of mind. I made him late for his courier route, though.

Chris: Emily, you love making people late for work, don't you?

Em: No, I don't. OK, yes I do. Sometimes. Only if it is important.

You know what, Chris? I never had any photos of you, not from your obit, or your face in a crowd, at a party, or anywhere. Your So Called Best Friend was the only one I knew who had a picture of you, and hell would freeze over before I ever asked him. I might ask Shane. He must have one he could copy for me. I might finally get that souvenir of you I've been missing all these years, since we threw out the old brown Davenport.

Chris: Ask him, Em.

Em: I just might do that. Thank you, Chris. From the bottom of my heart.

Chris: Thank *you* for remembering me. Will you thank Shane for me when you see him?

Em: Sure.

Now I'm going to watch *Shake Hands with the Devil* on the TV. It's about Romeo Dallaire and Rwanda.

Chris: Oh oh. Are you going to get all depressed about the state of the world again?

Emily: No, I think I'll be OK this time. Christmas is long over, so I won't be disappointed if there are no big miracles. I'll just be happy for the little ones. With Rwanda, at least I am familiar with what happened, as horrific as it turned out to be.

To me, Dallaire is one of Canada's finest soldiers. In the midst of chaos, the world left him with two hundred and sixty UN soldiers to protect the innocent, not enough guns to arm a hundred men, and orders from UN headquarters to do nothing. Two hundred and sixty UN peacekeepers. Thirty thousand innocents under his immediate protection. One million innocents slaughtered. You do the math, Chris.

Chris: If the numbers were that bad, what did Dallaire do to make him such a hero to you?

Em: He did the one thing, Chris. He showed up. And he stayed, even when headquarters told him to leave. He did the unthinkable for a soldier—he disobeyed orders. And he bore witness.

Chris: That's more than one thing. No wonder he's your hero. I forgot to tell you the last time we talked—victims of genocide dwell in a special place here, even more beautiful than where I live. And the sweet innocent little boys play all day.

Em: Hockey?

Chris: Hockey, soccer, basketball, marbles. Singing, dancing, painting. And the sun never sets for them. They can call it up whenever they want, make the dark clouds go away even when it rains, so the sun will make rainbows for their entertainment. It never burns their little souls, either; it just cradles them in its warmth. And, if they aren't sleepy at night, the sun creates fireworks for them: Roman Candles, Catherine Wheels, Spiders, Fish, Horse Tails, and even Time Rain.

Em: Aren't the little boys afraid of the explosives?

Chris: We took lessons from the Mexicans to get the effect exactly right so we wouldn't frighten the boys. We turned the booms and pops and whistles into mariachi music. Man, was it ever worth it! The boys usually invite us over. Some nights they want heavy metal music instead, so we change the music for them. Whatever they want. Just no war sounds.

Emily: Can I visit them when I get there?

Chris: If they invite you.

Em: Sooo, the sweet innocent little boys are OK?

Chris: They are very, very OK here.

Emily: And it is a hopeful place for them?

Chris: Very, very hopeful.

Emily: Explosives into fireworks, rocket launchers into Roman Candles, gun powder into Horse Tails, mortar shells into Time Rain, terror into Mariachi Music: thank you for telling me about this small miracle.

Chris: You're welcome, Emily.

Emily: Know what I love best about talking to you, Chris? Everything works out for the best. And little kids don't get betrayed by the adults they love. God protects the innocent.

Chris: He tries, Emily, He tries.

Emily: Can you ask Him to try for me? So Emily won't be left standing in the parking lot, holding on to one more secret while she waits for Luke to come back and fix this, take care of it like he said he would. Always waiting.

I'm some glad I never did tell him I love him.

Chris: Amen to that, Emily.

Mary

I am old now. I have no idea how it happened. It just did. Now I lie in the Queen Elizabeth II Hospital. The nurses are sweet here. They care for me and call me Mary and try not to hurt me when they move me around the bed.

I wonder about one thing. Siobhan is always here. I loved to see her when she first came, but now she should go home. She doesn't need to stay. She has a pre-schooler, and he needs his mother, and Luke needs her, too. She should be with them. So I keep telling her to go, go home. And she keeps telling me something about Monica sending her over. I tell her again, "Go. Just go."

But she doesn't go. So I study her face for a while, note all the changes in this formerly charming and delightful little girl. She has dyed the tips of her hair pink. Hah, maybe she does like the pink room after all! She also lines those lovely blue eyes with rings and rings of black pencil, like the nice East Indian lady who changes my bed for me. And she has changed her nose ring to a little silver stud. I like that better. As I watch her hunched over, chewing on the ends of her sweater, I say, "Vaughan." She peers up at me. I can see little drops on her mascara-ed eyelashes.

"Siobhan," I say, "Can I tell you a story?"

"Sure Granny." She smiles her brave little smile, the one she smiled the first time she ever smiled for me. So I say to her, "Did I ever tell you about the boy?"

Siobhan says, predictably enough, "Grampy?"

"No, dear. The boy from Cape Breton. The Indian boy."

She seems a little shocked and says, "Granny, we don't call them that now. Was he a Mi'kmaq boy?"

I don't know so I tell her so. That doesn't have anything to do with anything, so I go back to the story. "When I was a little girl I lived in Margaree Forks. You remember, luv, the place your mother took you to in the summers? The old home place? Do you remember picking strawberries in the summer with your great-granny? I did the same thing when I was a girl. Oh, they were so sweet and tasty, those tiny little berries! Not like the commercial ones. Now

254

mind you, right now I would give my eye teeth—if I had any—for a fresh berry from home, whether it be a tame one or a wild one. Did you notice they can't grow decent berries around Halifax? Not enough sun. If I'd known, I might not have agreed to retire here with your granddad.

What's that, Siobhan? You could ask your mom to bring some when she comes? Dear, they wouldn't be in season now, and by the time they are, I will be long gone out of here. I hope your mother is planning to come sooner than that. Well, good then.

So back to The Boy. There was a village close to our farm where some natives lived. What did you say? Oh. The Indian type native, not the 'I was born here' native. I know, it is funny how they do that in Cape Breton—use the same word for both. It can get downright confusing by times. I remember one time a neighbour of mine said she applied for a home loan under the Native Housing Program, and I said, 'Do you have native blood in ya?' Silly fool said, 'Oh no, dear, I'm just from here.' Anyway, that has nothing to do with the story, either.

One day, I was picking away, head down, not a care in the world. Nothing but green leaves, tiny red buds, and honeybees, as far as I could see with my head down. I should have stuck my head up now and then, because I was some shocked when I heard a snarl and a bark. I thought for sure I was about to get tangled up with a coyote, so I looked up quick as a whip and made to run. But all I could see was a shadow in the sun. What a shadow! About six feet tall with shoulders of the gods and slim hips and hair down to God knows where. I couldn't tell. Oh my, what a sight! All dark and surrounded by light.

So I raised myself up off my knees and dusted myself off. I better get fixed up, I figured, if I was about to be greeted by a god. Then the god spoke. But he sounded like snarls and barks all over again. I couldn't help myself, I had to laugh. Now I was just an ignorant girl; wouldn't have known a native language if it struck me on the top of my head.

We all spoke the Gaelic back then, and our language was full of pops and growls and barks too, but this god didn't sound a bit like that. Can you pour me some water? All this talk is making me dry. No, it's OK. I'll take a break a little later.

So I thought to God I was about to meet my Adonis. I read about him in school, our encyclopedia even showed pictures, and, my, oh my, this fella sure looked like him, even if he couldn't talk right. I figured Adonis being Greek and all, probably couldn't talk right, either. But I was willing to forgive them both if they would appear in my life like this. Just the once. And I could be Aphrodite.

Anyhow, as he came a little closer and out of the sun, I could tell he was not a Greek god, after all. So I felt a little less speechless by the time he got down to my berry patch. Then he totally surprised me. He asked me in English what the hell I was doing in his berry patch. I said, 'Go on with ya, this is my berry patch.'

He said, snotty as anything, 'No way. This is my patch.'

But that wasn't good enough for me, 'This is my patch and you're standing on my berries. Git off.'

To which he replied, 'You're trespassing. This is native soil.' Being kind of smart-mouthed at the time, I said, 'Is that native as in 'got Indian blood in ya' or native as in 'you're from here'? 'Cause I'm from here.'

Oh my God, to think of it now! It's a wonder he didn't heave me over his shoulder and run me back to my farm and fire me on the ground right then and there. Of course, that could be what I was going for all along.

Well, he didn't, because as it turns out, he was a gentleman. Instead, he took a big, deep breath and said, 'Young lady, you must leave here now. You are trespassing.'

I'd been listening to too much American radio, so I yelled, 'So sue me.'

By now, he was getting all red in the face and I was right tempted to call him a Red Injun. Then I thought better of it. He was an awful big guy. A lot bigger than I was. Daddy warned me once the Natives didn't take kindly to that kind of talk. I guess they couldn't see the humour in it, way back in 1940. Still don't. Even though the rest of us Cape Bretoners have to be the butt of all jokes and take it all in good fun. Oh Siobhan, I can feel a coughing fit coming on. Can you get me some water? I'm afraid I'll have to rest now. You can go on home.

Before you go, could you do me a favour and ask the nurse to come with my shot? Of course I want you back tomorrow. It's OK about your mother not being here. I'm having more fun with you, anyway. Do you think I would ever tell your mother this story? Not a hope or a prayer. We'll talk more tomorrow. Good night and God bless."

Later the nurse tells me I've got a touch of fever. I explain to her I'm a bit worked up about the beautiful boy of my childhood I've been telling my granddaughter about. My Adonis. She looks at me like I have two heads. I don't think she would even know who Adonis is. And she's wrong. I'm not too old for that 'nonsense'. Bitchy old Nurse Cratchit. Anyhow, I think my story cheered Siobhan up, and got her mind off her troubles.

Siobhan Takes a Ribbin'

Siobhan caught the bus back to Robie Street, for what felt like the fifteenth time in a row. Every night, she had to walk by the local scruffs smoking on the bench outside the pub by the bus stop. Oh, how she craved a smoke! But she had quit when she got pregnant with Liam, and the smell bothered Granny. She thought she had grown used to the little digs from the locals, but the other night one of them yelled out to her and, for some reason, she stopped and answered him. "Cape Breton," she said.

They all started cackling, "Caape Brehhton." So mature.

People making fun of the way she talked wasn't news to her, so she kept walking. Last night—same thing. She didn't respond and kept on going. Tonight, they were cackling again, and this time she couldn't understand what they were yelling out. It sounded like Katy to her. Curiosity got the better of her, so she turned back and confronted the guy on the end of the bench with the British accent. "My name is not Katy. Why do you call me that?" Then she took a good look at him. And wished she hadn't.

"Not Katy," he said. "KD."

"KD. What the fuck does that mean?"

"You know—KD. Cape Breton steak. Kraft dinner? Eh?"

"Haha. You're so funny," Siobhan said. "And no, we don't only eat Kraft Dinner. Or say 'eh' all the time. Not any more than you Brits do. Give me a smoke, why don't ya? Eh?"

So he stood up and gave her one. Then he followed her home. As he drew closer, he asked in his best British enunciation, "Who is your granny that she comes to live in such a posh part of town?"

Siobhan shot him a look and said, "What do you mean—posh? Nothing wrong with this part of town. What are you suggesting—we are some kind of snobs?"

"No. No, not at all. It's just that...well, these houses are huge. My home is a dumpy little row house. I'm curious, that's all. It's not like I'm gonna turn into a B&E maniac on you."

"Her name is Mary."

"Mary? I know her. She shops at the butcher shop sometimes. She's a sweet old doll."

"Yeah, well, that's my gran and here's her house, so good-bye. Don't let the gate kick ya on the way out."

"Hey, KD, come on, tell me your name."

"Siobhan. My name is Siobhan. S..I..O..B..H..A...N. Shhheh vaughn. Siobhan."

"OK, OK, I got it."

"Now take a hike."

"OK, don't get your knickers in a twist, KD. Night."

"Night."

After she locked the door, she realized she didn't know his name. She leaned against the locked door and thought, 'but I do know the colour of his eyes.' She leaned on that thought for, oh...ten minutes. Then she did the usual checking of closets and under the beds. Tonight the big house seemed bigger and emptier than ever.

Morning came soon enough. She drank her OJ and headed out to the bus stop. At least in the hospital, she didn't have to be alone.

The Lovely Boy

Siobhan seems a little brighter this morning. I wonder what's going on in that pretty little head of hers. I might not want to know. She is twenty-five now, after all. Maybe wiser not to ask, or even wonder. I'm feeling much more chipper myself, so I offer to tell some more of the story. She looks relieved to have something to talk about. Not exactly a brilliant conversationalist, our Siobhan.

"OK. Now where was I? Oh yeah, Adonis. And Mouthpiece. That being me. Seems to me I was telling you how big he was, and how fine. My, my, what a lovely boy! What's that, luv? Oh. I didn't mean to drift off. Sorry. Daydreaming, I guess.

So. He shoo-ed me right out of there. When I got home, I told my Da all about it. I'll tell you, I was as mad as a wet hen. Even after Da explained that, yes, if I picked on the other side of the big birch tree, I certainly was on their land and in the wrong. Well, nothing made me madder when I was sixteen than someone telling me I was wrong. I believe I stayed mad for two days that time.

Eventually, curiosity got the better of me. Curiosity always was my downfall. Off I went to the berry field, 'xact same place. I watched and watched for him. I expected him to sneak up on me any minute. All that waiting made me crankier and crankier. So I cursed—under my breath, of course—'The bastard. Where the hell is he?'

Then I glanced over my shoulder, in case Ma had crept up behind me and caught me using such foul language. I never did see the bastard again. At least not that year. No, he waited till I had turned eighteen to surface. A real test of patience, that boy. But then aren't all the best things in life?

We used to hold some grand dances in the Margaree Valley. We would go to the neighbour's barn and oh, how the hills would ring! Practically everyone could dance or sing or play something musical. Not like now where you young folks sit around and play that old boom box all day. It's called a what, Pet? iPod? Oh. About five inches long and paper thin? And only one person can listen at a time? Good lord, that must be worse than the boom box, if only one of ya can listen at a time. What do the rest of you do while the one fella is listening? Sit there and look at Stupid? You each have one of them, you say? Oh my.

Well, back to the story. So here I am at this grand Shindig and who walks right in, as big as brass. Adonis. All six feet of him. I don't mind telling you, I had to run to the outhouse some quick. I thought I might pee my pants. Of course, that might have been the effect of the moonshine. Anyhow, good thing about the shine because it gave me the courage I needed. I walked right up to him, I did, glared up at him and said, clear as day in good English, 'Where the hell ya bin?'

Then I threw up. All over him. OK, maybe looking back, the shine wasn't such a good idea. But if I hadn't had the false courage...well, who knows?

Then I couldn't find any of my own kin. Don't know where they got themselves off to. Must have been behind the barn, necking. Or drinking shine. I didn't look too hard. This gentleman, being a fine gentle man, offered to take me home. How could I refuse? First he needed to go home and change. Home for him wasn't too far, only down to Margaree Harbour.

So he took me home. I watched him skim that stinky shirt off of him. Well, then, I thought for certain my heart would stop! Drop me dead right then and there! Nobody home at his house, and that's just as well. I wouldn't have wanted them to find me laid flat out on their floor with a heart attack, especially with me being so young. It mighta left them in quite a bind. I'd love to see the notes from the coroner, reported to the Cape Breton Daily, headlined "Redheaded Celtic Wench Drops Dead in Kitchen of Mi'kmaq Home".

Of course I'm exaggerating, dear. But have you ever noticed when a man is genuinely comfortable in his own skin, how gracefully he disrobes? This man was the picture of grace, as I was to learn again not too long after.

By now I had pretty well sobered up and I didn't have a lot of sass left in me. So I didn't quarrel when he suggested he saddle up the horse. Oh, yes dear, we had cars back then. Tell you the truth, I think he was showing off. And well he should. There was a man who could sit a horse! I've never been much for horses; I like my feet on the ground. But I figured, what the hell? In for a penny, in for a pound. So I hopped up behind him. Man, could that creature fly! What with the moonlight and the air whipping by me and the feel of the horse between my thighs and his warm back in my arms, I soon revived and forgot about the unfortunate incident at the dance. So did he, it appears. For he stopped the horse up short and he hopped off and he said, 'Do you know where you are now?'

I stared down at him and I said—real clever like—'Strawberries.'

That's all I could get out of me. Well, he reached up, and I slid down onto him, and the next thing he pulled me on the ground, close by him. He said, 'You didn't think I remembered you, did you?'

And I said, 'No. But I remembered you. Ya Bastard.'

He looked a wee bit shocked, but then he threw his head back and roared with laughter. Right next to me, under the dancing moon. (At least the moon danced in my eyes. Coulda been the shine.) All those flashing white teeth and his warm red mouth, now dark and open and enticing. Like a cave I wanted to explore with my tongue and my lips to see if I could find a cool pool in that shadowy cave, something I could drown in.

So I gave him a sock on the shoulder, instead. Oh, wasn't I the great seductress! He rolled over on his side, and I could see the sparkle in his eyes. Definitely the sign of a devil inside, or so I thought. As I say, I was still an ignorant farm girl. He flipped onto his back, but this time he brushed his arm against mine, and when I didn't react, he did it again. And left it there! Oh my, the audacity! Then he said, 'You want to know where I've been? I've been up to Halifax getting my education at Dalhousie University. I'm going into law.'

Now, Siobhan, can you explain to me why every Indian I've ever met wants to be a lawyer? Or wants their kid to be. For us Irish Catholics, our parents all wanted to send one up for the priesthood. But not the Mi'kmaq. Did I say it right? Good. We used to say 'Mic Mac'. Since those developers named the big shrine to consumerism over in Dartmouth the MicMac Mall, I don't blame the Natives for wanting the proper pronunciation. Whose bright idea was it anyway, to name a shopping centre after our founding people? And what does wanton consumerism have to do with The People of the Dawn?

Where was I? Oh yes, we were lying in the berry patch with his arm under my shoulder and my head on his chest. I wanted to shout at him and tell him, 'What do you think I am—a poor ignorant farm girl? There's lots I know, too.'

So I did. I must confess, there wasn't much shout left in me. Not with his cool satiny night skin under my arm. And the dark shining eyes of his. I was having trouble remembering where his eyes ended and mine began. We were starting to get right tangled up in each other. 'Course, it didn't occur to me till I got home that I might be squishing strawberries all over the back of my lovely white party dress. Good thing my little sister noticed and warned me before Ma caught me.

Anyhow, as we were rolling around on the berries and I was searching for something clever to say to prove my point, he put his fingers to my lips and whispered, 'Shhh.'

Have you ever watched a man when he makes that 'sshh' sound? No? Next time, watch. I promise you it will be worth it. See, that's the thing, Siobhan. Love...well, it's all in the details. And no, I don't mean sex, Siobhan. I mean love. You're wondering about his name? I don't know. No, it's not that I don't remember. He never did tell me, and he moved away, and I never saw him again. I think he went to war. I met your grampy and left the Margaree Valley. So how can I say it was love and not lust? Oh, Sweetheart, you just know. You will know. Love, like God, is in the details. I'll tell you some more tomorrow."

Siobhan left the hospital that evening even more puzzled by her granny. She always heard it said the devil's in the details. But Granny said it's God who resides there, at least when it comes to love making. Granny said the devil was in his eyes, instead. So God and the devil showing up in the same place—what the hey? She would be glad to hit the sack that night and stop all this thinking about devils and strawberries and wild horses and dark shining lovers. All those images made her head spin and made her lonely for Luke.

She wasn't left lonely long. She woke up to the sound of the phone in her ear. The hospital calling. Bad news. Granny was sinking quickly now. It would be best to call her mom. So she did.

"Mom, you need to come. Now."

"Oh Vaughn, can't you take care of it? I have a big meeting Friday, and a deadline to meet, and..."

"Mom, you're not listening. You need to come."

"Oh. How much time do I have?"

"For Christ's sake, Mom, I don't know. Do you want to see her before she dies or only come to clean up the paperwork?"

"Siobhan, don't be cruel. Let me think. How soon should I book the time off from work?"

"As soon as possible. She asks for you every day."

"How long has this been going on?"

"Since I got here. It's you she wants. I texted you about it."

"Oh. Sorry, I didn't check my text messages lately."

"Mom, you haven't been listening. Big surprise."

"Well, I'm listening now. And you're with her, Siobhan. I can only go by what you say. Should we all come now—Dad, Chad, Aunt Renee?"

"How should I know, Mom. You guys work it out."

"What about Luke? Should I get in touch with him and ask him to go to Halifax and help out?"

"Gotta go. Gotta get to the hospital."

264

"Siobhan, don't hang up..."

It was a miserable day, nothing but reflections of fog and rain in the window pane. Mary couldn't get comfortable, no matter how many drugs they poured into her. At one point, Mary grew quite panicky and couldn't breathe. Siobhan thought her granny might die right there and then, with only herself present and accounted for. But the nurses came and calmed Granny, while Siobhan watched and waited. For someone, for death, for whatever was to come.

That night the guy from the smokers' bench beat her onto the bus. She walked past him as if she didn't know him. He followed her home again, anyhow. As she arrived at her gate, she turned on him and said, "Either go away or come in."

So he did. Come in. She led him around the big empty house, showed him all the closets and the dust under the beds, as she made her nightly rounds. After the grand tour, they settled into the den, which happened to be the smallest room in the house. He sat in her grampy's chair and said, "Come here, KD."

He reached for her, pulled her down on him, grabbed her hair, and turned her face to his. Siobhan was too busy looking for the devil in his eyes to notice him slipping his hand down her pants. Until she felt his fingers. She pulled away, said, "Slow down."

"OK, KD. What would you like to do—play tiddlywinks?"

She said, "No, slow the fuck down, is all," and moved over to the daybed.

He sat on Grampy's chair, eyes hidden under Grampy's desk lamp. Then he winked and slowly—and gracefully—slid his T-shirt off his body. Siobhan took a good hard look at him. Looked at what the cat drug in. Honey-coloured skin, all over. Not much chest hair. A little peach fuzz on his nipples. An inny at his navel. Honey-coloured curls, loose, almost girlish. Like the little Victorian girls with the ringlets in the picture Granny hung in the bathroom. But not quite ringlets. Not quite little Victorian girlish either, somehow.

He grinned up at her and said, "Do I pass inspection?"

Siobhan, never one to doubt or defend her intelligence or opinion, told him bluntly, "Depends. What else ha' ya got?"

Now he wore a full frontal smile. Another slow strip, a bit of a performance piece this time—flinging of socks and belt and pants. Then a few leisurely hip rotations before the Big Reveal. Not so graceful.

He stood in her grampy's lamplight, fully naked. Which left her fully clothed on the daybed. His smile began to fade, as she continued to sit and stare. "Hey," he said. "Your turn."

"Oh, what? Sorry. I wasn't paying attention."

"Shit. You sure know how to shrivel a guy."

"I'm sorry," Siobhan said. "Come here."

He walked his naked honey-coloured butt over to her and she put his little honey-coloured penis into her soft red cave of a mouth.

"Oh, that's better. So much better."

Siobhan thought, but didn't say—she couldn't because her mouth was full—'You really are a brilliant conversationalist.'

When that was all over with and out of the way, she laid back with her arm behind her head. He sat down by her and said, "Can we play tiddlywinks now? Honestly, I only came for the tiddlywinks. But at least I did come."

Siobhan thought, but didn't say, because it didn't matter enough, 'Brilliant. The guy is brilliant.'

Instead, she said, "Sorry, no tiddlywinks tonight. I think you better go home now."

"Come on," he said, "don't be like that. I'm not a bad guy. I want you to have fun, too."

Siobhan thought, but didn't say, 'Oh yeah, you're a right lovely gent, ain't ya?' Struck her so funny she burst out laughing. He grinned ear to ear like he must be the most charming, seductive, entertaining guy in the world to make her laugh so hard. A full-bellied, head-tossed-back laugh. Regardless, the laugh did her good. He started to massage her shoulders. Turned out he had skillful hands, and a gentle touch when it came right down to it. Maybe he would do. Any port in a storm, as Granny would say. But in a completely different context, of course.

So she let him do it. The usual moves, the exploratory fingers, the slide down her belly to her V, the bouncy curls between her legs. She could feel herself respond at last in that big cold empty house. Feel the warmth on her soft

266

spot. The wet dripping on her thighs. The shadows on the walls, the rough fabric under her ass, the arch in her back, the skin of his tight honey-coloured butt, the ghosts in the attic, the rain on the roof. The light from Grampy's desk lamp unveiled everything. Round, firm asses, arms and legs and tongues and cheeks and penises and vaginas. Hair and sweat and cum and tears. Tears that he wouldn't notice, or if he did, he'd think it was something certain women did when they came. He'd probably read it in Esquire, so it must be true.

Siobhan checked the clock, as they rolled apart. 11:11. Not much luck here tonight, if that's what 11:11 meant. Or did it mean the fairies are about to come calling? Or was it the angels? She couldn't remember, but she hoped it wasn't the angels. She'd rather they didn't come for Granny as she would like her to stick around a lot longer, at least till her ma got here. She grabbed a towel, shared it with him. He said, clever fellow that he was, "What I wouldn't give for a smoke."

"No smoking here. Granny's rules."

"How is your granny doing, by the way?"

"Not so good. She's dying." She had the satisfaction of watching his already limp dick go even limper, if that was possible, till it resembled an upside down squirrel's tail. Fuzzy and curved into his thigh, little pink end tucked under and hiding. She suppressed her laughter. Lord knows, if she had to explain the joke to him, she would never get any sleep!

"You know what? It's getting awfully late. I gotta get home. Mum will be wondering where I am," like someone straight out of Coronation Street.

Siobhan thought, 'Old enough to smoke, old enough to strip, old enough to fuck, but not old enough to leave home. Or stay in a big scary house with a girl who thinks she is about to become the biggest, saddest, little baby orphan in the whole wide world.'

Instead, she said, ever so politely, "Fuck off out of here, then. See ya."

Off he scurried, gathering clothes as he tried to find light switches and doors and his missing runners. She laid back and laughed again at the sight of his little squirrel, dangling and bouncing away, and his beautiful, ridiculous, honey-coloured ass, as it slipped out the door.

'Ah, sleep at last, and it better be a good one,' she thought, but didn't say, because there was no one listening, not even Luke. Luke was never there anymore. So she pulled the scratchy, woolly blanket Grampy always kept in the den up over her body and slept the sleep of the dead.

Where Are You Now My Lonely Boy Tonight

The next morning, Siobhan woke up and thought, 'I must get to the hospital straight away. No time for OJ this morning.'

Then she gave her head a shake and laughed, 'Straight away. I'm even beginning to think like a Brit. Next thing you know, I'll be worried about losing my knickers, like I did last night.'

She gave a little snicker and made a note to herself to find those knickers before Mother Dearest arrived. On the bus, she kept her head down and tucked her hair under her cap in case he showed up. 'Oh well,' she thought, 'I did get one thing right. His eyes were honey-coloured.'

When she got to her ward, she was some glad to feel Granny's arms around her and see her bright eyes. Granny looked a thousand times better.

"Granny, we've got a crisis in Cape Breton."

"What happened? Hurricane hit?"

"No, but it might as well have. Mom can't make up her mind when to come."

"Tell her: soon. Would you like to hear more of the story of the Lovely Boy?"

"Sure. Why not?"

"Where was I?"

"You and the Lovely Boy were rolling around in the berry patch, and you were smushing up berries with your dress."

"Berry stains. How romantic, eh? Ready?"

"Yup."

"Sooo. I guess you could say by then, we were grassing. Do you kids still go grassing? Grassing? Oh, that means rolling around on the grass, of course. Only not like when you're little. More like when you're barely old enough, and there is nowhere else to go, and no one else around, just a girl and a guy. No, actually, you wouldn't catch a cold. Don't believe everything your mother tells you; the damp won't kill ya, not if you've got a lovely warm body to roll around with. And the best part? You can breathe. All that night air. And—a big plus—

269

you don't need to worry about your stink with all the fresh air. Not even if you fart. Don't laugh, Siobhan. These things can be important considerations when you are picking out a love nest.

No worries about smells that night, once we got rid of the vomit. He smelt like all of outdoors and strawberries and sweet grass and...Siobhan, do you remember the aroma of sweet grass? Remember the little meadow at the home place? Go at the right time of year, and you'll smell it. No sweeter fragrance in the world. The Lovely Boy was the essence of sweet scents.

Promise me you'll go to that meadow one day, Siobhan, and breathe in the sweet grass and devil's paintbrushes and daisies and bay leaves and wild strawberries and brown-eyed Susans and wild heather. It became my favourite place to go when I wanted to be alone: to daydream, to read, or simply to breathe. You'll find it down by the cliff where the old stairs are. You think the sea washed the stairs away? How sad. Well, follow your nose, then.

So here we are grassing. But I forgot to tell you about his eyes. Dark as pitch they were. Little chips of coal. Dark and shiny and...Oh, I did tell you? Sorry. Did I tell you they haunted my dreams for years? No? I shouldn't say haunted, more like 'warmed'.

Coal mattered back then. It heated our homes, and it kept the men working, and it made the Island prosperous. Cape Breton never had it so good. There wasn't a house on the entire Island didn't feel a whole lot more secure with a basement chock full of coal. I know, I know—acid rain and black lung and all that. But it kept us warm. And his eyes kept me warm, that night and many nights that could have been lonely and cold without my memories of him.

Siobhan, would you mind if we left this for now? I am quite sleepy and I'd like to see if I can find those charcoal eyes, one last time."

Before Granny closed her eyes, she took a good hard look at her granddaughter. She saw such unhappiness in her eyes.

"Siobhan," she said gently, "what is going on, hon? Why so sad?"

With that, Siobhan burst into tears.

"Oh Siobhan, my sweetie, my pet, whatever is wrong? Come up here and tell Granny."

Siobhan dropped the safety rail and climbed up on the bed.

"Snuggle up here, Honey. Don't worry; I'll move the tubes out of the way. No, you won't hurt me. Shush now, shush. Cáilín mo Pháistín i, my baby girl."

Siobhan snuggled up and cried till she had no tears left and inhaled Granny's sweet scent, even over all the hospital odours, the fragrance of rosewater and Ivory Snow. Then she fell asleep. She slept till the nurse came and kicked her out. On the way to the bus stop, Siobhan worried that she might have disturbed her grandmother's sleep, destroyed her dream.

The next day Siobhan found her granny curled up in a ball, sleeping like a baby. So she waited and waited. Around three, Granny woke and gave her a big sly wink. Siobhan could tell the Lovely Boy had shown up just on time to give Granny some pleasure, before she met her Maker. She didn't tell Granny, and Granny didn't ask again, but Siobhan knew she was losing her own Lovely Boy, maybe this time for good. Her Lovely Lonely Boy. She just knew.

Chris Intervenes

Emily was busy getting on with her life and washing dishes, when Chris ducked in for a minute:

Chris: I hear that friend Kate sent you has been banging young chicks in alleyways.

Emily: Where'd you hear that?

Chris: Oh, I have eyes and ears everywhere on that man.

Emily: You should get rid of him, if you're so omnipotent.

Chris: Don't blame me. He's not my responsibility. Blame him on Kate.

Emily: I wonder why we say 'banging' when we talk about two bodies colliding. Sounds a lot more like a 'squish squash' to me. 'Squishing' doesn't quite connote the same thing either, though.

Chris: Not for men. So he got caught this time! Yahoo! Are you going to tell his wife?

Emily: No. Of course not. You shouldn't gloat, Chris. It's not attractive. Man, you're territorial!

Chris: Didn't we ever tell you that after you die you still retain some challenging characteristics of your world self? Otherwise heaven would be one big sea of unwashed souls, floating around, bumping up against each other, and basically going nowhere. We still need to work out some things that we didn't fix before we left the earth, or we can't move on to another dimension.

Em: No, you didn't. But thanks for the warning. Is that why you'd like to get into a pissing match with Luke, so you can advance? Doesn't sound very spiritually enlightened, and that's what I thought heaven was all about.

Chris: No one wants to get stuck in the same dimension forever.

I know you care about him and you feel like you need to defend him, but he really is a dweeb.

Em: That's unusually harsh talk coming from your neck of the woods. He's been called many things by me and Trudy—numbnuts, arsehole, dickwad, dumbass, nimrod, idiot—but dweeb is a first. Wasn't it you telling me not to call him names, not so long ago?

Chris: I could think of worse ones. Like misogynist. Would that one suit?

Em: No.

Chris: If the shoe fits...

Em: It doesn't fit. Hell, what do I know? He still hasn't answered that question about does he like kids, or just his own.

Chris: Does he like women universally, or just his own? Or not even his own, like my So Called Friend?

Em: I wouldn't even want to open up that can of worms. 'Do you like women, Luke, or just the ones who provide for you?' Wonder how many eons I would have to wait for a reply this time.

And no, Luke's not like your So Called Best Friend. Not a bit.

Chris: Let me beat him up for you.

Emily: Which him?

Chris: Both.

Emily: Now, all of a sudden, you've decided to become overprotective?

Chris: Yup. I didn't protect you when I should have, and I'm not missing my chance this time. God gave me a second chance to make a first impression on Him, so I'm taking it.

Emily: So when it comes right down to it, Chris, this is all about you and your redemption.

Chris: No it isn't. I'm just making excuses again. Bad habit left over from my lifetime. I was always looking for distractions when it came to you and I didn't pay enough attention. I didn't do the one thing and you paid for it.

Emily: In hindsight, I can see that your So Called Best Friend was jealous of you and me. Not the 'me' part; I don't think he ever liked women much, and *especially* not me. I stood in the way of you and him one time too many.

They claim sexual assault is often a lot more about power than sex. It has taken me years to understand where the balance of power went out of whack that night. And you weren't around to help.

Chris: No, I wasn't. Not that night and not for all those years. But I'm here now.

Em: And I'm glad you are. It helps.

This is something you wouldn't know, Chris. In Canada, they changed the law so they don't call it rape anymore. They call it sexual assault. Today, I heard a report on the radio about three cops who are being charged with gang sexual assault.

Chris: So no more gang rape? For the cops or the bike gangs? No more rape for the so-called best friends?

Em: Not anymore.

Chris: Still, a rape is a rape is a rape.

Em: That's what I thought.

Chris: 'Sexual assault' sounds so passive and way too formal. It's not even a dirty four-letter word, like it should be. I'll still call it what it is. And it shouldn't have happened to you. I wasn't much good at protecting you. I was never any good at telling you how I feel either, but I'll say it now. I love you, Em.

Em: Well, that's obvious. And required of you.

Chris: True.

That was awkward.

Em: Mmmm. Fat lot of good it does me now.

Chris: And I thought right this instant would be the perfect moment! Sheesh! Is that why you never told Luke you love him—no perfect moments to spring the news?

Emily: Could be. Thank God.

Chris: Bet you're glad you never told him you know him by heart, either.

Emily: You'd win that bet. Except that I do.

Chris: Do what?

Emily: Know him by heart.

Chris: Oh. Well, I know that. Like you do me. And Tessa and Kate. So we never end for you.

Emily: I wish he wouldn't always run away. I wish he would stay. For just one moment.

Chris: Didn't see this one coming though, did you? Didn't know his restless ways could disrupt your peace of mind, even after all this time.

Emily: No, I sure didn't.

Ninety Nine Red Balloons

Emily knew nothing about Siobhan's new responsibilities for her granny, her money worries, her sadness, and her sense of impending loss. Emily sometimes tried to imagine Siobhan: her ways, her hair, her shape, her looks, her attitude, her ups and downs. She looked hard to find a reason to care, and a way into Siobhan's world. She knew she should be stretching the muscles of her compassionate heart to include Siobhan. But it wasn't like imagining Kate and Tessa and Chris. She hadn't ever met the girl and she couldn't expand her imagination or compassion to include her. For some strange reason.

Meanwhile, back at Tracadie Bay, Emily was put in charge of another big event: Maddie's seventh birthday party. Maddie rose at dawn to greet the July day as it promised her sunshine, friendship, and lots of presents. At the end of the party, Maddie insisted on releasing balloons into the stratosphere, which caused a little disturbance between her and Emily. Emily tried, but had a tough time, explaining to Maddie about the damage released balloons do to the birds in the sky and the fishes in the sea. Maddie told Emily she shouldn't complain about the balloons because she, being Emily, talked to dead people, and Maddie wanted to share her balloons and her birthday wish with Emily's dead friends. Maddie thought they might have some extra influence with God, as this year's birthday wish was of the utter-most importance. Or so said Maddie. It's hard to argue theology with a seven-year-old. They'll always win.

Emily promised she'd check in with her spirit people to see if the message from Maddie had been received:

Kate: Acknowledged and processed. Maddie's dad will be sprung from the Japanese spa prison next week.
Emily: Kate, you're back! Where have you been?
Kate: Pulling strings on Maddie's behalf.
Emily: She'll be happy to hear that. Speaking of balloons and stratospheres, I have another Maddie story. Any jokes floating around heaven these days?
Kate: No. You got any?

Emily: Charlie told a good one at the birthday party:

' Three guys go up in a plane. One has a penny, one has an apple, and one has a bomb. The first guy drops his penny out of the plane. A few seconds later, they can hear a child crying. So they fly down to see why the child is crying. They find a little girl who is crying and she says, 'A penny just fell out of the sky and hurt my kitty.' So they fly back up. This time the second guy drops his apple out of the plane. A few seconds later they can hear someone crying. So they fly down to see who is crying. And they find a boy, crying, who says, 'An apple just fell out of the sky and killed my dog.' So they fly back up into the sky. This time the third guy drops his bomb. Then they can hear someone laughing really, really hard and loud. So they fly down to see what's going on. And they find a man out in his yard, laughing his head off. So they ask him, 'What's so funny?' And he says, 'I just farted and blew up my garage.'

Maddie loved that joke. Fart humour and seven-year-olds—still a winning combination. So then she insisted on telling me her joke. She said, 'I can make you say a letter.' So I said, 'Why?' And she said, 'There. Get it? Y? X Y Z? Get it?'

Did I ever tell you about the day I first met her? When I still lived in BC, Pierce dropped by my house to pick up some of Erin's stuff, and I went out to the car to meet his kids. I opened the back door and this little face peered up at me from her car seat. A dazzle of freckles, stringy hair and big blue eyes. Pierce's kids still hadn't met Erin at that point, even though Pierce had been seeing her for six months. So I introduced myself as Daddy's imaginary girlfriend's mother. Clair got it right away, but I'm not sure Maddie did.

Kate: Madison. What a pretty name.

Em: For a pretty little girl. That Maddie? Well, she's a quick little child. She thinks quick. Loves quick, moves quick, spills quick.

Kate: You're not playing favourites, are you?

Emily: I know I shouldn't. But Maddie wiggled her way into my heart quickest. What can I say? She's the perfect age, but then what isn't a perfect age for a kid? When she comes over to my place, she draws and colours and practises her 'school words' a lot. I'm trying to get her to use recycled paper, but she likes the crisp white look of two clean sides best, so she can really go to town with the ink. She's an inky kid, for sure. Ink everywhere—cheeks, eyebrows, clothes, my couch. Thank goodness I put a slip cover over the couch and chair.

One good thing—the ink blends in with her freckles and looks natural. If she uses the brown one, that is. Not so much so with blue or red or green markers, which she usually uses. I think I'll go colour with her. Or play hangman.

The next day was Wednesday. Book Club day. After Book Club, Kate called on Emily:

Kate: Em, I've been meaning to ask you. What has the Book Club been reading lately?

Emily: We did *Loving Frank*, about the marriage and affairs of Frank Lloyd Wright. I loved it. The author didn't spend all her time debating whether affairs make you happy or not, like I do. She told the story, instead.

Kate: What else are you reading?

Emily: A somewhat tedious biography of Queen Elizabeth and Mary Queen of Scots.

Kate: If it's tedious, why do you keep reading it?

Emily: The author shows some interesting parallels between the two queens; she just takes a hundred pages too many to explain it. But I learned a lot. And a little about the mysteries of this friendship you cursed me with.

Kate: Like what?

Emily: That friend you sent me? Methinks we art not unlike the Virgin Queen Elizabeth and the love of her life, Lord Robert Dudley. Forever unconsummated. Or more like Elizabeth and Mary: only to correspond endlessly and never to meet.

Kate: So that's where the curse comes in?

Emily: There could be worse things. The two queens tried so hard to get rid of each other. Elizabeth won. Mary hung. Or, actually, got beheaded. At least, I'm not constantly in danger of beheadment. Is that a word?

Kate: And you don't have to wear those heavy gowns and big neck ruffs.

Emily: And get blood all over my nice white ruff when the axe comes down for the beheading. Or should it be deheading? Like defrocking? You know—what happens to priests and virgins? But not at the same time. I hope not. Back then, they—the priest and virgin—would have each been 'burned for a witch' if they got tangled up in a mutual defrocking.

Kate: Lots of that going on during Tudor times. Burning, hanging, beheading and defrocking. They changed sects more quickly than Imelda Marcos changed shoes. All those variations of Christianity with just enough difference to give the Christians something to fight over. Now the Muslims are doing the same thing. Oh, the things you humans concern yourselves with!

By the way, did you know, the 'never meeting' increased the mystery between those two queens, so it lasted all their lives?

Emily: Yeah, the author theorizes about that a lot. She claims it could be fundamental to why they couldn't ever work out their petty quarrels. That and those insufferable religious differences.

Kate: Speaking of insufferable differences, how is the accursed friend I sent you?

Emily: I guess you could say my work here is done. Time to fold my tent and move on, if an obligation to teach the children well is all loving him was ever about in the first place. Now when I get a substitute teaching day, I practise on real children, so my yen to intervene in young people's lives gets satisfied. It beats worrying. Which is what thoughts of him replaced originally. I remember when they used to be bright shiny pennies, those thoughts. Before he knew.

Thanks to the bright shiny kids, I don't need him.

Kate: You could have written a book; called it *Loving Luke*. Then you could get our old book club to critique it.

Emily: Hrmph. Not likely. Besides, like Elizabeth and Mary, he's ancient history now.

Erin's stepson Clair is a better man, and he's only nine. I took him for a walk on the beach the other day; it turns out he's a treasure hunter and a beach comber.

Tessa: I'm not surprised.

Emily: He found a big foam net buoy and dragged it home. Well, it didn't weigh much, so he didn't exactly drag it. We agreed he looked like a cave man with a wild boar slung over his shoulder. He grunted one word all the way home: 'Supper'.

Tessa: So many women would be grateful to find a young man who can drag supper home.

Emily: I know. I'm the envy of the Book Club. He's pretty darn cute. Guess what else? He can read!!

Tessa: Wow. He's growing up so fast. How did that happen?

Emily: Now when he picks up a book he reads without hesitating, and he knows what it means. He can follow along without running his finger under each word.

Tessa: A gift of Grade Three?

Emily: It would seem so. He's my Alpha and Omega male.

Kate: I'm glad you've got a big man to help out, Emily.

Emily: Clair's not that big yet, Kate, only four foot two. But as a buoy-toting caveman, he's undeniably capable.

As for me, I just want to be normal. Be a good step-grand-mommy to the kids. Walk around the world like everyone else. Mind my tongue. Keep my opinions to myself. Agree. Set my mind to what's for supper. Stay out of the line of fire. Stop seeing meaning where other people see stones, and colours where other people see black and white. God, I think I'll even start going to church.

Kate: Did you know in *The Iliad*, stones represent the duality of all of us beings, the light and the dark, the yin and the yang, the Alpha and the Omega?

Emily: Oh. And I thought Luke was just a dull old stone, one I had too much trouble letting go of.

Kate: Maybe that's why. If you look for the duality, you might...

Emily: Anyway, I'm done with risks and I'm done with stones. I'm going for the New Normal from now on.

Chris: Does this mean you won't talk to us anymore?

Emily: Well, Chris, what do you think? Talking to dead people hardly fits with the New Normal.

Tessa: Em, you are such a sulk.

Chris: But who's gonna talk to me about granny panties and cute asses now?

Emily: Heaven's a bitch sometimes, eh, Chris?

Kate: Emily, you can't be serious.

Emily disappeared for a few days:

Kate: I'm glad you're back, Emily.

Emily: I went for a walk with Trudy today on the beach at Canoe Cove. Your beach. We were talking about how so many of your closest friends saw eagles right after you died. For me, it was red-tailed hawks. Why choose black and white when you can choose colour?

Kate: Wasn't that in a commercial selling TVs back in the sixties? Why choose black and white when you can choose colour?

Emily: Could be. TVs have come a long way. 3D and HD rule the five-hundred-channel universe now.

279

Trudy pointed out an eagle in the distance. I couldn't see it very well—got to start wearing those bifocals, I guess—and I said it couldn't be an eagle because I couldn't see any white. She said she could tell by the way it moved, and it might be a juvenile. I wasn't having it. My sinus headache had become quite painful, and I was not in the mood for any mystical signs. Frig that.

But this morning, on my way out the door to go to the hairdresser's, four eagles flew directly over my head. They were so close I could see all the mottled feathers on the underside of the two juveniles. They hung around and taunted the crows, who were vastly outnumbered for a change, and let me have a good look. Four of them.

Kate: Did you also like the free parking space I found for you in town and the 11:11 the clock flashed you as you were about to get out of the car?

Emily: Yeah. You're still on your journey, aren't you, Kate?

Kate: Yeah, I'm still a traveler travellin', travellin' on.

Like good old Tommy Hunter.

Emily: Thanks for letting me come along.

Kate: You're welcome.

Emily and Kate: So let me wander.

Emily: Wander.

Emily and Kate: All my life away.

Kate: It *is* your journey, Emily.

Emily: And I get to pick who I take with me.

Kate: As does Luke.

Emily: As does he.

Good Night Chris

After washing up one more sink full of dishes left by Erin and the kids, Emily hung the tea towel over the handle of the stove and stood by the kitchen window. Two foxes were playing at the shore, dancing around like they didn't have a care in the world. One fox, probably the female, was a bright red, the traditional Reddy Fox colour, while the other with the tawny coat looked like the hybrids that populated the Island now. After a few rounds of jigs and reels, the male raised himself up on his hind legs and started batting at the female with his front paws, teasing her, till she agreed to stand upright too and play the little clapping game, much like Emily and her childhood friends played. *Three six nine, the goose drank wine...and they all went to heaven in a little rowboat. Clap clap.*

As the golden sunset turned his coat to bronze, something about the male fox reminded her of Chris. Clever fellow, the fox used his paws to pull the red female in closer and settle her into a mating ritual. Embarrassed, Emily turned away, but not before she called Chris to her:

Emily: Something is bugging me, and I need to tell you. You know, Chris, in his own twisted way, your friend loved you too much. You were the light to his darkness; the Abel to his Cain; the compassionate Man on the cross to his unrepentant thief. Saving you from drowning could have been his best chance to become a better man. And then you died after all and took it all away from him.
Chris: I know. But I *did* care about him. More than Abel cared for Cain.
Emily: You more than cared. You loved him in spite of himself. Like Jesus does. Christ, you even looked like Jesus, or at least the paintings of Him we grew up with in our small towns.
Chris: Must have been the beard.
Emily: It was more than the beard. It was in your eyes and nose and hair and skin and body. You were a truly beautiful man, in every sense of the word. In spite of knowing you would die young and the drugs you tinkered with to suppress your spirit, you carried so much light. There were a million other

281

reasons why I loved you, but most of all, it was the light. You were a very special person, not just to me, but to so many people who were touched by your light and your love. You shared the light of your love with us, all of us, even your desperate friend, and we reflected it back to you. You were surrounded by light and you never knew.

Chris: I don't know what to say. Thank you?

Emily: And you were honest. You didn't say things you didn't believe, not like I did, just to make people feel better. If you didn't want to be unkind, you simply kept your thoughts to yourself. When you spoke, you meant the words you said. One night you opened up long enough to tell me we were meant to be together, if you would have only been given a longer life so we could both grow up and become a couple, have each other's babies and the whole bit. But you, this most honest of men, never told me you loved me.

Chris: I loved you Emily. Not like Jesus, I was never spiritually mature enough— I couldn't even remember to say those three words out loud—but like me. The best I could with what little I knew. I loved you then and I love you now and I will love you always.

Emily: And me you. When you would come back to me, it could be in complete darkness, and I would know you by your scent. Skin and hair as clear as all of outdoors, overlaid by the faintest hint of Export A tobacco. And we would make love. On a mattress on the floor, against a bathroom wall, on a flimsy fold-up cot, in the back of my car. We would find each other. The pleasure of having you to myself ran deep into my bones and warmed my soul. You would give of yourself so freely then, as if you could make up for all the people and things that kept us apart and all the times you went away from me. With the silken threads of our love-making, we would spin a cocoon of our own conception to soften all the harsh edges and make the rest of the world go away. I've never been loved like that, not before and not since. You were the love of my life.

Chris: And you mine.

I'm so sorry Emily, but I can't talk to you anymore, not in broad daylight and not in the darkness of night. I have to go, Emily, and I can't come back.

Emily: Don't go! I won't call you up again. I promise I'll wait for you next time.

Chris: It's not because you called. Or couldn't be patient. You have been so patient, all of your life, Em. It's just that, once again, I've simply run out of time.

Emily: Please stay, Chris, just a little bit longer.

Chris: I can't. This is all the time we get. Listen to me, Emily. You could find another man to love, a good man to love as much as you loved me. Even more if you want. I wouldn't mind. Not now.

For the second time in her life, Chris was gone. But this time, he left Emily's heart full of peace.

Stay

August arrived and brought with it hot muggy days and plenty of sultry nights. Trudy invited Emily to keep her company at the McNeil family cottage for a couple of nights and help her explore her favourite beach, the one the locals called The Beach We Don't Tell Tourists About. Trudy had already invited the three Ps and two of her other brother's kids to come along the next day. She wanted to celebrate the end of her radiation treatment by soaking in one last blast of the sun, deprived as she had been all summer. Emily insisted Trudy wear long sleeves and a straw hat, at least, whenever she went out in the sun. With so many friends lost to cancer, Emily wasn't taking any chances with Trudy, even if the doctors did think they got it all, that Trudy was cancer-free, if there is such a thing.

After months of silence, Luke called Emily's cell phone and asked to see her in person, so he could make a proper apology. He yapped on about his life of the last few months, opened up to her more than he had in a long time, till Emily complained of telephone ear and begged off. Emily hoped maybe the cold war had ended. Trudy gave Emily permission to take Luke along to the beach the next day, with the one proviso being he behave himself and leave the drama at home.

Late at night, Emily and Trudy sat back on the deck chairs and gazed up at the starry, starry night. Emily hated to break the silence but she had something on her mind. "Trudy, remember a couple of weeks ago when we went for a walk at Canoe Cove? We saw another bloody eagle, and you said, for about the umpteenth time, 'Look! See, it's Kate waving to us, letting us know she's still with us, here in spirit.' I hadn't heard from either Tessa or Kate in ages and sometimes I get sick of pretending birds can send us love signs from beyond the beyond."

Trudy said, "You said something grumpy about doubting very much it could be Kate waving hello and you preferred red-tailed hawks, anyway."

"I still do. I forgot to tell you about the next day. Guess what I saw when I was heading to work the next morning."

"An eagle?"

"Four eagles. Two adults and two juveniles hovering around the hydro pole right outside my door. I stepped off the porch and there they were, dancing around as if they'd just found a Maypole for eagles. Kate died on the first day of May. Did you remember that?"

"No, I didn't. We should round up the kids next spring and hold a May Day dance to honour Kate. We could invite Maddie and Clair. Maybe Tessa would show up, too."

"I like that idea. Remembering the date should be a piece of cake. No need to mark it on the calendar."

"So tell me more about Kate's eagles."

"The adult eagles didn't stay long, but the young ones hung around for several minutes, swooping and playing. I had a good laugh about it, said 'OK, OK, Kate, I get it. I'll never doubt you again. Very funny'."

"Do you think Kate sent you the two juveniles to remind you not to behave like such a juvenile yourself, to have a little faith?"

"Could be. Four eagles might be a bit of overkill, but I did get the message."

"Whatever it takes. Good thing Kate and Tessa still hang around to help you out with your dysfunctional relationship with God. I heard you're not speaking to Him again."

"That would be your fault, Trudy. I've been too busy taking you to chemo and radiation treatments and cursing a god who would come up with a most ridiculous notion called cancer to sing or pray or do much of anything pleasant, God-talk wise."

"Not His fault, though. And I'll be alright. I ain't going nowhere any time soon. Still, it's good Tessa and Kate help you sort Luke out, since you won't talk to God, and offer to help with your girls, too."

"True. Pour me another glass of wine, will you, Trudy. It must be five o'clock somewhere."

Trudy laughed and sang,

"'Pour me something tall and strong

Make it a hurricane before I go insane.'"

Em tried singing along, "'I ain't had a day off now, in over a year

285

My Jamaican vacation's gonna start right here

If the phone's for me you can tell them

I just sailed away.'"

Trudy said, "No, that's not what comes next. You're too drunk. It goes,

'It's only half past twelve but I don't care'".

"Oh yeah, 'It's only half past twelve but I don't care

It's wine o'clock somewhere.'"

"Not *wine*, 'it's five o'clock somewhere'. Get it right. But if you *had* got him drunk on homemade wine, you could have had him, Em. If you had only pushed it a little, taken him out to the hay loft and got it on. You're still a hot Mama."

"Or taken him out to the back forty and shot him. Case solved."

"That too," said Trudy. "Except then you'd be a pistol-packing Mama. And we don't shoot people."

"Oh yeah, I forgot. In Canada, guns don't kill people, people with guns kill people. We could call ourselves the Prince Edward Island National Rifle Association—the PEINRA."

"Drunk PEINRA people with guns could shoot people. If I was Luke, I'd take the wine cure. Was it the kid?"

"No. Canadian kids don't shoot people. Even if they pay their dues to the NRA."

"No, Silly, I mean was it about the kid? Is that why you couldn't seduce Luke?"

"Yeah, little Liam. It's always about the kids."

"True," said Trudy. "They don't ask us to bring them into the world and then turn around and fuck it up on them. You mad at him?"

"Naah."

"Emily, where did you go? Did you just fall down and go boom?"

Trudy found her off the corner edge of the deck, lying flat out on the grass, staring up at the stars, and trying to get Trudy in focus. After Trudy stepped down off the deck, picked her up, dusted her off, set her back up on the Adirondack rocker, and told her to 'stay', Emily confided a bit of her conversation with Luke. "I'm a little worried about him. No one should be forced to work with an agent who is no good and books him too many gigs too close

286

together. He's killing Luke, and Luke won't say no. He needs to slow the fuck down."

"And who's the biggest obstacle to that?"

"Luke."

"And total financial ruin, of course."

"Of course."

Trudy asked, "How are he and his wife doing?"

"He says something happened when she was in Halifax looking after her granny last spring. It can't have had to do with the granny, 'cause she's still alive and kicking. Luke claims Granny's a tough old bird. He says Siobhan's been pissed at him ever since. He has apologized about a hundred times for neglecting her while he was chasing music all over the Maritimes, and for never bringing enough money home to her, but she says that's not it. Siobhan won't tell him what's wrong. She decided a break would be best for both of them. So he's staying at Tommy's for a few days. Siobhan and a bunch of her friends have gone up to Montreal for a Metallica concert, see if she can clear her head."

"What's she like?"

"Who—Siobhan?"

"No, Granny. Yeah, Siobhan, Stupid."

"I don't know. Haven't met her yet. According to Luke, she's level-headed enough. Can't imagine she'll be taking a walk on the wild side at the Metal concert or anything. She's got a young kid. She keeps saying, 'It's me, not you.'"

"Who?"

"Siobhan."

"No, I mean who is the 'you' she keeps saying it to?"

"Oh. You're sure you're not drunk, Trudy? Gettin' me all frickin' confused."

"No, but I should put you to bed. I can't remember the last time I saw you this drunk. Unless it was the last time Luke showed up on your radar."

"'To Luke, I mean. She says it to Luke. She don't talk to me."

"Where's Liam?"

"Not here."

"Of course not. Or he'd be starving hungry. I mean, where is he staying? With Luke at Tommy's?"

"No, he's staying with the tough old granny and Siobhan's mom. Granny moved home to Cape Breton to be closer to family, in case she gets sick again. They leave their little kid behind while they go find themselves. Fuck, I don't know what gives with those two and their fucking first world problems."

"Em, to tell you the truth, I sometimes wonder what all the fuss is about. He's not even all that good looking."

"Shit. You mean the lens I held up for you to see him with wasn't pink enough?"

"Not rosy enough at all. What little glow it had disappeared for me after your sister Nora told me how he kept you waiting that time you drove all the way to Halifax for his big gig at the Misty Moon. A man who keeps a woman waiting all alone on a barstool is just rude."

"That was a long time ago. A year and a half at least."

"My point exactly. Why do you even bother?"

Emily didn't answer her and she didn't tell Trudy about Luke's one night stand, either. Too private. She wasn't *that* drunk.

Sandfire

The next day Luke showed up at the beach, fashionably late, a few minutes before Trudy was about to head out without him. Trudy would have preferred to take her recently divorced brother, the father of Johnny and Jake, but he had to fish. Trudy had been trying to get her brother and Emily together for months, but no luck so far. In total, that made six boys—Patrick, Philip, Paul, Johnny, Jake, and Luke—and two women.

As for Emily, she hadn't seen Luke since that day in the spring when she ran into him at Tommy's, and then only through a blur of crying baby, tangled sheets, and naked bodies. So, she took a good hard look. He had shaved off his beard, and his newly liberated chin and cheeks met with Emily's approval. She wondered if that was the answer to the mystery of that original kiss: no prickly hair scratching her lips when his made contact with hers. If *that's* all it was...well. The beginning of lines around his eyes and a slight slump to his shoulders reminded her that even Luke would age eventually. She thought he might look a little stressed.

All eight beachcombers knew that on The Beach We Don't Tell Tourists About they could walk for hours, and it would never feel like a chore. They could always find something more to discover a few steps down the way. The boys played Superheroes and made capes out of their towels, as they wandered off to the far end of the dune across the channel from the lighthouse. The youngest, Jake, complimented Luke on his pretending skills. Luke had traded towels with Jake when Jake's got soaked, so Luke may have had an extra 'in' with him. Jake was only six; not so hard to please.

After a few kilometers of running around attacking each other and inventing new action heroes, Luke and Jake caught up with Emily and Trudy on the sandbar where they were digging clams. Emily wanted to try burying the clams in seaweed and steaming them over a pit fire for supper, the way her parents had prepared lobster when she was a kid. The most succulent lobster she had ever tasted came from those beach parties with her folks, so she couldn't see why a seaweed fire wouldn't work for clams, too. She hoped to get the recipe right. No salt needed, thanks to the seaweed. How much seaweed was enough to cook in, but not so much as to smother the flames? She was discussing this with Trudy when Luke interrupted.

"Hey, Em," he said, "Remember a long time ago you asked me if I liked kids? I figured out later on you meant did I like kids universally, or just the ones in my little corner of the world, where Liam lives. Did I pass the test today? As you know, I'm not much for tests."

"Oh my God, Luke, don't tell me you finally caught on! Now go play with Jake, ya big goof. And keep the kids off the dunes and away from the marram grass."

Emily kept right on digging for clams with her toes and filling her fishnet bag. No time for Luke. She had serious work to do. Trudy was trying out the latest clam diggers' innovation: her neighbour had taken the rubber end of a toilet plunger and screwed it on to a broom handle to create some superior suction on the wet sand. The perfect clamming tool. Trudy offered to let Emily try using it. After all her digging around, Emily's pedicure appeared to be pretty well trashed, no Tutti Fruitti polish left to save. She was a bit fascinated by the new contraption, so she and Trudy traded methods.

The afternoon seemed timeless. Until Emily felt a little shiver in her spine, glanced up from her sand-plunging work, and said, "Trudy, look across the way to the harbour. Can you see how the waves are skiffing along, like they are in a wicked hurry? Out past the third sandbar—see how the water is changing?"

And it was—from a bright sky blue to a dark angry navy blue, a military colour.

"Not good," Trudy said as she started to fret and frown. "Did you notice how quiet the gulls and terns are? Look, over towards the lighthouse. See the Great Blue Heron trying to fly and pushing against the wind? He must be wrung right out, poor scrawny gangly bastard."

The light darkened all around them, as if someone had turned down the master dimmer switch of the sky. To the east, a huge black cloud headed their way, from across the bay. "Luke, gather up the boys", she yelled.

Luke threw down his yellow Superman towel and immediately read their situation for what it was—they were about to be hit with a good old fashioned PEI weather bomb. As the five boys drew closer, Luke and Emily both

290

hollered to them over the roaring of the wind to run back to the car, as fast as they could. The rain came pelting down, bouncing off the sand, as the boys' feet rose and fell with the familiar urgent rhythm of a game of Chase, only this time the chase was real and they were the prey. Thunder rumbled overhead as the black cloud pursued them. Just as ferociously, lightning lit up their path in sheets of yellow light. Emily yelled out to Luke, who reacted by telling everyone to drop to the sand and cover their heads with their towels, as marble-sized pellets of hail shot down on them.

Emily landed next to Luke and whispered that they needed to do something to keep the kids from panicking. Stories are what she knew, so stories would have to do. She just got past "Once upon a time" when she turned towards Luke as a lightning bolt skipped across the ocean, erupting directly in front of him, and hitting the sand a few inches from where she lay shivering under Luke's bare chest. The sand appeared to melt and turn into glass. The brilliant, dancing light refracted from the sand and transformed into glints of oppositional crystals, creating mirror images of stone and sand and sea and sky. Emily witnessed Mother Nature as She had her way with the tiny innocent little grains of sand.

Emily didn't share her encounter with the kids, only with Luke. She didn't want to frighten them, as the boys were soaked and shivering, and the little ones were close to tears. Luke asked them all to sing with him "The Night that Paddy Murphy Died." Which they did at the top of their lungs, shouting against the wind and the rain and the thunder. As the song said, it was a night they'd never forget.

Midway through "Paddy Murphy", as the boys roared out, "Some of the boys got loaded drunk and they ain't got sober yet", the dark night disappeared. Poof! And the bright sun returned. The boys gathered up their wet towels and headed to the parked cars. But not before Luke convinced them all to jump in the waves one more time to celebrate. The kids, who were giddy with relief, kicked up the water and pushed and shoved each other into the waves. Then the three Ps, Patrick, Philip and Paul, grabbed their Aunt Trudy and heaved her into the ocean.

"No fair," Trudy cried. "Three against one."

"Let's get Emily!" hollered Luke.

Emily squealed as the water hit her chin and splashed in her eyes. "Wait till I catch you, Luke. You're in big trouble, Mister!"

Trudy and the boys chased one another all along the shore, which allowed Emily a few moments with Luke. She thought he'd like to hear about the beach shrine she had found for Kate. Before she could begin to describe it, though, Luke said, "We got you beat in Cape Breton when it comes to shrines. You know those old cast iron claw-foot tubs? We cut them in half and stick the half with the curve and no taps into the earth, curve end up, and...Voila! Instant shrine! We usually use one of the old wooden fish boxes turned on end for the shelf. Stick a buoy on top so people can locate it and you're all set. All you need is one of those white, glow-in-the-dark, plastic Virgin Marys for the religious touch. We stole one from my gram when we made ours."

"You're kidding, right, Luke?"

"No, Scout's honor. Those Virgins are spooky in the dark. I think Gram got hers when she went to Sainte-Anne-de-Beaupre Basilica in Quebec. Ever been?"

"No."

"Now there's a shrine. Spectacular, Gram said. I've never been, either."

"I'll have to add it to my list."

"The bootlegger down the road did something similar with an old Cape Island lobster boat, only for a different purpose. He took his chainsaw and split the boat in two, right across the middle, and stuck the half with the bow into the ground, bow up. Then he made a little door in what used to be the floor so we could get into the pointed end up hull. Instant outhouse."

How could Emily ever top such genius?

By the time they walked the rest of the way back and climbed the stairs up the steep bank to the red clay road, they were all exhausted, or as Jake put it, "I'm pretty well shook!" Trudy explained 'pretty well shook' was one of Jake's grandmother's expressions. An old soul, that Jake.

Trudy loaded the McNeill kids into the family van, while Luke asked Emily to sit in with him for a minute, let him catch his breath. So she climbed into his van and waited for him to speak. He hadn't gotten around to that apology, and she was curious about how long he would take. She had time.

As she waited, she thought about what she had seen when the lightning continued to flash over and all around Luke, after it created the miracle of glass from sand. She had looked into his eyes and seen something there that chilled her, beyond the hail and wind and lightning and thunder of the late summer storm. At first, the jade green flashes in his irises tugged her in and threatened to overwhelm her common sense. But then she caught a glimpse of something deeper, a canyon of green glass leading down to the core of him, and pulled herself back from the edge.

The crisis was over, they were all safe and warm on the shore, but still Emily shivered. She pulled Luke's sweater close, tucked her knees up, and wrapped it around her. Something about the cavern of light in Luke's eyes reminded her of the sense of tumbling down through time she had felt when she gave birth to Christina twenty-four years earlier. At the height of her un-medicated agony, she had experienced a strange connection to generations of mothers, cascading down through eons of time, back to the Bedouin days, back to the well where women have drawn strength for eternity. This time the sensation had nothing to do with birth and everything to do with Luke, though, and the vision she glimpsed in the mirrors and crystals as he lay with her in the sand did not bode well for either of them. As she sat in the truck and waited and worried, she forgot she was supposed to show him how indifferent she was to his words and his apology, and burst out, "Luke, what is it? What is going on with you?"

Luke turned away from her, leaned over, and laid his head on the steering wheel. "You know the black cloud that chased us today? I feel like it's been coming for me."

"Well, it wasn't. Now you're anthropomorphising. It was just a storm, nothing supernatural, or to do with you or me. Oh, you mean before today. Like, all along?"

"Yeah, all along. I couldn't outrun it today."

"No. Because we used some common sense."

"Most days when it shows up, I can't get out from under it, climb over it, or race ahead of it."

"Is that what you've been running from? Chasing tail and going nowhere? Good God, Luke, in front of your son?"

"Yeah. Stupid, I know. And I know I'm only going to hurt Siobhan and Liam."

Emily thought, 'and me. I wish you'd say "and you, Emily". For once.' Instead, she said, "So stop. Get your crap together."

"I know I'm going to fuck it up. You don't have to tell me. But it feels like it doesn't matter what I do, I could be Mahatma Ghandi, and still, I'll end up abandoning them. And there's not a damn thing I can do about it."

"I heard Ghandi did that too, abandoned the women and children for the sake of the greater Ahimsa. He wasn't perfect, either. You'll be alright, Luke." Emily hated being prescriptive, but she was grasping at straws here. First she'd heard of Luke's Big Existential Crisis. Was that what it was, or was it something deeper, more ominous?

"Yeah, well." Luke had nothing more to say. He put the van in gear and headed for Trudy's cottage. Now she'd probably driven him back inside himself. Men!

Late that night, after filling up on rubbery clams, hot dogs, and s'mores from the bonfire, the kids bunked down on the floor of the cottage, Luke withdrew to his van to sleep off the day, and Trudy and Emily sat out on the deck again, only this time without the homemade wine. In many ways, it had been a sobering day. Emily asked what Trudy thought Tessa would say about it all. Trudy laughed and said, "Doomed. Tessa would say you are doomed. She sent you this, though, as a souvenir of the day. I found it when I picked up my beach towel after the storm." She handed Emily a piece of newborn glass, about three inches long and a minute deep.

Emily's cell phone buzzed in the night. She woke with a start, remembered where she was, found her purse under the coffee table, and fished out her phone, trying not to wake the McNeill boys. Luke.

"I'm sorry."

"I know."

"Tell me a story, Emily."

So she did. It was 3 am, after all.

Emily and Luke

"I hope you have your cell phone charged because this could be a long story and a longer night. And I can't talk loud or I'll wake the kids. So put your listening ears on. I am going to Halifax again next week, so I think I'll start there. Should I call it 'Emily and Luke' or 'Luke and Emily'?

Emily and Luke

Your booking agent conveniently plans a gig in Halifax, but neither of us knows the other is scheduled to be there. My sister, Nora, convinces me to go downhill to the downtown—and when you stay at the Prince George Hotel, it's all downhill from there. We find a bar on the waterfront that is about as low down as you can get, called the Divers Down. But someone changed the sign to Dive Down. And someone else scribbled Diverse Down above it. We sweet talk our way through the line-up and—Oh! There you are! Singing, "River Boat Fantasy". We can hear you warbling, 'Cocaine kisses, moonshine Misses.' You know a lot of old songs for a young dude.

This time when you take a break, I walk right up to you and tell you, 'You could let yourself come home for an hour now and then. Not to the Prince George, but to good old PEI. Meet me at Campbell's Pond. We could go fishing and see what we could catch. I could tickle you under the chin, like my Dad taught me to tickle trout, catch you and check to see if you are a man or a fish. A better time for you than riverboat fantasies of whiskey, moonshine, and a rock and roll band with a reefer in your hand. And my kisses would be sweeter than those cocaine infused ones.'

You could tell me stories. About the ones that got away (but you'd have to leave all those women out of it). I haven't been trout-ing for a long time. I would like that. And we really would only catch trout. Or a cold if it was in the middle of winter. We'd have to build a campfire and toast s'mores.

295

Or we could forget about gooey snacks and do "The Bearcat", dance around and howl like David Wilson's guitar. I don't know if a bearcat is a cat or a bear or half of each, but either way, if you were a trout, you'd make a delicious bite for a bear or a cat.

Like an obedient trout, you could land yourself at the Prince George Hotel tonight. A trout would be a good incantation for you, as lately, much of what you've been up to is a little fishy. Through pursed lips, you ask the desk clerk if he knows if I've checked in. Your flapless fish ears hear him say, 'Oh yes, yes, we all know Emily. She's always so friendly and quick to make conversation to shorten our day. Yes, Mr. Trout, she's in room 302, and she said for you to go right on up. Do you need a little help with your tail? We would not want you to catch it in the elevator.'

When you get to my door, I welcome you with a hug and a cold beer and invite you to come in and sit down. You slip and slide over to a chair and curl up, (since there is no other way for you to sit) and tell me about your day, and I reach over and take your fin in my hand. My fingers dance across your slimy skin. I decide to kiss you, release your inner fish, so it can swim away. I spring you from your aquarian existence, for the sake of the story.

So now my fingers can dance across the somewhat hairy skin on the back of your hand. I ease your fist open, just enough to form a cup with your palm. It's been a rough day, and you don't want to let go of all that tension, not yet. I don't ask you to or expect you to. I'm just happy to lean my cheek into the palm of your hand.

Gradually, you unfurl your body onto the chair and ease your legs out over the carpet. I can touch your eyes now with my lips. And I do. Your palm feels empty to you without my cheek, so I put a little round object into it. I have warmed it against my breast as I was waiting for you. And you feel the warmth radiating from your hand and see that it is a piece of a coiled fossil. A fossil that reminds you of a shell. A shell that reminds you of me. And you make the connection. I am the shell. The shell that you can slide into when you are feeling crabby, like a homeless hermit crab, or too alone. The shell that will make room for you and give

296

you another home to go to when you need to switch from the one you inhabit every day. So you slide into the shell and wrap yourself up and feel the warmth of all those soft curves. You burrow in deeper and deeper until, at last, you know that you have come home. A different home. A home that has been created just for you. A home that will shelter you from the squall, wash around in the storm surge with you, take every wave the way that you do every day of your life. She will tumble with you in the waves, this shell, and you will both come out unscathed. For just one moment, she is you and you are her and nothing comes between us. And, for just one hour, you and I make the rest of the world go away.

You have a lot of words as you lay there curled up inside our shell. You talk. I listen. I become the listener I should have been for you. You tell me stories of all the lives lived when we had permission to love each other. You have quite an imagination. Wow.

I listen and hold the fossil, which I originally thought was just a nice rock, in your hand and let you feel the energy of infinity. You may be disappointed to learn this, but it is not the hot, lust-fuelled heat of seduction. The heat in your story and in your stone is warm and gentle and old and patient. And wise. It carries the wisdom of the ages. So do you. You have grown so much that you have outgrown the shell I found you in three years ago. And, being a stagnant shell and all, I can only move forward if you carry me on your back. I make the home and you make the journey, like we have been doing since we met.

As I lay there with you inside of me, if I know one thing to be true, it is that I love you even more than I love your words. Even more than I love anyone's words, including my own. And I know it is true for now and will be true for however many more millennia you and I have left to do this dance together.

Are you still awake, Luke?"

"Yeah."

"Can you see the sun coming up? It's splitting the trees over here by the cottage. I need to get some sleep."

"I don't think I'll sleep tonight. You've said some things I need to think about. You and me and the dawn...well, it's always scared me a little, Emily. I wish I could come over to the cottage and talk to you."

"You'd have to crawl over a half dozen boys sleeping on the floor. It's just a story, Luke. But still, don't you ever wish for s'more?"

Acknowledgements

Emily's Letters could not have been written without the music that surrounds me as I write, either in my head or from my stereo. I take a few pokes at musicians, but the respect I have for the life they live so we can have a soundtrack for our lives runs deep. Wherever possible I have received permission for use of lyrics. For lyrics, snippets of songs, or inspiration for wording, I would like to acknowledge:

Lennie Gallant for sharing the title of his wonderful song "Emily's Letters"
Garth Brooks "Too Damn Old"
Francis James Child for collecting "The Cherry Tree Carol", believed to have originated in the 15th century
April Wine and Myles Goodwyn for "You Won't Dance With Me"
Trooper for "Here for a Good Time"
Bob Marley for "Girl I Wanna Make You Sweat"
The Trews for allowing me to have a little fun with "Man of Two Minds"
Leonard Cohen for "I'm Your Man" and so much more.
The Who for the classic album "Tommy"
Lynyrd Skynyrd for "Sweet Home Alabama" and "Simple Kind of Man"
Eagles for "Take It to the Limit"
Bruce Springsteen for "Fifty Seven Channels" and "Baby I Was Born To Run"
Eric Church for "Like Jesus Does"
Eva Cassidy for "I Know You by Heart". I can hear her singing with Tessa, who also died too soon.
Kelley Mooney for her version of Leonard Cohen's "Hallelujah"
Fastball for "The Way"
John Prine for "The Sins of Memphisto"
Bob Seeger for "Turn the Page"
Neil Young for being Neil Young.

Meatloaf for "Dashboard Light", which really should have found a place in *Rocky Horror Picture Show.*

Dan Seals for "You Bring Out the Wild Side of Me", "Addicted" and "They Rage On". Also, excerpt from "You Still Move Me"

Rickie Lee Jones for "Chuckie's in Love"

Queen for "Fat Bottomed Girls"

Michael Jackson for "Beat It"

The Rolling Stones for "Dead Flowers" and "Brown Sugar"

Tommy Hunter for "Travellin' Man", popularized by the Canadian TV series "Littlest Hobo"

Alan Jackson and Jimmy Buffett for bringing "It's Five O'clock Somewhere" to the bars, and the song writers for writing a great drinking song.

The Rose Vaughan Trio for "Stone and Sand and Sea and Sky"

Great Big Sea for popularizing the traditional Newfoundland song "The Night That Paddy Murphy Died"

David Wilson for "River Boat Fantasy" and "Bearcat"

In case you, dear reader, would like to source some of the poems and books that influenced Emily:

God Loves Laughter by William Sears

The Island Acadians by George Arsenault

On Mexican Time by Tony Cohan

Come Away: Song of Songs by Anne Hines

The Beekeeper's Apprentice by Lori King

"How to Know if He's Amazing in Bed" Cosmopolitan Magazine July, 2006 issue

What is the What by Dave Eggers, based on the life of Valentino Achak Deng

Shake Hands with the Devil by Romeo Dallaire. Movie by the same name directed by Roger Spottiswoode and cowritten with Michael Donovan.

Loving Frank by Nancy Horan

The Gaelic expression "Cáilín mo Pháistín I" means 'my baby girl'
And, yes, there is an ice cream called Island Fantasy. But you'll have to
come to Prince Edward Island to try it.

Thank You

My deepest thanks and gratitude to an old friend who came back into my life when we both needed a project—my editor Norma Murdoch-Simos. She took on this scrambled mess and did everything humanly possible to make it 'presentable' for the big world. We had so much fun back when we were young adults and now again with Emily. Maybe someday the distance between Prince Edward Island and Greece will not seem so far, and we can sit on the deck, like Emily and Trudy, and tell our stories face to face.

Also to Ivy Wigmore for the first editorial assessment and the encouragement to carry on with *Emily's Letters*. And thanks to Joan Gallant for help with the final proof.

To my sister Aggi-Rose Reddin for all the invaluable technical support and 'fixes'. And to my friends who became my first 'readers': Ellen Niles, Mary Armellini, Sue Woodworth, and Edna Reid. You're the best!

Special thanks to Brad Fremlin, whose photographs capture PEI in all its moods, for the generous use of his photos for the cover design. Sue Woodworth thanks for catching the light on my naked face one morning and turning it into my author photo.

Thank you to Katie Perry at *www.littlebikedesigns.com* for the cover design.

To my husband Sonny for your patience when writing takes me too far away from you. And to my three daughters for always encouraging me to write, even as I was wiping your tears and cleaning your sick-up and driving you to soccer games and dance class. You are the true loves of my life.

˙·.¸.·´¯`·.¸.·´¯`·...¸><((((º>

Vicki resides in Rustico, a beautiful coastal community on the North Shore of Prince Edward Island. With her husband Sonny, she has raised several businesses and three lovely daughters. After much life experience, Vicki is now free to follow her passion for writing. Vicki is currently working on her autobiographical book "C is for Cancer C is for Caregiver". She can be reached through her website www.vickireddingauthier.com.